SAVANNAH
FROM SAVANNAH

DENISE HILDRETH

MARION COUNTY PUBLIC LIBRARY
321 MONROE STREET
FAIRMONT, WV 26554

WestBow
PRESS
A Division of Thomas Nelson Publishers
Since 1798

visit us at www.westbowpress.com

Copyright © 2004 by Denise Hildreth

All rights reserved. No portion of this book may be reproduced, stored
in a retrieval system, or transmitted in any form or by any means—electronic,
mechanical, photocopy, recording, scanning, or other—except for brief
quotations in critical reviews or articles, without the prior written permission
of the publisher.

Published in Nashville, Tennessee, by WestBow Press, a division of Thomas
Nelson, Inc.

Publisher's Note: This novel is a work of fiction. Names, characters, places,
and incidents are either products of the author's imagination or used fictitiously.
All characters are fictional, and any similarity to people living or dead is purely
coincidental.

Library of Congress Cataloging-in-Publication Data

Hildreth, Denise, 1969–
    Savannah from Savannah / Denise Hildreth.
      p. cm.
    ISBN 0-8499-4455-4 (pbk.)
    1. Women—Georgia—Fiction. 2. Mothers and daughters—Fiction.
3. Savannah (Ga.)—Fiction. 4. Young women—Fiction. I. Title.
    PS3608.I424s285 2004
    813'.6—dc22   2004005932

Printed in the United States of America
04 05 06 07 08 — 6 5 4 3 2 1

114-308

b15291510

This book is dedicated to those who have ever known loss,
and those who have had a dream only to watch it crumble.
May you realize this side of heaven that God redeems
all things, even those that seem unredeemable.

CHAPTER ONE

S avannah is my name. It's also my world, my home. I didn't cherish it until I left. And when I returned, it was because I had something to prove.

My mother, Victoria, was born and reared in Savannah. My name is explained by her love for this city—that and my belief that she had a craving to spend the rest of her life announcing her daughter to every living creature as "Savannah from Savannah." For a time I thought she was just being cute. Then I realized that this was really how she intended to introduce me for the rest of my natural existence.

"Savannah," she said when I confronted her, "one day you will thank me. When you are famous and the whole world knows you as 'Savannah from Savannah,' children will envy you and long to be named after you. And me, well, I will be your mother."

By the age of thirteen, having no desire to be any child's envy, I went around my eighth-grade class and had all my friends sign a petition requesting my name be legally changed. Afterward, I walked straight up to the courthouse and into the office of Judge Hoddicks, one of my father's best friends. I withdrew my two sheets of moderately legible names from the pages of *The Hobbit,* where I'd stashed them for safety, spread them on Judge Hoddicks's desk, and informed him I would like to change my name to Betty.

"Why Betty?"

"Because my mom doesn't like any name that ends in a *y*. Just try calling her Vicky and see what happens to that southern charm of hers. It will fade like a vapor."

He directed me to a chair in his stunning office, with its rich mahogany bookcases and coffered ceiling. I passed the time reading my well-worn copy of Tolkien's classic until the glass-paned door opened and my mother made her entrance. I thought maybe he wanted to witness the meltdown of a southern woman in high heels and Mary Kay. But her arrival proved it was all about her ability to command any room as well as this city's inhabitants.

She looked fabulous—perturbed, but fabulous. Vicky always looks fabulous. She has never appeared in public in anything lower than a two-inch heel. She doesn't own a pair of jeans, and she wouldn't be caught dead with curlers in her hair, without makeup on her face, or without being fully accessorized by seven a.m.

Ten minutes later, as we left the office, I vowed that even if I called her Victoria to the world, she would always be Vicky in my mind. I took one last look back and asked Judge Hoddicks to give me a call if there was anything he could do. He assured me he would.

Today, eleven years later, my legal name is still Savannah Grace Phillips. To Judge Hoddicks, however, I will forever be Betty.

I have spent a considerable amount of my life trying to convince people that Vicky isn't my real mother. I mean how could I come from a woman I don't understand, a woman no one understands? Anyone with half a pea-pickin' ounce of perception can tell that Vicky and I are nothing alike. We don't talk alike, act alike, or do anything else alike.

And you wouldn't know I was hers by my looks, either. I have two inches on her five-foot-four frame. And I don't think our hair is the same color, although no one really knows what her original hair color was. My hair has always been golden brown and straight as a stick. Vicky has been blond, frosted, and redheaded. The best color of all was when she wanted to be platinum blonde, and woke up the morning of the annual Savannah Chamber of Commerce Ball with the majority of her hair lying broken off on her pillow. But we don't talk about that much.

The only remote proof that Vicky could actually be my mother is that I do, on rare, necessary occasions, feel the need to freely express myself in, shall we say, clear tones. My father, Jake Phillips, has the amazing ability to sit back and breathe before responding. I, however, like Vicky, tend to speak before thought has had a chance to register. This is a most exhilarating, dangerous trait that we share. Vicky has managed to envelop hers in charm. I have only managed to envelop mine in something begging to be refined.

I have tried to channel this intense need to freely express myself into the written word. Every Big Star notebook I've saved from school contains either words to songs, short stories, or entire movie scripts. In high school, I ran for student-body president just so I could write a speech. The speech was so good I didn't even have to campaign to win. I appealed to the students' deepest cravings: food, exemption from finals, and football. Tie those three things together and then close with a poem called "The Man Who Thinks He Can," and, well . . . my fellow students were mush. The poor girl who lost had her own campaign manager and spent so much money on pencils and posters that I almost felt bad for beating her.

That moment allowed me to catch a glimpse of how words can impact the human spirit. A few months later, a short story about an eighty-year-old named Lula who wore purple hats and sang show tunes at area nursing homes, à la a Victoria biography, secured me a scholarship to the School of Journalism at the

University of Georgia. College taught me how to craft my gift, a gift that would propel me into the highbrow world of publishing. I envisioned my books in the window of Barnes & Noble and day-dreamed of people rushing in to catch the latest novel by Savannah Phillips—or "Savannah from Savannah," as people back home would forever require me to be identified. And that probably would have been my life, had it not been for some intervening cir-cumstances and a newspaper.

For four years of college and two years of graduate school, Vicky sent me a subscription to our local paper, the *Savannah Chronicle*. She never acknowledged it, but when there is a half-page ad on page 3 that reads "To our Savannah from Savannah, wishing you all the best in your new passage, Love, Mom and Dad," you just kind of know. My first week of college, feeling somewhat liberated yet homesick, I picked up my mail and headed to a McDonald's right off-campus to grab a Coke. Then I would take my Coke over to a small café across from my apartment and get a chef's salad with Thousand Island and blue-cheese dressing on the side. There, along with caffeine and fat grams, I consumed every article and ad in the paper.

For years, I considered Savannah a town of the near-dead and dying, a place frequented by people who'd come to pick out retirement facilities. I had never realized that it was so vibrant, alive. The main reason for this newfound impression appeared every Wednesday and Friday at the bottom of the front page of section B. Beside her column in the local section was a picture of a distinguished-looking lady with frosted hair, probably in her mid-fifties. Gloria Richardson. Her smile looked genuine, and her human-interest stories made me believe that unexpected kindness and prevailing strength just might exist in Savannah after all. So twice a week for six years, I spent lunchtime rediscovering the place I thought I knew and had longed to leave.

One Wednesday in the last weeks of the final semester of my master's work, I picked up my mail and my *Chronicle* and headed to McDonald's, and then the café. With Coke and salad at the ready, I flipped through the envelopes first and paused at a return address labeled "Fiction Achievement Award." I couldn't believe the results were already in.

Over the past six years, I had dedicated myself to consuming other writers' work and sharpening my own. For my thesis, I turned in a 450-page novel about four female college dropouts who left home to discover the world. It was a delightful tale of searching and survival, crafted over an agonizing two years. My dean entered the novel in a fiction contest for unpublished writers. A portion of the winning story would be published in a leading literary magazine, and leading fiction houses would consider the manuscript for publication.

Surely I held in my hands a rejection letter, sent out first to the really bad entries. Not only was I not picked to win, but my book was so bad they wanted me to know two weeks early how truly pathetic I am!

I sat up straighter in my booth and tore the letter open. "Let the guillotine fall quickly," I said.

Dear Ms. Phillips,

After careful consideration, we are pleased to inform you that your novel, *Road to Anywhere,* has been selected for the Fiction Achievement Award. An excerpt from your novel will appear in a future edition of the *National Literary Review.* We look forward to meeting you in person on May 15 with Taylor House Publishing in New York. All pertinent information has been sent to Dean Hillwood at the University of Georgia. The awards ceremony will be held on May 16 at the Waldorf Astoria. We have reserved a table for you and nine of your guests.

Congratulations. We are pleased to help you pursue your dreams of becoming a successful author.

Sincerely,
Jeff Peterson
Chairman, Awards Committee

"Oh my stars! Oh my stars!" I said, throwing the letter into the air and jumping out of my booth. I caught my Coke before it traveled south and smiled at a surprised couple at the closest table. This was a moment to savor. I had finally achieved what I'd spent years working for.

I have no idea who I passed or who passed me on the dance back to my apartment. I'm not even sure what route I took, but I made it back, walked upstairs to my room, and sat down on the edge of my bed. I opened the letter and read the words again and again. I walked over to the phone and laid the envelope and letter down on the desk. For the first time, the addressee information on the envelope registered with me. Though the letter itself was addressed to me, the envelope read, "Victoria Phillips."

At first I laughed, thinking how funny that they had mistakenly used my mother's name instead of mine. Then reality surfaced. There was no way in the world they would know my mother's name unless they knew my mother. A weight drove me into my chair. I couldn't move. I couldn't breathe.

What had she done? Why in the world would she get involved? I had worked so hard, trying to make this novel good enough to win on its own merits. Two hours passed, as did two classes. Around three that afternoon my eyes turned from the window to the phone. I picked it up and dialed.

A thick New York accent greeted me. "Taylor House Publishing."

"Jeff Peterson, please."

"May I tell him who's calling?"

"Yes, yes you can. Would you tell him it is Victoria Phillips from Savannah, Georgia," I spread the southern belle accent so thick the receptionist would be talking about it for the rest of the day.

"One moment, Ms. Phillips," and with the press of a button, I was dumped into the land of Muzak.

"Well, Mrs. Phillips. So, good to hear from you," said a lackey's voice. Disgusting. "So your daughter has received the results of the contest. I trust she's happy."

After all the years of mimicking Vicky, I could have auditioned for *Saturday Night Live*. "Oh, she is, Jeff, she is. She got the letter today, as a matter of fact, and she was thrilled."

"It turned out to be a really fabulous piece of work." Was that a smirk in his voice?

"Well, I just wanted to thank you again for your help and discretion in this matter."

"Don't mention it. I look forward to meeting you and your daughter next month."

"Oh, you don't know how much I look forward to meeting you. Good-bye."

"Good-bye, Mrs. Phillips."

And with that, my dream ended and my mission began.

CHAPTER TWO

I need you, now," was the only other call I made.

"I'll be there as fast as I-16 will take me," said the voice from the other end.

To kill the next three and a half hours, I did what any normal college student would do in her moment of uttermost stress—I cleaned. But I didn't clean just anything. I cleaned the bathroom. From top to bottom, spic-and-span, take-a-nap-in-the-shower kind of clean.

Screams from my best friend, Paige, snapped me out of the world of the ceramic celestial. "Oh my word, this is worse than I ever dreamed. You could have a picnic in here. I came as fast as I could." She walked over to help me pull off the kneepads, rubber gloves, and galoshes.

"I'm not well," I said as I derubberized. I stood to give her a hug, realizing only then that my body had participated in contortionist activity. Paige threw her arms around me, then, forcing me back, stared at me eyeball-to-eyeball. "You look horrible. Let's go get a Coke." And she headed for the door.

I never moved. With no inflection or emotion I said, "I don't want a Coke." For a moment Paige was paralyzed.

"What?" Her flip-flops brought her back over to me. "Come in here." She led me into my bedroom and pushed me across the room to a small sofa at the foot of my bed. "Sit down. You *aren't* well, are you? You talk; Paige will listen." She took the floor and wrapped her petite frame into a ball, positioning herself as she had countless times through the years, ready for me to let loose.

I wanted to pace, but I didn't have the energy. So, I just began at the beginning. I told her of the letter, Vicky's name, and the call to New York. She listened intently. "Paige, I've tried for years to figure out what I wanted to do with my life. Years, I tell ya! Finally, finally I figured out I love books. I love to read them, and I love to write them. So, I changed my major to English and literature, you know, and I felt like the world opened up to me.

"Through all of this, the one thing Little Miss Vicky couldn't do was stay out of it. First she tried to get me a job hosting the Athens news before I had even finished my first semester. Then, she tried to get me a radio broadcasting gig covering the capitol."

"But she hates Atlanta," Paige said, getting up to search the room for food.

"There are chips in the top drawer of the dresser and some bottled water in the closet."

"No Diet Coke?"

"No! Just water. No ice, no cup, just room-temperature water kept in a closet. Now, please, this is my crisis."

"Who keeps chips in a dresser and water in a closet?" she asked.

"You are here to console, not critique."

"I can't console well without food." Paige finally discovered the Doritos and some water, and she walked back to the sofa with a look of hungry dismay.

After a full minute of Paige's futile attempts to open the bag, I jerked it from her hand, ripped it open, and gave it back.

"Focus," I said.

"I am, I am, continue." She munched a Dorito.

"Then she tried to get me the role of the narrator in *Joseph and the Amazing Technicolor Dreamcoat*."

"Oh, I remember that," Paige said, starting to laugh hysterically. "The whole role is singing, and you're the worst this side of Arkansas."

"Yes, well, thankfully, I know I can't sing and declined the audition. But that's just what she's poked her nose into since college. Who has time to talk about the previous eighteen years!" I was finally coming alive.

Paige pulled her fingers through her hair, trying to push her bangs out of her eyes. "You just put cheese powder in your hair," I told her.

"Oh, it's just us. Who cares?" She put her hand back into the bag to retrieve another chip. "But you know what? I think it's time you quit whining about your mama and get on with your life." She stuffed another chip in her mouth. "You know what really amazes me?"

"What?"

"I can't believe you figured this out. Me? I would have spent the rest of my life thinking what a coincidence it was that my mother's name was on *my* letter." She was totally serious. "But you've always been that way. You could figure out just about anything, about anyone. You remember when someone stole your student-council speech from your locker?" She snickered.

"Yeah," I said, laughing myself at the memory.

"You turned that school and half its students and staff upside down until you finally sneaked into Kimberly Malloy's house and found it in a shoebox in her closet. You are shameless!" Now her snicker had turned into a belly laugh.

"Hey, I was doing good until her mother sneaked up on me with a can of Mace, ready to attack the behind that was poking out of her daughter's closet." That image made us both hysterical.

"At least you weren't cleaning her bathroom," Paige said, laughing so hard she fell off of the sofa.

"Maybe that's it," I said after we wiped our tears and regained our composure. "Maybe I don't need to write books. Maybe I need to uncover stories. Maybe I need to write for a newspaper or something."

"Yeah! You could move back home and write for our paper."

For the first time in the last six hours, I was actually having a rational thought. "You're right, Paige. I could. Maybe this book-writing thing isn't what I was really supposed to do. Maybe I'm supposed to be a journalist after all." That said, I began to pace. "Maybe I could go home, write for the paper, and uncover stories. The first will be 'Tales of Victoria.' That's what I need to do. I need to go home and write stories that terrorize my mother." I was beginning to like this whole idea.

"You need to just go home and do what you're good at."

"I was able to prove that Victoria rigged this contest. There's no telling what I could uncover around our fair city. We've had a very productive evening, my fine friend."

"Yes, we have. Can we eat now?" she asked as she stood to brush the Dorito crumbs off her shirt.

"Are you not totally sick? You just ate an entire bag of chips."

"We'll call that an appetizer," she said, then she threw her arm around me and led me toward the door.

"OK. I need a Coke anyway."

Leo's has the hottest chicken wings north of Hades, accompanied by what Leo calls "raw fries," thinly sliced potatoes cooked either almost raw or crispy, like I like them. Paige and I munched on celery and blue cheese and ate ourselves sick, then we headed back to my apartment to crash. Around three a.m. we had exhausted both conversation and ourselves. Paige got up with me at seven thirty, and by eight I was in class and she was headed home.

After my second class, I went to the mailroom and reached into my mailbox, excited to examine the paper and discover where the *Savannah Chronicle* could most effectively utilize an investigative reporter. But that morning's edition held more distracting information. "Local Humanitarian and Writer, Gloria Richardson, Dead at 62" announced the headline. I read in disbelief, feeling as if a friend I loved deeply was gone. This woman, who had made such an impact on my life, was dead of cancer.

Who knew how many articles she had written about people who overcame insurmountable odds and helped others, in spite of their own circumstances? All the while, she could have been writing her own story. She chose, instead, to keep her battle a secret. Maybe it was the cancer itself that drove her to write some of her more moving pieces. Who could be sure?

As I closed the paper, I thought about the last six years. Lines from past columns began to fit themselves together in my recollection, as if taking over my senses. Then came thoughts of short stories and novels I had written, chased by images of my misguided mother and the decisions I was now forced to make because of them.

It was time for me to become a writer. A good writer. A life-altering writer. A Gloria writer. I knew what I would do. I would decline the award. Better yet, Vicky would decline the award on my behalf and with sincere regret for all of Mr. Peterson's troubles. I would return to Savannah. I would make my own mark right on Vicky's doorstep.

The front page of the *Savannah Chronicle* declared a Mr. Samuel Hicks the editor at large. Within the hour I dialed the number, went through a truly southern receptionist, a rude secretary, and finally landed a rather winded-sounding Mr. Hicks.

"Uh . . . uh, Mr. Hicks, my name is Savannah. And this is probably not the way you normally handle business, but I, well I, uh, I really felt like I needed to speak to you immediately. I'm here at the University of Georgia, and for the last six years, I've consumed every article Gloria Richardson has written. Each one seemed more, well, more powerful than the one before."

The phone was so quiet on the other end, I finally asked, "Are you still there?"

"I'm here," said a perturbed voice.

"I know her death has left a tremendous void at the *Chronicle*. I also know that no one will ever totally fill the place that she has left, but I believe I am capable of carrying on her vision, and—"

"Young lady, I'm not sure who you are or what you think you are capable of, but I won't be hiring anyone to fill Gloria's shoes. No one can. We have only entry-level positions available at this time. If you are interested in a job, you can send in a résumé and some writing samples to our human resources department. Now, I have to get to work." And he hung up.

I decided at that exact moment that I would have Gloria's column in less than a month. Vicky wouldn't be allowed to know. At least not until I decided to tell her.

CHAPTER THREE

After graduation, I hit the road for home in Old Betsy, my eight-year-old black Saab. She's a little tired. The fabric on the ceiling is beginning to detach in a couple of places, but that will be an easy fix. When I actually have time to fix it.

Vicky wanted my dad to buy me a Lincoln Town Car for graduation. She felt it would be safer. "Safe" being the operative word. Safe from anything and everybody. No one would want to be seen with an eighteen-year-old girl in a Lincoln Town Car. My dad graciously salvaged my reputation and refused.

Something happens to me just north of downtown. Savannah begins to fill my senses. No matter what the time of year, I'm forced to roll down my windows and tug open my sunroof, allowing myself to both feel and smell home. I've memorized the story that the streets tell in progression, culminating in the enchantment of the place I call home, the Historic District.

I know this city. I know it the way a couple who have been married fifty years know where the lines came from around each other's eyes. I know its stately oak trees covered in moss, its Bradford pear trees blooming in clouds of white. Savannah holds all my secrets shared with best friends, my first kiss, my once-upon-a-time dreams of foreign lands and great adventures, and my discovery of faith. It is 2.2 square miles of history and life's simple pleasures. It was built of twenty-four squares, many of which held a church, cathedral, or synagogue, and a neighbor who knew not only your name, but your dreams.

During my high-school years, these were the streets we drove in unforgettable joy, riding with heads stuck out the window. These streets were also home to our own Barney Fife, Sergeant Millings. He always hid on the corner of Oglethorpe and East Jones Streets, waiting for any opportunity to pull one of us kids over and fortify his claim that no one under the age of forty-five should be driving.

We Phillipses lived in Atlanta until my eleventh birthday, when my father, Jake, sold his multimillion-dollar accounting firm at the ripe old age of forty. My mother had longed to return to the place she called home since I could remember. So Dad said good-bye to insane hours, the pressure of a hundred employees, and an hour-and-a-half commute. He bought a small coffee shop on East State Street in Savannah, packed up the Phillips clan, and settled in to spend the rest of his life enjoying his family and his job.

Jake's Coffee Shop is located on Oglethorpe Square, between the Chatham County Legislative Building and the courthouse. His shop is the place where people start their days with some good old-fashioned brew, as he likes to call it. "If you can't spell it or pronounce it, you surely shouldn't drink it," he is fond of saying.

I proved to be his most difficult customer. I hate coffee. I've tried. I've tried it every way but in milkshake form, and I may have had it that way as well. But I hate it. I am a confessed Coca-Cola addict. It is one of life's greatest joys, especially McDonald's Cokes. They are magical. Their magic lies in that powerful, burning sensation that brings alive every sensory organ known to man. My first taste of a McDonald's Coke sent me soaring. I had more energy than a carpool of five-year-olds and never forgot the taste. Sure, I had had Coke before—but this, this wasn't Coke; this was an experience.

When we moved to Savannah, I commenced my search for the Golden Arches immediately. A quick survey of the area revealed not one within the Historical District. Appalled and persistent, I did what any committed McDonald's Coke connoisseur would do: I picketed. For one week, I picketed in front of our house before and after school, even sacrificing my after-school recreational reading hour. "Do you people not think I deserve a break today?" I asked the passersby. "Don't you know I need to start my day with a Coke and a smile? Well, do you see me? I'm not smiling."

Mother was mortified. "My stars, Savannah Phillips, I'll build you one in the backyard with its own play land if you will just get yourself inside." I refused to be swayed, because we don't *have* a backyard. We have a courtyard, overtaken by a lap pool and flowers with names that no one on the face of the earth beside Victoria and Martha Stewart can pronounce.

By the end of the week, I was worn down. I had been honked at, laughed at, and exploited on the evening news. To top it off, I was dying of thirst. That Friday, Dad picked me up from school and took me straight to his shop. He blindfolded me and led me to the back room. The removal of my blindfold revealed my very own McDonald's Coke fountain, courtesy of a good friend who owned a franchise. Dad knew an eleven-year-old prepubescent girl didn't need any extra drama, especially when she had no trouble creating her own already.

On this beautiful May afternoon, when the front of my house on Abercorn Street came into view, the world was in perfect order. And I was certain I was home. Why so certain? Easy. There were two six-foot signs spanning both of our front balconies. The sign on the balcony to the left of the front door read "Welcome Home," and the sign to the right read "Savannah." I truly wished Vicky could have found a more discreet way to express her excitement.

The house was built with brick made by slave laborers. The people of Savannah in that time believed that if the brick was so inexpensive, it couldn't be good enough. So they covered the brick with stucco and scored it to make it look like stone. By the 1970s, the same brick that years before had been deemed worthless and in need of covering began to be valued for its actual worth at ten dollars a brick. Its value had homeowners all over Savannah removing their stucco. The brick on our home is undeniably stunning.

There is more ironwork in the city of Savannah than in any other city in America, the majority of it unquestionably on my house. Two balconies in front of the second-floor windows flank ornate black-painted wooden doors. They are rather simple, but beautiful nonetheless—well, before they were mercilessly draped with vinyl communiqué. Ivy climbs the brick wall and reaches around the front of the house from East Jones to Abercorn. There is also a beautiful iron fence that follows the curves of the house in front of the lower windows.

When I pulled into the driveway, my little brother, Thomas, who is all of six-foot-one, came flying out of the side door. He had my door opened before I could even reach for the handle.

"I'm sure you hate the sign," he burst, "but you would have hated Mom's first one even more. She had it evenly distributed with 'Home' cut in half." Thomas turned to face our front stoop, pointing first to the left side. "Welcome Ho"—he stopped long enough to point to the right—"me Savannah. We'd've had tourists making you the next Savannah attraction."

"The eighth wonder of the world, I'm sure."

He planted a kiss on my head. "Don't think so highly of yourself. Fortunately for you, she declared you would rather she cook for you anyway. By now she thinks the whole thing was her idea, and she's totally satisfied."

"Thank you for preserving my reputation." Duke, Dad's golden retriever, came pounding out the side door and stood stately at Thomas's side.

"Duke, you haven't changed a bit. Except maybe gained about

fifty extra pounds!" I grunted as he put both paws on my shoulders and licked me, obviously expecting me to reciprocate. "Someone has got to get this dog on a meal plan."

"He's on Mom's-leftovers meal plan. She refuses to spend money on actual dog food for him."

"Who does that surprise?"

"Well, she might not have a choice. The vet told Dad Duke needs to lose fifty pounds. So Dad started walking him." He stopped and patted Duke on the head. "I think Dad's lost more than Duke has, though."

"Yeah, there's not much pleasure in a fifty-pound bag of Alpo when compared to pork tenderloin." Duke's ears perked up at the mere mention of pork.

"What are you doing here anyway?" I asked, finally stopping long enough to give him a hug. "I thought you had another week of school." As he walked around to open the trunk, I smiled at his neatly cropped hair.

Thomas was in his third year at The Citadel Military Academy in Charleston, South Carolina. Vicky was sure he had enrolled to embarrass her, but he had dreamed of going to The Citadel ever since Judge Hoddicks's son Roger filled his head with stories of life as a cadet. When Thomas came home after his first month with his head shaved, Vicky called the general who was the head of The Citadel and threatened abuse charges.

"Have you seen my child?"

"Yes, ma'am. In fact, I have another five hundred that look just like him."

"Well, it is criminal, I tell you. Criminal." She then headed to her room. Dad followed her and, legend has it, made it clear she would call and apologize. Now, Dad lets Vicky think what she will, but trust me, he is the one who has this ship under control. She made that call to the general, albeit brief and very private, then gathered herself, returned downstairs, declared Thomas too thin, and began to cook a feast.

"I finished up exams early," Thomas said, bringing me back to the present.

"Lucky you."

"I'd say lucky *you* by the way Mom has tried to make your graduation the talk of the town. You might need me here to keep you out of the limelight. Especially if you plan to tell Mom about your new career move. All I have to do is bring up women in the Corps, and she will resurrect her letter-writing campaign to the South Carolina Legislature."

I had called Thomas to warn him of what I was doing, knowing he could help me with the excruciating task of adjustment. We walked around the sidewalk to the front of the house and up the stairs to the double front doors. In old Georgian homes, the entrances were built on the second floor in an effort to limit the dust and dirt that entered the houses from the horse-drawn carriages traveling the dirt streets. The servants lived on the lower level. Today, most homeowners rent out the lower levels as apartments, but Vicky never has. She, instead, made it a haven where Thomas foolishly relocated his room. Vicky walks around in sheer delight, believing her baby will never want to leave.

As we reached the top of the front steps, I stopped and turned around to take a moment to breathe in the essence of my life.

"Been a while, huh, Vanni?"

Wrapping my arm around the young man who alone could call me by such a name, I closed my eyes and allowed a smile to cross my face. "Mmm hmm . . . it's been too long." We walked inside.

I hadn't been home at all my last semester, trying to finish my story and finals. It seemed like forever. Yet, the looming foyer bombarded me with familiarity, right down to the smell in the air, which proclaimed that fried chicken was on the menu.

The oriental rug still encompassed the majority of the black-marble floor. Two black Armthwaite chairs flanked the opening to the left of the foyer, which held the dining room. One massive arrangement of flowers that Mother replenished on a weekly basis brought it all together, creating an abode that could compete with the pages of *Veranda*.

The magnificent staircase with a wrought-iron banister and an oriental stair runner in complimentary tones of rich black, peach, and pink curved around the back of the foyer. I peeked into the "parlor," as Vicky called it. A living room to any normal person, but not to any person living in Savannah. In front of the window sat the early 1900s burlwood petite grand piano, one of my mother's most treasured keepsakes. My father had it shipped from London as a wedding gift.

Above the fireplace in the parlor hangs a picture of Vicky in a white organza gown with hand-beaded flowers all over it, adorned by a bow on each sleeve. All I can say about her hair is that it is big. I have no idea what it is with pageant people and big hair. Maybe they are just trying to make themselves look taller, but most of the time it spreads as wide as it does high. Draped across her is a sash declaring her "Miss Georgia United States of America." She stands stately in this twenty-seven-year-old photograph, her hand draped ever so deliberately, yet casually, across the back of a French colonial chair. Below the portrait in an acrylic box rests her Miss Georgia United States of America crown. Thomas and I call it the "Ode to Vicky." This parlor is her own private sanctuary, where she comes often just to stare at her picture, remembering who knows what.

Thomas came back through the front door, setting down the rest of my bags. "Happy thoughts, I hope."

I couldn't help but laugh as I picked up my bags. "Humorous thoughts. I'm going to get cleaned up for dinner. What about you? Because I have something I want you to do."

"What? I'm not telling Mom anything for you."

"I need you to go take down those banners. Please, they are humiliating. And as long as we keep her inside, she won't even know they're gone."

"Would you like me to hang them up in your room?"

"I will refrain from telling you what to do with them, because I am a southern lady." I turned my back to him and headed up the stairs to a landing that connected four bedrooms. Mine was in the far left corner.

Mother has revamped this house completely three different times and rearranges furniture and accessories on a bimonthly basis. But she is not allowed to touch my room. It is where I can come and know that things will be like I left them. The color of my room is yellow. It reminds me of sunshine. My bedroom suite consists of a wrought-iron bed and a pine dresser that sits to the left of my bed in front of the windows. A pine armoire stands directly across from the bed, housing those things that make young adulthood tolerable: a TV, a stereo, a VCR, and a recently added DVD player. My mother, an only child, had wanted to put my grandmother's antique bed-room suite in my room after my grandparents died, he from a heart attack, she from heartbreak. But I don't do dead people's furniture. I'm more than glad to love 'em while they're living, but once they're gone, well, I don't want to be sleeping on their furniture.

My bed is flanked by floor-to-ceiling bookcases. On these shelves lie my greatest treasures. Pictures of some of my best mem-ories with my closest friends are stuck between the books that have shaped me. Chaucer's *Canterbury Tales,* Lewis's *Chronicles of Narnia,* and Fitzgerald's *The Great Gatsby.* Brontë's *Wuthering Heights* is still wuthering as far as I'm concerned, but some things were just required reading. I also have numerous biographies, some that were authorized and others that weren't. There is the one about the Onassis women that is rather enlightening; a book of Ronnie's love letters to Nancy Reagan, which leaves little room for most men to stand a chance; one of Hillary Clinton that my mother told me I couldn't leave in her house; and the one of George W. Bush she bought to replace it.

When he won the election over Al Gore, she acted like a giddy school girl. She even calls him by the pet name his wife gave him, "Bushie." I told her she needed to get a grip. She told me I needed to appreciate her respect for world leaders. I asked her to name one other world leader she actually knew.

"Oh, you know, the lady with all the shoes. I hear she's pretty good."

"Imelda Marcos?"

"Yes, that's her," she said, acting as if she had said it herself.

"Did anyone ever tell you she went to prison?"

She told me I was getting a little snippy and needed to watch my tone, that she was still my mother. But I saw through the protest. My mother has a crush on the president. I know it, she knows it, and anyone who catches her watching Fox News knows it.

Some books inside this bookcase have changed me. *Roots* by Alex Haley first came to television when I was in elementary school. Mom wouldn't let me watch it, thinking it would be too troubling for my tender years. But she was so glued to the TV set downstairs that I sneaked in the first four nights of viewing without her knowing. My father eventually caught me and held me in his arms while we watched together. He did his best to explain, at least as much as he was able to understand himself. For the next week's show and tell, I brought no show, just tell, and all I told was the story of *Roots*. My teacher finally assured me I had covered all that could possibly be covered. I assured her there was more, but one week was all I got. For my thirteenth birthday, Dad gave me the book.

Gone with the Wind rests there too. That one was Vicky's gift for my thirteenth birthday. "Everyone needs to know her heritage."

"It's fiction, Mother," I told her.

"Fiction to some; reality to truly southern women." I will never tell her that I have actually read the book, or that Scarlett is my secret heroine. In fact, no living soul will ever know, because my mother would see it as cause for public celebration.

Scanning to the bottom of my bookcase, my eyes caught the biography of John Wesley. It is one of my two most precious books, and the sight of it caused me to laugh. I was forced to read it by the pastor of Wesley Monumental United Methodist Church. My longtime friend and eventual boyfriend, Grant Lewis, conned me into sneaking inside the church one Saturday night during our eleventh-grade year, all because he wanted to see who could stay inside the longest without getting freaked out by the shadow figures coming through the fifteen stained-glass windows. We both lost it at the same time when we heard footsteps on the hardwood floor.

"What was that?" Grant whispered.

"God coming to tell us we shouldn't be messing in His stuff."

"No, He only comes on Sunday. It has to be John Wesley's ghost."

"Well, rest assured, he'll know for certain whose inane idea this was by the time he heads home."

About that time, Pastor Mason walked up the stairs and laid his Sunday sermon on the pulpit, eliciting from me a scream loud enough to make Grant scream too. All this lively noise culminated in a scream from Pastor Mason louder than the aforementioned. Not to mention he also went airborne, jumping so high that his knee hit the edge of the pulpit. By the time he hobbled over to turn on the lights, Grant and I were frozen. I couldn't have run had I tried. I knew then that, just like in dreams, fear prevents retreat.

Pastor Mason hobbled calmly toward us, removed us from the red-carpeted runner, and sat us firmly on the front row of the stiff wooden pew. I was too scared to speak, and Grant never opened his eyes.

Then Pastor Mason decided that if we felt it necessary to come to church so early for the Sunday service, we must be in need of a powerful sermon. So he climbed to his pulpit—well, limped actually—and proceeded to preach.

You would think, due to my state of mind, that I'd have trouble remembering his sermon, but I think it is precisely because of my state of mind that I do remember. Surely part of my punishment in heaven for pulling such a stunt would be to recite the sermon verbatim. And I still pretty much can. His message was titled "The Door."

He began by describing the front doors to people's homes and likened them to Jesus being the door to life. Then he compared Jesus to shepherds and spoke of how shepherds are the door to the sheep pen. No one gets to the sheep unless they go through the shepherd. Then he finished with this word: "Each of us should be a bridge builder to that door, the door of Jesus Himself." I wasn't sure I got it, what with all those mixed metaphors, but I'd certainly remember it.

For the benediction, Pastor Mason made us sing four stanzas of "Christ Is Risen" and assigned a twenty-five-page report on the life of John Wesley. Somewhere between the message and the singing, Grant passed out from holding his breath. When Pastor Mason finally left us alone, I was at the altar praying that God would somehow forgive me, and Grant came to long enough to roll around underneath the pew in hysterics. I didn't speak to Grant again until I had written my report, and I have kept the book on John Wesley's life safely tucked away ever since.

John Wesley is known for starting Sunday school in Savannah. It is told that as a little boy he escaped his room in the attic one night when his house caught on fire. He said that night he realized there was a destiny for his life. Wesley loved people, all people. He preached to the Spanish, the Italian, the French, and the English. "The world is my parish," he said. So I guess you could say he was a door to the world. His only desire was to leave something life-changing in his wake. I didn't know if I'd ever leave a wake, but I hoped I could leave something, be a door to someone, somehow.

The other book that has changed my life is my grandmother's Bible. Though I wasn't willing to take her bed, I was pleased to take her Bible. So, it rests here as well, with all her hopes and markings, and new hopes and markings of my own. My greatest treasures are in this room. The past six years, however, have led me to believe they are in this home, in this city.

I only hope I'm still Vicky's treasure by the time dinner is over.

CHAPTER FOUR

In the land of lard you don't have to be told what's for dinner; each offering has a distinct smell of its own. There is the fried-steak smell, the fried-pork-chop smell, the fried-green tomatoes, squash, or okra smell; and the greatest of them all, the fried-chicken smell. As for the smell of Victoria's fried chicken, well, let's just say it is so sinfully delicious that I am forced to call her Victoria when referring to it. My mother is in her element in the kitchen, where she dances around like a virtuoso in apron and high heels.

My first evening back revealed all things as they were: Dad at the table going through the mail, Duke at his feet, Thomas nowhere in sight; he rarely was. This world of mine was still mine.

I set the table and pulled out serving dishes. When all was ready, a yell went out for Thomas to come to dinner. Upon his arrival, we all took our usual seats—me across from Dad and Thomas across from Vicky. And there in front of us was a piece of heaven, a platter of fried chicken à la Victoria.

We also had fresh corn on the cob, butter beans, macaroni and cheese—and not that boxed kind either. Vicky would have needed rehabilitation if anyone in her home cooked something out of a box. The only thing she bought in boxes was cereal, and that only after my father took a liking to Frosted Flakes. If it wasn't homemade, Vicky declared it wasn't worth eating. This caused a bit of a controversy every now and then, but I'll just leave that to the imagination.

No, OK, I'll tell. One evening some new neighbors invited us for dinner. Vicky usually liked to have new families over to our house so she could supervise all culinary activities, but this couple was insistent that they cook for her after all she had done to help them get acclimated to the city.

Upon arrival, Vicky gave me a dirty look for having gum in my mouth. "Would you mind telling me where your trash can is?" I asked our lovely hostess.

She stopped putting ice in the glasses and pointed me in the direction of the pantry. "Sure, honey, it's right over there."

Vicky was standing next to me when I swung the pantry door open to get to the trash can. There, in full view, were boxes for just about anything you could imagine. There was macaroni in boxes, rice in boxes, soups in boxes, cakes in boxes—and the crowning transgression—entire meals in boxes.

Poor Vicky grew white as a sheet. She politely excused herself, grabbed my father, and pulled him into the half bath beneath the stairs.

I heard snippets of "I wouldn't feed Duke . . ." and ". . . snowball's chance in Dixie." Then I heard a male voice say, "You will and you'll like it."

Dad must have been immensely clear, because she returned and we all convened at the dinner table, where Vicky sat staring at her plate. As our hostess passed her a perfectly acceptable meal, she asked, "Victoria, is anything wrong tonight? You look kind of peaked."

Vicky came out of her trance long enough to say, "No, nothing's wrong." She then picked up her fork and let it slowly work its way through the food without ever bringing it to her mouth.

My dad glared at her from across the table, but even that didn't work. Finally she asked the lady, "So, how do you make this, this, this lovely casserole?"

"Oh, it's really easy. In fact, I think I have another box of it in the pantry that I'll give you to take home."

Well, I honestly thought Vicky was going to expire right there. But with one more glance at my father, she ever so slowly put a minuscule amount of food on her fork. It crept to her lips, where she placed only the tiniest bit into her mouth. I was mesmerized.

When the first bite entered, she feigned chewing. The next thing I knew, her eyes were watering, and she started coughing and gagging and holding her throat. She jumped up and asked the lady, fist clinched around her throat. "What's in here?" The poor hostess, horrified, ran to the trash can, pulled out the empty box with my chewing gum stuck on top, and began to read out loud every ingredient on the back.

When the lady got to an ingredient she couldn't pronounce, Vicky said, "That's it! I'm deathly allergic to that." Waddling over to my father, still holding her throat, she grabbed his arm and feigned gasping, "Jake, you'd better get me to the emergency room immediately."

My dad hadn't budged and didn't budge. He simply looked at her and said, "You can walk yourself home, get the car, and drive yourself to the emergency room. The kids and I are going to finish dinner with this kind family, and we will check on you when we get home."

I don't know if our poor hostess was more horrified by what she had done to my mother or by how my father was treating her. Her husband did his best not to break out in sheer hysterics, and I just sat back and enjoyed the drama. Thomas never looked up. He was still enjoying every bite of his boxed dinner. Vicky glared at my father, touched the lady's arm gently, apologized, grabbed her purse, and waddled home.

When the door closed behind her, Dad looked at the sweet

hostess about to collapse in tears and touched her arm. "Victoria has episodes like this quite often, but trust me, she'll be back to normal, oh, I'd say by early morning. Now, let's enjoy this excellent meal." He looked at both of us, smiled a smile we knew all too well, and we stayed another two hours.

"Lord, we thank You that Savannah is home. We thank You that we can be together. We thank You for this meal we are about to receive and the amazing hands that so sacrificially and lovingly prepared it for us from scratch." I thought it rather shameless to try to schmooze your mother through prayer, but I would take whatever worked. "Amen," Thomas closed.

Vicky started right in. "Savannah, has Dean Hillwood let you know when you could expect to hear the results of the contest?"

Thomas was on that like a duck on a June bug. "Mom, did I tell you that I'm going to bring some of the guys home this summer? They haven't quit talking about your biscuits since the last away game and—"

"Thomas, that will be great, but I was speaking to Savannah. She and I haven't had time to talk in weeks. She's been so busy." She turned back to me. "So if you win, will you move to New York or try to stay here?"

I wiped my mouth and refolded my napkin. "There is something you need to know about the contest."

"Tell your mother anything, darling."

"I spoke with my dean before I left school, and he totally agreed and is supporting me. I hope you can do the same."

"Now, honey, your mother loves you more than Dean Hillwood. I'm sure anything you do I will support." My eyes caught Dad's. I knew he would support whatever decision I made. As long as I was making an honest living and enjoying what I did, he would be happy for me.

"Well, I've been doing a lot of thinking over the last couple of months, and I've made some decisions for my life. I did receive the results of the contest." Poor Vicky leaned in so far her chin was about to touch the gravy. "And I won, actually."

"Oh my stars! I knew you would win," she said with a little too much enthusiasm. "I just knew you would. You were created for this, Savannah. You are just going to be amazing! Oh, but you can't move. Will you have to move? Surely you won't have to move immediately, if you have to move at all. I mean, can't you write books from anywhere?"

"Yes, I can write from anywhere."

"Yes! Right! You could. You could write them from right up there in your bedroom."

"Yes, I could, actually."

"Oh my stars! Oh, well, let's eat. Let's just eat and eat and eat and then go get dessert and eat some more," she said, laughing at her own delight.

"I'm not finished, Mother," but she didn't hear a word. I was forced to reach over and touch her hand. "Mother, Mother . . ."

"Oh, yes, darling, what is it? If you have something else to tell your Mother, just go right ahead."

"I did win the contest," I said, pausing to take a deep breath, "but I am not accepting the award."

"You what?"

"I turned it down. But before you go off in the other direction, let me finish."

"Savannah Grace Phillips, I cannot—" she began. Dad reached over and touched Vicky's arm and nodded in my direction. She looked slightly perturbed but conceded. "Continue, Savannah," she said through pursed lips.

"Go ahead, Savannah. We're listening," Dad said, softening his brow.

"I've been doing a lot of thinking. I love to write. I really do. In fact, until this contest, I thought that really was what I wanted to do with my life. But when the opportunity came, something didn't feel right." I studied Vicky's expression, but she offered nothing but staged melodrama.

"I can't believe this! Something didn't *feel* right," she started.

"Victoria, let her finish."

"Do please finish, Savannah," she said, stabbing at a butter bean.

I looked over at Thomas for support. He gave me a wink and a smile. "It just isn't right for me. I believe there is something else."

"Something else? What? A street hustler? A Falcons cheerleader? Heaven help us all." A brief clutch of her chest caused the entire table to flinch.

"I believe I have a different mission in life than to simply write novels. And that's basically all I have to say." I picked up my fork to eat my now-cold dinner. Then I let fly the arrow that would certainly strike with practiced precision. "Oh, there is one more thing. I want to live here, here in Savannah. And if I can, Mother, I'd really like to stay at home, at least until I can find an apartment."

My, my, my, a verse and a chorus of "Sweet Beulah Land" could have been sung about that time. You would have thought the last five minutes were a distant memory by the light that came on in Vicky's black eyes and the smile that crept its way back into position. I knew it was evil, but it was necessary. For a moment, my thoughts went to visions of the inevitable Vicky meltdown when I indeed found my new place. All could be certain she would die a thousand deaths, each of which we would suffer with her.

On the whole, the entire adventure went well. She offered a few brief groans, a few sighs, and a few, well, I'm not sure what they were, but they didn't quite fit the gasp category. Dad sat meditatively across from me as well, never picking up a bite of food. Thomas looked up only between bites.

As the production came to a close, Dad got up calmly from his seat, kissed me on the head, and whispered in my ear, "I'm not sure what you are up to, but I know you have a plan." I looked up and he smiled at me—that smile that is definitively Dad. Then he sat back down, content to finally eat his chicken.

I felt a hand on mine. I looked over at Vicky and saw tears coming down both cheeks. She just smiled at me, either out of pity or pleasure, I'm not quite sure, and patted my hand like she does. Then she said, "Eat your chicken, darling." Even cold, Victoria's chicken was still the best I had ever eaten.

"Jake, why don't you and Thomas clear the table so Savannah and I can go for a walk?"

Dad hesitated, thinking I'm sure that the whole pat-on-the-hand, tears-in-the-eyes presentation at the table was a momentary diversion, and that I might be in for the reeling of my entire human existence. "Victoria, she's a grown woman. You can't make her decisions for her."

She kissed him on the forehead and headed to the foyer. "Yes, but she'll always be my daughter. We'll be back shortly, I promise."

She never asked me if I wanted to go for a walk, but I followed her to the foyer, and Duke followed close behind, both of us with our tails tucked between our legs.

"Grab your sweater. It might be cool," she said. Vicky took her elegantly embroidered sweater from the coatrack by the door, and I grabbed my gray sweatshirt off the armchair. Duke seemed content to stay behind, but I made him come for protection. He and Vicky have issues. She's had little regard for him since Dad refused to name him Magnolia.

As we walked down the stairs and turned the corner to East Jones Street, the air still held a slight chill, but I could feel the hint of summer in the distance. We headed straight to walk the squares.

It took an entire square for Vicky to get to the point of this excursion. We had taken only two other walks like this one since we moved to Savannah. One was the prerequisite birds-and-the-bees talk. I'm not sure how it ended. I just know that by the time she was through and I realized that she had participated in birds-and-bees behavior on at least two separate occasions—well, it absolutely rocked my world. Then there was the going-off-to-college talk: always be a lady, wear clean underwear in case you get in a wreck, don't give your heart away, don't talk back, and call home once a day. I obliged by calling three times a week. And I never understood the clean underwear part anyway, because after a wreck, who could be sure what was bad hygiene and what was simply a by-product of the wreck itself?

I had a feeling, however, that this conversation was going to be different. Why? Because for the first two blocks Vicky never said a word. She didn't talk about the weather. She didn't talk about the McCollums, who live next door, and their grandchildren, Penelope and Priscilla. She didn't tell the latest gossip about crazy Mrs. Weitzer, who lives across the street, or dirty old Mr. Dickerson, who lives two doors down and has a habit of gazing through windows. She didn't even talk about the new flowers planted around Lafayette Square. She didn't talk about what was happening down at the Chamber of Commerce, where she served the city as director, or the coffeehouse. She didn't talk about her latest recipe or award. She didn't even talk about how glad she was to have both of her children home. No, for two solid blocks, my mother remained absolutely and miraculously silent. Then, it began like this.

"Savannah, I remember those countless times as I would rock you in the wee hours of the morning and stare into your precious face, dreaming of what you would become. For years I tried to make you me, but I realized some women weren't meant to be like me," she said, placing her hand daintily on her chest while I nodded in adamant agreement.

"I used to think you would be a great pianist, until I heard you play."

That gave us both a moment of confirming laughter. "Ain't that the truth."

"Savannah, don't say 'ain't.'"

"OK," I said in mock appeasement.

"We tried you in ballet, and then we saw you dance."

"Thank you for saving me," I said, laughing again. We were coerced into stopping so Duke could take care of his business. We both stopped talking because it was hard to have any meaningful conversation with that going on.

"I don't know why that dog has to do that," she said, crinkling her nose and turning away.

"Because he's a dog."

"I don't care. He should be more discreet. Out here where anyone can see. Did you bring something to pick it up with?"

"There is no way I'm picking that up!"

"That is the law around here, Savannah."

"Well, you should have told me that before we started this thing."

Victoria sighed in disgust. "I knew we should have gotten a lap dog."

When Duke was finished, we picked up our walk and she picked up her thoughts.

"But when you brought home your first creative-writing piece in middle school, I knew then what you had been created for. I don't believe I have ever read words more simple, yet profound, more compelling or endearing in my entire life."

"That's a bit overstated."

"No, it's not. You engulfed me with your story, and you made me cry at your ability to express yourself so tenderly yet with such strength."

Duke yawned and shook his head.

"All that at thirteen?"

"Yes! You were a very gifted child." Her use of the past tense gave me pause. "You got that from your mother. So I nurtured your imagination. You went into theater and writing. And I always believed that one day you would be one of the greatest writers of your generation—melodramatic, maybe, but phenomenal nonetheless."

"Can you imagine, someone from our family melodramatic?"

"Well, they say every family has one."

"Yes, they do." I could not believe the poster child for melo-drama had just labeled me the same.

"I've pictured your face in the bookstore windows and thought about how we could advertise your first book signing here in Savannah. Well, anyway, tonight, listening to you, I realized that your life isn't about what I want. Your life is about doing what you believe is the absolute best thing for you."

When we reached the edge of the Dueling Zone in front of the cemetery, Victoria stopped and turned to face me. The duel-ing zone was used years before for unresolvable conflicts. It had been avoided by us since our last flip-flop confrontation. Duke didn't realize we had stopped until his leash extended fully and he was forced to come back or gag to death. Victoria looked down and patted his head. I thought about checking her temperature, her pulse, her latest psychiatric evaluation, but I figured this was one of those once-in-a-lifetime moments that just needed to be left as is.

"Savannah, everything in my life that I ever wanted I have achieved. I was crowned Miss Georgia United States of America."

"Yes, you were."

"I married the man I have always loved, and he has loved me better than I probably deserve," she said hesitantly but not totally convincingly. I held my tongue.

"I have two children who are exactly what I wanted. I live in the city I adore. I have a job I love and the anticipation of some-thing eternal beyond this world. I don't need anything else except to see my children achieve the same happiness I have been fortu-nate enough to enjoy. If you find that in staying here and seeking out a new dream, then I will support you wholeheartedly." And with that she kissed me and hugged me as only a mother can do.

Somehow Vicky made me believe her. How she could try so hard to secure my victory in that contest and not fight harder at this moment wasn't clear, but she didn't. And it felt genuine. She really seemed, at that moment at least, to want for my life what-ever I wanted for my life. We would see.

"Thanks."

"Well, we believe you will make the right choices because we believe in you. Now, let's go home before your father thinks I've killed you and thrown you into the river," she said, and she hooked her arm in mine.

As we headed home, I took in all the changes that had taken place while I'd been gone. "I see the Adamses repainted their house. When did they do that?"

"Oh, that was an issue. Jane Ann wanted a rich cream and her husband wanted a gray. They were both wrong; I thought yellow would be perfect." We continued up the street, leaving the yellow painted-brick house behind us.

CHAPTER FIVE

I have always been a jogger, well, since the eighth grade. It is the one form of enjoyable exercise that middle-school P.E. offered, and since then, running has been a way of life. I conned Paige into joining me for all of two days. Then she lost interest and retreated to her indoor life.

My freshman year in high school, though, my motivation for jogging changed. It happened one Sunday morning at the church we attend on Tybee Island, in my usual place on the tenth pew, left-hand side. I had not expected to encounter any life-altering milestone that morning, and so I was caught unaware. Pastor Brice took his place behind the acrylic podium and began his simple message titled "The State of Your Soil." It was all about a gardener's inability to plant a crop of any substance or value unless he first prepares his soil. He used the parable of the sower and the seed from the Gospel of Matthew. And he let us know in the most tender of ways, that unless we spent time preparing the soil of our hearts through prayer and actually dusting off the coffee-table Bible, no seed would ever take root.

Since that day, morning has been my "tilling time," beginning with a jog. I put on my earphones and play some inspirational music. Then I head home and read from my grandmother's Bible, digging for the same treasures she did before me.

I've come to realize that those moments in the morning have done exactly what Pastor Brice said they would. Focusing on my heart, focusing on my life, taking time to actually ask the Lord to show me His will—I've seen things take root.

This particular morning I grabbed Duke and we headed toward Forsythe Park. I greeted the lightness in the air with thankfulness that the heavy heat had not yet arrived. Spring in the South is simply a wish.

As Duke and I trotted along, a curly-headed beast on a bicycle attacked from out of nowhere. Duke turned around so fast that his leash wrapped up my legs like a bad mess of Christmas-tree lights, leaving me in a dreadfully knotted heap. The maniac came to an abrupt stop, and I tried to unwind my legs from my neck as graciously as possible.

"I'm so sorry," he said, half apologetic, half laughing. "Here, let me help you." He tried to untangle Duke's leash from around my legs. Duke thought this whole thing was a game and couldn't decide who needed licking more, me or Evel Knievel, so he just lavished us both.

"I'm OK. Really, it's no big deal," I said, trying to act cool as my feet finally touched the sidewalk again. He helped me up and handed me Duke's leash. Duke clearly wanted him to stay, but I was ready for him to go. "Really, I'm OK. But *you* need to slow down a tad on that thing," I said, raising my right eyebrow.

"Yeah, slow down a tad. I haven't heard that word in a very long time."

"What word?"

"Tad."

"I didn't say tad!"

"Well, I don't have time to argue over a young, attractive woman like yourself using the word *tad,* because I'm kind of late for work. I'm really sorry. Are you sure you're OK?" he asked again as he headed over to pick up his blue bike off the concrete.

"Yes, I'm OK, really," I said, making it clear I was oblivious to the fact that he had called me both young and attractive. "It's all of five thirty in the morning. Where on earth do you work?" I asked, trying not to notice how toned and tanned his arms were as they grabbed the handlebars and his muscles flexed magnificently.

"Oh, just up the street. Maybe we'll bump into each other again," he said, an irritatingly straight, beautiful white smile lighting up his annoyingly dramatic dark eyes. "But if you're OK, I really have to go."

"I'm OK. So just go," I said, shoving my hand at him.

He departed with a smirk, and Duke watched as he and his bouncing black curls rode up the street in the direction of Bay Street, forcing me to have to watch as well. Grant was the only man who had ever turned my head, and that head had been stuck inside books for so long, even Grant hadn't been able to turn it in years. Duke and I had a long talk about his leash, and I tried to "till" as best I could, but I confess I was a tad distracted.

How do newspaper people dress? Do they wear their *hair back, or down, or what?* I pulled up my wet, stringy hair, then let it fall, then pulled it up just to let it fall again. Duke was sitting at my bathroom door with a cocked eyebrow. "Do they walk around with pencils behind their ears and their shirttails out, always racing around on a deadline? I should have gone in yesterday before I came home and scoped out the joint."

After great deliberation, I settled on a simple black pantsuit with a pale blue tank underneath, slid myself into my black mid-heeled mules, certain flip-flops were inappropriate, and pulled my hair back in what I hoped was a Lois Lane do. She's about the only newspaper reporter I knew. Then I was on my way, sneaking out to join the world of the employed.

When I turned left onto Bay Street off of Abercorn, I could see the sign SAVANNAH CHRONICLE hanging vertically from the side of the building up ahead. Those two words seemed to mock me, "SAVANNAH CHRONICLE, and you don't know anything about us."

True, but that was all about to change. I walked into the office and wasn't greeted by anyone. I came early, wanting to catch Mr. Hicks fresh before the onslaught of appointments and crises. The receptionist's desk was empty, and the people who were there were running around in such a tizzy that they noticed nothing but the path ahead of them, if that. I decided to make myself at home and find Mr. Hicks's office without assistance.

I searched the first and second floors without encountering so much as a hello, and decided to make my way to the third floor. As the elevator ascended, the fear in my mind did as well. *Maybe this is the week he decided to take his wife and kids to the south of France. Or maybe he doesn't even have a wife. And he probably doesn't like kids. In fact, he probably would hate the south of France. Or maybe he's a nice man who likes everyone and was just upset the day I called because of the loss of Gloria. Who knows?*

The elevator doors opened, and I heard his booming personality before sighting the body that went with it. "So much for fresh, free from crisis, and no appointments." I eased up the maze of aisles, following the noise toward a half-open door. The words coming from the office were loud and direct. "I told you yesterday I didn't want to see you here this morning. So go to your office, pack it up, and get out of here. And if I see your face around here at lunch, I'll pack you up and throw you out myself."

I began to perspire. Southern ladies don't "sweat," Vicky says. She could have been proven wrong ten times over that morning, however. As I neared the door, the name placard that read "Mr. Samuel Hicks, Editor at Large" confirmed my fear. From my vantage point, his office looked rather sparse but possessed a fabulous view of Bay Street. Then, the object of his torment came into view—an elderly woman, whose black hair had strands of gray, and whose etched chocolate hands made it evident she was in her glory years. I couldn't make out her soft words, but Mr. Happy Hicks's roaring verbosity didn't allow for much of a reply anyway.

I sat down in a chair on the other side of the door, which kept me out of view. "So that's Mr. Hicks," I said to myself. "Just like I thought, a man who takes vacations in his recliner with the remote control, who hates children, his wife left him years ago because he didn't know how to be nice, and when he dies, only a handful of people will come to his funeral, and they will only be there because he owes them money."

And the longer I sat there contemplating this afflicted life, the madder I became. I should have let it go. But who could? Someone stronger maybe, but self-control was a quality I had yet to successfully till. I saw no reason to start today. When I heard her faint whisper and then the power of his voice begin to consume the air again, I stood and took a moment to set my course. Fortunately, one of my professors had been a hard one to melt, until I stole his heart with my Georgian graciousness. Well, maybe not completely stole his heart, but he did at least quit glaring at me. I wasn't confident that a similar tactic would work here. But wars had been won with less. Then the spirit of Vicky welled up inside me, and I decided this wasn't a moment for graciousness. The only appropriate approach for this brute was "The Vicky." No lady should ever be spoken to in such a rude, ungentlemanly, and unacceptable manner. So, I spun my little heels around, steeled my jaw, and let Vicky take over.

As Mr. Hicks jerked his head to see me standing there, I realized he was a rather calm-looking man in his late fifties. The precious lady turned and smiled a beautiful white smile. She sensed rescue had come. I pushed the door open the rest of the way, and it flew so fast, I'm certain the doorknob stuck in the wall. For a moment, I wished he had been standing behind it. I walked over to his desk, where he had already assumed a seated position, his slight belly from too many fast-food lunches poking out in front. I put both hands on his desk and leaned over where he could see me clearly.

"What can I do for you, young lady?"

"Actually, I don't need anything from you now. At first I thought I wanted to work at your newspaper. But I can tell you're not a man who appreciates talent or even people, for that matter."

That statement caught his attention, and the lady crossed her arms and leaned back in amusement.

"No, anyone that would speak to a precious lady like this"—I patted her on the arm— "the way I've heard you speak to her isn't a man that deserves fine, raw talent. This lady has probably worked for you for years. Met your deadlines, listened to your rantings, spent sleepless nights wondering what would possibly make someone like you happy. She comes into the office every day and isn't allowed to drink McDonald's Coke or even have pictures of her golden retriever on her desk."

"She doesn't have a golden retriever, and she drinks coffee."

"Like you know what kind of dog she has."

"Yes, I do. She has a cocker spaniel."

I looked at the lady, hoping he was bluffing, but she nodded with a smile.

"Well, the point isn't what kind of dog she has; it has to do with who she is. She's a human being who deserves your respect. She deserves to be treated like a lady and respected for her, well, for her age if for nothing else. There's wisdom behind these gray hairs, gray hair you probably contributed to. Lord knows she's probably spent a lifetime having to make sure you're happy. And frankly, I don't want to spend the rest of my life doing the same."

Mr. Hicks was having trouble stifling a grin, which incensed me all the more. "Are you through?" he asked as he folded his arms and rested them on the top of his stomach.

"No, not quite. I came here today to get a job. Gloria Richardson's job. But I am leaving here disillusioned and dismayed. You wouldn't appreciate me. You probably didn't appreciate Gloria any more than you appreciate this fine lady."

"It's Ruby," she said with a smile and a nod of apparent satisfaction in Mr. Hicks's direction.

"Thank you, Ruby, nice to meet you. I'm Savannah. Anyway, I have decided I wouldn't want to work for someone who would treat anyone the way Miss Ruby has been treated here today. So for all of the beleaguered souls, I quit."

"Is that so?"

"Yes, and remember you could have had your Gloria back by next week, only her name would have been Savannah. You could have published stories the next generation could appreciate and the older generation would have respected."

"Yeah, that the older generation would have respected." Miss Ruby snickered.

I looked at her, shook Miss Ruby's hand, and turned on my heels, not so gracefully. Fortunately, I gathered myself prior to disaster, and proceeded to walk toward the door. Vicky was good, but Savannah had just raised the bar.

"Hold it just one moment, young lady." I turned around cautiously to face the now-standing and rather looming figure in front of me. "Do you mean you are just going to come in here and rant and rave and then leave without ever allowing anyone else to speak?"

"Well, I . . ."

"Now it is time for you to listen. Miss Ruby, would you like to tell her what was happening here today?"

Miss Ruby walked over to me and took me by the hand. "I just want you to know, Miss Savannah, that is the kindest thing I've seen anyone do for someone else in a long time. I thought kids your age didn't think about much else than the opposite sex and mooching off their parents." I decided then never to introduce her to Paige. "But on Mr. Hicks's behalf, I must tell you, he was making me go on vacation."

Her face lit up and every ounce of blood drained from my own. "Oh."

"Yes, that's what I was telling her. This woman, as you can tell, is here before anyone else and works after everyone else leaves. She doesn't go on vacation unless absolutely forced and hasn't taken a sick day in thirty years."

"Don't need a sick day, Samuel. I'm healthy as a horse. My husband's no longer living, all the kids are grown, and I just enjoy being here," she said, looking at me with a wink. I tried to smile back, but I was totally incapable. I no longer had a book deal and had just successfully rejoined the world of the unemployed without ever having left.

"So see, Savannah. Things aren't always as they appear. Now, if you'll excuse us, I'd like to talk to this lady for a minute," he said.

"Sure, I'm sorry. I hope you have a great vacation," I said, nodding to Miss Ruby. "And I hope you have a pleasant day as well, sir."

"Savannah, I was actually talking to Miss Ruby. I'd like you to stay for a moment," he said, smiling. "Ruby, I meant every word I said. Get going."

"I'm going, I'm going. Savannah, if you don't make it in the newspaper world, you'd make an excellent defense attorney," she said, patting me on the arm. She left the room, and her chuckle trailed her up the hall.

Then there were two. I looked at him with a pathetic grin, and he motioned for me to have a seat. "So you're the one I told to send me some of her writing. Do you always follow instructions this well?"

"Well, I wanted to make sure you read my articles. I didn't know where they would end up if I simply mailed them."

"You're a brave soul, Savannah."

"I believe I just knocked on the door of stupidity myself."

"Well, that too," he said chuckling, his belly bouncing as he laughed. "I've only seen that kind of passion one other place before."

"Where's that, sir?"

"In Gloria Richardson. She had it from the moment she arrived and it left with her. Don't get me wrong. We've got excellent journalists. But passion and an ability to write are two different things. You'll have to learn to harness your passion, Savannah. And I'm not sure if you can even write, seeing as I never got what I asked for."

"I have some samples with me, though I can't imagine you'd actually want to read them now."

"Well, I do. Leave them with me, and I'll call you later."

I retrieved what I had brought and placed them on his desk. "Does she really have a cocker spaniel?"

"Yes, his name is Sam, after me, and he just turned eight. And she takes her coffee with cream, no sugar. I know the people who work with me, Savannah. And I know them well."

"Hmm." And with that I pulled the embedded door closed, certain I had left a couple of lingering impressions.

CHAPTER SIX

I needed a Coke. A Coke and a good book. I headed to Jake's.

Only eight fifteen and Jake's was already lively. The atmosphere and the company, even more than the coffee, is why people return. In the past thirteen years, I don't think Dad has lost a customer. Judge Hoddicks, Jake's most loyal patron, is in every morning at eight, and Mr. and Mrs. Leonard Culpepper, who live above the coffee shop, follow moments behind. The Culpeppers have two decafs with no sugar and extra cream. They firmly believe that caffeine after seven a.m. will keep them awake.

Jennifer, Hope, and Karen from the Legislative Plaza next door pick up their usuals around eight thirty, before they head into the office. They get cappuccinos later in the day at that other coffee shop, the mere mention of which is not allowed at Jake's. But they wouldn't miss seeing my dad at the beginning of their day for anything.

Most everything in the Savannah Historic District, besides restaurants and that other coffee shop, closes around five. My father's main business comes from his square alone, and he figures when they are gone, he can go home too. Dad is home no later than five fifteen. Oh, and he is closed on Sunday. He, like Chick-fil-A, operates by the motto "After six days of work, everyone needs a day of rest."

As my face registered with old friends, there were hugs all around. Louise and Mervine, twins who came out of retirement to work with Dad, stopped midpour, abandoning countless customers.

"Mervine, this child is too thin. Savannah Phillips," Louise continued, "sit yourself down while we try to find you some food." They flitted around the counter that separates the tables from the back offices, storage rooms, and Coke machine, leaving their customers to fill their own cups.

Richard, one of the sweetest men I know and Dad's right-hand man, was standing behind the counter refilling a couple of obvious tourists' cups when he heard Louise's commotion. Richard's sixty-five years showed only faintly on his dark skin, as gray had begun to infiltrate his coarse black hair. He grabbed me and hugged me the way only Richard can, hugging me so hard it would take hours before I would breathe correctly again.

"Savannah Phillips, I can't believe you finally got out of school. I thought you were going to stay until they made you leave," he told me, his beautiful smile lighting up his face.

"You didn't hear, Richard? They did kick me out. Vicky came by and told them unless they changed the color of the brick on campus, she wasn't going to pay the rest of my tuition." Richard laughed with me as I pulled up a chair at the counter.

Since the death of notorious Savannian Jimmy Williams, my mother has done more for Savannah's architectural integrity than anyone in recent history. Jimmy Williams is the man from the acclaimed book *Midnight in the Garden of Good and Evil,* a book that put Savannah on the map for things many like my mother would rather have kept off. He came into this city bringing his own demanding perspective and rather extravagant taste and colorful lifestyle. Prior to his death he purchased and restored seventy-two homes. The publication of his story caused this city's tourism to increase by 46 percent.

Since Williams's death, Vicky, a member of the Historic Review Board, started a program in conjunction with the Savannah College of Art and Design, a co-op in which the students work with the city on the restoration of historic homes and landmarks. They have beautifully restored more than fifty of the downtown-area homes, turning them into museums of Savannah's history and stores reflecting Savannah's taste and style.

Vicky also helped to pass a law that banned changes on the outer structure of any home in the Historic District without those changes first being approved by the city. It passed easily in the state legislature. The only thing that still rankles her is that some modern buildings were grandfathered in, including one up the street that she refuses to drive by, walk by, or discuss. She wanted to have them torn down, but no one was brave enough to tackle that one. She is this city's greatest lobbyist and advocate. She is the government's greatest thorn. But Savannah loves her. I think one day she'll run for mayor. I also think she does most of this in hopes that someone will write a book about her. Then she can say, "Jimmy Williams may have increased tourism 46 percent, but I, Victoria Inez Phillips, increased tourism 54 percent and didn't have to murder a soul to do it." Not that a few of us haven't died a thousand deaths in the process.

"Your mother will eventually learn that not everything requires her opinion," Dad said as he appeared from the back room, Coke in hand, and pulled up a chair next to me at the counter. His six-foot-one frame is still sturdy at the age of fifty-three, a brief eight years older than my mother. He was probably considered "fine" when he was young, though I can't say I'm comfortable ascribing that kind of adjective to my father.

"Well you can dream in Technicolor if you wish," I pronounced, "but as long as there is breath in ol' Vicky, there will be a helpless victim on the other side of her opinion."

"Dreaming in Technicolor is something I do often," he said, laughing that genuine laugh I have grown to love. None of that fake southern stuff just to make you feel good. Jake only laughs if it's funny. He also cries when his kids make him proud and lights up like a fifteen-year-old schoolboy when Vicky enters the room. "But you don't need to talk that way about your mother. And it is 'Mother,'" he added. Dad got up to wipe off a table that had just been vacated by two businessmen. "What've you been doing this morning?"

I stopped for a moment to watch him in this environment that he loved. He looked happy. "Oh, nothing much really. Just rode around for a bit to see what has changed."

"You look mighty nice to have been just riding around," he said, giving Richard a wink.

"Oh, well, I've been trying to look a little more professional. You know, with graduating and everything," I said, apparently unsuccessful in my attempt to convince anyone, including the two women who had just come out of the back room with a banana and a muffin.

"Do you have a busy morning?" Dad asked.

"Nope." I pulled a book out of my bag and waved it around. "I have a little time to kill before lunch."

"Well, we could use an extra pair of hands round here," Richard said. "Why don't you go grab an apron so you don't mess up your new look?"

I gave Richard my best woeful sigh and put the book away. Then I headed to the back of the store, grabbed an apron, and proceeded to fill cups.

Above the counter at Jake's hangs a blackboard that features daily pieces of wisdom or, as my father calls them, "Thoughts for the Journey." Some folks take these little thoughts to heart, like the one that read, "A man who works hard is guaranteed success." Dad said he saw more activity on the square that day than he had seen in years. Or the other that had people falling all over themselves trying to live right: "Live righteously and rewards will seek you out. Live like the devil and misfortune will pursue you."

Some people, like Vicky, take the ones they like and leave the ones they feel don't apply. She was especially offended the day Dad had written, "A quarrelsome wife is like a constant dripping." She thought he had it up all day, but he only put it up when he saw her come out of the courthouse and head over toward the shop.

"Are you calling me 'a constant dripping,' Jake Phillips?"

Dad simply smiled, removed her hands from her hips, wrapped his arms around her defensive body, and whispered in her ear, "No. You, my love, are a consistent nurturer." To this day, whenever Vicky begins her constant dripping, Dad, or any of us nearby, lets her know that she is consistently nurturing that which has been nurtured enough.

Today Dad's thought for the journey read, "Anxiety in the heart of man can make him depressed, but it takes only one nice word to make him happy." Surely I had caused enough anxiety for the entire population of Savannah already that morning, making this a justifiable penance. So for the next three hours, Dad and I determined to get rid of everyone's anxieties with a nice word. We complimented suits, hairdos, grandchildren's pictures—we even complimented things that really shouldn't have been complimented at all, like Mrs. Taylor's new wiry-haired, rat-looking dog. When it came through the door, Duke ran to the other side of the counter where he would be safe from such a rodent. Dad made over that dog until Mrs. Taylor was beaming from ear to ear.

By the time the morning and midmorning rushes had cleared, depression had vacated the streets around Jake's Coffeehouse. I was even feeling better myself.

As I walked to my car, I could feel the heat challenge the coolness of my skin. Crawling into the black car and its warming conditions made me dread what the actual summer would hold. I pulled out of my parking place and was forced to stop as a group of ubiquitous tourists made their way across the street in front of me.

They give themselves away too easily what with their visors, hanging cameras, walking shorts (which no one should be walking in), sneakers with crumpled-up socks, and even colored socks with loafers. Fanny packs and guidebooks usually finish off the colorful ensembles. Some visitors take the opportunity to wear hats they aren't brave enough to wear in their hometowns. And everyone over fifty has a jacket on, just in case our 100-degree, humidity-filled afternoons might turn into a chilled breeze. Tourists keep Savannah alive, however, and they love to try locally owned places like Jake's, or Clary's Café, the restaurant I was aiming for before this flock of poorly attired geese stopped me.

Clary's is perched directly across the street from my house. Paige and I have patronized Clary's for their BLTs since I can't remember when. We have been friends since my second week at the Massey School. We were paired up for a history project in Mr. Gilbert's class, and the rest, as they say, is . . . When I left for the University of Georgia, she stayed here in Savannah to go to the Savannah College of Art and Design.

I parked my car beside my house, crossed the street to Clary's, and arrived inside to, no surprise, Paige's absence. Paige was always late, whether it was fashionable or not.

Her parents—Sheila, my mother's best friend since childhood, and Patterson Long—own a beautiful antique shop on Abercorn Street right across from Saint John the Baptist's Catholic Church. Paige doesn't care much for antiques, but she is one of the most skilled painters I have ever met. I would've commissioned her to create the cover for my first book, had my original dream still been intact. Paige has been selling paintings since she was in high school. Her parents, out of sheer pride, put her first paintings up in their store. By the time she graduated college, she was so popular and had sold so many paintings, she opened up her own little area in the back of the antique shop. But Paige had recently declared at least partial independence by moving into her own apartment in the Lafayette Building—right next to her shop on the square.

Paige entered Clary's in total Paige style: out of breath. "You are not going to believe what happened."

"Try me," I said, leaning back in my chair and knowing I was in for an interesting narrative.

"I got pulled!"

"You got pulled?"

"Yeah! There he was. Mr. I-don't-have-anything-better-to-do-than-pull-over-people-for-no-reason Millings."

"He does need a life."

"He needs a mint. Have you smelled that man's breath?" she asked as her entire face contorted in horror.

"Can't say I've gotten that close."

"Well, hold on to your hat, Hannah; it won't be long," she said, flipping her hair, which was really too short to flip.

"Did you flash him a smile? Offer him money? Bribe him with a portrait?" I laughed as I took a sip of the chocolate shake my favorite waitress, Helen, set down in front of me the very moment of my arrival.

Paige slumped back in her chair. Then, as if getting a second wind, she sat up, patted me on the arm. "So, how did your meeting go?"

Before I could reply, Helen returned. The waitresses here rarely change, and Helen is an icon. She cusses like a sailor, smokes like a forest fire, and talks like a man. She has been reprimanded for the first two offenses a trillion times; the third is out of her control. Oh, and she has a photographic memory. She has never written down an order, and she gets each one right every time. Even down to a table of ten. "Girls, I'm so glad to see you both. But, Savannah, you are too skinny and, Paige, your hair is too blond. I'll have your BLTs out in a minute." And away she went.

"Why is it that you are always skinny, and all she notices about me is my hair color? I've had this same color for five years."

"And I've weighed the same since my senior year in high school."

"Anyway, didn't I ask you about you and your job?"

"Well, I have successfully told Vicky about forgoing the book deal and kept it a secret that I am trying to get this job at the paper."

"Aren't you the woman?"

"Well, I'm not so sure I'm all that, not after this morning."

"Savannah, what did you do?"

"Why would your first thought be, what did I do? Why couldn't it possibly be something someone else did?"

"Please. What did you do?"

"I pulled a Vicky," I told her, crinkling my nose.

"No!" Both hands slammed down on the table, her eyes wider than a hoot owl. "You pulled a Vicky on the very man who could give you a job? That's a tad audacious."

"Did you just say tad?"

"Probably. My mother uses it all the time."

"Well, thank the Lord! I must have picked it up from you. I was afraid I had picked it up from my mother. Well, it was really a huge mistake." Paige sat in complete and total silence and listened to the rest of my story. Helen brought our lunch and Paige finished most of her BLT before I'd taken my first bite.

By the time I was through, all she could say was, "Get out."

"I did!" I told her, laughing.

"Do you think you'll hear from him?"

"Honestly?"

"Honestly."

"Well, since he didn't call security, odds are I'll hear something." I took a sip of my shake.

Paige looked up and nodded, then swallowed and said, "There is something I need to tell you."

"OK. You are way too serious. What is it?"

She paused long enough to make me look her in the eye. Then as she always does in her rare serious moments, she placed her hand underneath her porcelain chin. She gave up on tanning years ago after a severe burning episode. Now she wears SPF-105. "I heard that Grant is getting married."

"Well, we all want to get married one day, don't we?" I said, hoping she was just joking.

"Savannah, I'm not joking. He met this girl from Converse College while he was at Clemson. They started dating after he got out of school and started working for his dad's firm. She is graduating this month, and they are supposed to get married this summer."

Grant and I had only seen each other a couple of times since I started graduate school. He had been my best friend through middle school. Then in high school we realized that we felt more for each other than just friendship, and we dated through my senior year in college. Until this halting moment, I had somehow thought that he and I would one day get married. He was the only guy I had ever cared about. Now, I knew that things had changed since graduate school, but we still talked.

Our last serious conversation had taken place one morning at my dad's shop, right before I went back to school for my master's and he started full-time at his dad's architectural firm on Oglethorpe Square. I'll never forget how beautifully golden his skin was from spending most of his summer on the ocean. I stared at him through the front window at Jake's, where I sat at a table facing the sidewalk.

He walked in wearing wrinkled khaki shorts and a T-shirt, which, like the majority of his wardrobe, bore the name of a local store or a race he had recently participated in. "Out for a day of fun?"

He gave me a gentle kiss and sat down. "Actually, I'm working today."

"Dressed like that?"

"I'm helping Dad do some things in the yard," he said, laughing.

"When do you start your real job with your father?"

Instead of answering, Grant sat and reached across the table to take my hand. "Savannah, I think we have some decisions to make. We've done this relationship thing for four years now. Except I'm not sure I would even call it a relationship. I need more. I think it's time. I want us to take our relationship to the next level. Really focus on our future."

I blinked, wishing I had an answer he would want to hear. But school required everything of me. And at that time, I was so consumed with writing, I didn't know how I could offer a real, committed relationship much of anything. "We've got all the time in the world for that," I responded. "You know I love you. I've always loved you. And next to Paige, you're the best friend I've ever had. I just need to get this master's behind me. And I just can't commit to any more right now."

I'll never forget the look in his eyes when he left that afternoon. He hugged me a little longer than usual. But school would be over eventually. Then there would be time to solidify our relationship. Obviously, Grant hadn't been clear on the plan.

"Earth to Savannah," Paige said, waving her hand in front of my face.

"Do you even know her name?"

"I think it's Eliza or something like that. One of those real southern kind of names."

"Oh, more southern than *Savannah?*"

Paige rolled her eyes.

"Do you think he really loves her or does he just want to get married?"

"Savannah, you know Grant isn't going to marry someone he's not in love with."

"Maybe she's dog ugly."

"No such luck, my friend. I saw her over the Christmas holidays. He brought her to an exhibit. She was very tall and very gorgeous." Paige turned up her nose in mock disgust. "I mean legs up to—"

"That really is enough. I bet she's fake. I bet there isn't a thing on her that's real."

We wrapped up our lunch and declared that we would do this every Monday.

"Call me as soon as you hear something about the job. And no cleaning excursions. It's going to be OK." She sealed her solace with a hug.

I watched as she faded up the street, the consummate artist, from the way she dresses to the way she walks. If she weren't my best friend, I would hate her, so irritatingly perky and cute.

Looking out over the same street I had viewed only hours before, I was amazed by how a morning could change things.

CHAPTER SEVEN

The beauty of Savannah is that it is a place where people come to fulfill dreams. Sure, we have a lot of old money, the kind that joins the Oglethorpe Club and are members of the Garden Club. But there are a number of people who simply come to make their own way, start a business, raise a family, and leave their mark on their own little corner of the world through life and love and loss.

As I walked down River Street, I took a left on Perry, crossing in front of Chippewa Square, which holds the familiar statue of General Oglethorpe, Savannah's founding father, and the concrete wall behind the bench where Forrest Gump had his box of chocolates. The city was planned on paper before Oglethorpe even arrived and before Forrest was a thought. Oglethorpe's friend Robert Casteel was an architect in England and later jailed in debtor's prison. It is said that England's prisons were dismal beyond comprehension. Casteel died there of smallpox, and Oglethorpe dreamed of creating a new life for the poor, the debtors, and the religiously persecuted. Savannah was his canvas.

In 1733, Oglethorpe's Savannah had four laws. Law Number

One: No hard liquor, only beer and wine allowed. He didn't want any lushes in his society. That lasted only in dreams. Law Number Two: No slaves. Oglethorpe wanted Savannah built as a place of equals. That was repealed in 1751, thanks in large part to Eli Whitney and the cotton gin. Law Number Three: No Catholics. Oglethorpe feared they would be sympathetic to the Spanish and try to take over this new colony. So much for the religiously persecuted. Law Number Four: No lawyers. That was repealed in 1755, you guessed it, by a lawyer. But until there were lawyers, Savannians needed a way to settle their disputes. So the citizens built the Dueling Field, on the backside of Colonial Park Cemetery.

As I turned my gaze from the familiar square, I couldn't help but notice the gray-sided home on the corner whose basement had been transformed into a quaint little bookstore. I have never passed a bookstore without going inside; it's sacrilegious.

During my school years, I spent most of my time and money at E. Shavers Booksellers on the corner of Bull and East Harris Streets. My life's original plan was to open up a little bookstore in the basement of my own home. Since reading William Golding's *Lord of the Flies,* I believed kids needed a place to experience the world of adventure and make-believe, a safe place to get lost in the turmoil of undisciplined youth. Remembering *my* dreams made me realize I had left little room for someone else's. Grant had probably figured that out long before.

Trying not to contemplate Miss Converse's false beauty any further, I opened the tucked-away door and stepped into an enchanted land, Katherine's Corner Bookstore.

Everything was neatly categorized and organized. There was history, fiction, nonfiction, new releases, and, of course, local-interest titles in a prominent display in the front. I laughed when I saw the book that featured pictures of my home—well, not exactly my home. A local publisher doing a new book about Savannah asked Vicky if she would allow them to shoot a couple of our rooms for the book, because our home is on the Historical Register. Well, you would have thought she had been crowned Miss Saint Patrick's Day Queen. We thought she was going to make us move to a hotel for a week so nothing would be touched once her interior designer came in and did a "fluff."

My mother worked frantically to make sure everything was perfect. But in the end, the only pictures that didn't develop correctly were the ones they had taken of the inside of our house. By the time this was discovered, it was too late to do another photo shoot. Dad would have refused to go through the torture again anyway. So instead of this lovely book having pictures of Vicky's décor, the publishers used photos someone had taken of the previous owners' interior.

You won't find this lovely picture book lying around in Vicky's parlor, that's for sure, but a very nice book it is, even if Vicky's fluffing has been omitted.

A striking lady, probably in her late forties, appeared from behind a bookcase. She caught my eye and smiled, her beautiful dark eyes reflecting the soft track lighting. "Can I help you find anything, honey?" she asked.

She was carrying a stack of magazines to the rack by the front door, and the sun caught her salt-and-pepper hair, a rarity in these parts. Southern women, for the most part, don't want you to think their hair has ever seen gray, even if they're eighty and walking with a cane. She wore little makeup, but a stunning color of red lipstick and simple jewelry complemented her natural olive complexion perfectly.

"No, I was just walking and saw your great little store here. How long have you been open?"

"Only about a month. But the remodeling took over a year, so it's really nice to just feel settled."

"Where are you from?"

"Here originally, but I moved to Birmingham with my husband when we were first married so he could work in his father's business. When my husband passed away, I decided to come back home," she said, taking outdated magazines to the counter.

"Oh, I'm really sorry."

"Well, thank you. Jim suffered for almost two years with cancer. So I was ready to let him go. Don't take that the wrong way, but when you love someone like that, the last thing you want is to see them suffer."

I nodded.

"Eventually, letting go is easier than holding on. Our children are grown and have all moved away, so I decided there was no better time than now to try out my dreams," she said, indicating the store with a sweeping gesture.

"Well, I think you've done a wonderful job with your dream. It's perfectly quaint."

"I hope you'll feel free to stop by anytime. Do you live around here?"

"Yes, ma'am. On Abercorn Street across from Clary's."

A flicker of recognition came to her eyes as she posed my most dreaded question. "Oh, are you Victoria Phillips's daughter?"

"Yes, ma'am. And Jake's too," I added for my own peace of mind. "Savannah, Savannah Phillips," I said, holding my hand out, hoping she would not hold my heritage against me. "Do you know them?"

"Well, I've met your father," she said, grasping my hand in a solid, confident shake. "Hello, Savannah, I'm Katherine Owens."

I smiled back, still wondering.

"I stop in at your father's place now and then. He is a doll. And so is that sweet Richard. Now, your mother I haven't met yet, but I've heard a lot about her."

"I can only imagine."

"I heard your mother is responsible for much of the recent restoration around here."

"Yes, she is. There's something about her and this city."

"Then perhaps that explains your beautiful name?"

For some reason Katherine's question didn't irritate me. I smiled. "Maybe so."

She smiled back. "So are you just here for the summer?"

"No, I just finished my master's and moved back here to find a job," I said, then added, "Actually, I've found the place I want to work, but I'm not so sure if they're going to want me."

"Oh, really! What do you mean?"

"That's a long story. But let's just say that I should hear something by this evening."

"You sound like a rather interesting character," she said with a faint laugh. "Well, Savannah, it was a pleasure to meet you. I'm going to go back to my cataloging. New fiction is on the back wall, and new nonfiction is right beside it."

"What do you suggest?"

"Well, this one isn't new, but I've been rereading some classics lately," she said, reaching into a shelf and pulling out Harper Lee's *To Kill a Mockingbird*. "It takes me back."

"I love that one too," I said, taking the book from her extended hand. "Atticus Finch, a man to be admired."

Leaving the bookstore to head back home, I noticed the decorative fish spout she had put on her gutters. Another indication of the lady she was, so understatedly overstated. She captured my attention without ever changing the volume of her voice. Not like my mother, who had a Chamber-of-Commerce Victoria voice, and a hold-on-to-your-britches "Mama's home" kind of voice. Katherine was just a lady. A lady to be admired.

The note on the kitchen counter read, "Vanni, Mom has a late Chamber meeting. I'm meeting Dad after work to do some things at the shop. Dinner is on your own, unless you want to come grab a bite with us later. Love, Thomas."

The phone rang, commencing a desperate search for it. Thomas never left it on its cradle, so I didn't stand a chance of getting to it before the person on the other end hung up or was sent off to voice mail heaven. Fortunately, it was close by, underneath the newspaper on the kitchen table.

"Hello."

"Savannah Phillips, please." I knew immediately who it was.

"This is she," I replied, trying to hide the terror in my voice.

"Ms. Phillips, this is Mr. Hicks. I've been reading your work this afternoon, and, well, it's not bad."

"Thank you, sir." *I think.*

"I've decided I'm willing to give you a month to prove yourself. I'd like you to start a week from Monday. You can run one human-interest story each week, in two parts. And I'm not going to tell anyone you are Gloria's replacement until I know that you can handle the pace around here."

"I understand."

"Most of our entry-level positions start at four hundred dollars a week, with one week's vacation after the first year. We offer one week's sick leave your first year and pay health insurance."

"I don't believe this position is entry-level, sir. My articles will probably be the most-read next to your headline news. Doesn't that alone make me more valuable?"

"So what do you think you should be paid, young lady?"

Put on the spot, I backtracked. "You know, Mr. Hicks, four hundred will be fine, actually. I really need six hundred to be able to move out into an apartment. But I'll just work up to that."

He probably believed I was playing him. But I really did need six hundred dollars a week. "How about we meet in the middle, Savannah? I'll give you five hundred and a week's vacation this year. But you need to remember, the newspaper business isn't a place for getting rich; it's a place for creating change."

He got the no-rich part right. I just hoped I could eat. But decided it would be a good excuse for having to eat at my mother's. Then I almost got mad, realizing if she hadn't ruined my publishing deal, there's no telling what I could be making right now. "That will be wonderful. Thank you."

"Oh, and one more thing, you'll make sure you don't interrupt conversations you are not privy to."

I simply replied, "I'll be there."

"Very well. I'll see you Monday. Your first story is due Tuesday."

Tuesday? One could spend a year or two writing a book. How in the world was I going to have two articles ready in a little over a week? "That's no problem," I said. "Would you mind if I came in tomorrow and went through Gloria's research materials?"

"Not at all. I'll make sure Rich Greer, our weekend editor, knows you're coming. I'll see you in a week." And with that he hung up the phone.

I set down the phone and did a jig around the kitchen. I was going to be Gloria. I was going to be a newspaper writer. Grabbing my cell phone, I got in the car to go to Jake's and called Paige immediately.

"You goob! I can't believe you are not answering the phone!" I said when her voice mail answered. "I got a call from Mr. Happy Hicks! He's giving me the job! For at least a month, he says, but in one month he'll be mine. Call me!" I pulled up right in front of Dad's store, almost knocking over two elderly people in plaid shorts. I apologized as best I could.

Richard was behind the counter pouring some decaf for a young woman. "Put the cup down, Richard." As soon as he did, I gave him a bear hug and a big kiss on the cheek. Then I grabbed him by both arms, looked straight into his eyes, and said, "I got a job, Richard. A real job."

Richard let out a big whoop and spun me around behind the counter. My foot caught an empty coffeepot, and it crashed to the floor. Out came Dad, Thomas, Louise, and Mervine.

"Savannah, you got a job?" my dad asked.

"Yes, I got a job. Can you believe it? I pulled a Vicky and it worked. I got a job! I mean it could have blown up in my face. But really, it was the perfect thing to happen. He saw my tenacity, my drive, my passion he called it. He—"

"Breathe, Savannah," Dad said.

Louise and Mervine scurried away and were back in no time with a cherry floating in a big old Coke. "Special occasions require special things," Louise said. Mervine, well, she just shook her head. In thirteen years I had never heard Mervine do much more than agree. Maybe she was mute, but now didn't seem like the right time to ask.

"Vanni, you're the man!" Thomas hooted. "I never dreamed you could get a job so quick. Who's paying who?" He leaned against the door that led to the back.

"And what kind of job did you actually get?" Dad asked.

"Well"—I spread my arms wide and grinned—"You are looking at the next human-interest writer for the *Savannah Chronicle*."

Richard, who was trying to clean up the mess we had made and actually give coffee to the lady at the counter, set down the cup and said, "That was what Gloria Richardson did. My, my, my Savannah, those are some mighty big shoes for your dainty little feet."

"Savannah, that's fantastic. When did you decide you wanted to do this?" Dad straightened his apron over his crisp short-sleeve green polo shirt.

"Well, it all started with that paper Mother kept sending me." I filled him in while everyone else returned to thirsty sojourners.

When I finished, he said, "I'm very proud of you."

"I learned something along the way, too. Ya wanna hear?"

"Shoot," he said, leaning on his elbow and giving me his undivided attention. Something he had always done. From skinned knees to broken hearts, Dad knew when the world needed to stop.

"I saw a lot of people pass through the halls of academia, Dad. But they were so caught up in themselves. Everyone wanted to be the best, you know, have the perfect talent or the loudest applause. But no one seemed to see the real joy in the fact that they had a gift at all. Do you know what I mean?"

"How about I see where you're going to land."

"Well, it's like they missed it. Like the guys who sacrificed everything to be the first in the college draft, even if it meant giving up their character. They had the gift but missed the purpose."

"A lot of people do that."

"Well, I don't want to, Dad."

"Then always be gracious, Savannah." Dad paused in a way that said I'd better listen up. "Your gift will make room for you. Sometimes it will bring you before great people. But it isn't *your* gift, Savannah; it's simply been entrusted to you. So hold it modestly. And remember, wisdom will be needed for every decision you make, just like you needed it for this one."

"That's why you're here, isn't it? To keep me humble and give me wisdom?" I kissed him on the cheek and raised my half-empty glass. "Here's to gifts."

Dad raised his coffee cup and added, "Here's to a paycheck."

We closed up the shop, but everyone stayed, and we spent the next three hours talking over Chinese takeout. Everyone had suggestions for what my first story should be. Then they all added their two cents about how I should tell my mother. The real beauty of the moment, however, was that I had a job she didn't even know about.

Everything was perfectly situated—the pillow, the light, the book, my water—when the slight tap on the door interrupted the quiet. Vicky peeked in.

"I hear you had a rather eventful day!" she said, sitting down on the edge of the bed.

"Yes, I did. But who told you?" I asked, laying my book across my chest and trying to conceal my annoyance.

"Your father, but that was about all he gave me. He said you would want to tell me yourself."

"Oh, he did, did he?"

"So what happened that is so exciting?"

"Well, first tell me about your day. You're in mighty late." I knew this would buy me a little time to get my story in place. And like Paige, it never took much to sidetrack my mother. Past adventures proved that.

Like after she tired of decorating our home she went on a Fact Finding mission for our fair city. When Vicky found out there was a store named Jezebel on River Street, you would have thought the sun had stopped shining on the South. Vicky worked herself into a lather, sure the heathens had come to town and pretty soon we were going to have massage parlors on every corner doing "Lord knows what!"

"I'm sure the Lord knows what," I told her.

She got mad that I would even suggest that the Lord would know what went on inside a massage parlor.

Then one day we heard that she had actually gone inside Jezebels. Well, we figured whoever owned that store had been subjected to a big-time come-to-Jesus meeting. But the store owner, now one of Mother's best friends, told us later that Vicky was so overtaken by the green linen ensemble in the window that she stayed until three that afternoon, trying on clothes and telling her life story. She denied it was true. But then we saw her leave the house in an outfit in the lovely shade of green.

"Oh, a few members of the Chamber are trying to change my mind about some of the tour guides having to dress in original southern dresses. They want everyone to wear those khaki shorts and logoed button-up shirts. I still can't believe you were able to talk me into allowing that in the first place," she said, poking me under the covers. "It's so unprofessional."

Vicky is colossally concerned with the impression Savannah visitors take home with them. She feels if they don't want, even long, to return, then she has failed as the head of the Chamber. So she decided a couple of years ago to make sure that every aspect of our social graces was operating, well, with grace. It began with her incognito rides on the local Savannah touring trolleys, horse-drawn carriages, or walks in one of the walking tours. If the tour guides didn't entertain the visitors, if they didn't know Savannah history as well as they did the ins and outs of their own families, if they didn't create a total feeling of consummate hospitality, Vicky would inform the guides' bosses of their inability to "capture their audience."

"Just remember," established tour guides tell the new recruits, "real tourists don't wear high heels. If you spot one, it's her. And if she doesn't leave your tour crying, you are over."

She still has no idea they are onto her. And I'm not about to tell her. There's nothing more amusing than driving past a trolley car and watching the guide with more motions than a synchronized swimmer, while Vicky sits in the back in her pink hat and large sunglasses. She looks like a bad Susan Lucci impersonator, thinking no one knows who she is.

Where I really feel Mother has gone over the edge, however, is in this crinoline controversy. Back when I was in high school, I passed one of the tour guides in a full-length peach dress, with about forty-five layers of crinoline and a huge bonnet with roughly the same number of flowers on top. She was giving a tour dressed up in this garb with the heat index at 110 degrees. Her makeup had melted, and she had mascara tracks all the way to her chin. Most of it had pooled at the top of her lace collar, which looked as if it was choking her. Poor thing was trying to blot herself with a tissue and spin a parasol at the same time.

I came home and told Mother, "This is totally inhumane. You should at least give those poor pitiful souls a choice." I didn't figure anyone would choose to wear those ridiculous getups, and Vicky didn't either, so she compromised by breaking it up half and half. God bless the miserable creatures who were at the cutoff line of the crinolines.

I closed my book and laid it on the nightstand and put my arms behind my head, thinking we might be here for a while.

"People get enough of the authentic here without making others endure human torture."

"Well, you start snipping away, and pretty soon we're no better than Charleston."

"Mother, Charleston is beautiful, and I doubt they make their people dress up like bad southern belle impersonators just to make tourists feel they've had a real cultural experience."

"You don't think they wear those kind of dresses in Charleston?"

"No, Mother. Charleston is progressive, and you need to be careful not to hold Savannah back from what most would see as progress."

"But I love those dresses. The girls look so sweet in them," she said, having no recollection as to why she had come into my room.

I rolled over on my side and yawned, hoping this would not be a terminal discussion.

"Well, I still haven't decided," she said, not moving.

"You mean you kept those people in a meeting for almost five hours without reaching a decision?" I asked in mock disbelief.

"Yes, but I'm too tired to worry about it anymore tonight. I'll think about it tomorrow." She leaned over and kissed me good night. When she reached the door, she turned back around and cut out the light. Standing in the doorway, the hall light created her silhouette. "I know you think I forgot why I came in here, but you obviously aren't ready to tell me your news. So I'll just let you tell me when you're ready." The door closed behind her.

"The lady is good," I said to the door.

CHAPTER EIGHT

G ood morning, Mother," I said, greeting her with a kiss. I sat down at the counter to enjoy my breakfast. *Maybe she would still let me come by for breakfast and dinner even after I move out,* I thought. *My word, I'm not going to be so well off that I can do it all. Everyone needs a gradual transition, don't they?*

She was prancing around in a beautiful cream linen sundress with matching cream mules when I entered. "How did you rest, darling?" Her hair was somewhere in the brown family today. This is as close to her real color as we'll be seeing this side of heaven.

"I rested great. It's nice just to be home in my own bed."

"Well, I'm so glad you're here, precious. This is exactly where you belong, with your mother and your father and everything that makes you comfortable," she said, fixing me a plate. I knew why she was there. She knew why she was there. And even cleaning my bathroom from stem to stern wouldn't prevent this conversation from having to take place eventually.

"OK, you've been patient long enough. I'll tell you," I said, trying to scarf down some bacon before I began. "I got a job."

"You got a job? Already? Where?"

I knew she didn't think I could get one without her, but I refrained from needless gloating. I responded, "At the paper. I am going to write human-interest stories."

"Savannah, oh my word, well, that, that is wonderful. Is that what you really want to do?"

"Yes, it is. It's exactly what I want to do. Well, I've got a busy day, so I'd better get going." I poured myself just enough juice to wash down the entire scrambled egg I had just crammed in my mouth.

"But, Savannah, I had our day planned," she said, puffing out her lip like a spoiled two-year-old child. "There are some new neighbors I told we would meet for lunch, and then I was going to take you and show you some of the houses that the college finished since you were home last. And I'd like to know more, more about this, this job thing."

"Mother, we'll do all those things, I promise. I have to go to the paper today. And I have to start early."

"Today? So soon? And in those shoes?"

"Yeah, I've only got a little over a week before my first story is due." Then I went in for the kill. "And while we're talking change here, I think you need to know that I'm going to move out as soon as I get enough money."

"But, Savannah ..."

With my hand in the air to try and stop her graciously, I headed to the door. "You know, the funny thing is, I never would've even thought about the paper had it not been delivered every day while I was at college. It was so strange too, because I never ordered it, nor did I ever have to pay for it. Oh, well, I guess it was just meant to be. I'll be home for dinner."

Most things in the South run slowly even Mondays through Fridays, but tack on a weekend and, well, let's just say, snails could outrace a southerner. But not at Jake's. The environment was rather frenzied for a Saturday in Savannah.

"Big day?" He handed me a Coke glass filled to the brim.

"Yes, and an eventful morning too. I told Mother that once I get a couple of paychecks I'm going to get my own place."

"I think you should, Savannah. You're a grown woman, and you need to pave your own course and create a life for yourself. So where are you going to live?"

"I have no idea." I leaned back against the counter and took a long swig of my Coke. Dad picked up his coffee and took a drink himself.

"How did your mother handle such eventful news?"

"Didn't give her time to do anything!"

"How did you accomplish that?" he said with a laugh.

"Walked out the door after revealing that her newspaper was what led me down this whole path in the first place."

"You are shameless."

"I know."

"No dramatic unfoldings? No emergency-room scares?"

"No, but I expect to be confronted eventually with everything from heart palpitations to the fact that 'criminals loom in the streets seeking single females who live in apartments all by them- selves,'" I said in perfected Victoria.

"Ooh, that one might even scare me."

From my parking place across the street, I could see through the windows that lights were on everywhere, and people were obviously working feverishly preparing the Sunday morning copy. I tried to forget that the only thing I knew about newspapers I learned reviewing books for the Massey School *Ledger*, a job I was given because I was the only one who actually read them.

The second semester of my junior year at UGA, I decided to take a literature class with a required-reading list of fifteen books. It included Emily Brontë's *Wuthering Heights,* F. Scott Fitzgerald's *The Great Gatsby,* Hemingway's *The Sun Also Rises,* other titles you might recognize, and some that might make you cock your head the way Duke does when he has no clue what you're trying to tell him. That course was a turning point for me. After that class, I knew there was a place for me. I needed to hone my craft, polish my abilities, and learn how to place my words on a page the way they were uniquely formed in my mind before my fingers ever typed them. This was my masterpiece to create. No one alive could create it the way I could. No one could copy it or duplicate it exactly. So I poured myself into what I already loved. I thought it had proven faithful.

Yet here I was, staring at a newspaper building with a questionable sting still in my gut. *I should be staring at the front door of the largest publishing house in the nation,* she thought. *But, no, I had to have some intervening circumstances.* Circumstances that had diluted my world into a city. With all the changes of the past month, I still wanted to leave a mark that would last. A mark that would change something or, dare I believe, someone the way Gloria's mark had changed me. Whether I liked it or not, destiny hovered in front of me, daring me to enter. Before leaving the comfort of my car, I decided to leave all preconceived ideas behind with it, taking in my confidence instead. If I left that behind as well, I might never find it again.

Between her continual *"Savannah Chronicle,* please hold," the receptionist mouthed she would be with me in a moment. After putting the 111th caller successfully on hold with or without permission, I told her I was here to meet Mr. Greer. She declared it loud and clear over the intercom and went back to find that caller number one had hung up hours ago.

Mr. Greer was a small, elderly gentleman with a nice smile, strong hands, and a round little bowling-ball tummy. "Savannah, nice to meet you. Follow me, and I'll show you Gloria's office." We walked through a maze of cubicles to the back of the building. He walked with such a spry step it was hard to keep up. As I wove my way through the great gray abyss, I pitied the poor people who had to spend their lives staring into such a dismal sea. I had spent six years of college writing in parks, sitting in coffee shops, or staring out my window into a stunning courtyard. We proceeded to the same elevator I had ridden only once before. The numbers on the buttons were nearly invisible from years of being poked, and the elevator creaked so loudly, I held on in hope that the doors would open to actually reveal the next floor and not some helpless state of in-between.

The doors opened to the infamous third floor, and we walked straight ahead in the direction of Mr. Hicks's office. Situated next door, looking out over Bay Street, her name still declared on the door, was Gloria Richardson's office. I was almost afraid to go in. I stopped by the door and looked up at Mr. Greer to make sure it was OK to enter. It almost felt wrong, almost disrespectful. "It's OK, Savannah. I'll check on you in a little while. If you need anything, my office is right around the corner there. I hope you find what you're looking for."

"Thanks. Me too," I said. I peered through the glass wall for a moment, wanting to be absolutely certain I should enter at all. It was clear that all of Gloria's personal things were gone, but everything else was in pristine and perfect order. I finally gathered the courage to enter, slowly turning the knob, and letting the door slide gently open. The sun was already illuminating the office, but my aversion to dead-people's belongings prompted me to turn on the lights anyway. For a moment I took in the fact that this office was amazing. "Can you believe this view?" I asked out loud to no one.

A faint scent of lavender was in the air. Maybe her fragrance or a scented candle. I sat down slowly in her chair and ran my hands across the smooth leather arms. The stapler and tape dispenser were in exemplary condition and fastidiously positioned. The Post-it notes and paper clips looked as if they had rarely been used. I opened her top drawer to find nothing more than some notepads.

I swiveled the chair around to stare out the wall-length window and repressed my intense need to grin. My eyes made their way to the two black metal filing cabinets against the wall. I walked over and opened the top drawer to find everything perfectly labeled and color-coded. Though an amazing writer, the woman obviously suffered from an obsessive-compulsive neatness disorder. My only neatness disorder manifested itself in the bathroom area.

I sifted through each folder, feeling as if I was somehow violating her privacy. I was sorting through this woman's life. These files held the questions, mysteries, and discoveries never revealed in her columns. They held her decisions of what to print and what not to print. They held her legacy. They held secrets I was sure I shouldn't see but couldn't keep myself from opening.

Four hours passed before the startling sound of knocking broke the spell. I looked up and felt the burning sensation in my neck muscles. "Come in."

"Savannah, you've been in here a long time. You OK?" Mr. Greer asked, tugging at his pants to pull them up frighteningly higher.

"Yes, sir. I'm doing fine."

"Would you like some lunch? I'm going out to grab a quick bite."

"Oh, that would be great. I'll have whatever you're having."

"Oh, you will, will you?" he said with a chuckle. "Need you some cottage cheese and prunes? You look a little young for those things."

I laughed myself. "Well, how 'bout you grab me something more accustomed to my dietary tract."

"That would be a cheeseburger and French fries, I presume."

"You would be a phenomenal presumer." I returned to my work, and he returned quickly for someone who should probably move a little slower. The prunes probably kept him in a hurry everywhere he went. I ate simply to keep my stomach from distracting me and went straight back to reading.

Each story was like a life lesson. And each article was neatly cut out and paper-clipped to the inside of each folder that housed the related interviews and research. In the last drawer of the second file cabinet, I came upon closed files. Some were closed due to lack of information, some for lack of validity, and others because the subject had changed his mind. By all notions of modern journalism, not many reporters kept stories from going to press because the subject changed his mind.

After peering at the clock and seeing it was already five thirty, my stiffening body made it clear it was time to go home. Mr. Greer had said good-bye an hour ago. I stood up to close the file drawer and heard something bang inside. I reopened it and looked to make sure the files hadn't fallen. I closed the door again and heard the same sliding, banging noise. Opening it once more, I reached my hand between two files to feel down inside the bottom of the drawer. At the back, my hand found something square, about the size of my palm.

It was a tape recorder. I pulled it out and found a tape inside. I pushed "play" and immediately heard a woman's voice asking a question. It had to be Gloria. It freaked me out, sitting there in her office, holding her voice in my hand, so I shut the tape off. I put the tape player in my purse, knowing it wasn't stealing, because it would be returned to its rightful place. But I wasn't about to sit there and listen to it in her office.

I could smell dinner from the street. Duke was at the door and politely rolled over so his stomach could be rubbed with my foot. I took my flip-flop off and gave him a courtesy rub.

Vicky wanted a lap dog. Duke would oblige, but he's not exactly what she had in mind. She told Dad that if Duke knocked over one more antique with his tail, the dog would be living in the coffee shop. I believe Vicky might be gone before Duke, but we'll let time play that hand.

In the kitchen, Dad was already setting the table and Thomas was filling the tea glasses, both talking to Vicky as she set dinner on the counter. She had prepared fried pork chops, fried potatoes, steamed cabbage, and fried cornbread patties. No wonder Dad and Duke were having to go for walks. It was that or become terminally clogged.

"Savannah, were you at the newspaper all day?" Vicky asked.

"Yes, I was. And it was so interesting. And you should see my office. It's awesome. It overlooks Bay Street and has a wall of windows. I know it will be a lot of work, but I'm totally prepared."

We fixed our plates and sat down at the table. With grace said, Vicky revealed her latest idea. "I've been thinking about our talk this morning."

"Our talk?" I asked.

"The apartment, darling. I understand that a young woman would want her own place." Poor Thomas about spewed pork chops at that. Dad even perked up to listen.

"Well, thank you, Mother. I'm glad to hear that."

"And you know, I know a place that just came on the market that I think would be perfect for you."

"Well, that really isn't necessary. I want to do this on my—"

"I insist, Savannah. I've already called, and we have an appointment to see it tomorrow after lunch." And without any further conversation or debate, she proceeded to recount the events of a day worthy of a movie script. How so much can happen to one lady on a Saturday is beyond my power of imagination. I zoned out somewhere between the hair salon and manicure and picked back up with Duke taking a dip in the swimming pool.

"Well, it is warm for May," I said. It wouldn't have mattered, however, if Duke had been teetering on the edge of heatstroke and utter demise; the fact that the pool would have to be excavated of dog hair was reason enough to keep him out.

"I don't know why you didn't take him with you this morning," she said to Dad.

"Because he was sound asleep on Thomas's bed, and I didn't figure they would get up before noon. I couldn't imagine Duke doing much damage in an afternoon," he said, smiling at me across the table.

"Well, Thomas didn't actually get up until one and left around two, so the damage that Duke caused happened in less than an afternoon. Your dog is amazingly talented."

Duke had been called "your dog" since the naming episode. Now, if she had gotten her way, Magnolia probably could have taken a dump in her pool and she wouldn't have thought a thing about it.

"Well, we'll get the pool cleaned out," Dad calmly assured her.

I sneaked away somewhere between Duke's need for obedience training and the city's need for a flowering fish garden in front of the Chamber of Commerce. I had a more important conversation to listen to.

CHAPTER NINE

My purse rested on one of the glass tables that flanked each side of my bed. I knew what was in there; I just wasn't sure it was for me to hear.

It has to be OK, I assured myself. *She would want her work continued.* I took my purse and retrieved the tape recorder, popping the tape out. Side A was clearly marked, but there was no other labeling of any kind. Odd for a woman who could have won the Savannah Labeler of the Year Award.

A scratching and sniffing noise at the door distracted me. I cracked it open to see Duke wearing a look that cried, "Rescue me. Bring me into your sanctuary. Save me from the wicked throes of men. Purge me from this madness."

I opened the door wider and he ran straight to my bed, perched his hairy body on my cream coverlet, and sprawled himself out where his back paws reached my duvet. I made him scoot over and proceeded to rewind the tape.

I pushed play, and that voice, that unfamiliar voice, the one I had heard in my head for years, was more commanding than I had ever imagined. The tape began with questions of the interviewee's past. I listened intently. The woman who responded to Gloria's questions seemed familiar, but I couldn't place her voice. "So, tell me," Gloria asked, "When did you begin competing in the Miss Georgia United States of America Pageant?" For a moment I thought the other voice would betray itself as my mother's. But when the answer came, it was certainly not the voice of Victoria. This was driving me crazy.

Apparently, the lady Gloria was interviewing was there to tell the tale of why she believed the pageant was rigged the year she competed.

"Can you tell me the events that led you to your conclusions?"

The lady paused before saying in a soft and kind voice, "You know, Gloria, I really don't think I want to talk about this. It's been a long time, and I've moved past this. I really don't think it's necessary to go over such silly events. I hope I haven't wasted your time."

Gloria responded just as kindly, "Of course not; here, I'll just cut this off . . ." And with that, the tape went dead. I tried both sides. There was nothing else.

I leaned back against Duke almost afraid of what I held in my hand. Downstairs resided not only the queen of pageants, but the queen of the Miss Georgia United States of America Pageant. If this pageant was rigged—if it had ever been rigged—I needed to know. She needed to know. Everyone needed to know. "But who cares about pageants anyway?" I said to Duke. He put his head on his paws. "They're silly. They have no value. You prance around the stage in your skivvies. You wear heels of inhumane height. We're just going to put this back inside my purse here and forget we ever even heard such nonsense. Gloria was right not to pursue such a silly story. That's not a human-interest story. That's silliness. Don't you agree?" His expression said he did.

I walked into the bathroom to brush my teeth. In the mirror, a little bit of mildew in the bottom of my shower caught my eye.

Two hours later, Thomas found me. "What's wrong with you now?"

Some of my hair had come loose from its knot on the back of my head, and I blew it out of my eyes. "What do you mean, what's wrong with me? There's nothing wrong with me. Does something have to be wrong with a person simply because they want to have a clean bathroom?"

"Chill, Homer."

"Just because you're totally comfortable living in filth doesn't mean I am. Bathrooms carry more germs than Duke's mouth. Ever thought about that when you step into that shower of yours?" I finished off the grout in the far corner of the bathroom, underneath the farthest cabinet. Then I sat down, took off my rubber gloves, and looked up at Thomas, giving my hair one more quick blow. "There, I'm through."

"You are your mother's child."

"Why in the world did you say that?"

"Because Dad has more money than—"

"Do not say God; that's totally sacrilegious."

"I was going to say Bill Gates."

"No, he doesn't."

"Well, more money than most, and Mom refuses to have anyone clean her house."

"She doesn't think anyone can do it as well as she can."

"That's sick. Why would you clean your own house when you could afford to have someone else clean it?"

"Thomas, I'm way too tired to talk about our mother's issues. She does it because she is a control freak. And besides, someone might try to steal her tiara."

Thomas began staring at Duke's mouth. "Did you know dogs' mouths are supposed to be one of the cleanest places known to man?"

"You are here why?"

He came over to kneel down beside me. "To say good night. You can deny it if you want, but between dinner and now something happened. No one cleans the bathroom for pleasure, my dear

Vanni. Especially you. Are you sure you don't want to tell me what's wrong?"

"There's nothing wrong, Thomas," I said, standing up in front of him. "I simply wanted to take a shower in a clean one, that's all. Now if you'll excuse me . . ." With that, I closed the door on his perfectly positioned nose.

"OK. Whatever you say. But I'm just two floors down," he hollered. I heard Duke pad after him.

After a nice long, hot shower, bed captured me. Reading would be nice, but sleep was persistent. Dreams of tiaras, big hair, spiked heels, and that voice held me captive. Everyone in my dream had that voice. I woke up one time in the middle of the night with fists flailing, trying to prevent someone from wrapping a sash around me. By the time morning came, I was simply glad to have survived the night.

Sunday in the South means church. Sunday in this house, even if we lived in California, would still mean church. I hadn't been to our church in months: Babies had been born, people had been buried, and marriage vows had been spoken, and no doubt Vicky knew about each one. But bless her heart, I hadn't given her enough time to tell me what she had been doing, much less what anyone else had been doing.

Mother descended the staircase as though it were a runway. She had brought back hats on Sundays in Savannah. And everything always matched. Today she had chosen a pale blue ensemble trimmed in cream, her feet adorned by lovely Via Spigas in cream as well. She was accessorized with pearls this morning, and the whole grouping was topped off by a beautiful cream hat encompassed by a stunning pale blue bow, accentuated in the center by pristine blue silk hydrangeas.

Dad looked sharp in one of his navy suits, white crisp shirt, and light blue tie with white polka dots. He only wore suits on

Sundays anymore. He wouldn't even wear them on Sunday if he didn't feel one should wear one's very best to church. Mom thought one should look divine. I chose pleasant; Thomas settled for doable. In fact, I don't know how he got past her, in his wrinkled no-pleat khakis, flip-flops, and stretch-cotton shirt sleeves rolled up, but he did. He pulled off flip-flops on a Sunday! In fact, he pulled off a million things I never could.

I wore a simple black skirt and white blouse. Feeling rebellious, I let the blouse hang outside of my skirt. I pulled my shoulder-length hair back in a sleek ponytail, about the only way I wore it anymore, valuing the thirty minutes it saved me by not having to blow it dry. I debated wearing flip-flops but didn't desire war. A pair of black mules completed the look, and I was off to accomplish the day.

Dad and Vicky left about thirty minutes early so she wouldn't miss greeting anyone. Through the years, many in the city have thought of my father as a pushover when it comes to Vicky. This perception is usually reversed when they meet him. Dad was the one who let her know that we would travel thirty minutes to Tybee Island to go to church, because he thought it was best for the family. Pastor Brice's church has a little bit of everything; it is an integrated place of culture and worship. My dad believes that you should worship in places where all people are accepted.

"If you only see people there who look like you, you're missing what you've come for," he told us.

Mother loved the church but felt that as the head of the Chamber of Commerce she should attend church in one of the historical churches downtown. "You are more than welcome to attend any church you want," he said, "but you will attend it alone. The kids and I are going to Pastor Brice's church, with or without you." Today, Sister Victoria is one of our church's official greeters.

Thomas and I got to spend some time together on the ride over. He opened the door to his 1995 Jeep, a gift for graduation—not new of course, but nice nonetheless. "Glad to see you're learning how to be a gentleman."

"Glad to see you're still too chicken to wear flip-flops."

I slid into the car, and he closed the door. Dad didn't even buy new cars for himself, so he sure wasn't going to buy one for us. He knew you lost ten thousand dollars by driving a car off the lot, so he made sure the ten thousand was lost by someone else before he drove it away. It wasn't by frivolousness that he had retired at forty. Now Vicky, she would pay extra just so she could have it.

The Jeep was unusually clean. "Did Mother make you take her someplace?"

"No, things were growing in the back, so I figured yesterday was a good day to get it cleaned up. You just lucked out," he laughed.

"No, I would have just driven myself. What else did you do yesterday?"

"Well, me and Jeff Bryson—you remember him from Louisiana?"

"Yeah, sure . . . no, I honestly have no idea."

"You know, the guy from New Orleans who goes to The Citadel with me? He came home with me last summer for a couple of weeks. He won Mom over because he told her Savannah was far more beautiful than Charleston."

"Oh yeah, I remember."

"Well, he was here visiting his girlfriend, Mary Thomas, who went to Saint Vincent's and now goes to the College of Charleston. I went with them to the beach to surf and hang out. After your meltdown, we went to City Market to listen to a jazz band. I got so sunburned, though, I could hardly sleep," he added. "What did you do?"

"It wasn't a meltdown. My bathroom needed cleaning."

"Was it the apartment thing? Because I'm not ever leaving."

"Why should you? Free room, free laundry."

"Don't forget the food."

"No, how dare I forget the food."

"Why would you leave?"

"If you have to ask, you wouldn't understand." I knew he would continue to think it was the apartment that had me troubled. No one else needed to carry the burden of that tape until it was clear what it was really about. Not even Thomas.

We pulled up to the church just a couple of minutes before service started at ten. You could see Vicky's brim a mile away. She greeted us as she had every Sunday for the last thirteen years, straightening our shirts, spitting on her fingers to flatten one of Thomas's cowlicks. We often went in one of the other entrances just to avoid her spit and shine, but because we had parked in the front of the church today, we had to go through the front entrance.

"You two go get a seat and sit quietly." As if that thought would be lost on us in some way. We just smiled and did as we were told. Wonder what would've happened if, instead, we had chosen to stand in the back and carry on loud conversations, just to prove we were too inept at coming up with such a conclusion ourselves.

Inside, Thomas and I hugged necks, said hellos, and sat down about midway back on the left-hand side. Vicky and Dad sat on the second row on the right-hand side. The music started, and no one saw their seat again for almost forty-five minutes. The music rocked the house, then came down to a soothing pace. Each song gave me a reason to rejoice, reflect, or respond. Some clapped, some stood silent, others raised their hands in a form of surrender, but each responded in the way that expressed his own heart.

When the special song was over, Pastor Brice took the platform in his usual unpretentious way. He acquired his congregation's respect without demanding it. Today's message was titled "The Life You're Looking For." For the next forty minutes, Pastor Brice made it clear that the direction for our lives could be something we've yet to discover. Then he told us what was necessary in a person's character to achieve the ultimate destiny for his or her life. I listened as if every word was spoken directly to me. I felt as if he had followed me around for the last two months, cataloging my life and culling a message from my mayhem. But somewhere between his reading of the Scripture and his final point I felt a calming, even an assuring, that the decision I had made was necessary for wherever I was going.

After a magnificent meal of roast and potatoes, Vicky was sitting in wait. "OK, let's go. I want to show you your new apartment."

I eased myself out of the chair and followed her reluctantly to the front door. "Don't get too excited. There are no guarantees that I'm going to move into this apartment."

"You're going to love it. I promise." And she took off out the front door and across the street. I had barely closed the door behind me when she turned around in front of a townhouse almost directly in line with her own front door, flung her arms wide open, and declared, "Ta-da! Isn't it perfect?!" I sat down right on our top step. "Savannah, get up. You're going to love this."

I got up and walked over to the Mini-Me. It was made with brick, just like her house; had an iron railing in front of the door, just like her house; and had ivy growing halfway up the wall, just like her house. The only difference was the red front door. "Why didn't you pick the one next to it?" I asked as I stood beside her. "Its door is black."

"It didn't have as much charm. Come on, Bett loaned me her MLS key." Bett Thomas is the only *real* real estate agent in town. Others try, but she's the master.

"Of course she did. But there is really no reason for me to see this, Mother. I'm not going to live across the street from you. I may as well not move out at all."

"Oh, OK. Well, good, let's just go home then," she said, turning her little three-inch heels around quicker than she could rename a street Victoria Valley Drive.

"Is that what this is about? Did you do all of this so I would stay home? Well, get your hiney in that house and show it to me then."

"Savannah! I'm going to have whiplash if you keep spinning me in circles like this." She opened the door.

The place was breathtaking. It had plantation shutters, hardwood floors, built-in bookcases, and a newly remodeled kitchen and master bath. It had three bedrooms and two baths. And it was simply perfect.

As she closed the door behind us, I stood my ground. "Well, if I was even willing to live across the street, it wouldn't matter, because I couldn't afford this place anyway. It's probably $1,500 a month."

"Actually, it's $2,500 a month," she said, "but I'll help you pay what you can't afford."

"How would that have me independent and making my own way?"

"Savannah, give me a break. You'll be living by yourself. I won't even bring you dinner, unless we have tons of leftovers." She smiled. We walked back through our front door. "Well, I think it's perfect, and if you let it go, you'll be sorely disappointed," she said to my back as I dragged myself up the stairs.

"It won't be the first time," I called back. I spent the rest of the evening in travail over the fact that I needed a story. She and Dad went up the street for a Bible study, allowing me to use that time to get a snack and head back upstairs.

Duke and I conversed about the Abercorn address and relocation. He was all for it. And the thoughts of how nice it would look decorated did have a certain appeal. "I would technically be out on my own." Duke panted in agreement. "No one would have to know Vicky was supplementing the rent. It would look nice with some furniture and my bedroom suite." Somewhere between choosing toile or damask, we both surrendered to sleep. And somewhere in the middle of the night, Vicky slipped me a lovely sample of a new-address acknowledgment for one Savannah Phillips at the address across the street.

CHAPTER TEN

There is something about dogs that just makes life better: they have a way of listening without giving opinions, following you wherever you go, and being totally comfortable with no agenda at all. What an ideal relationship. After slipping on my Nikes, I headed out with Duke. I talked to him for a couple of blocks, then I put my earphones on to listen to my new weekly tilling CD, Jonathan Pierce's *Run to You,* I put the button on repeat. "I could walk to you, but I'd rather run," came the lyrics, giving me the motivation to keep up the pace.

After the second mile, I stopped to give Duke a break at the doggy fountain. The break was really more for me, because Duke was in much better shape since he and Dad started working out. I sat down on a bench at the south side of the park and saw a familiar face approaching out of the corner of my eye.

"Savannah?" Grant called.

I took off my earphones and swung them over my shoulder. "Hey, Grant," I said, wondering if hugging him was appropriate anymore. Hard to believe I was actually having to ask myself that question.

He bent down and hugged me instead. "I saw Duke and knew you weren't your father. I heard you were home. How're you doing?" he asked.

"Oh, I'm doing great!" I said, sounding ridiculously fake. "How're you doing?"

"I'm doing pretty well. Work is good. Dad and I manage pretty well together." He was wiping his beautiful tan face with a white towel. "I have had some things change, though. Do you mind if I sit down?" he asked, waving to the empty side of the bench.

"No, not at all," I answered. Duke came up from his water break and shook his head right in front of us, soaking us both. "Oh, that's attractive, Duke," I said, laughing. Grant smiled, causing both his green eyes and perfectly white teeth to flash, as they did any-time something amusing or thought-provoking happened.

"Savannah," he began rather cautiously, "I've wanted to call you for a while, but I didn't know where to begin. I met someone my last semester at school. Her name's Elisabeth." So much for Paige's accuracy. "She's a sweet girl. After you and I had our talk, I decided that I had to get on with life. So she and I started dating after I graduated. We've been dating almost two years now, and we're getting married next month. I wanted to tell you myself, but figured your mom would tell you first," he said, laughing. I had long since grown accustomed to people laughing after they said my mother's name.

"Well, she didn't tell me anything, which means somehow this has escaped her realm of knowledge. How that is at all possible, I am totally unaware. But Paige told me yesterday."

"Well, we haven't had a need to tell that many people around here. Elisabeth's from North Carolina, so we're getting married there, but then we'll move back here after the honeymoon." He spoke in such a matter-of-fact tone. Did he not know this news was only a day old to me?

"So do you love her?" I blurted, then slapped my hand over my mouth. "I'm sorry. I can't believe I said that. Of course you love her. You wouldn't marry someone you didn't love. Why would any-one marry someone they didn't love? No one marries someone they don't love. Well, maybe if it were for money, but I'm sure this isn't about money . . ."

"Yes." He paused, then softly touched my arm. "I do love her, and you're right. I wouldn't marry someone I didn't love. She's a wonderful girl, and she really loves me. And she's Methodist too!" Another laugh.

"Well, what more could you ask for?" I asked, all the while wishing he would say, "I could have asked for you." But he had asked for me. And two years ago, I had let him get away.

He looked me directly in the eyes. "Not much. I'm a lucky man. I've loved well, Savannah. And I loved you well."

"I loved you too, Grant. No, I *love* you too. But you know me, I believe that the decisions we make are for a reason. You've been one of my best friends for as long as I can remember. I know what your expressions mean. I can tell what you're thinking by the way you squint your nose when you're perplexed, or by the different rubs you have for your head. There's the stressed rub"—I demon-strated—"and the thinking rub." My laugh was much more awk-ward than his. "I know all of these things about you, and I still let you walk out of my life. And that day led us to this day, a day I didn't plan, but apparently a day that was meant to be. You deserve to be loved well," I said. Grant looked down at the top of Duke's head. I touched the bottom of his face and lifted his chin so I could see those green eyes as we closed this chapter of our lives. "You're a wonderful man. One I always appreciated, but never quite the way that you deserved. I wish you the greatest happiness." I turned to go and heard him call out my name, differently than I had ever heard before. He was letting go.

"Savannah, you would like her. She would have been your kind of friend."

"If she likes you, I know I would like her," I said.

He stood up and brushed himself off. "And she would like

you," he said. "Everyone likes you." He smiled at me as only he can, then he turned and jogged away.

Duke and I stood there. Walking away felt somehow treasonous. Downright sacrilegious. But Grant—Grant hadn't just walked away; he had jogged. There was no slow step, no hung head, no discreet wipe of the eyes. But I couldn't move. Moving meant letting go. Moving meant good-bye.

Duke's whimper forced me back to Forsythe Park. "Me too, boy. Me too."

Dad's Land Rover was sitting in the street when I rounded Abercorn Street. My mother was perched at the door, his hand eclipsing hers as they rested on the edge of his open window. This was how love looked: undivided attention and last-minute conversations. It looked through the same eyes after twenty some years and yet still held a reluctance to part, an anticipation of the next time they would see one another. I looked at Duke sadly. He looked at me as if he knew what I was thinking. Well, he had never known love either. There was the chocolate lab up the street, but Dad wouldn't let him anywhere near her. I walked up the steps a tad slower than usual.

I distracted myself by taking inventory of my closet. It was certain—I possessed no appropriate newspaper reporter attire. It was time to shop. I decided to walk because summer would be here soon, and months would pass before I could again walk without perspiration settling behind my knees and in the creases of my arms. Today was beautiful and warm, but not cruel. As I passed Katherine's bookstore, a customer emerged with a sack full of books. Thinking maybe something inside could spark my interest and give me an idea for a human-interest story that might actually interest a human, I decided to go inside.

People were browsing most every nook and cranny. Many looked like tourists. An elderly gentleman dressed in plaid pants picked up Vicky's book with pictures of someone else's home. He skimmed through and set it down and progressed to another about ghosts. Savannah has a ghost story around almost every corner, which appalls Vicky to no end. When she found out Disney World copied the exterior of the Hamilton Turner Inn for the facade of their haunted mansion, well, she wrote Mr. Disney himself, totally oblivious to the fact that he had been dead for years. And this past year, Savannah was voted the most haunted city in North America; and well, let's just say, had my mother learned of it, Washington would have been notified.

Katherine was behind the counter when I came in, and she saw me immediately. A customer was waiting to check out, and she thanked him and invited him to stop by again before leaving Savannah. With her greeting, my pulse went haywire. The voice on the tape. Katherine was the one who had a story to tell. A story she never finished. Afraid my expression would give me away, I pretended to interest myself in a display. My new friend had a secret.

When she spoke again, I jumped. "Well, Savannah. I hoped I'd see you again soon. I didn't know it would be this soon, though. I see you've got your book with you. Wanting to return it already?"

"No, no, I usually carry one around. You know, in case there's any lag time. And I . . . well I . . . I hadn't planned on stopping in so soon, but I just needed to do a little research, you know, take a few minutes to browse." I picked up the closest thing to me, to show that I hadn't really come to expose her deep, dark, buried secret.

"Well, you research all you need to," she said, turning her attention to Mr. Plaid Pants's wife, Mrs. Polka Dot.

More people came and went, so I spent some time browsing through the new autobiography section, trying hard not to stare at Katherine. My mind raced with a thousand questions, all begging for immediate answers. Katherine walked around the bookstore like she owned the place. Well, you know what I mean. She has a quiet confidence that invites you in and encourages you to stay, but you know you're in her domain. I tried to act interested in the autobiographies.

There were more stars' faces on the covers of books than you could find on the walls at the Chamber of Commerce office. Vicky had all the stars take a picture with her and the Chamber staff before they left town after filming their movies. Then she would shoo everyone out of the way and get one of her own. She has pictures with Julia Roberts, Tom Hanks, Denzel Washington, Kevin Spacey, and Clint Eastwood. They all hang in her office at home. Not that anyone knows what that office is for. Come to think of it, no one knows what her office is for at the Chamber either, because she's usually standing in someone's front yard talking or sitting on the back of a trolley car acting like she's not who everyone knows she is.

Eventually, Katherine got a moment of reprieve from her busy spurt and came back to where I was. "We just got a lot of new books in. You should look through the titles and see what you find."

"Do you read a lot?" I asked, not wanting to blurt out the real question lying beneath the surface: "What on earth were you doing in a pageant and what on earth do you know?"

"As often as I can."

"Do you mind if I ask what you're reading now?"

"You'll laugh," she said, putting her hand up to her mouth to hide her blushing face.

"Trust me, after the books I tell people I've read and loved, you won't find me laughing at you. Try me." I hoped she would reveal that she had just picked up the latest edition of *Pageant Scandals and Recovering Drama Queens,* which would be a perfect segue into my questions.

"Well, I was going through our young-reader section the other day and found one I hadn't read in years. I couldn't remember much about it except how much I enjoyed reading it the first time. So, I picked it up again."

"OK . . . and it is . . . ?"

"I'm rereading *Lord of the Flies,*" she said, squinting in mock embarrassment.

"No way!" I hollered, belting her on the arm. She lost her balance and almost tumbled into the shelf in front of us. I grabbed her and helped her stand upright. "Oh, I'm so sorry. Did I hurt you?" I asked, half laughing, half humiliated.

"No!" she said, laughing quite hysterically. "I'm fine, but I didn't quite expect that response."

"That is like my favorite book of all time. I reread it about once every couple of years."

"You've got to be kidding."

"No, I am dead serious. And trust me, I don't use the words *dead* and *me* in the same sentence unless I'm totally serious. That's my favorite book. I just think it is so telling of human nature when every form of law is removed, when every boundary is released, and we are expected to create our own. That struggle alone is mesmerizing. It has to be one of the best books of all time."

"Well, don't we have similar tastes? But no more talking about me. You said you came by to do some research. What are you researching?"

It still felt bittersweet coming off of my lips. "I'm working at the paper. I'm going to write human-interest stories."

For a minute she didn't speak. "Oh, well, well, that will be wonderful, Savannah. Are you taking Gloria's place?"

I responded as quickly as I could so she wouldn't think I was avoiding her questions. "Well, I don't know that anyone will ever take her place, but I hope I can at least write stories as provocative and transforming as the pieces she wrote through the years."

"Yes, she is—well, she was a wonderful writer. I loved her pieces." She turned to straighten the books she had knocked out of place when I sent her reeling. Her silence made me feel like I needed to say something. I wanted to make her comfortable, make her trust me. The more open and honest I could be, the better the opportunity in the end.

"It's been a crazy journey for me."

She turned her attention back to me. "Really? How so?"

"Can we sit down?" I asked, motioning to the steps beside us.

"Sure."

For the next hour, we had the luxury of uninterrupted time. Absolutely no other customer entered the store. It was a divine appointment. I told her about the fiction award and publishing opportunity, leaving out the part about my mother but adding the revelation of my destiny and the countless papers that had made their way to UGA.

"Those articles consumed me. And now I'm here, back where I started. So, we'll see if it works. But none of it will work without a story," I said, getting to my feet, hoping she would burst from the exhaustion of having held such a tale of disrepute for so long that she could no longer control herself. But control herself she did.

She stood up. "Well, I'm sure you'll find exactly what you need."

"I'm sure I will. Thanks for listening. I've got to run and buy some appropriate clothes for this new job," I said, motioning to the T-shirt and denim Capris I had on.

"You'll do wonderfully, Savannah. Now go get beautiful."

"I'm not looking for miracles, just closed-toed shoes."

She laughed and walked me to the door. "I hope I'll see you soon."

"Oh, I'll see you soon. Very soon, I'm sure." And with that, I walked out the door, realizing I had a story. The story just needed to admit it should be told.

CHAPTER ELEVEN

I entered through the back gate that leads directly to Paige's portion of the antique shop. I did this to avoid any questions her mother might ask, because they would be the same as my mother's. She, like Vicky, never wears jeans and prefers heels over anything else. The fact that Paige and I came out so alarmingly normal still amazes us both.

As I came through the door, Paige was wrapping up a painting for a customer, a lady who owned one of the hospitality centers up the street. She was planning to send the piece to her daughter in Augusta for her birthday. We said our hellos, and I went behind the counter to unwrap the lunch I'd brought. Before Paige sat down, she turned the Open sign around to Closed.

"You're going to have people so confused on when you're open and closed that they're going to start coming by at night just to try to catch you."

"The joy of having your own business," she mused.

"Speaking of having your own business, have you met Katherine Owens? She owns Katherine's Corner Bookstore."

"How long have you known me?"

"Too long."

"Have you ever seen me with a book in my hand?"

"She carries magazines too."

"Oh, well then, no, I haven't met her yet. But I have all intents and purposes of meeting her soon." She took a bite of her chicken wrap.

I told her all about Katherine and how lovely she was and about going into Gloria's office and finding the tape and then realizing it was Katherine's voice. "Why do you think she didn't want to tell her story?"

"Maybe she's really the Beauty Queen Serial Killer and decided at the last minute that she liked her life of freedom. She didn't want to chance the world knowing her deeds of devastation," she said, slurping like Hannibal Lecter.

"You have too much imagination," I said, rolling my eyes and taking another bite of my sandwich. "Would you help me think? OK, she mentioned the pageant was rigged. But then she closed down. I mean, if Miss Georgia United States of America is rigged, that could mean that Vicky's win was rigged."

"Savannah, if you think you've had trouble with your mama in the past, you are asking for trouble of colossal proportion if you go tampering with her tiara."

"Who does beauty pageants? Who would know something about this? You know everyone, Miss Social Queen."

"Hey now, I've never been the queen of anything. You beat me, remember?"

"Homecoming queen doesn't count. Besides, Vicky bribed half the campus with promises of pizza and Coke for lunch."

"There was Emma Riley," she said, hardly stopping to breathe as she engulfed what was left of her wrap.

"Emma Riley. Oh, that's right. Emma did pageants forever. She was one of the most beautiful girls I've ever seen. Didn't she win Miss Queen of Everything and move out to California with a beach bum or something?"

"You haven't heard about Emma?"

"*No,* I haven't heard about Emma. What? What!"

"Well, after she lost Miss Georgia Whatever, her life went to pot. She didn't come out of her house for about six months, married the biggest loser in Savannah. Now she comes out every now and then, but no one hardly recognizes her because she looks so terrible. Has a busload of children with dirty faces and nasty tempers."

"You've got to be kidding me."

"Nope. That is the truth as I see it from here."

"And you see pretty much everything from here."

"Absolutely. That's why I chose this corner."

"Maybe I need to visit Miss Emma."

"Maybe you need to get your inoculations first. She's a scary lady now."

"You are such the overreactor."

"Fine. Go see for yourself."

"Watch me chase this crazy story. I'll waste my first week and end up coming here to interview you and make you sound like you're some great gift to the community. I'll be writing obituaries by next week."

"You laugh. You probably are supposed to be writing about me. I'm a human-interest story," she said seriously.

"You're a human-interest story all right. A young girl with rich parents who let her sell her paintings in the back of their store on the days she chooses to show up. People will only be interested in seeing if your parents ever thought of adoption," I told her, picking up my fork to dig into my key-lime square.

"I've accomplished extraordinary things for my age."

"Yes, you have. And I probably will share your story one day, but most everyone around here knows your story, and mine too probably, thanks to our respective mothers. But my first article has to be a bang. I have to leave them knowing that someone worthy of Gloria's position has arrived."

Paige swallowed the first bite of her key-lime square. "Oh, Savannah, this thing is delicious. Who made this? And if it's a man, is he married?"

"Yes, it's a man, and I have no idea if he's married."

"Where did you get this food?"

"It's a new place. Wright's Café, over off of West York."

"Well, it's divine." Then, with her mouth full, she managed to say, "No, I know you're right. And it sounds like this could be, hopefully, a wonderful discovery."

"Yes, I really think it will." We talked for a while longer, and I told her about my run-in with Grant. We both agreed that I should leave it at that and spend the rest of my life avoiding him and Miss Converse, but I wasn't sure how long I'd be able to keep that up. Paige loved my new clothes, hated the shoes, and sent me off with instructions to check for a wedding band the next time I was at Wright's Café.

Things were running as usual when I entered Dad's coffee shop. Customers were coming in and out, giving Duke the usual devoted attention. Duke had decided to spend some time lying out on the sidewalk in hopes that some unwitting lady from the courthouse would forget Dad's ban on feeding Duke the remainders of bagels and muffins.

Inside, Judge Hoddicks was at the counter, picking up his late-afternoon fix. He had an assistant, but not a day went by that he didn't step out of his robe and into the Savannah sunshine for a little banter with Jake. "Hi, Judge."

"Hi, Betty!" he said, grabbing me in a bear hug. I love that he still calls me Betty. "I hear you're here to stay."

"Can you believe it?"

"No, I thought for sure we'd lose you to one of those states up there in the North, writing your books, getting famous, and referring to us as those crazy people from the South."

I laughed. "I did too! But then I came to the conclusion that I'm as crazy as the rest of you."

"Well, you may not be happy about it, but I sure am," he said with a kiss on the cheek and a smile as he headed for the door. "Jake, give Betty whatever she wants, and put it on my tab!" He walked out, never turning around.

"You got it, Judge," Dad said, wiping off the counter and laughing at his old friend. Before I got situated good, Mervine came from the back, set a Coke down in front of me with a little nod and a sheepish smile, and disappeared again.

"Dad, have you ever in all these years asked why Mervine never talks?"

"Well, I just figured that Louise talks enough for the both of them, and Mervine's never felt that anything else needed to be said. But I overheard Louise telling Richard one day not to let her shy, quiet personality fool you, because she talks a blue streak at home. So how was the apartment?"

"The Mini-Victoria across the street? I looked at it, realized I would have to have ten roommates to afford it, and said thanks but no thanks."

"Has that stopped her?"

"You are such a funny man. What do you think?"

"I figure she's got a contract on it as we speak."

"And new-address postcards for me to mail out."

"So what are you going to do?"

"Keep looking. But I must admit, it was fabulous."

"With your mother, I have no doubts," he said, getting up from his chair and heading toward the back. "So why are you declining?"

"Because it would defeat the purpose," I said, following behind. "You aren't making your way in the world if your mother is paying your rent and bringing you dinner."

"I'm glad to hear you say that," he said. He turned around and started two new pots of coffee.

"I'm sure you are. But I'll find one. My friend Claire's got her real-estate license and she's going to look for some things."

"Well, that will be nice," he said, giving me a kiss.

My mother's voice was coming from the top of the stairs, sounding loud and irritated. I rounded the corner, peeked inside her room, and was greeted by her derrière protruding from underneath the bed skirt. I leaned up against her door, not wanting to miss whatever might be unfolding.

Her head finally popped out from under the bed, most of her hair all crowned nicely on the top, giving her a nouveau-retro kind of undone look. In her hand she held the shoe that matched the one already adorning her right foot—except for the nicely mangled heel and chewed up sling-back strap, evidence of a bored golden retriever with bitterness issues.

The look on her face was priceless. She grabbed her heart, feigning a heart attack from my unsuspected presence, and proceeded to tell me that Duke was going to be living at Jake's.

I went into my bedroom to hide out until she left. I heard the clicking of what I assumed to be a different pair of heels go down the stairs and out the door. I gave her a few seconds to come back in case she forgot something, having learned this trick after getting caught on two occasions by her return for forgotten things.

The first time she caught me with a BB gun shooting at squirrels. The next time she caught me talking on the phone to Grant after we had both been put on phone restriction for the episode at John Wesley's church. I wasn't sure why she was leaving so late in the day, but then I remembered that it was Monday, and every other Monday evening she hosted a meeting of the local historical society at the Owens-Thomas house right after work, to discuss issues that needed to be dealt with in the Historical District regarding renovations and gaudy décor.

Having waited a sufficient amount of time, I headed to the attic and found a box marked "Pageant Keepsakes." I opened it, trying to disturb as little as possible. Inside her box of keepsakes rests what most would consider trinkets of self-absorption. We all had a sneaking suspicion that Vicky crawled up here to peruse her little box of mementos, because every now and then you would see her walking around with pieces of insulation in her hair.

I've often wondered what it was that took her all the way to first runner-up at the Miss United States of America Pageant. After all, it's hard for any young woman to look at her mother objectively. Young women see their mothers with guarded fear, ever cognizant that they are looking at what they could become.

Vicky competed in the Miss United States of America Pageant in 1976, the 200th anniversary of our Declaration of Independence. She chose a Statue of Liberty costume for the introduction of contestants. To her dismay and horror, over half of the girls wore their own Statue of Liberty costumes. I don't know how she thought her costume would be original, but obviously, common sense wasn't a prerequisite for competition in 1976. I told her she should have dressed up like Uncle Sam, because no other woman at a beauty pageant would dare dress up like a man. She could have won most original for sure. She didn't laugh.

After moving aside her rather torched torch and gingerly placing her lovely silver-sequined statue costume on the floor, there on top of dried and crushed roses, banners, and other memorabilia was the 1976 program book. I pulled it out and laid it aside, then replaced everything with hopes that she would never notice. I was kind of surprised that her box wasn't wired.

I began to flip through the pages carefully. If a beauty contest was rigged, the tampering would most logically begin with the judges or the auditors. I studied the page bearing their photos. Judge number one, Marcus Smythe, hailed from South Carolina. He looked kind of cartoonish, with thick gray hair, bow tie, and a sports coat. He was a local television personality there in the Low Country.

The second judge was a lady named Dr. Beverly Corzine from Tennessee, a Vanderbilt graduate and a physician in Nashville. She looked rather elegant, despite the super-fixed hairdo from the seventies.

The third judge was a dowdy-looking lady named Madeline Taylor. She looked downright manly and mad. My, what a combination for a pageant judge! She was a retired schoolteacher, and she wore her hair in a pageboy with chopped-off bangs that looked as if her granddaughter had made Grandma a beauty-school guinea pig. She wore glasses on a cord around her neck. Well, all you saw in the picture was the cord, but with those squinty, shifty eyes, you were sure glasses were hanging somewhere nearby. She hailed from Florida. So much for her joy of retirement in the Land of Sunshine.

Then there was judge number four, a distinguished-looking gentleman from Jackson, Mississippi. Wearing a coat and tie, he looked to be in his late forties. His name was Randolph Cummings III. He was a Mississippi attorney who also ran the local community theater in Jackson.

The final judge was a former Miss Georgia United States of America herself, Francis Margaret McEntire. She was from Atlanta and was a graduate of the University of Georgia, recently married and with a new baby on the way, her bio declared. So these were the five people who would decide which young lady would be dedicated to hosting local barbecues and talent competitions, visiting snotty-nosed kids in schools and kissing all over them, and cutting ribbons at the openings of local funeral homes and furniture stores. What excited a woman about all of that was beyond the power of my imagination. In 1976 at least, twenty-one women apparently found such a lifestyle worth coveting.

I turned the page. A section with no pictures read, "Auditors for the evening are Lynn and Larry Templeton of Templeton and Associates Accounting Firm of Macon."

After looking at my mother's program I didn't know much more about pageants than I did when I began, but I was intrigued by the thought that anyone would bother rigging a pageant in the first place. It seemed ridiculous and petty. Even so, it had happened at least one time, at least as far as Katherine was concerned. I had a week to kill, and I might as well kill it well. Then I caught myself. "I don't have a week to kill," I said out loud. "I have a week to produce a human-interest story. Lord, help us all." Fortunately, the Lord knew I really meant it.

CHAPTER TWELVE

Before anyone came home for the evening, I left a note on the kitchen counter that I was having dinner out. Across the street at Clary's, maybe, but it was "out" nonetheless. I ate dinner and consumed two shakes and three Cokes, all the while staring at my house. I watched as every light turned off, including the ones inside Clary's, and they told me to go home or clock in.

Standing on the steps to my house, I knew my growing dread wasn't over the apartment taunting me from across the street. My real concern was how to confront Vicky with the possibility that the Miss Georgia United States of America pageant had once or ever or always been rigged. Over dinner and liquid chocolate, I had asked myself a million questions, most of them regarding my mother's reaction.

If for one moment she thought she had not won her title because she was the best in the show . . . well, it would be a ruin like no other. I would be released from the family. My scooping abilities would become the bane of my mortal existence. My name would never be spoken again.

The more I thought about it, however, the more I concurred

the drama might actually be worth watching. But then again, this claim of Katherine's, accompanied by proof I would have to uncover, could destroy my mother's greatest achievement. That in and of itself was, at its core, unfair.

And so I decided I would not share an ounce of this with my family until I could prove that it was true. At least for tonight, I wanted my mother to lay her head on her pillow believing that she was still a former Miss Georgia United States of America simply because the judges thought she should be. I wasn't willing to take that from her . . . unless I absolutely had to.

I tried to be as quiet as possible, slipping up the stairs and closing the door behind me. No sooner had I turned the light on and flung my shoes across the room than there was a knock at my door. I opened it to find Thomas and Duke peering back at me.

"Can we come in for a minute?" he asked.

They plopped themselves on the bed, and I headed to the bathroom to apply Noxzema and brush my teeth. "It looks like you already have."

He watched me lather my face.

"Is that what all girls do before they go to bed?"

"Well, I'm not sure what all girls do, but it works for this one."

"I kind of always imagined that Mom just took off her entire face and sat it on a foam head next to her bed, then put it back into position in the morning," he said, rolling on his back and sticking his feet up in the air as if he himself were Duke.

I couldn't help but laugh, and I accidentally stuck a Noxzema-covered finger in my eye. "Ow! You are just wrong. But, in my twenty-four years of existence I have only seen her without makeup on one occasion, and I was in preschool. I asked her to hurry up and put it on, and I've never seen her without it since." I wiped my face clean and started to brush my teeth.

"Well, she looks good even without it. Anyway, I just wanted you to know that she told me tonight about the apartment she found you. Dad told her to let you make your own decisions."

I stopped in the middle of my brushing. "Wellimnodgonatakit. Whaddoyouthankshe'ldoweniteler?"

"Besides attach a tracking device to your car, who knows?"

I spit, rinsed, and wiped my mouth, then walked back into the bedroom and sat on the edge of the bed. Looking straight ahead into my bathroom, I spotted a glimpse of dirt. "Do you think my bathroom is clean enough?"

"Have you ever thought of therapy?" He jumped up and patted me on my head as if I was Duke and they departed. I just watched as he closed the door.

"Have you ever thought of therapy?" I mimicked. "Blah, blah, blah." I decided to go downstairs to grab a glass of water before I put my pajamas on and went to bed. I rounded the corner to walk through the den that is attached to the kitchen, flipped on the light, and let out a scream. Sitting there on the sofa in the now brightly lit family room was Vicky. The last thing I had been expecting to see was a person in that room, and the last one I actually wanted to see at that moment was my mother.

Once I retrieved my nerves from the far corners of the earth, I continued to walk past her to the kitchen. "What are you doing sitting here in the dark?"

"I was waiting on you, actually," she said. She turned around to face me but remained in her chair. "I wanted to talk to you about your new place."

I kept my back to her as I filled up a cup with ice and water from the door of the refrigerator. "Mother, I'm not taking that apartment."

"Why not? It's beautiful. And it's right here."

"Mother, it's like I wouldn't have even moved away. I would be right across the street. I may as well stay here. And that's not going to happen," I added quickly.

"Savannah, I don't know why on earth you would think you

need your own apartment anyway. It's just silly. You have a beautiful room upstairs. You have someone to cook and clean for you. You don't have to worry about paying rent or any of those other things that could happen to a young lady . . . alone . . . all by herself . . . in a strange place . . . with strange people," she said in a rather entertaining form of mock fear.

I turned to look at her. She had still not moved from her chair, but she now had her arms wrapped around her knees and the most exaggerated of wide-eyed expressions. I walked over to her and sat on the moss-green velvet ottoman directly across from her floral chair. "Mother, let me tell you something. There comes a time when a young woman has to take the opportunity to become just that, a woman. Lest you forget, I have lived the last several years in my own apartment at school. Now, instead of living in my own apartment hours away, I'll be living in my own apartment possibly blocks away. But not across the street." I took a moment to be a touch melodramatic and reached out to pat her leg, then I stood to be able to part the room after my final statement.

"You should actually treasure this experience, Mother. This move is a testament to how competently you have raised me to be self-sufficient and a major contributor to this city, your city. That fact alone should make you as excited for this new adventure of mine as I am. I will now become part of your city, something you can share with your countless visitors, an asset to your community. I will now officially be a part of Savannah, all because of the excellent way in which I was raised," I finished, feeling manipulative but successful, because with each sentence her lamentable stature straightened in confidence and pride. And with the knowledge that I had probably just created an even greater monster, I departed.

The moment I saw him, I ducked behind the edge of the building. Grant made this walk every morning, from his house on 345 Habersham to his dad's architectural building. In years past

I had craved discovery, even choreographed it a time or two. But now, sight of Grant brought rejection and undue trauma. So as he rounded the corner of Lincoln Street, I rounded the corner of Jake's and entered the back door slightly winded.

Coming through the door, Dad spotted me. "Grant's out front grabbing a coffee. Would you like to say hey?"

"Grant hates coffee."

"Doesn't seem to anymore. Maybe he's picking it up for his dad."

"Or maybe for his floozy."

"Savannah Phillips! What did you say?"

"I said I'm feeling a little woozy. I might need a double this morning."

"That's what I thought you said." He placed the cups in the sink and wiped his hands on his apron while I got what I needed from the Coke machine. "It sounds like you had a rather eventful evening last night with your mother," he said, heading to the coffee maker.

"It was a rather brilliant performance, if I do say so myself. However, it was all true. And I have been raised exceptionally well." I kissed him on his cheek and headed for the door.

"Yes, and educated in the art of manipulation by the master."

"I'm not sure what time I'll be home," I added on my way out. "Would you let Mother know I'm going to grab dinner out?"

"No, you can call your mother. I am not your messenger, young lady."

"OK, OK, I'll call her. But I'm not sure if I'll get her. I might have to simply leave the message on her voice mail. Oh, that wretched piece of machinery. It has totally devoured a culture's ability to address each other personally. Modern technology will be our society's eventual downfall."

"Technology and wimpy children will be our death."

As I grabbed the door handle and pulled it open, the smell of Savannah mingled with the brewing of freshly roasted coffee. I turned around. "Dad, if you knew something that could possibly

hurt someone you love, but the knowledge of that truth could prevent its ability to hurt even more people, would telling it be worth
the risk?"

Dad set down his pot and turned to me. "I have no idea what
you are talking about, Savannah, and Lord knows if I really want to.
I can tell you, though, that life has taught me that revealing truth
isn't always easy. But allowing someone to be hurt knowingly is
unforgivable. Just make sure that what you reveal is actually true."

"That's what I thought too," I said. I headed out the door and
into the alley, then back to the front of the building. Richard was
outside standing by the door, watching Duke watch his beloved
chocolate lab cross to the other side of the square.

He never turned to look at me. "Poor thing. Never gets quite
close enough."

"He is a woeful creature." I turned to look at the lines that had
now grown distinctively deeper through the years in the corners
of Richard's eyes. They were from his endless smiles and bouts of
laughter. Next to my mother, Richard knew most everything happening in this town. The reason was that he did more listening than
talking. Richard listened as people shared their stories, and he
knew when they wanted his advice and when they simply wanted
his ear. He was like your best hairdresser or priest.

"Richard, I have a question for you."

"Shoot, Savannah," he said, still observing Duke's frustration.

"Do you remember Emma Riley? She graduated from Massey
School a couple of years before me? Really pretty girl who won
all the local pageants?"

"Oh, that's a sad story, Savannah," he drawled. "A very sad
story. Seems she married herself a drunk, had four children like
stairsteps, and barely gets by. I hear he beat her and the children.
It's a very sad story."

"Do you know where she lives?"

"Actually, I hear she finally listened to reason and moved away
from that jerk."

"Richard! That doesn't sound like you."

"Sorry, Savannah. Things like that just make my southern gentlemanly ways fade out with the northern breeze. Seems she moved into the apartment underneath her mother and father's home once her divorce was final, changed her name back to Riley, and her folks help her take care of her children. But I don't know that she's any better than before." He stopped and looked at me as if to remove himself from the land he had drifted to. "What in the world you readin' now, Savannah Phillips?"

"Oh, it's *To Kill a Mockingbird*."

"Child, you haven't changed a lick. We're going to bury you with a book."

"Eww. No talk of such things." I kissed Richard and patted Duke. "She probably drinks out of toilets, Duke. I'm sure she's not worth it." He sighed a heavy sigh, refusing to be consoled, and dropped himself back to the heated pavement.

CHAPTER THIRTEEN

The Savannah morning sun had shifted into assault position. No one in this square would be able to escape it until late in the afternoon. It had already attacked the sides of my Coca-Cola cup and left me with a wet hand. I just about ended up bathed in Coke as I tried to find a napkin in my glove compartment, put my cup in a cup holder, and answer my ringing cell phone all at the same time. I grabbed the Coke before it cascaded down the front of my white linen pants.

"Hello," I answered, sounding rather discomposed for such an early hour.

"Well, Miss Sunshine apparently has already forgotten that she has a real job and the possibility of moving out of her home in a very short while."

"Miss Sunshine just about rained on herself. Did you decide to work today, or do you want to come out and play with me?"

"If I don't sell some artwork, I can't pay rent."

"Yeah, right, and if I hadn't gotten a job, I'd've been kicked out of Vicky's house. Anyway, I'm headed to Emma's house now. Sure you don't want to come?"

"You mean you're just going to go over to her house, show up on her doorstep, and say, 'Do you want to tell me your story?'"

"Well, I was planning on it until you said it like that. Do you have a better idea?"

"No, I don't have any idea. I just hope you're still packing that BB gun in your trunk. You might need it. And don't tell her I said anything about her. I don't want her sending her children over to me for art lessons, if you know what I mean."

"I have no idea what you mean. Well, I've got to go. I'm here."

"Good luck, brave soul."

The front of the Riley's house was as beautiful as it had always been. Mr. and Mrs. Riley were well-respected in the city. They ran a local restaurant down on River Street that was a favorite of tourists and locals alike. They weren't very assuming people, but they were stunningly beautiful, thus Emma's flawlessness. I couldn't imagine that this beauty from high school could be as haggard as Paige and Richard made her out to be.

There wasn't a doorbell by the apartment door, but there was a beautiful gold-plated lion's-head door knocker. I clutched the ring that it held in its jaws and tapped it with three determined strokes. There was no sign of the door opening for an extremely long moment, but I could hear movement. Every shade in the downstairs apartment was drawn. After what seemed like enough time for Vicky to both groom and accessorize, a hand lifted the corner of the blind and a blue eye peeked out.

"Who is it?" the eyeball asked.

"It's Savannah Phillips from up the street. I would like to speak with Emma, if it's possible."

The door opened to reveal something I wouldn't have believed possible. The natural beauty from high school was now just natural. Truth be told, she didn't even seem natural. She was only two years older than I, but she looked as if she were my mother's age. In fact, my mother looked better than Emma. Emma's once sun-kissed blond hair looked as if it hadn't had contact with a brush in years.

Her skin, which used to be so golden and fresh, now looked sallow and worn. Her eyes were once a stunning blue. Now they lacked any life at all.

Almost too shocked to speak, I mustered up something to the effect of, "I just finished my master's work and heard you had moved back home, and I wanted to see how you were." I felt like an idiot and knew I probably sounded more like an idiot than I actually felt.

She stared at me, revealing she didn't believe much of what I'd said. "Savannah, we hardly ever talked in school. Why would you want to talk to me now?"

I decided since honesty had worked in my life up to that point, there was no reason to ruin my track record. The worst that could happen would be a door slammed in my face, or a challenge to make her beautiful again. "Emma, actually you're right. I'm not here to just talk. I wanted to ask you a few questions for a story I'm working on. Do you mind if I come in for a minute?" She just stood there, staring, glaring. "I promise I won't take long, and if you don't want to talk to me, I will take my things and leave," I said, motioning to my satchel that was hanging on my side.

To my surprise, she opened the door to let me in. I didn't know, however, that I was going to need a backhoe to make it past the foyer. The place was dirty, excessively cluttered, and filled with the stale smell of cigarette smoke. Emma walked ahead of me in a white tank top covered in I didn't want to know what. She had on what looked like men's boxers, and she kicked the toys out of her way to get down the hall to the small living room in the back. She never apologized or even spoke in the process; she just sort of shuffled. She shuffled stuff out of her way and removed clothes from the sofa, motioning for me to sit.

If Vicky had come with me, she would have snatched up Emma, told her to get ahold of herself, then taken her to the bathroom and scrubbed her from head to toe. I, on the other hand, planned to sit there on that sofa and hope I didn't have Cheerios stuck to my behind when I got up. Emma lit a cigarette, revealing the early lines that had formed around her mouth and the yellowness of her teeth. She really was a pitiful sight.

"What do you want, Savannah?" she said flatly.

"Emma," I paused for an extremely long time, having no idea how in the world to even begin this conversation. "Emma, I'm sure you know people around town have speculated for years about what has happened to you. Some say your life turned upside down when you lost the Miss Georgia United States of America Pageant."

She took a long drag from her cigarette, but her face registered a moment of shock. "Is that so?"

For a moment I believed she might put her cigarette out on my arm. So I responded quickly. "Well, yes, and if I told you I was working on a story that might reveal that the pageant was in some way rigged, would you be willing to tell me your story?"

At that question, I was sure I saw a scant ounce of emotion in Emma's eyes. I'm not sure what kind of emotion, but something. Something there reflected a brief recollection of a life past, a faded memory. It was almost as if in one transient expression I saw her experience a reality long since forgotten. As if with one volatile query she was confronted with the reason for who she had become. But it left before I could catch it with my own expression. Her original apathy returned. "I wouldn't care to tell you anything about beauty pageants. Now if you'll leave, I need to go get my children from upstairs." She stood up and headed back to the door.

I would make one last-ditch effort, see if I could retrieve her past and make her confront it. I stood as if to follow her but remained at the edge of the sofa. "Emma, you were once one of the most beautiful women in this city. What happened to you?" I was probably crossing a line, but I believed someone needed to shake this girl up and make her confront her demons. And if my mother wasn't here to do it, who better than me?

She turned around and glared at me in the most menacing of ways. I decided this was probably how all beauty queens looked without sequins and tiaras, false eyelashes, and imitation body parts. For a moment, I thought about escaping out the back, not sure what women like her were capable of; but I decided, whether I ever published a story or not, this girl needed serious help. It was time for intervention. And if I was to be the interventioner (if that's even a word), then so be it.

"I mean, well, um . . . look at you!" I said, pushing back my fear, getting even bolder, and taking a determined step forward. "When is the last time you have taken care of yourself: brushed your hair, washed your clothes, picked up after your children?" I asked, gesturing at the mayhem. "When is the last time you looked in the mirror and saw someone you liked? I may not have known you well growing up, but I'm not dumb enough to think this is the real you." The more I talked, the stiffer her upper lip became and the redder her face. Right before I thought she was going to explode on my head, I decided I would show myself out, but not without one last statement. Unfortunately she beat me to it.

"Who do you think you are coming into my home, with your little preppy-looking self? You have no idea what my life is. You live in your little fantasy world, with no responsibility and no one tugging at your sleeve twenty-four hours a day. You spend time sipping lattes and hanging out with your prissy mama."

Well, heaven help the child who talks that way about my mama. I can tell you any story about her I dare please. But Emma's words brought me to life in a way that, honestly, to that point I had never seen myself. "First, let me tell you one thing. I don't drink lattes. I drink Coca-Cola. Second, I have responsibilities. But I actually take care of them."

"So do I," she said, glaring.

"Oh, do you? Well, I make sure at the end of the day when I lay my head on my pillow that I did the right thing, the right way, and at the right time, with hopefully the right motives. I don't let others suffer at my hands."

"Does anyone look like they're suffering around here?"

"Well, I don't call ten years of T-shirts living the high life. And third, my mother is one of the finest women you will ever meet. It would do you good to learn how to be half the woman that she is. No, it would do us both good." With that, I passed her in the carved-out path and turned around to add one final thought.

"Emma, I don't care if you tell me anything about your experience. I might've been sent here for one reason alone today, and that was to let you know you need to remember how to live. You have four reasons upstairs. They should be enough to clean yourself up, make something out of your life, and do those things you were created for. Because I assure you this isn't it. And if you need to figure out where to start, you would benefit from talking to my mother. She has a way of helping people see the good in themselves. I think you've forgotten that you have any."

She walked over to the door and opened it, making it clear she had tired of my dissertation.

"I'm sorry to bother you. I hope you have a good afternoon." With that, I walked out of the already opened door, and she slammed it behind me.

"Well, that went well."

I needed a mandatory rest period. There was only one place that ever gave me real quiet—the Savannah College of Art and Design Library. I took my station next to the window, so I could keep my eye on who was coming and going up the street.

As I opened up my satchel, I saw him. His bike was still blue and his curls still curly. He passed by the window, and just as I turned my head to watch his departure, he turned back and caught my eye and smiled a "I know you're watching me but don't want me to know" kind of smile. I returned a raised eyebrow and upturned lip. *Cocky little something, aren't you? I wasn't even looking at you. I was just looking out the window trying to create an adequate opening for my first article. You need to get a job anyway and quit riding around the street like some troubled youth with nowhere to go.*

I began an Internet search to find out how I could get copies of the Miss Georgia United States of America program books. The Miss Georgia United States of America Pageant Web site opened to the playing of their theme song. "What a lady, dressed as royalty. With such grace, she has arrived. Can't you see her magic and splendor? Isn't this world greater for having her?"

Ooh, bad rhyme, I thought to myself as the song continued. "Here she comes. Walking on air, she comes. Don't you wish you were her? The lady divine, Miss Georgia United States of America."

"Ooh, so sad. So very, very sad," I actually said out loud. I had heard the song a thousand times. Vicky walked through the house singing it to herself. But hearing it from a computer speaker solidified the fact that it truly was wretched.

Searching the Web site, I found the past issues. Some poor soul had been forced to scan every page of every program book over the last fifty years. Grateful, I began the tedious search for Katherine's picture. She would have to be somewhere before Victoria, who was crowned in 1976.

I found her in 1972. I couldn't believe it. Despite more than thirty years, she looked exactly the same, without the gray, of course. And the few laugh lines from a good life that had since formed around her eyes were undetectable in the photo. Underneath her picture it read "Katherine Powers, Miss Savannah United States of America, sponsored by the Savannah Chamber of Commerce."

Finding Katherine, I began to research the judges for her the year she competed. There I saw Mr. Randolph Cummings III himself. I began to scan through the years and learned that Mr. III was a judge from 1970 through 1992. Then in 1993, Mr. Randolph Cummings IV came into the picture as a judge. I went back to Katherine's program and looked at the auditors. Her auditors were Mr. Lyle Wilcox and Mr. Stanley Harvard. But looking through the programs from '71 and '73, Mr. Wilcox and Mr. Harvard hadn't audited before or since. The Templetons audited from 1973 until 1996, and then a different set of auditors was used every year after that.

My mind raced with a thousand questions. *If the pageant was rigged, by whom? Was it by the directors, a rotund older fella named Mr. Carl Todd, or his daughter, Miss Carline Todd? Was it this Mr. III judge, who never seemed to go away? Or was it these one-time auditors? And were they fired for what they did that year?* It was up to me to make this puzzle work. It was up to me to make it all work before Tuesday. Because by Tuesday, Savannah needed a story and Mr. Hicks needed a reason to fire me. I determined I would have mine; I only hoped that it wouldn't afford him his in the process.

The Atlanta phone book popped up on the Internet and pulled up Wilcox, Harvard, Pratt, and Dean. What could it hurt to call and ask for a meeting? The worst they could do would be to say no. I dialed right there on my mobile phone and heard a friendly voice. "Wilcox, Harvard, Pratt, and Dean, may I help you?"

"Yes, hello. I was trying to reach Mr. Lyle Wilcox or Mr. Stanley Harvard."

"Oh," she said, pausing. "Well, they have both retired, but Mr. Wilcox's son, Raymond, and Mr. Harvard's daughter, Suzanna, both work here. Would you like to speak to one of them?"

"Do you mean they've retired from the company or have they retired, period?"

"Well"—she dropped her voice to a whisper—"Mr. Wilcox retired about two years ago from the company and died immediately after his retirement. Mr. Harvard retired over ten years ago and just passed away last month. So, I guess you could say they have both retired, retired."

"Well, in that case, how about I just speak with Mr. Wilcox, Mr. Raymond Wilcox?" I said.

"Oh, he's in a meeting right now, so you can't speak with him."

I decided not to remind her that she had just asked me if I

would like to speak with him, so I went on to request to speak to Suzanna Harvard.

"Oh, well, she's in that same meeting. In fact they are all in that meeting. By the way, who is this?"

"My name is Savannah Phillips. I'm from Savannah, Georgia, and—"

"Oh, isn't that cute. I bet you go around telling people you are Savannah from Savannah." Her laugh was increasingly irritating.

"Actually, no I don't say that to anyone. You know what, I don't think I'll leave a message. I think I'll just try back another time." I hung up and decided to see if maybe Mr. Wilcox's or Mr. Harvard's wives were still living. Searching under their personal names, I could find no listing for Mr. Wilcox, but Mr. and Mrs. Stanley Harvard were in Buckhead. I picked up my phone to try again.

"Hello," said a voice from the other end.

"Hello, Mrs. Harvard?"

"Yes, this is she. May I ask who is calling?" she responded warmly.

"My name is Savannah Phillips, and I am calling you from Savannah, actually," I said, pausing to see if she would want to add anything of her own to my recent statement. She didn't, so I continued. "I'm working on a story about the Miss Georgia United States of America Pageant. I know it has been a long time, but I saw your husband's firm was the auditor in 1972, and I wanted to know if I could discuss that event with you."

"Young lady, that was a lifetime ago and an experience we don't fondly recall. I'm not sure what you are working on, but I can assure you, you won't find any information here."

"Well, I understand that it's been a long time, and to you it probably isn't even worth discussing. But what if I told you that what happened could still be affecting the pageant today? Would it matter at all to you then? I mean, I'm not sure that pageants matter at all to you. They don't matter much to me myself. But—"

"Pageants are of no consequence to me one way or the other. But whatever some women want to do is their own business.

Stanley had nothing to do with those pageants. He only audited them for one year, and then he quit. So I don't really have any information to give you. Are you some kind of reporter or something?"

The way she said "reporter" had an air of sleaze to it. I had never thought that people might see what I do as somehow less than ethical or necessary. But if they hadn't met Gloria or read her work, then their only point of reference was the media they were forced to endure on 24/7 news. The kind that can make news from nothing during a slow news cycle. "Actually, I write human-interest stories for the *Savannah Chronicle*." No point in her knowing that I had yet to write my first story. "I believe I have found something of interest to Savannah. It revolves around the year your husband was an auditor. I just wanted to come and talk with you about it."

"You and I have nothing to talk about."

"I'm not asking you to promise anything. I'm just asking for the opportunity to talk with you."

"This would be a waste of both of our time, young lady."

"Ma'am, I know I'm young, but I believe that everyone should have the opportunity to do their best in anything and be granted their due successes accordingly. I'm not a big beauty pageant person, but if that is a young woman's dream, she ought to at least have the opportunity to pursue that dream fairly."

The other side of the line was quiet for a while. "I'll meet you tomorrow at noon at the Buckhead Diner. Do you know where that is?"

"Yes, ma'am. It's my favorite restaurant in Atlanta, and I'll be there by eleven thirty. I'm sure we'll leave liking each other."

"Well, we will leave, but I don't know how much we will like each other." All that followed was a dial tone.

CHAPTER FOURTEEN

I parked Old Betsy a couple of houses down from 13 Oglethorpe Avenue, where Claire was waiting. We hadn't seen each other since my fall break, when we had spent a morning catching up over breakfast at The Lady & Sons in the City Market. She was already looking tan, and it was just May. She looked like a real real-estate agent in her seersucker pantsuit and strappy pumps. I walked toward her and we greeted each other in the only acceptable way below the Mason-Dixon line—with a hug. A real hug. Not a half-pat or a half-tap. But a grab-you-and-let-you-know-somebody's-got-you kind of hug.

"Claire, I can't believe how tan you are. It's only May. When have you had time to lay out?" I asked her.

"Savannah, where have you been? We don't lay out anymore around here; that stuff will kill you. We use Tan Beautiful that they sell on TV. You just wipe it on, let it sit, and vavoom, you've got a tan. Looks natural, doesn't it?"

"It looks amazing. But I'll stick to the real thing. What's the joy of living this close to the ocean if you don't ever lay out on the beach?"

She laughed. "Wait until we hit thirty. Then you'll be asking me what the number is to QVC."

I turned to look at the cute white house in front of us. "This is a charming place."

"You're going to love it. It just came on the market yesterday. I heard some young couple bought it and want to rent out the bottom. Number 13A, that could be you," she said as she opened the iron gate.

"That would be amazing. You should see where my mother wanted me to move."

"Already heard and already have."

"This city is pathetic."

"This city is Savannah," she said as she flipped on the light inside. We entered the quaint little apartment in the den area. Directly behind it was an open kitchen and a small area for a breakfast table. Down a small hall toward the back of the house was a bedroom and bath. All in great condition, with what appeared to be the original hardwood floors and moldings. "Isn't this quaint?"

"Yeah, it really is. What's the rent?"

"It's eight hundred a month. It's a little more than you said you could afford, but this is Savannah."

"Well, I think I could swing that. At least until I have to get a new car."

"Oh, that car will outlive you!"

I laughed. "You're probably right." We walked through one more time and I checked out the closets, which were small but doable; and then tested the appliances, which were older but in good condition. "This really is great. I think it will be perfect. Do you think I have a couple of weeks, until I get paid?"

"I can find out who the owners are and ask. I don't even think they are moving in for another month. Heard they wanted to do a few renovations."

"Well, maybe it would work out perfectly," I said as we made our way outside and headed to our cars.

As we went to the other side of the street, Grant came walking toward us. "Well, hello, girls. What are you doing over here on this side of town?"

"We could ask you the same question," Claire chimed in.

"Oh, I'm coming to check on my house. I just bought #13, the white one right up there," he said, pointing. I simply watched another dream slip its way into the sewer that was quickly becoming my life.

"You've got to be kidding—" Claire started.

"Well, you must be doing well at the architectural firm." I glared at Claire, who retreated. "It looks like a beautiful place."

"Yeah, times are good, I guess. I thought it was a great place, and Elisabeth loved it. We're trying to rent out the bottom, though, so if you hear of anyone, let me know."

"We'll do that," I assured him. "Well, we've got to run."

"Yeah, me too. See ya'll soon, I'm sure."

"I guess you'll want me to look for something else," Claire said in shared hurt as we watched Grant walk into his new house.

"Yeah, that would be a good idea," I said, opening my door.

"We'll find something. Keep your chin up."

"We've nowhere left to go but up. Call me." And I drove away from my second lost opportunity at freedom.

I could hear Vicky before I even entered the kitchen.

"People are just tacky. Who would spend millions on a home and just put tacky right out in plain view? They'll have to get rid of it. They didn't get it approved, and they'll have to get rid of it." Vicky added the clanging of pots and pans along with her own jaws for effect.

"Victoria, you don't need to be involved in everyone's business. When a person spends that much money for a home, they should be able to paint it purple and attach a helicopter pad on the top if they want to."

"Jake, that's not how it works."

"Yes it is, Victoria. Whether you and your little fashion committee think it is fashionable."

"I don't have a fashion committee. I have a historical review committee."

"Call it what you will, but you spend too much time in people's business."

My mother was still grumbling like a food processor, preparing what looked to be spaghetti when I came in and sat on the stool by the island. "What's all the commotion about?" I suspected this little ruckus just might prevent me from having to have any conversation about my day at all.

The pots were clanging louder than had been heard in a good year. "Oh, you wouldn't believe it, I tell you. People are just crazy. Just lack the sense God gave a pea turkey."

"What in the world is a pea turkey?"

"Savannah, don't bother me about the way I talk. You know good and well a pea turkey isn't anything more than a pea turkey."

"OK. So who lacks the sense God gave a pea turkey?"

She turned to stare at me, waving around a small frying pan in her left hand. "This couple down the street invited me over today to see how everything had been decorated since they moved in. They're from South Carolina. What does that tell you?"

I was sure at that moment my mother had ADD. Decorating and South Carolina had nothing to do with each other. In fact, most of what she said didn't seem connected. She could change the direction of conversation as quickly as she changed the color of her hair. Why did it take me so long to notice things? Apparently, I had spent my life too preoccupied, and at that moment I needed to pay more attention to what was going on around me.

"Savannah, are you listening to me?" I was surprised that she noticed I had wandered off the subject as well. Maybe I had ADD too. I didn't think so. But who could be sure?

"They're from South Carolina."

"Oh, right. So you can just imagine where I'm going with this. I go inside, and their house is horrendous. I mean everything is Pepto pink. The walls, the trim, half the furniture."

"The furniture?"

"Yes, and their poodle even looked like she was pink. It could have been the tones bouncing off of the walls, but by the time I left I thought my aubergine suit had turned pink."

I dodged the waving pan and added, "Well, aubergine is a variation of the pink-purple family."

"Savannah, stop. I know what color aubergine is."

"OK, continue."

"Now, anyway, beyond the house being horrendous, she told me they had just gotten a satellite. It had come in today. I told her that was great. That she would love it. That we had one as well. Then we proceeded to her patio and gardens." Her eyes went so wide you would have thought she had seen a two-headed pink pelican. "Well, this, honey, was a satellite big enough to call in Star Trek, Alien Nation, and any other outer space extraterrestrial you would desire. It was big enough for E.T. to phone home, I tell you."

"Ooh, E.T., huh?"

"Yes, and it had its own concrete slab. It takes up half of their backyard and can be seen from two different streets. All I said was, "Well, honey, I do believe that's the largest television apparatus I have ever seen."

"Half the backyard?"

"Savannah, small children could get overtaken by that thing. They could be snatched up by Galaxy Network and lost for eternity. But it won't stay. I won't allow it. They are in the Historical District, and that home is on the Register, and I'm not allowing some big canker sore—"

"I think you mean eyesore."

"Thank you, I mean eyesore like that to exist in this city. Pretty soon people would be calling it artwork and hanging it off the sides of their houses. It wouldn't end, I tell you. And then we would be known as the satellite capital of the world. I can hear the advertisements: 'Come to Savannah, where you'll get beaches, good food, and any channel in the galaxy.' Now that's just not what I intend to let happen." And with that, she turned back around to actually use the frying pan she had been torturing me with.

By the time we actually ate, watched a little TV, and went to bed, Vicky was still mumbling under her breath. I washed my face and spent some time in prayer. I crawled into bed not knowing what tomorrow would bring, but certain my future was much brighter than Satellite Lady's.

CHAPTER FIFTEEN

I got up before anyone else so I could make a quiet exit. I wrote a quick note saying I had some work to do until late that evening (which I did), I wouldn't be home until late (which I wouldn't), and I would see them in the morning (which I would). Adding the only thing necessary to prevent a return to a thousand questions, I jotted a note to my mother offering lunch tomorrow. That invitation alone would save me from being accosted by a woman perched atop a chair in the dark when I got home.

A new bronze button-down with a patterned skirt in cream and bronze seemed appropriate for my lunch appointment. I pulled my hair back in a low ponytail and slipped on a pair of cream-colored slides, which I'm certain Vicky paid entirely too much for. The entire ensemble was topped off with a Louis Vuitton backpack, a graduation gift I never asked for.

Heading west on Interstate 16 allowed me about two and a half hours to drive, catch my breath, and sort my thoughts. How was I possibly going to be able to write a story about a rigged beauty pageant and not make a debauchery of Gloria's good name? She wrote stories of conviction. She wrote articles that made readers believe in something, even someone. She unearthed a moral compass that came from something more profound than herself.

I wasn't sure which way my own compass pointed half the time, and I probably wouldn't be able to help anyone else find theirs. The only thing I knew on this day was that I had her job, a possible first story, and a knowing in my heart that this was what I was supposed to do. At that point, those were the only things I could trust.

This is for a purpose. This is for justice. If Emma really lost because of unethical behavior and her pathetic existence is the end result, then this does have a purpose. Emma needs me. She might not know it, but she'll thank me for this when it is over, I thought.

The parking lot at Buckhead Diner off of Piedmont was pretty full at eleven thirty. As I pulled up, I realized that neither Mrs. Harvard nor I knew what the other looked like. Voice recollection would be our only connection, other than the "are you her?" look in each other's eyes.

The hostess put my name on the waiting list. I told the super-model hostess my guest would be a Mrs. Harvard and then sat down at the curved booth under the window. Scanning the waiting area, no one seemed to look like a Mrs. Harvard, not that I had any idea what a Mrs. Harvard would look like. There was a couple all cozied up in the corner, acting as if there was no other person around their love nest. They were totally unsympathetic to the fact that someone in the room had just been forced to hear her one-time boyfriend and future husband tell her he was marrying another woman. I found them annoying.

A group of thirty-something women chattered away by the door, as if this was their first day of adult conversation in the last millennium and they were making up for lost time. With each woman hardly taking time to breathe between sentences, it was a miracle that they even knew what the others were saying. I'm sure as long as the words returning weren't "Mama" or "gimme," it didn't matter much.

The young couple took their seats without ever removing their hands from each other. *I'd love to see what you two look like in fifty years.* Looking back now, Grant and I had never been that way. He hadn't competed with another man, just my own selfishness. It made me wonder if I had ever loved him the way real lovers do, those who finish each other's sentences and can't walk without holding hands.

The group of jabbering women forced me back into the moment as they walked to their table. Around eleven forty-five, the supermodel led me to mine. A young waitress made her way to my booth by the far window to take my drink order. Coke seemed adolescent, so I asked for water with lemon.

At noon sharp, Mrs. Harvard walked through the door, looking just like the seventy-some-year-old wife of a "retired" accountant from Atlanta should. As her low-heeled, closed-toed, cream pumps brought her stately frame to our table, I stood to greet her. She placed her small and wrinkled hand into mine. We made our introductions, and I invited her to sit down.

"It's a pleasure to meet you, Mrs. Harvard. Thank you so much for coming." I waited for her to get comfortable in the booth.

She nodded her freshly styled, frosted gray hair. She straightened her dainty pink-and-white striped piqué skirt, then ran her hands across the matching short-sleeved jacket accented with pearl buttons. I glanced at her matching pink purse. "Well, if I hadn't given you my word, I would've canceled this silly meeting. I don't know why on earth you are fooling around with something that is thirty years old and of little importance to most people."

"Well, I'm bringing it up because of the people it was important to at one time."

"'At one time' may be the key words, young lady."

That "young lady" thing was so irritating. "Well, apparently not. After thirty years, a woman I know actually felt she should tell someone." Mrs. Harvard seemed to debate whether she would stay. Her pause allowed me to add another thought. "And it was obviously something that either your husband or his partner was troubled enough by, or caught red-handed doing, that they never performed the task again."

The waitress arrived in time to prevent her from grabbing her knife and flinging it in my direction. "I think I'm going to need a Coke, young lady," she said, looking at the waitress and then returning her glare to me. I figured if I was the source of causing a seventy-something woman to actually "need" a Coke, then we might get somewhere.

"Savannah, is it?" she asked. I nodded back at her with as genuine a smile as I could muster. "Savannah, let me tell you something about my husband, God rest his soul," she said with a quick bowing of her frosted head and crossing of the chest. "If there is one thing that Stanley was, it was honest. He never wanted anything to do with anything or anyone that wasn't totally honest. So, if you are here questioning his character, then I'll let you know right now our conversation is finished."

"Mrs. Harvard, I'm not here to destroy anyone's character. I am simply here to find out why in 1972 a young lady who competed in the Miss Georgia United States of America Pageant left feeling rather confident that the wrong girl was chosen."

"I'm sure girls feel that way every year. It's a beauty pageant; only one girl can win."

"I know that. But this is a different situation, and I'm here to find out what Mr. Harvard might have known, or Mr. Wilcox for that matter. Did a judge have a complete change of mind? Or, for some ridiculous reason, did your husband change the scores?" I asked, keeping my eyes on her knife.

The waitress came back again, and Mrs. Harvard, who had never opened a menu, looked at her and ordered blue cheese chips. "I would like a Coke too," I added.

"Well, you're just an adventurous little soul, aren't you?" Mrs. Harvard said, moving her straw around in her glass and never taking her eyes off me. "So, Nancy Drew, why would my husband quit if he had something to gain? I would think he would continue for-ever if he was making a profit, wouldn't you?"

The giggling sounds from the booth across from us pulled my attention in their direction. There they sat. The two young lovers, oblivious to common decency. I wanted to slap them. By George, for a moment I wanted to slap her. But I was too busy watching them to remember her. And when I did, she was still in full discourse.

"Let me tell you why: Because he didn't. Because my husband was the auditor for that pageant for one year. One year too many. And, to kill your curiosity, it was my husband who realized that something underhanded was going on. So if you thought this is where you would find your story, you are sadly mistaken, young lady." I noticed her run her frail fingers around a simple gold wed-ding band that still graced her ring finger.

"Then who is the story, Mrs. Harvard?"

"You're the reporter, Savannah."

"So you're not going to give me anything?"

"Oh, yes, young lady. I'm going to give you something. I'm going to give you a piece of advice. You need to decide first if this is even a story worth telling. If it is, you need to make sure my hus-band's name is never mentioned. And then you need to figure out where the real story is, because you've looked in the wrong place."

"Can't you throw me a bone?" I asked, exhausted.

"Yes, I'll give you a bone. Longevity is the key here, and what would be gained is the question. If you're going to be a reporter, you need to ask all the questions." With that, she stood up, laid her unused napkin on the table, picked up her pink purse, and pranced herself out of the diner.

The waitress arrived with a plate of blue cheese chips. "I'll need another Coke," I said, staring at the plate in front of me. "And you can keep them coming."

Mrs. Harvard left me feeling like an idiot, totally speechless and with the check. I didn't even have my first paycheck, and she had

left me with the stupid bill, which I paid only after I had successfully made myself sick on blue cheese chips. Walking out to my
car in a stupor, I was half-fuming, half utterly confused, and completely full.

*Why in the world would she even agree to meet me if she wasn't
going to tell me anything?* I thought as I drove. *My word, I drove three
hours to talk to her. This is a joke. I'm going to go work for Paige. That's
what I'll do. I'll stay at home, make the basement an apartment, and work
for Paige on the weekends, live on Daddy's money and Mother's cooking.
And I'll make prank phone calls in the wee hours of the morning to a little
old frosted-haired, pink-and-white-striped prima donna in Atlanta.*

CHAPTER SIXTEEN

Thursday brought rain inside and out. *Lord, let it be a monsoon and every restaurant in town flooded. And let Vicky be forced to go into work for crisis management.* Then I heard her voice downstairs and knew there was no such luck. The alarm clock read ten. I hadn't slept in until ten in years. Of course, with my usually uneventful life, I usually slept like a baby. But all my new adventures proved tiring.

The knock on the door had to be one of a perfectly manicured hand.

"Ugh."

She opened the door anyway. When she saw me still under the covers, she walked over and placed her hand on my forehead. "Savannah, are you feeling OK?"

Removing my head from underneath her hand, I scooted past her to the restroom to brush my teeth. "Yes, ma'am. I'm fine. I just had a longer day than I thought."

She followed right behind. "Well, I thought you would meet us at Bible study last night. But when you didn't come, I got worried. Then, you were resting so soundly when we got home, we didn't want to wake you. What in the world were you doing all day yesterday?"

Fortunately I had already crammed the toothbrush in my mouth, and most of what I said was purposely unintelligible. "Welunfortenlswthsu."

"Oh?"

"Thniwentwfentishrwolkintomir."

"Hmm, really."

"Yehannremtadlokrutsfioiinhn."

She just nodded and continued anyway. "OK, well, sounds like fun. I want you to meet our new director of tourism. She's an absolute doll, and I just know that you'll love her. I invited her to lunch with us."

I was about to look at her with an "I can't believe you invited someone else to lunch with us" kind of look, but then I realized that with someone else there it would give me the opportunity to avoid discussion about what I had been up to. I rinsed out my mouth and straightened. "That's a wonderful idea."

"I knew you would think so. It's too late for you to eat breakfast, or you won't want lunch. We're going to meet her at eleven thirty at the Gryphon Tea Room for tea and sandwiches," she added as she left. "I'd say you need to get a move on, and please try to dress a smidgen more, well, more delicate, OK?"

I peeked my head around the corner and watched as her Karen Kane blue linen sundress and matching blue linen overshirt swayed behind her, and her camel-colored BCBG mules clicked on the hardwood until she was gone.

Staring at my closet, I tried to deduce what Vicky defined as a "smidgen more delicate." But since I didn't even know what that meant, there was no way to accomplish it, was there? The best solution when I couldn't read minds—comfort. I chose a comfortable, long, and loosely fitting black skirt with tiny white polka dots and a black linen vest. There was a mysterious shoebox in the front of my closet that said Kate Spade. I pulled it out and opened it to find a pair of black open-toed sandals with one wide strap across the top.

Inside was a "delicately" written note. "I thought these might be a pleasant alternative to flip-flops." They were rather cute, and they would make her happy, so I caved. They were undeniably comfortable too, but she didn't need to know everything.

"I wondered if you were ever going to get here," Dad said as I came through the back door around eleven.

I poured myself a Coke and sat down at a stool by the prep table in the back. "I had a rough day and even longer night. I had to go to Atlanta to interview someone for the story I'm working on. Then I forgot I had promised Mother lunch, and that thought kept me up another six hours."

"Your mother is looking forward to your lunch, so you need to be nice," he said in all seriousness. "So, when are you going to tell us about this story?"

"Well, I haven't really told anyone anything about it. I'm not sure when I'm going to talk about it. I'm trying to get all of my sources and facts together first."

"Like a reporter?"

"Yeah, that real-reporter kind of thing. Can't give all my stuff away."

"So how was the apartment Claire showed you?" he asked, sitting down beside me.

"Great, just great."

"Oh, that good?"

"Yeah! Grant and Miss Converse would be my landlords!"

He laughed, then stood up and went toward his office. "Ooh, nice. Your mother's offer is looking better and better, isn't it?"

I followed him. "No way! I'll just keep looking. Stay focused. I'll find it. Something safe, affordable, and conveniently located to my life."

He rummaged through his mail, smiling. "You think all that's out there?"

"Yes, I do. Anyway, I don't have any more time. I've got to go meet Mother and this new director of tourism she invited to have lunch with us," I said, walking to the back door.

"Oh, you're meeting Amber today."

"Why are you smirking? I hate it when you smirk."

"Well, you should have a wonderful time. Yep, you're going to have a fabulous day," he said. I heard him laughing all the way out to the front of the store.

The Gryphon Tea Room is off Madison Square on Bull Street. Mother was sitting in the front window waving at me as if we hadn't seen each other in a week. It was then this figure leaned up from behind her, as if they had gone to the same how-to-wave-like-a-beauty-queen school. Then it all came together: the wave, Dad's laugh, hair that looks like a Pantene commercial: I was having lunch with Miss Savannah United States of America. "You will pay, old man."

I walked in and went up the few steps that led to the elevated area of tables that flanked the big picture window in the front of the store. They both sized me up and down. But when Vicky spotted the shoes, it was evident she approved. I smiled back at her knowingly.

"Hey, I'm Amber," she said. The six-foot-tall frame stood up to shake my hand like an overexcited Jack Russell terrier. "Your mother has told me so much about you," she added, still shaking. I pulled my hand from her grip.

Casting a raised right eyebrow in my mother's direction, I said, "Well, I haven't heard much about you."

"Oh, well, I've heard Savannah this and Savannah that. Everyone in this whole entire town knows you and loves you. And your mother. Oh, Miss Victoria is just the sweetest thing," she said, patting my mother on the leg as my mother smiled at her and looked at me, wanting to see me nod in agreement. I thought I was going to gag at the "Miss Victoria" thing and was too bewildered at this creature in front of me to realize that my mother wanted my element of approval.

"Your mother and I have been friends since I was Miss Queen of Tulips United States of America three years ago. And now that I'm Miss Savannah United States of America, well, let's just say, we've been practically inseparable," she said with a giddy laugh. I raised my right eyebrow, gave a nod in the direction of my mother, made mental note of my father's torture to come, followed by a deep breath for the woman in front of me who had yet to breathe herself. With the same thought, I realized that Amber's experience was exactly what I did need to talk about. Maybe this was providence. Maybe this was exactly what was supposed to happen to me today.

"Then, she helped me get this job and, well, I just know you and I are going to be the best of friends. I mean, I feel like we are sisters already because your mother has treated me like a daughter." I settled in, certain we would never be good friends, nor sisters. She may act like my mother, look like my mother—in a pageant, fixed sort of way—she might even be a better fit for my mother, but Vicky was still my mother.

"Well, it sounds like you and my mother have a lot in common," I said, looking up gratefully at the waitress who had come to save me from another Amber monologue on her joyous entrance into our world.

While "Miss Victoria" and "Miss Amber" placed their orders, I mentally orchestrated the conversation for the afternoon. There were two choices: Let them dictate the next hour to hour and a half and leave exhausted and in need of therapy or dictate it with my developing journalistic skills, which, unbeknownst to them, had failed miserably the day before.

"So, Amber, is it?" I asked. I paused, trying to use up minutes.

"Yes, Amber. It was my mother's favorite stone, and she has

always said I was exactly what she ordered, and so she named me Amber. How did you get the name Savannah?" she asked. Then she flipped her hair back with her perfectly French-manicured nails, revealing her absolutely flawless skin, but not following my lead in the slightest.

"Oh, it's a long story."

Vicky missed the clue. "I named her Savannah because I grew up here and have always loved this city. It was my favorite place and she was exactly what I ordered as well."

"Oh, that is one of the sweetest things I've ever heard. Isn't she the sweetest lady you would ever want to meet? I could just put her in my purse and take her home," she said, lifting up her pretty little designer bag and opening it up like she wanted Vicky to hop in. I knew at that exact moment that attempting to follow any journalistic agenda was hopeless.

I was sitting at a table with two women who didn't quite measure all the way up to the normal scale. They were normal on their own scale, the beauty queen, live and breathe, never-had-a-greater-dream kind of scale. That scale required little interactive conversation. So, I just sat back, drank my Earl Grey tea, ate my crab cakes, and watched them dine on skimpy salads, water with lemon, and the fancy house tea while they told their own stories back and forth as if hearing them for the first time. That is exactly what I did for two solid hours.

Amber sipped her water with her left pinkie sticking out as if she was competing even now. "Savannah, your mother said you were never interested in beauty pageants." I nodded emphatically, assuring her she was exactly right. "Well, I've competed in pageants ever since I was little. I'll never forget the very first one. It was called 'Little Miss Savannah.' I've lived here all my life, so that's why I competed in 'Little Miss Savannah.'" I about rolled my eyes, figuring she was certain I couldn't have come up with that on my own. This made me feel fortunate that I hadn't moved here until I was old enough to ensure my escape from such things.

"I was pathetic. I'd never been in a pageant before, and my mother had never seen a pageant for little girls, but I entered it anyway. We had to compete in swimsuit and "party dress," they called it. So, my mom bought me a metallic fuchsia swimsuit and white sandals, that are back in style now, you know, the kind where the strap goes between the toes, not those flip-flop kind of things. I can't believe people even wear those today. Can you, Miss Victoria?" she asked, looking over at my mother.

"Well, they do make some cute ones nowadays," my mother said rather diplomatically. I propped my foot up on her side of the booth.

"Well, I don't think ladies should be caught dead in those things. They ought to outlaw them this side of the Mason-Dixon line. They are just ghastly. Anyway, my mother bought me those cute ones where the strap comes up between your toes then con-nects to a strap that buckles around your ankle. Now, the white and fuchsia kind of clashed. I probably looked like all feet," she said, laughing at her own story. She put her hand over her chest as if it was almost more than she could handle.

During her treatise I gave a few nods, a few smiles, and a few raised right eyebrows, assuring them I was mentally present. My mother kept looking at me to gauge my politeness level. She even cast a couple of "this girl is a little too much" expressions my way. I was glad she had us to compare to each other.

"Oh, I bet it was as cute as it could be," Vicky said to re-assure her.

"Well, I doubt it, and it only gets worse from there. Then, Mama bought me a pretty little pastel pink church dress—notice I didn't say party dress—and she put black patent-leather shoes on my feet, with white knee-socks," she said, doubling over in laughter. Even I knew that would have been a pretty pathetic combination.

"You're not serious," Vicky exclaimed in true horror. "She put a pink dress on you and black patent-leather shoes?"

"Yes, and sent me out there on that stage to compete against eight-year-old pros with absolutely no modeling experience of my own. I clomped around on that stage from one end to the other. I had no idea what in the world I was doing, but I was too young to know any better," she said, beside herself in hysterics now.

"That is just awful. You poor thing. Were you scarred?" Vicky asked in all seriousness.

She paused long enough to pick up a piece of lettuce and place it in her mouth as if she might blow up like a house. "No. In fact, when we were walking to the car, my mother said, 'I bet you won't ever want to do that again, will you?' I told her that if I could get a new swimsuit, a new dress, and two new pairs of shoes, I would do it anytime. At that moment, she created a beast. That was how the journey of my career began," she said, meaning every word she had just spoken. She had made a career out of beauty pageants.

Mother picked up a slightly larger bite of her own salad. Vicky at least appreciated food. She had a great figure for her age, but she wasn't obsessed about her weight. And her excellent cooking was something she wasn't going to let only other people appreciate. But in public, she ate a little more refined. "So what did you do next?"

"Well, my next pageant was the Miss Snow White Pageant. My mother had gotten it down by now. I had me a great party dress. This pageant actually had talent too, and I am a rather fabulous little singer. I mean *American Idol* didn't appreciate me when I competed for them last year, but, well, that Simon Cowell, he's just a mean ol' meany."

I determined she was of the ADD family too. "A mean ol' meany, huh?" I tried to stop myself, but it came out anyway.

"Yes, just downright rude. I told him he needed to come to the South and learn some manners. I didn't know what they taught him over there in England, but here we didn't say such cruel things to people."

"What did he say to you?"

"It's just too horrible to repeat, Savannah."

"Oh, we won't tell anyone. I promise." I figured I could blame rumors on any one of the other thirty million viewers who'd already heard. "Your secret is perfectly safe with us. Right, Mother?"

Even Vicky was dying to know about this, so she chimed in, "Yes, absolutely. Not a word to another living, breathing soul."

"Well, OK. But I promised I would never even give him the privilege of repeating it. He had the audacity to tell me I sounded like the girl in the movie *Shrek* that made the bird explode. And if I sang much longer, he was certain he would have exploded."

My hysterics were lost on her. "So anyway," she continued. "In that pageant I competed in talent and swimsuit. And I won. I didn't win talent but I did win the overall title, which let me compete in the state pageant. The girl who had won first runner-up and talent here in Savannah was able to go to the state pageant too. She beat me at state, which I still don't understand how that happened, and I won't tell you her name, because you probably know her, and I don't want to sound petty." She came up for air. "But after that, I had the bug and knew that one day I wanted to be Miss United States of America."

"Oh, Amber, you've got to tell Savannah some of those stories you told me, about what the girls did while you competed in pageants. They are just hysterical," Vicky prodded.

"Oh yes, do tell," I added.

"Oh, I did see some funny things through the years. The funniest though was this one poor soul who I competed with my first year in Miss Savannah," she said. She must have noticed my perplexed look, when she said "first year." "Yeah, I competed in Miss Savannah United States of America three times before I won. And this will be my fourth time in Miss Georgia United States of America.

"Anyway, one of the girls was going to wear a dress her mother had made for her evening-gown competition. It was a one-shoulder-strapped evening gown in royal blue." I had no idea how this girl remembered all of this stuff and wasn't about to stop her to ask. "So, when she competed she didn't think her gown fit well, but she went out there anyway. After the pageant was over and she went to take her gown off, she realized that she had worn it backward. Worn it backward!" she said, heehawing and slapping the table. Vicky laughed as if she were hearing it for the first time too.

"Can you imagine walking out in a dress where your, your"— Amber leaned in closer and said in the most delicate of whispers— "where your boobies are in the back?"

I was ashamed I had even leaned in for that one. "She didn't know she had her dress on backward because it didn't have a tag in it since her mother had made it. Her mother came backstage and asked her if she couldn't tell"—here we went again, as she leaned in—"that her boobies were in the back."

I could only picture that poor girl being traumatized for the rest of her life. She would forever be known as the girl with her "boobies in the back."

"I bet her mother dressed her for the rest of her competitions," Vicky said, finding her own self rather charming.

Amber showed a hint of compassion for the young lady who would forever be checking the tags in her clothes before donning her attire for the day. "Actually she never competed again." Her sadness left as quickly as it had come, and the giddy storyteller was back.

"Yeah, I've seen a thousand incredible sights in my years. I've seen girls add 'extra personality' by winking at the judges during their swimsuit competitions when their mothers meant for them to add it in their talent competition. I've seen girls play drums who shouldn't have, dance who couldn't, and sing who, well, let's just say dogs in the near vicinity are still not the same." There was a final pause as she placed her napkin over her half-remaining salad.

"Oh, this has been fun, hasn't it, girls?" she said, getting a nod and a smile from Vicky and as much as I could muster from myself. "I do hope we can do this again soon. I have a thousand more stories. And, Savannah, I just loved getting to know you. You are one of the neatest people I have ever talked to."

"Thank you, I'm glad we had this time together too."

"Well, I need to get home. I'm meeting with a dress designer today to see if she can copy a dress I saw Julia Roberts wear to the Academy Awards last year. I think it would be simply elegant to compete in. You know Julia Roberts filmed a movie here? I was an extra in it. She and I would have been great friends too, but they wouldn't let me get near her," she said, rolling her eyes. I was amazed at the discernment of the Hollywood elite.

"Well, kisses, kisses!" she said, leaning over to my mother and pretending to kiss her on the cheek. She came at me, but I shot out a hand and practically punched her in the stomach. And after another ferocious shake, she turned to descend the stairwell in true beauty-pageant style. Her tight white Capris were paired with a black sweater that had one shoulder out and a small sleeve on the other arm, seemingly similar to that backward-dressing victim. Her three-inch heels met each step with grace and ease. But she turned back suddenly, her pretty, preppy purse dangling from a dainty arm. "Oh, my word, I almost forgot. I've got to run to the drugstore and refill my subscription. I have allergies, you know. And no one wants to see a beauty queen with her nose dripping."

"I think you mean prescription," I said, trying to stifle my embarrassment for her. My mother cut me a glance because she knew it wasn't polite to correct people in such a manner. But as far as I was concerned, my politeness quota had been tapped an hour and a half earlier.

"Yes, that's what I said, prescription. So see you precious little ladies later." And she went back into cascading mode.

I could not control myself any longer. "Oh, Amber." With the mention of her name, she stopped and turned in model pose to see whatever it could be that I wanted now.

"Yes?" she asked still in full stance.

"I think . . . oh my goodness . . . I think I see your tag sticking out in the front of your sweater." The look on her face was worth the two hours I had been forced to surrender. As she pulled the front of her shirt out to make sure there wasn't a tag resting on her neckline, I decided to deliver her.

"I'm just joking," I said, laughing. She didn't laugh back. "Actually, I was hoping you'd let me see your Miss Georgia United States of America program book sometime." Vicky looked at me with wide-eyed disbelief. Why in the world would I be asking for such a thing from Amber? I tried to dispel her thousand questions by adding, "The one thing I always enjoyed about Mother's was checking out the hairstyles." I know it sounded totally lame, but Amber would think I thought it was chic and Mother would think I just wanted to make fun of them. Both would believe that either was reason enough.

"Sure. I'll drop it by this evening," she said with a quick wave and a wink, and with that, pageant's greatest ode to itself walked out the door, and the eyes of every man in the room followed close behind.

Mother wiped her mouth and placed her own napkin in her plate. "Savannah, thank you for being so kind. At least until those final moments."

"It wasn't too hard when you don't have to say anything for two hours," I said emphasizing the last five words. "Mother, truly, you must think that girl is over the top," I said, getting up from my seat and holding out my hand to help her up as well.

She smiled and took my extended hand, "Slightly!"

"Slightly?"

Then she laughed, wrapped her arm around my shoulder, and walked with me down the stairs and out the door to the street, whispering in my ear, "Drastically! But you have to admit she is very entertaining."

"If that's your choice of entertainment," I said. It was a comfort for me to remember that somewhere underneath it all Mother was more human than I often gave her credit for. She gave me a kiss and said she was going to shop awhile. I sat in my car watching her walk down the street. She entered a quaint shop up from the Tea Room. In spite of it all, I was thankful that she was mine. And even more grateful that she wasn't the girl who would be forever known as Miss Boobies in the Back. Some things were just too horrific even for willing participants.

CHAPTER SEVENTEEN

Amid thoughts of high heels, bad talent, and evening-gown malfunctions, Mrs. Harvard's words raced through my mind again and again: "Longevity is the key, and the question is what could be gained." As far as I could tell, only two people had been involved in this pageant promenade longer than dirt: Mr. Cummings III and the director himself. As most things dysfunctional start at the top, that seemed the place to begin.

I headed back to the library to see what Mr. Cummings III was up to now. I wasn't even sure if he was alive to be up to something at all, since his son had taken over judging for him, but I'd start at the top and work my way through those Cummingses until I reached Adam if need be. The Jackson, Mississippi, phone book held a Mr. Randolph Cummings III and IV.

I was probably stupid to just pick up the phone and call cold. What was I going to say, "Hey, Mr. Cummings, are you a creep? Do you take pleasure in rigging a beauty pageant? Do you not have a life?" As soon as I asked myself that, it was clear the real question was missing: Why? Why would Mr. Cummings be willing to fix a beauty pageant? What would he gain? Why was he the one chosen to change his scores, if indeed he had? Either he was a man with no backbone or he was a man who had something to lose.

I didn't stand much to gain by a phone call. What was he going to do, give me a confessional right over the telephone line? This would take a trip to Jackson, Mississippi. Work started Monday, so unless I was planning to do a story on why people had fish heads on the downspouts of their gutters, I needed to head to Jackson.

I wrote down both the business and home addresses and phone numbers of all of the Cummingses, then made my way to Jake's for a talk. Nearly there, I heard the clicking of high heels and the whooshing of cascading following close behind. My greatest horror and newest fear called out, waving her arms in front of her face and all but skipping down the sidewalk. "Savannah, hey it's me, Amber. Remember, we just had lunch together?"

"Yeah, I remember!"

"I have that program book you wanted. In fact I brought you all of mine. I was going to run them by your house, but figured you probably hadn't even had time to get home yet. Do you want to sit down and look at them together?" she asked, hopeful. Looking at the stack of rather large program books, I politely declined.

"So you've done this three times already?"

"Yes, I know they say third time's a charm, but to be honest with you, the third time su— Oh, my word, I almost said something very unladylike. Slap me and call my mama. But I believe four is fabulous, fantastic, and philanthropic. I'm not exactly sure what *philanthropic* means, but it is just a great word to say."

"No, it's OK, I understand," I said, looking at her with pity at the possibility that she actually thought *philanthropic* started with an *f.* I was still trying to gauge whether she was imbalanced or simply overprocessed. "And sorry, I would love to sit down and go through these with you, but I have to take a really quick trip. But

I promise, I will get these back to you very soon. Maybe we can even have lunch again." I could have slapped myself.

"Oh, that would be wonderful. Let's do it soon. I have a thousand more pageant stories to tell you. I know, let's meet Monday."

"Actually, I start work on Monday and my friend Paige and I, well, we set aside that day every week to catch up. How about Tuesday?"

"Oh, that'll be just fabulous. I'll try to go back and see if I can find some more pictures to show you. I could even bring my crown. Oh, Savannah, we are going to have so much fun! You take care now. I'll see you soon," she said, beaming. "I just know we are going to be the best of friends."

I smiled the best I could, thanked her for the books, and headed for my car.

"Oh, yoo-hoo! Savannah!" the voice came again from behind.

"Yes," I said, slowly turning to take in her radiant glory once more.

"There is a pageant tomorrow night in Hinesville."

"Where in the world is Hinesville?"

"Just a hop and a skip up the interstate. Seeing as you wanted to see my program books and all, I thought you might want to go with me. I love to scope out the competition."

At that moment I was presented with one of the greatest dilemmas I had been forced to encounter in my young life: whether to actually go see a pageant of my own free choice or refuse to allow my reputation to fall under such ill repute. *Well, it would only be for research,* I thought. *I haven't been to a pageant since I was old enough to say no. I probably need to be abreast of what happens in pageants. Did I just say* abreast? *If I go to that pageant, let alone spend an entire evening with Amber, I might come out of there robed in velvet and clogging. I can't do it. I just can't put myself through such needless affliction.*

"You know, that might not be such a bad idea," I said. "I haven't been to a pageant in years. But I'll need to meet you there.

I'll have to leave as soon as it's over because I have to get out of town early the next morning."

"Oh, Savannah Phillips, you will have the most wonderful time of your life. There's singing and dancing," she said, twirling herself around the sidewalk. "It's sheer magic. I'll get you directions and save you a seat, and I'll give you all the inside information on the contestants. You'll wish you had entered." And with that, she skipped, sauntered, and cascaded away.

I got in behind the wheel and hated myself. I was almost certain I hated my job at this point too, but the one thing Amber had accomplished was make me feel amazingly better about my mother. In light of this new acquaintance, I realized Vicky wasn't quite so unnatural after all. Then I was consumed with intense desire to see what Amber looked like in these program books resting on my lap.

The first one I opened was 1998. There she was, Amber Topaz Childers, Miss Rose Petal Queen United States of America. Both she and her mother must have had a thing for jewelry. This was the first time Amber had gone to Miss Georgia United States of America. She looked exactly the same. She was obviously dedicated to her look.

I perused the remainder of the contestants because they captivated me. My eyes couldn't help themselves. They were drawn to the hair, the makeup, the smiles, the queens. A picture snapped me out of my hypnosis. The portrait of Emma Elizabeth Riley, Miss Savannah United States of America, rested beneath Amber's.

This was the Emma Riley I had known. She was undeniably the most beautiful girl in the entire school, possibly all of Savannah. She was perfect without being plastic. She was every beauty pageant's dream contestant, and she won every pageant around town. She even won Miss Massey School her freshman year. She was the first freshman to ever hold the title. My mother said she waited two years after high school to compete in Miss Savannah United States of America. She wanted to be prepared, older, and more mature. Town talk has it that the entire city was shocked when Emma didn't return Miss Georgia United States of America. She never competed again and, according to Paige, thus began her spiral to spandex.

The beautiful face stared back, forcing the question of how she had lost. And having witnessed her ability with the flute, even I knew she was talented. The girl could kick behind on that little sideways piece of machinery. Flipping over to the judges' page, there I saw the face of Mr. Randolph Cummings IV. The director, Mr. Todd, had turned the reins over to his heir apparent as well, Carline Todd. The Templetons were still around, tallying up all of these fine scores.

The 1999 program book showed Miss Amber decked out in sequins, mane pulled up and sitting aloft her head. This was the year following Emma's defeat, and Amber was now Miss Macon United States of America. But this year, Mr. Cummings IV was gone and the Templetons had been replaced by another Atlanta firm. I scanned her next book, and neither Mr. Cummings IV nor the Templetons had returned. It was definitely time to head to Mississippi. Questions needed answers. And as soon as I was through being terrorized by tiaras, I would see what stories Mississippi had to tell.

For a woman with no job, a flight to Mississippi would be impossible. For a father with a credit card, all things were possible. So I headed in his direction. I would broach the subject on two levels, honesty and flattery. Oh, and the fact that he owed me for sending me off to lunch knowingly with those two. When these three merged to form a plan, the humidity of May turned into nothing more than a gentle breeze. I spent an undue amount of time outside Jake's with Duke, talking through my rhetoric. He got bored, so I reluctantly entered, heading in the direction of the Coke.

I caught Dad's eye and motioned him in the back room. "I need to speak with you for a moment."

He finished wiping remnants of the afternoon tourist traffic off the counter and followed me into his office. "What's wrong, Savannah? Surely lunch couldn't have done enough damage to require a private conversation."

"What you did was wrong."

"Welcome home, Savannah."

"Oh, so now you're saying I really owe you."

"Let's just be thankful your reputation is still intact."

"Well, the thing I need to talk about is . . . well . . . I don't feel like I can tell you everything right now, mostly due to the fact that I don't know everything right now. But I do know that I need to go to Jackson, Mississippi, this weekend to do some research, and unfortunately the Bank of Savannah is empty."

"I wasn't aware there was a Bank of Savannah."

"Well, there is, in its dwindling state. So I need to make a withdrawal from the Bank of Jake."

"Oh, yes! I know that one very well. Your account there is busted, however."

"I promise you, I wouldn't ask if it wasn't essential. I also promise I will pay you back everything even if I have to stay at home a week longer than I want. But I really need to do this, and I really need you to trust me without asking a lot of questions."

Dad reached into his pocket and pulled out his wallet, from which he took his platinum American Express. "Savannah, if there is one thing I know about you, it's that you wouldn't be asking me for money and offering to stay at home another week longer if you didn't feel it was absolutely necessary."

"You're a smart man."

"Very smart, don't forget it. I also know you have bigger reasons for everything you're doing that I will learn about soon enough. Whatever it is, all I ask is that you do it well and that you be careful," he said, handing me his card, kissing me on my cheek, and walking toward the door.

"Dad, thanks. I love you totally separate of the fact that I'm holding your credit card in my hand," I said, laughing.

He turned back around, laughing himself. "I love you too. And trust me, it is *totally* separate of the fact that you are holding my credit card in your hand."

With that he disappeared to continue his commission for the day. "Listen to the wise people around you, and live a life that is always learning."

Richard said people had been asking Dad and him questions all day long. "There's been more learning going on in here than I've seen happenin' in a schoolhouse in fifty years!"

CHAPTER EIGHTEEN

My entrance caused most eyes to turn my way, except those belonging to the elderly man in the back, who squinted at the books in front of him. I watched as Katherine headed to a little boy who was sitting in her reading corner. "Well, Savannah, good morning. I think I'm going to offer you a part-time job. You're here almost as much as I am."

I closed the door behind me. "Too much time on my hands. But that will change come Monday."

"Is that when you officially begin your new job?"

"Yes, and my first story is due Tuesday."

"Well, tell me all about it," she said, patting the stool next to her behind the counter. "And did you find you some reporter clothes?"

"I'm not sure I even know what reporter clothes are, but I found some clothes to wear to the newspaper and at least act like a reporter."

"So what's your first story going to be?"

I had prepared myself for this question on my walk over. This was why I had come. "Well, all the details haven't been worked out yet. So, I'm really not certain at the moment. I've got to do some more research and make sure all the facts are accurate."

"Well, that's wise of you, Savannah." The squinty, elderly man made his way to the cash register with a large-print book in hand. I could tell by the way he squinted at the bills in his wallet that this checkout would take a while.

The magazine rack was nearby. I picked up a couple of magazines to add to Paige's library while Katherine waited for the gentleman to exit. He packed up book and billfold, and I paid for Paige's literary advancement. "Well, I hope you have a great night, Katherine. I've been snookered into some rather interesting activities myself."

"Did you just say snookered?"

"I'm absolutely certain I did not just say snookered."

"So what is your big activity?"

"Oh, there's a pageant up the road, and the reigning Miss Savannah United States of America, who is certain I'm her new best friend, wants me to attend. I haven't been to one in years. So, it will be interesting to see what happens. Have you ever been to a pageant?" I asked. I am shameless.

"I've gone to a few in my time. But not for many years. I'm sure you'll have an interesting time. Come back and see me soon." She closed the register, patted my hand, and headed to the back of the store.

"OK," I said, trying not to sound deflated. I whispered to her disappearing back, "But if you get bored and want to come along, let me know." A few tourists, who had dressed, well, just wrong, watched my departure. Who knew how they could justify such attire, but they did.

Sergeant Millings was on West Harris Street at Madison Square, writing up a ticket for a shiny blue bicycle leaning against a light pole. "Hello, Sergeant Millings. Heard you saw Paige the other day."

"Gave her a ticket, all right. That little thing flittin' round here doin' thirty-five in a twenty. She shouldn't even have a car. You kids ought to ride the trolley or somethin'."

I stopped in front of the bike. "Yeah, I know. So why are you giving a bicycle a ticket? I'm certain it wasn't exceeding the speed limit."

"Are you trying to be smart, Miss Savannah?" he asked, looking up from his notepad.

"Now, have you ever known me to act smart?" I asked, smiling from ear to ear as I continued past him. "Now, you have a wonderful afternoon, you hear?" About the time I approached Drayton Street, the cries of one bicycle boy pierced the everyday noise. There was no need to turn around to watch his curls bounce in the wind.

Miss Amazon Amber had left directions no fewer than four times on the voice mail. I erased them all right before my departure in hopes no others would be left for my family to retrieve.

At the Hinesville High School Auditorium, the princess of pink came cascading down the steps to meet me. Her pink pantsuit was complemented by the tiara sitting atop her blanched tresses. There were as many rhinestones on her suit as her tiara. I was sure my subtle attire of blue jeans and leather jacket would be appreciated by overstimulated observers. She scampered and sparkled toward me, calling out my name for every entering entourage to hear. "Ooh, Savannah, we've got to hurry. You do *not* want to miss the opening number," she said, grabbing my arm and pulling me inside. "I've got your ticket, and Trina and Tina, my good friends—of course I just call them the twins—well, they're saving us a seat."

"Yea!" I said, clapping my hands together in feigned excitement.

The auditorium was abuzz. Faces were flying everywhere. Pictures of women's heads had been stapled or taped atop paint stirrers and people were waving them all around like bad Home Depot advertisements. We made our way to our seats, which were close enough to the judges to read their scorecards. I prayed no one would know me. Our seating companions, Trina and Tina, were adorned in splendor as well. Trina's tiara hailed from Sandersville,

Georgia, and Tina earned hers in Swainsboro. "Hey!" they sang in unison.

Sure of the fact I would never say "hey" again as long as I lived, I said, "Hello."

"Oh, Amber, she's just as cute as you said she was," Trina—or was it Tina?—exclaimed. There was no way I was capable of spending the evening figuring out which was which. "Yes, you are, Savannah. You're just cute as pie. And you look just like your mother."

"Yeah, we all just love Miss Victoria," they said, finishing each other's sentences. I was like a spectator at a tennis tournament.

The curtain rose, whisking us away into the wonderful world of waving and whipping. *Whipping* was the term I created for young ladies as they came to the edge of the runway and whipped themselves back around. "Ooh, she shouldn't have worn those tacky shoes with that dress," Amber said as she leaned over to my ear. "I don't know who told that child strappy was in, but she looks like Elvira."

Then Tina or Trina chimed in and said, "Oh, my goodness. Would you looka there? Tinisha Tettweiller has entered herself in another pageant. That child has competed in twenty-four preliminaries in the past two years. She should just stop."

I hoped they didn't truly know how many pageants Tinisha had been in. The fact that they were counting would be far more disturbing than Tinisha's obsessive-compulsive pageant disorder. When swimsuit started, I couldn't help but ask, "*Where* did she get *those?*"

Amber leaned over. "Honey, that's what we call taping."

"Taping?"

"Some girls have cleavage by natural graces. And others have to create their own. They just lift those babies up, tape 'em underneath, and voilà—you've got cleavage."

Why am I here? I slumped even further into my chair.

"Honey, you think that's bad," Amber continued, not noticing my discomfort. "I've seen girls tape their entire stomachs!"

I turned to stare at her in disbelief, but the commentary continued for the next two and a half hours.

As fifteen ladies competed in swimsuit, I endured talk of thighs, taped parts, and cellulite. For talent, I tolerated commentary on pitch, poor choices of songs, and bad Barbra Streisand impersonations. And for evening gown, those three girls were downright shameless. They ripped those poor girls apart for wearing velvet in May or insufferable shades of purple. One girl could be seen only from the nose up because of the boa that flanked the top of her purple velvet dress. Throughout the evening, a petite brunette, who sang the tar out of "Quiet Please, There's a Lady on Stage" and donned, shall we say, a stunning dress that looked to be hand crocheted, captured the audience's attention and applause. Even Amber and Friends seemed to like her.

While the trio was captivated by what was going on onstage, I turned my attention to the judges and their interaction with the auditors. And as the late-forties, overmanufactured hostess bantered and babbled to kill time, the auditors feverishly tallied the scores in full view of the audience.

When the hostess declared it was time to announce the winner, a young, tall drink of water named Lancy took home second runner-up honors. Tinisha was going to have to live with the title of first runner-up and another notch on her tally. And the petite brunette named Valerie was declared the winner. Being the novice I was, it seemed the proper lady had won. As far as I could tell, Hinesville could rest tonight knowing its pageant wasn't rigged.

Amber took me by the arm and escorted me from the building. "Well, did you enjoy yourself or what? Have you ever had so much fun in your entire life? I'm telling you, I could go to one of these a night!"

"Oh, well, wouldn't that be exciting? I'm afraid that might just send me over the edge though. I mean, how could a girl stand such a ruckus every night? Those people got wild in there," I said, politely extricating myself from her embrace.

"You should see it when they get nasty. That's when it gets really good. When mamas are yelling at each other across the auditorium, and daddys want to meet in the parking lot. Oh, girl, Hollywood couldn't write things as good as I've seen over the years. So what did you think about the winner?"

"I thought she was cute. She seemed like she was the best on the stage to me."

"She's a little short, though. It's hard to distribute all that weight when you've got less of an area of distribution."

"She didn't look like she had much weight on her at all."

"Well, she wore a black bathing suit. And you know what they say about black bathing suits."

"I'm certain I have no idea."

"You only wear black when you're trying to cover up something. So, we'll see how she looks when we get to Miss Georgia United States of America."

"Do you ever get tired of saying that entire phrase?"

"No, not really."

"What do you say we shorten it?"

"What did you have in mind?" She looked at me as if I might be close to committing some form of sacrilege.

"Nothing major. I just thought maybe we could call it Miss Georgia US of A."

"No, I don't think that would be appropriate," she said, heading toward her car.

"Are you serious?" I asked, stopping in the middle of the parking lot.

"Yes, I am. Women spend years trying to achieve such an honor. I think it cheapens their efforts not to give them the courtesy of announcing their complete title."

"Well, I will hereby take note of such an argument."

"Thank you, and I will take note of your desire to be proficient." I knew she meant efficient, but there was no point in correcting her. "Now, I've got to head to the victory party up the street at the mayor's house. All the queens are invited. Sure you don't want to come?"

"Oh, well, I would love to, but I've got such an early morning."

"OK, well, I'll see you for lunch on Tuesday," she unlocked the doors to her Mercedes coupe with the click of a button.

"Oh, yeah, Tuesday!" I said under my breath, inserting my key into Old Betsy and giving the door a tug.

"Don't forget!" she said, climbing into her plush car.

"I wouldn't dare," I said, straightening my cushion so I wouldn't fall to the floorboard.

CHAPTER NINETEEN

I needed to talk to my mother. Crazy, but true. Because in the middle of this madness lay a dream of Victoria Phillips. And swirling around it like a vulture was me. Even though she had ruined my dream, the thought of destroying hers ate away at me. I needed peace. I needed my mother.

"Hello, darling. I just love caller ID. What are you doing up and out this early?"

"I could ask you the same thing."

"Oh, a ladies' store is having a sale and the owner is letting me come by early to look through things before the rush."

I knew good and well she was talking about Jezebel's, but I would let her maintain her anonymity.

"Mother, do you know what a wonderful lady I think you are?"

For a moment she did not respond. Then, totally serious: "Savannah, are you drunk?"

"You know I'm not drunk. I do not get drunk, and besides, it's too early to be drunk. I know we clash every now and then over dumb things, but I really do love and appreciate you." I almost felt like a knot was forming in my throat.

"Savannah, are you crying? Is someone holding a gun to your head? Are you about to be murdered? Where are you, darling?" I could see her making a mad dash up the street past the Francis McNary Antique Store.

"Mother! I'm fine. Really. I just needed you to know how I feel."

Sounding as if she were slightly winded, she managed, "Well, I love you too, darling. So if you're not dying, are you needing something?"

"No! You act like I've never told you I loved you before in your life."

"Well, you've never said it quite like this before."

"OK, so let me say it like this, and don't ruin the moment."

"Well, thank you. Those are some of the kindest words I've ever heard," she said, now tearing up herself.

"Don't cry. Please, Mother."

"OK. Thank you." Then the sound of a horn blow pierced the receiver. There she was, standing on the sidewalk in front of an antique store in heels, cell phone attached to her ear and snot running down her nose, stopping to pant and blow. It was most Victoria.

"So, where are you? Do you want to come join me?"

"Actually, that's why I'm calling. I just need you to listen for one moment and not ask me any questions. I need you to just trust me."

"Savannah, I do trust you. You know that."

"Mother, you just asked me if I was drunk!"

"Well, I knew you weren't," she said, trying to sound convincing.

"I have to go to Jackson, Mississippi—"

"Jackson, Mississippi? For what? Why in the world are you going to go to Jackson, Mississippi?"

"Mother, I told you, no questions. Trust, remember?"

"OK, right, no questions, just trust. No questions. All right, I think I'm ready."

"I'm working on a story. But I need more facts on it before I can put it to print. I'll be back as soon as I can tomorrow."

"But what about—"

"Mother, no questions. Dad has given me all the money I need, and he knows no more than you, so please don't hound him. OK?"

"OK. But I don't like it. And that wasn't a question. That was a statement," she said all rushed so I wouldn't interrupt her.

I decided to turn to my method of distraction. "Oh, and I really like my shoes, Mother. Thank you for getting them for me."

"I knew you would like them. Kate Spade, she's the in thing right now. I think you would love a lot of her things. She makes the best handbags you have ever seen. And her stuff is timeless, you know, not trendy. I hear she even makes luggage now. Oh, Savannah, that would have been great for your trip. Not that I think you should be taking this trip. Again, that was not a question."

I figured Mother realized there was no one on the other end of her phone by the time I reached the airport. I checked in at the American Airlines counter and traveled with only one carry-on. The restaurant and small shopping area at the airport betrayed my mother's touch. Her influence seemed to surpass reasonable jurisdiction. Here, twenty miles away from Savannah, I sat in a town square that she had created in the middle of the airport. She felt people should have the "Savannah experience," as she called it, as soon as they stepped off the plane. So all of the small shops and stores were built on a square with real trees and small park benches.

Thomas said that when the square was initially finished, Vicky came by to make sure everything met with her approval. When she touched the ficus tree next to the women's restroom, she let out a yell. The tree was artificial. Today, Savannah's rumor mill has it that every tree, plant, bush, and phony flower ended up on the sidewalk in front of the designer's house, accompanied by a note that read, "Whatever you sow, that will you reap. Enjoy! Victoria

Phillips." Then she hired Thomas and about six of his high-school buddies, paid them with food, and created the parklike setting travelers now sit in.

The passengers on my flight were rather sparse, and I had a row to myself. The relative peace gave me time to reflect on the week's activities. But Emma kept coming to the front of my mind. If loss had the power to destroy someone's life, then a multitude of issues were at stake in Emma's. I mean, I had lost a thousand things through the years, but none of them—not even Grant—caused me to surrender myself to defeat.

Maybe my defeat was different. Maybe I wanted to lose. But everyone should know how to lose with grace. How can you ever appreciate winning, truly appreciate winning, if you've never known what it's like to lose? Even as whacked as my mother is, I have seen her face defeat gracefully. She has shaken hands with the winner of the annual Rose Day event, when her roses, though stunning before the tornado, looked a little haggard after. Then she shook the hand of Dolores Armstrong, Judge Hoddicks's secretary, after Dolores won the annual Fried Chicken Cookoff. Now I will tell you, on that one Victoria got bamboozled. There is no way anyone can touch my mother's chicken. But ever the pro that she is, she walked up to Dolores, hugged her, and even held up a piece of Dolores's chicken for the picture in the paper.

But Emma . . . Emma had given up on life. She had let defeat swallow her whole. She had even allowed it to steal her own family from her. This beautiful woman had come to the unthinkable place where she saw beauty in nothing. All because of a loss.

There was a deeper lesson here, I knew. I would search for it later. For now, I would search for the story that would bring her and Katherine vindication.

The clock on the dashboard of the rented Jeep Liberty read 12:09. My notebook held the street address of both Mr.

Cummingses. I scoured the map, searching for the location. I turned the key and the car started, eliminating my half-hope that I would be forced to spend the night in the airport, leave with nothing, and start work on something far less complicated.

Confrontation was nothing new to me. Twenty-four years of living with Vicky had freed me of trauma or trepidation at the prospect, and the Mr. Hicks and Emma episodes had recently sharpened my skills in this area. But I was about to confront people who lived by a different code. People who for some reason chose to select pageant winners based on something other than merit. The thing that gnawed at me was the fact that I had no idea what that something was.

Maybe it was just because of friendship. Maybe Mr. Cummings and the pageant director were so close that they would do anything for each other to make sure that the other was delivered the greatest results for his efforts. No, real friends have character. You can't be one without it. Maybe it was blackmail. No, that wouldn't last for thirty years. If it did, one of them was really smart and the other remarkably stupid. No, it had to be greed. People do amazing things for money. Yes, it had to be money.

As I processed my thoughts, it became clear that my destination was wrong. When I turned onto the interstate, the Golden Arches greeted me. Once I had acquired the necessary Coke, I knew what I had to do. This couldn't begin on Mr. Cummings's doorstep. It had to begin behind the scenes of his life. If the fraud was about money, then we were headed for one more ride. I just hoped I would still be in the driver's seat when we reached the destination. I pulled out my cell phone.

The voice on the other end sounded like it was chewing something. "Hello."

"Hello. Judge Hoddicks, it's Betty. I hope I didn't catch you at a bad time."

"No, honey. We're just finishing up some pork chops. A big ol' Saturday afternoon spread. Do you want to join us? All the kids are here too. I'm sure they would love to see you." I heard him tell everyone it was me. A resounding group "hello" came through on my end of the phone.

"Actually, Judge, I'm in Jackson, Mississippi, and I need a huge favor."

"You aren't in jail down there, are you? I'll have someone's head if they've done anything to you. Where—"

"No! No! I'm fine. Actually I'm working on a story and wondered if you knew anyone who could let me into the courthouse today. I know most courthouses are closed on Saturday, but I need to do some research. I only have today and tomorrow to get everything accomplished. I might end up in the unemployment line before I even see a paycheck if I don't."

"Betty, you hold on. I have an old college buddy who's a judge right there in Jackson. Hang on the line and I'll call him real quick on my cell." The hand-off went to Mrs. Hoddicks first, who said hello and then passed me around the table. By the time the judge returned, I had been fully updated on every cold, engagement, death, and baptism within the last six months of the entire Hoddicks family.

"Betty! His law clerk will meet you there. Where are you, anyway?"

"I'm only about five minutes from downtown."

"Well, the courthouse is right in the heart of their city. The clerk will meet you at the side door on the south side. He has been told to get you whatever information you need. If you have one ounce of frustration, honey, you just call me back. I'll come down there myself and get you what you need. You hear me?"

"Yes, sir. I'm sure I'll be fine. I can't thank you enough. And if this goes well, I'll get you free coffee at Jake's for the rest of your tenure."

That made him cackle. "Well, that would be great! Jake will appreciate it."

"He'll appreciate you helping me even more. Thanks again."

The Jackson County Courthouse looked imposing in the glow of the afternoon sun. I parked in front and walked around to the south side. Standing by the side door was a handsome young law clerk, probably about my age. He held out his dark hand and introduced himself.

"Gregory Taylor."

"Hello. Savannah Phillips. Nice to meet you. Thank you for doing this."

He did not seem at all perturbed at having been called in on the weekend. "Well, follow me, and we'll try to find what you need." He opened the side door and led me down a dark hallway lined by frosted-glass doors. The hall deposited us into the lobby. The vastness of the courthouse was impressive and possessed a sense of awe and quiet reverence. The hallowed halls brought to mind the lives salvaged and lost inside. "I sure am sorry to take away your Saturday. I know how people in the law field enjoy a moment of reprieve."

He surrendered a beautiful smile. "Oh, it's no big deal. I needed to come in and get some work done. You just gave me a reason to have to do it. So, what exactly do you need?"

"I need whatever information you have on Randolph Cummings III and Randolph Cummings IV." At the mention of their names, Gregory stopped dead in his tracks.

"Do you know that Mr. Cummings, both of them, are two of the most respected and influential men in this city? If you are trying to dig up anything unseemly about them, you won't find it here." His drawl took the edge off his charming but matter-of-fact tone.

"I hope I don't. But there is only one way to know. I need to see every certificate, every license, every death notice you have on record for this family." Then I added my own southern charm for good measure. "And Judge Hoddicks said if I had any problems he would be more than glad to come up here and help me get whatever information I need."

"Well, let's not waste any time then," Gregory replied politely.

He led me to a door that took us to the basement. "Are there any lights down here?"

He flicked on the light. "Don't worry. There's nothing down here but thousands of boxes and a few rats. And the lights usually scare off the rats."

I looked at him, grateful for lights. "How long have you been here?"

"I've clerked for Judge Tucker for two years now. I finished law school last year, but I worked for him every summer during those long years, so coming here full-time just seemed like a natural progression."

"Sounds like it."

"Well, this is it. Almost everything you want to know about anyone in the city: tax records, licenses, certificates, all right here." He pointed to about a hundred separate rows of shelving that ran the full length of the courthouse and were stacked with boxes from floor to ceiling. "It looks like you'll have everything you'll need. Everything is filed alphabetically, so that will help."

"Immensely."

"There are some cubicles over there in the corner," he said, motioning to four small work stations that lined the front wall. "I'll be in my office, and you can buzz me at #22 if you need anything."

"You can't bring your work down here?"

He laughed, "No, but I'm just a phone call away. I promise."

"I hope you were planning on working late, because I don't know if I'll be through before morning," I said, heading to one of the cubicles to unload my stuff.

"Honestly, I'm in no hurry. If it's morning, I'll just be that much further ahead. If you get hungry later, call me and I'll order us some pizza. And if you can't find something and need my help, just let me know."

"I'll forget to call, I'm sure. How about we just decide now on six o'clock? I'll buy if you'll order."

"That would be fine by me."

"Thanks, Gregory. I really appreciate your help. I know this is no one's idea of a good time on a Saturday."

"Obviously, you and I have different measures of that. Working until sunrise has always been my idea of a good time."

As he disappeared up the stairway, the masses of cardboard boxes brought me back to reality. Having no idea what I was looking for or what I was doing here, the only thing I was sure of was that if one rat trespassed on my territory, Gregory was going to find his hiney firmly planted in the cubicle in front of me.

As I worked my way down the aisle marked CU, I found a box that read "CUMMINGS, Randolph II, III & IV." These people had so much stuff, the three of them were worthy of their own box. The box was bulging. I slid it off the shelf with a thud and scooted it across the floor with both hands until it rested beside my work area. Then I grabbed my cell, called the hotel, and asked them to cancel my reservation. I wouldn't be needing a bed tonight, just caffeine. I would definitely need caffeine.

CHAPTER TWENTY

The Cummingses' box was sectioned off in three different places, by II, III, and IV. Each Cummings had his own section of business ventures and licenses and records, with IV being smaller than the first two. Mr. Cummings II's file began with the title deed to what was apparently his first home. It was followed by a marriage certificate, only one that I found, and then numerous business licenses.

"Well, at least he's the husband of only one wife. That's a nice place to start." Someone was going to have to talk to me or I would go crazy down here. Mr. II had his own law firm, which was now Cummings & Cummings Attorneys at Law. The formal corporation name change was enclosed. His son had been added in 1962, and he held a partnership in a local grocery store and owned a Burger King franchise and numerous other business ventures that seemed to be locally operated companies right here in Jackson. The file ended with the death certificate of one Cora Lee Cummings on September 14, 1985, at the age of seventy-five, followed by Randolph Cummings Jr. on October 19, 1991, at the age of eighty-nine.

The file of Randolph Cummings III, like his father's, began with a marriage certificate. On June 20, 1956, at the age of twenty-three, he married Patricia "Patty" Gwendolyn Stryker, who was only seventeen. "That's just sick. She was only a baby, snatched up by some worldly-wise attorney."

The IIIs purchased their first home only two weeks after their marriage, the address of which matched the one I'd written down. Mr. III joined his father's law firm in 1962. He then purchased a local theater, an arcade, a pizzeria, and a coffee shop. Dare Jake know he and this man had anything in common! As I rummaged through the rest of his papers, most documenting his numerous real-estate investments, absolutely nothing seemed to suggest he would care at all who in the world won a beauty pageant.

Heading to Mr. IV's folder, a tiny file in the back caught my attention. It was marked "Patricia Cummings." Her folder held evidence of two businesses: a local jewelry store and P&R Printing Co. The jewelry store seemed a logical business for any woman. But the printing company, for some reason, I found rather odd.

About that time, I heard someone coming down the stairs. Not even imagining that almost five hours had passed, the hair on the back of my neck stood up. But then I saw the pizza box and Gregory's face.

"Surely it isn't six already?" I tried to stand up, realizing quickly how long I'd been sitting. *"Ow!"*

"Yes, it's six. Have you been sitting there this entire time?" he asked, laughing at my pitiful attempt to rise. He reached out his hand to steady me.

"I didn't realize I'd been looking at this stuff for so long. Do you have any way for us to find old newspaper articles around here, or could we only do that at the paper?"

"Whoa, Snoop Dogg, why don't you sit down, eat a bite, and tell me your story?" He set the pizza on top of my desk and pulled up a chair. He had brought two extra Cokes down with him. I had finished off mine hours earlier, so I was grateful for the thoughtfulness.

"Good idea. I *am* starving."

He grabbed a piece of pizza, propped his Nikes up on the table, and leaned back in his chair, letting me know he was ready for the scoop. As he took a bite of pizza, I noticed his muscular calves. They made me confident his favorite pastime was running. "So, Miss Savannah. What in the world are you doing here on a Saturday night, hundreds of miles from home, in a basement at a courthouse in Jackson, Mississippi, snooping into the lives of some of Jackson's most prominent and influential citizens? Surely, this is a good story."

I leaned back as well. "You'll think I'm an idiot. Shoot, half the time *I* think I'm crazy, chasing some wild concoction of a story that no one gives a horsefly's rear end about."

"Did you just say 'a horsefly's rear end'?" He slapped his hands on his khaki shorts in amusement.

"Yes, have you never heard that before?" I realized then that I myself had only ever heard my mother say it.

"No, can't say that I have. And I don't know that you need to say it around anyone else," he said, going back to his pizza.

I started eating my pizza with fervor, trying not to chew and talk at the same time. "Thanks for the advice. So, if I tell you what I'm working on, do I have attorney–client privilege?"

"Only if you pay me."

"How much do you charge?"

"Well, tonight I have a special going. Tonight I am only charging one dollar per client per visit."

"Are you telling me I only have to pay you one dollar for the entire visit and I will have the undivided attention of your services?"

"It is your lucky day."

"That's a mighty cocky smile, Mr. Attorney Wannabe. But here." I grabbed the satchel beside me, pulled out a dollar bill, laid it on the table, and pushed it toward him. "I hereby pronounce you my attorney. And whatever I tell you is strictly confidential and can never be repeated."

"Absolutely. I'm all yours. Compensation has been exchanged and privilege is granted. Shoot with your concoction." He took a long swig of his Coke. He was a tall, good-looking fellow, with a quick wit and true southern charm. His blue-and-white T-shirt complemented his flawless dark skin, and his calm demeanor made him easy to talk to. For the next hour my new attorney listened to everything that had transpired in my life in the last two weeks. He sat rather mesmerized and quiet the entire time until I mentioned P&R Printing. Gregory's wheels began turning themselves.

I wiped my mouth and took another drink of my Coke. "What are you thinking?"

"I'm thinking, what would a pageant need with either jewelry or a printing company?"

"All beauty pageant women wear jewelry; that's a given. But money, not jewelry, causes people to rig pageants. So unless she's selling diamond tiaras and has the market on the whole Miss United States of America Pageant, that's not where she's making the money. Now for printing, they have to print these." I reached down and pulled out Amber's and my Mother's ridiculously large programs. You'd better not touch this one without gloves," I said, pointing to Vicky's book. "You might be a lawyer, but she, my friend, is CIA material."

He feigned difficulty lifting them as he brought each one to his side of the desk. "These things are huge! Why in the world would they need something this large?"

"This is how pageants make money for their prizes."

"I thought they had sponsors for prizes."

"They do for some, but the girls also sell program pages to businesses in their local cities. The money from those pages, at five hundred dollars a pop, offsets the expenses of the pageant and pays for scholarships."

"Savannah, there are over five hundred pages in here. That's $250,000. Combine that with sponsors' goodies and ticket sales, and somebody's making some money. I think your story is on the money. Follow the money, Savannah," he said, and he closed up the empty pizza box and walked it to the trash can.

Turning around so I could see him, I said, "What am I going to do, break into bank records and find out if someone received large sums of cash after the pageant money was collected? I don't have the time or the capability to do something like that."

He walked back and sat down. "Savannah, you don't always have to *prove* things, sometimes you just need to *know* things."

"I have no idea what you're saying," I told him, putting my head in my hands and sighing from sheer exhaustion.

"I'm saying, what do you know?"

"What do I know?"

"Yes, what do you know?"

"Nothing."

"OK, what do you *think* you know?"

"I *think* I know a judge changed his scores."

"Go on."

"I think I know which judge, who at face value has no motive and a wife who owns a printing company."

Gregory opened two program books in front of him. Each had its own list of acknowledgments to vendors who had donated their work. In both books, some twenty-five years apart, on line three, thank-yous went out to P&R Printing Company for the printing of program books, letterhead, and the new Miss Georgia United States of America personalized stationery. "Look, it's right here in black and white. Now, even if P&R printed these monster books out of the goodness of their hearts, it's unseemly at best. No judge should have any dealings with a pageant in a manner like this. It muddies the water."

"Well, sure it does, but it all but says right here that they did the work free for sponsorship purposes."

"Sure, they did it free. Can you imagine the stink if they had charged for it? That would be blatant misconduct. But what if their free services are a cover-up for a kickback? And what if their kickback comes with a perk for the pageant director? 'You help me and I'll help you.' The Cummings get a whopping tax deduction, and the pageant weasels their way out of a whopping printing bill. This really isn't that hard to see."

"What am I going to do, walk up to their door with a bunch of what ifs? 'Um, ma'am, I think, though there is no way on God's green earth I can prove it, that you are taking a kickback on the inflated price of advertising pages in a pageant program book in order to manipulate scores for a pageant director in Georgia. Now, don't let your foot kick me in the behind too hard as you *throw me out your door!*' Are you whacked? *I'm* going to be the human-interest story by the time you're through with me."

"Savannah, you should have gone to law school. You don't go in there declaring what you don't know. You put them on the stand, letting them assume you know everything. Then, eventually, they give themselves away. They're either frustrated you've got it wrong, or their expression reveals how right you really are." He stood and paced as if he were trying the case of a lifetime.

"You're saying I need to act like I know all this as fact in order to prompt a response?" I asked. "Would you please quit pacing?"

"That's exactly what I'm saying."

"What do you think we are doing here, acting out parts in a John Grisham novel?"

"Well, at least he knows how to write a good legal thriller, plus, he's good-looking like me and from Mississippi too."

"You are incorrigible."

"Yes ma'am, I know I'm adorable, but back to the business at hand."

"So, after I get sued for slander, you'll be my attorney, right?"

He waved my dollar in front of my face.

I couldn't help but smile back. "And that's about all you're worth, too. We'll probably end up in jail together."

"Well, at least you like me!"

"Yeah, at least I like you!"

After spending two more hours examining possibilities, I felt I needed more. I needed facts, not assumptions. "Let's go on a tour of Jackson. Let's go check out some printing companies and some of Cummings's office buildings."

"We can go look, but I will not allow you to step out of the car."

"You can lock the doors."

"I can and I will," he said, getting up himself. We walked out to his car and he opened the door for me to climb in.

"Nice car for a law clerk," I said, admiring his shiny silver Volvo.

"Thank you. A man's got to have a nice ride."

The tour of Jackson began. We traveled through the Historical District, and Gregory gave me a tour of some of the oldest African-American churches in the nation. He also showed me where Medgar Evers lived. Then we progressed to an area of town where the Cummingses owned the entire block. All in a row on West Capital Street stood Cummings Enterprises, Patricia's Precious Stones jewelry store, and P&R Printing at the top of the street.

"Here's the Cummings Compound, as we like to call it here in Jackson."

"So they're not quite the sweethearts of Jackson as you first led me to believe?"

"Well, they're high-profile, influential people. They own most everything in this city, including a few people. So, it is my job to protect this city. It is your job to protect your own behind."

"So, since behind protection is my job, what do you say we get out and take a walk up the street?"

"You're a persistent little creature."

"Yes, I am. Let's walk." Things were pretty quiet for a Saturday evening. A few people were walking about, and I could hear music and laughter coming from up the street.

"So how did you get here?"

"I was born and raised here."

"And law school? Was that always the plan?" I asked as we admired the grand entrances of the Cummings Compound.

"That was a father's dream for his son. Then it became the son's dream for himself."

"My dad would be happy at this point if I were simply self-sufficient, seeing as I had to use his credit card to get here."

"I would agree with him, seeing as you've yet to pay for the pizza."

"I haven't left yet. I'll pay you for that pizza."

"Savannah, you've had me so distracted I didn't even realize where we were. If someone sees us back here, we'll have more tongues wagging than a carpool of St. Bernards," he said as he noticed that I had drifted to the back of the Cummings's buildings.

"I just wanted to see what they had back here," I said, walking over to the back door of Cummings Enterprises and wiggling the handle, knowing it would be locked. It was.

"You can't go inside. You're going to get yourself arrested and who's going to come get you out?"

"That would be your job, Counsel."

"Not on your life."

"Gregory, look," I whispered, pointing to an open window. "Give me a lift."

"I will not. I will leave you behind, right here all by yourself."

"OK, then, I'll lift myself," I said, reaching as high as I could, barely able to grasp the tip of the window sill. I jumped up and was able to get a weak hold on the inside trim, all the while trying to glide my right foot up the side of the brick building. But with nothing to hold on to, I collapsed into a heap on the asphalt parking lot.

"You're pathetic."

"You're pathetic for not helping me."

"This is breaking and entering. This is a federal offense, a reason people go to jail and others are disbarred."

"This is not breaking and entering. The window is open. So, technically it is only entering. And I've seen enough *Law & Order* to know that many a defense is won on a technicality. Now please, you don't have to enter. Just give me a boost."

"That is being an accomplice to a crime."

"I will tell anyone who asks that I forced you."

"With what, a high heel?"

"I don't wear high heels," I said, pointing to my flat black sandals.

"Well, whatever you are going to do, you need to hurry. In Jackson, Mississippi, a black man in an alley with a white woman makes for nothing good in the eyes of busybodies."

"Just a quick hoist. You go back to the car, drive around the block, and I'll meet you at the courthouse."

"You don't even know how to get back to the courthouse," he said, exasperated. He bent down.

"Trust me, I'll find it. And you can go back to work. Now please, hoist!" Gregory relented. As I put my foot in his hands, he hefted me with enough effort to give me a firm grip on the window.

"How in the world . . . is *this* . . . a human-interest story?" He panted as he struggled to push me the rest of the way through.

"I'm a human and I'm interested. That's all you need to know." In reply, he pushed me so hard I flew through the window, landing on both head and shoulders and causing a loud crash as I toppled a picture frame.

"What happened? Are you all right?" he called in a half-whisper, half-petrified yell.

I poked my head out of the window and peered out. "Let's just say it is now officially *breaking* and entering. Go; I'll catch up with you later." I closed the window that separated us. I used my shirt tails to collect the broken glass as best I could, all my years of watching courtroom dramas having made me cautious. I laid them all back neatly on an unsuspecting employee's desk and headed through the dark corridors in search of . . . anything. I found a rag in a kitchen area and used it to open and close doors, searching by the dim parking-lot lights streaming in the windows.

When I began to think my first crime spree would prove utterly pointless, I noticed a cracked door. Behind the door was a dark staircase that led to purgatory for all I knew. But I had to go. While descending the dark stairwell, it became undeniably clear that I had taken leave of every good sense I had ever possessed. "Mercy," I said out loud, "I am in Jackson, Mississippi, breaking into an office building, searching for something, I don't even know what. I've sunk low. Desperately low." Sinking even further into blackness, it was evident by the lack of any light that this room had no windows. I felt safe enough to search for the light and finally found a switch. The light was blinding.

Once my eyes adjusted, I began to take in the environment around me. The room resembled the courthouse basement, with row upon row of shelving bearing boxes upon boxes of documents. I meandered down each aisle, searching for anything marked P&R Printing. Near the back were about six rows full of boxes for P&R Printing, which had been in business for over thirty-five years according to the dates on the labels. About halfway through row three, I found thirty-some boxes marked "banking records." I began in 1972, the year of Katherine, and searched for anything linking P&R Printing to the Miss Georgia United States of America pageant. I found absolutely nothing.

After what felt like hours of absolutely nothing, I turned the corner and saw a box marked "Personal." Pulling out my handy-dandy rag, I carefully opened the lid. It, like the last thirty-something boxes I had drifted through, was filled with nothing but papers and cards. Then the name Todd caught my eye. But this name wasn't Carl Todd, the director of the Miss Georgia United States of America pageant or of Carline Todd, his daughter. This name was Catherine Todd.

I painstakingly pulled the file out and laid it in front of me. Inside were twenty-two neatly rubber-banded notes. I opened each one. They were personal notes from Catherine Todd, thanking "Patty" for the jewelry and printing. In each she made reference to the "special gift enclosed," and each note was dated. Going immediately back to the bank statements and following the date of each note, a major deposit, identified simply as "Gift," was made exactly one week after the date of each letter into Patricia's personal account. Each deposit ranged from fifty to seventy-five thousand dollars, far more than any reasonable printing bill would have been.

I sneaked back upstairs and pilfered around until I found a copy machine. I made copies of each letter and each deposit, then returned the originals to their proper places. Exiting the same way I had entered, I took extra care to wipe the window and sill free of any fingerprints. As I turned the corner to return to West Capital Street, I tucked the photocopies underneath my shirt. I sensed a car come alongside me and heard a voice say, "Get in the car."

I hopped in, and every ounce of adrenaline left me, causing me to go limp. "I thought I told you I'd meet you back at the courthouse."

"You would have never made your way back there, even by morning," Gregory said as he pulled into his parking place in front of the courthouse.

"Well, thank you. Let's get inside, so I can show you what I got."

We descended to the basement, and for the next couple of hours I told him what I had found. He determined that no matter what the money was for, whether for jewelry or for the printing, it was unethical at best and, at worst, motivation enough for a judge to alter his vote.

I decided I wanted to meet the Cummingses before I left. Gregory decided I was certifiable. But he prepped me nonetheless on how I would need to present myself. I wasn't sure I would take all of his advice, but I would use what I thought was worth using.

Somewhere in the wee hours of the morning we both fell asleep in our chairs, our heads lying on opposite sides of the desk.

"Hello," I said, not sure where I was or how I got there.

"Savannah? Did I wake you up, darling? It's nine o'clock," said the familiar voice from the other end.

"Yes. But that's OK. I needed to get up anyway." I slowly tried to extract myself from the chair I had become one with during the night.

"Savannah, I heard through the grapevine that you made a visit to Emma Riley the other day." She stopped for a moment, but I knew what was coming.

Who knew how she knew, but no one here was surprised. "Oh, you did?"

"Yes, now I don't know what you are doing or what you are working on or why in the world you went to talk to Emma. But you and I are going to talk tonight and I want to hear everything. I have a feeling that what you are working on involves pageants because there is no way this side of Texas that you would voluntarily ask someone to show you her pageant program book."

"Now, that's not necessarily true."

"Oh, yes it is. You would rather be hog-tied and drug through cow manure across the whole state of Georgia than to have to sit down and look at one of those books." I wasn't sure where she came up with that, but she was pretty accurate on this point. "Nor is there any reason that after all these years you would seek out Emma Riley. So, just plan on me being up whenever it is you get home. I love you, and be safe. We'll talk tonight. Good-bye now."

CHAPTER TWENTY-ONE

The Edison Walthall Hotel is where everyone goes for Sunday brunch, mostly because the food is fabulous, but also, though no one would admit to it, to be seen. Gregory knew that Mr. and Mrs. Cummings III and IV went to the ten o'clock service at Saint Peter the Apostle at 123 NW Street, followed by an eleven fifteen brunch at the hotel. This was Judge Tucker's normal routine as well, when he was in town, which he wasn't this weekend, which was why Gregory knew it. At least that is what he testified to. He also knew that the Cummingses were usually home by twelve thirty and enjoyed working in their yard on Sunday afternoons. "I see them there working when I get out of church," he told me.

"I thought we'd take our own trip to the Edison for some Mississippi brunch," he said in his most southern of accents. "That way you can see what all the highfalutin Jacksonians look like."

I returned with my best Scarlett impersonation: "Well, that is a wonderful idea. How about I let you drive since you know the way?"

After cleaning ourselves up, we walked outside into a beautiful Sunday morning. He opened the door for me, and we traveled a short distance to the hotel. It was only about eleven, but the place was already busy.

"Do you people not go to church around here?"

"We go to the early service, Miss Savannah. We might miss something happening if we go any later than ten or ten thirty. But if you want to go to a happening place, come with me. We don't get out until about one. Then everyone goes to my mother's house for fried chicken."

"Gregory, are you sure we aren't related? We stay in church till pretty late too, and fried chicken is our favorite Sunday meal."

"It is the South, Savannah. I could be your cousin."

"Wouldn't that be a hoot!"

"Yes, I would find it rather amusing."

"Sorry I kept you out of church today. I'm sorry I kept myself out too."

"That's OK. Even though you need extra repentance for your escapades last night."

The Edison was a beautiful hotel, with a brunch I hadn't seen the likes of in years. They had eggs, bacon, sausage, beautiful fresh fruit with real cream, and a place to make omelets or pancakes. They even had a beautiful display of desserts, if you had another sweet tooth after you got through licking Aunt Jemima off of your plate. The waitress smiled at us politely but gave us the once-over, trying to figure out if we were a couple. She sat us at a small booth near the back of the room. As the waiter poured the water for us, I asked Gregory a question I had never asked a person before.

"Gregory, do you still find it difficult living as a black man here? I mean, not just in the South, but in America in general?"

"You'd be surprised, Savannah. Sometimes you see it in their eyes or hear it in the inflections in their voices. Sometimes it's subtle; other times they don't even try to hide their feelings. You even see it in churches."

"In churches?"

"What rock have you been under?"

"I'm not sure. We have every imaginable race in our church."

"You are the exception. Racism exists on both sides on what should be the most unsegregated day of the week. But it's everywhere. I see it in the way people refuse my gaze or move to the other side of the street. You want to scream at them, 'I'm a lawyer, not a criminal.'" Then he added with a laugh, "Of course, most people think lawyers *are* criminals."

I had to laugh at that one too. "They need to meet my lawyer, because he's dirt cheap."

"Well, I hear his prices might be going up."

"Not mine. I'm locked in at a lifetime rate."

"Well, anyway," he said, looking down and putting a lemon in his water, "it does get old at times, but some things have become a way of life."

"Some things should never become a way of life." I took a drink of water. "Thank you. You have been a great help and have come up with many wonderful ideas, I might add. I don't know that I'll use them all, but they were good nonetheless."

"Savannah, look casually at the door. That's Mr. and Mrs. Cummings III. Oh, and that's their son and his wife coming in right behind them," he whispered.

The presence of the stately looking older couple commanded the room. They moved spryly for their age, and I could tell they were regulars. People rushed immediately to service them. Mr. Cummings was tall and had an air of authority about him. His hair was totally gray, and he wore tailored glasses. Mrs. Cummings was statuesque. Her hair was white and she wore a vibrant red suit with matching red pumps. Even her lipstick was a bold red.

The son followed, looking like a younger version of his father. His wife followed him, looking like a cartoon character.

"Where did he get her?"

"From the hills of Tennessee, they say. Dumped wife number one, brought this beauty in, cleaned her up, and now he takes her out. Kind of like I did for you," he said, flashing his big smile. I raised my right eyebrow and he kept on. "They say she's had more sucked out of her than the Mississippi River. I think she's been pulled and plucked so much she'd probably bounce back if you threw her up against a wall."

"You are cruel."

"But knowledgeable."

We watched as the foursome took their seats. Every time someone came through the door and walked by their table, they would stop to speak to the Cummingses.

"This town loves these people."

"As I said. They are all but gods here, and you're going up against them with recent-college-graduate bravado and, dare I say, a few stolen facts."

"I'll be hung by morning."

"You'll be fabulous, Savannah." His tone had become serious. I looked at him. "You know something happened. Something that was wrong. You had gut instinct. You did your research, albeit somewhat criminal. You hold a smoking gun, and if by chance there are more rounds in the chamber, you at this moment are the only one who can do something about it."

We finished our breakfast and kept our eyes on the Cummingses as they finished their own and eventually left. We paid our check, and Gregory took me back to my car. For the thousandth time, we rehearsed how I should play my hand. I retrieved my stuff from his trunk and climbed into my car. Before we left, he walked over to my window. "It was nice to meet you, Savannah. You are proof that good things come out of Georgia."

"You are proof that good people become lawyers. Atticus Finch would have liked you," I said, patting his hand as it rested on my rolled-down window.

"I would have liked him too. Good luck. You'll be a great journalist. I expect to read that article you're going to write," he said, smiling and standing back up to return to his own car.

"I'll make sure you get a copy of that article," I said, smiling back. With that, Gregory climbed in his car and led the way to a grand house on the outskirts of downtown. The sign at the entrance of their driveway read "Cummings Estate." As he pulled away, I saw him wave through his rearview window. I returned the wave and hoped I could recollect our plan of attack. But I knew the one detail I would never forget—Gregory.

The straight driveway ran for almost a quarter-mile. The house was directly in front, so as I drove, it was always in my sight, becoming larger and larger the closer I got. Stopping in front of their home, I took a deep breath. Who knew how this was going to work? But the only way to know would be to actually evacuate the car and find out. Even removing my seat belt seemed like a daunting task.

As I closed the car door behind me and began to approach the house, the front door swung open. The older lady who only moments earlier had been in her Sunday best was now changed into denim trousers, a white T-shirt, tennis shoes, and a wide-brimmed straw hat, her red lips still vibrant. In her left hand were a pair of gardening gloves, and in her right, what appeared to be fruit tea. Following close behind was the rather intimidating figure of her husband. Well, intimidating until I got a look at his bad case of chicken legs in old Bermuda shorts and the same black socks he had surely worn to church under his suit. He also wore a white T-shirt and a large straw hat to protect him from the glare of the intense sun.

They didn't see me until they reached the bottom of their steps.

"Well, hello, young lady. You startled me," Mrs. Cummings said, almost tossing her glass and forcing me to catch it.

"Oh, I'm sorry, ma'am. I thought you might have heard me pull up."

She laughed, "My hearing's not as good as it used to be. I probably wouldn't hear a burglar if he was standing in my bedroom."

"Well, don't spread that around town."

That caused her to eye me suspiciously. Eventually she relaxed, realizing I didn't seem the burglar type. And a burglar probably wouldn't drive straight up the driveway and head to the front door on a Sunday afternoon. No, burglars climb into open windows and rummage through people's private, personal files.

"So how can we help you, young lady?" Mr. Cummings asked, turning his back to me and beginning his Sunday gardening ritual. "I hope you're not selling something."

I walked up and extended my hand to Mrs. Cummings, who hadn't moved from the bottom of the stairs since her initial discovery of me. "No, sir, I'm not. My name is Savannah Phillips. I live in Savannah, Georgia."

She put down her gloves and iced tea and shook my hand. Then laughed, adding, "Well hello, Savannah from Savannah. People probably call you that all the time!"

I tried not to glare or smirk, but I knew immediately this lady and I were not going to like each other. "Did you say 'Phillips'?" Mr. Cummings asked, looking over his shoulder briefly.

"Yes, sir, I did," I answered.

"So why are you here, Savannah?" Mrs. Cummings continued, turning to find her own spot in the garden.

There I sat with two backs staring at me. I decided to go for the jugular. After all, I had been suspected as a burglar and I had been called "Savannah from Savannah."

"Actually, I'm here on business."

"Oh?"

"Yes, I'm working on an article investigating voting irregularities and possible bribery at work in the Miss Georgia United States of America pageant," I stated calmly. Both pairs of hands stopped gardening. Neither head turned around. "Yes, it seems that thirty years ago some questions were raised about the possibility of a rigged pageant. I met with Mrs. Stanley Harvard of Atlanta's Wilcox and Harvard accounting firm. I've also met with a couple of former contestants."

With that, Mr. Cummings turned around and rose. He seemed much nicer seated. He approached me in what was still a frightening swagger for a man of some seventy years. "I have judged many a pageant in my day, young lady. Girls make accusations all the time. They get upset and start screaming foul. But if you came here looking for some story to quench a thirty-year-old question, you might want to take your assumptions and head on back home to Savannah." Then he just stared at me.

"So, does this mean you don't want to give me any type of statement?"

"I don't give statements to accusations or conjecture. So, no, I'm not giving you a statement on anything," he said, remaining perfectly still. By this time, Mrs. Cummings had turned in front of her hydrangeas to view the action.

Seeing that everything was going pretty much as rehearsed, I turned around to head back to my car. The walk back allowed me to take some deep breaths and collect my parting words. Opening my car door to make it clear that I was leaving, I turned around, letting one foot rest on the frame and keeping the other planted firmly on the ground. They needed one final thought to ponder on their Sunday afternoon among azaleas, boxwoods, and hostas.

"Well, it was nice to meet you both. I hope we see each other again. You know, before I leave, I'll share one more thought with you. As I was down at the courthouse last night, going through all of your records with the blessings of Judge Tucker, I discovered that Mrs. Cummings owns a printing business and a jewelry store. I also noticed that a printing company by the same name does all the printing for the Miss Georgia United States of America program books and has for roughly the last thirty years. The one thing that didn't seem to make sense however, was"—I paused for *Law & Order* effect—"why the Miss Georgia United States of America Pageant would use a printing company in Mississippi." Slapping myself in the head I added, "Then, I realized that P&R

Printing Company wouldn't register with anyone as being yours. So I put two and two together and came up with this scenario: Maybe your printing company has a deal worked out with Mr. Todd, the Georgia state pageant director, that for every page that is sold, your printing company gets a kickback and, for those kickbacks, Mr. Todd gets a vote of his choice."

Mr. Cummings put his hand under his chin and took one step forward. I pulled my door to me for protection. "Then I came across some banking sheets," I said, reaching inside and pulling a copy of the sheets from the front seat. "They showed a large deposit, every year, exactly one week after the pageant." Then risking the possibility that they might investigate my breaking and entering, I proceeded cautiously.

"Then I found someone to help me." They never had to know who. With any luck they would spend the next two months interrogating their staff. "And with their help I found these letters," I said, holding up copies of Catherine's letters as well. "This wasn't hard to get. There are even dates and transaction amounts here. So, I'm sure that if I need any further information, Judge Tucker will get me anything I need to help progress this little Mississippi steamboat right on up the river."

I bent down to act as if I was getting in the car, but popped back up for the *coup de grâce.* "It would be nice if I found nothing, but a good journalist must be thorough. If you change your mind about giving a statement, you can reach me at the *Savannah Chronicle.* You can just ask for Savannah from Savannah, OK?" With that I gave a big smile and a wink and climbed into my car. Mr. Cummings didn't move a muscle as my car turned in front of him. I rolled down the passenger window and leaned toward it. "Oh, and tell your son I'd like to talk to him as well. I won't bother him today though, seeing as Sunday should be a day of rest. But, I would love to discuss his years of service, specifically the year that Emma Riley lost. He might want to know what she's up to now. Take care." I gave a final nod to each and drove off.

I couldn't tell by either one's expressions if I'd receive a call. But I didn't figure any of us would sleep much tonight. If I was right, they'd call. If I was wrong, well, my story on Victoria's violets would have to be one of the most creative pieces I had ever written.

CHAPTER TWENTY-TWO

I used the twenty-five-minute drive from the Savannah airport to listen to my Jonathan Pierce CD. He was a cutie, that one. I couldn't help but wonder if he was married. But a guy like that wouldn't want a newspaper writer from Savannah who was doing her first story on a rigged beauty pageant.

On the outskirts of town, I picked up my cell phone and checked my messages. There were three. The first was from Vicky, telling me what was for dinner, saying she hoped I got home safely, and that we would talk later. I had no doubt. The second message was from Paige, wanting to get together for dinner. And the third message was from Gregory, wanting to know how my encounter had gone. He left his number.

I wasn't about to address Vicky any sooner than necessary, so I decided to call Gregory. He picked up on the second ring.

"Hello."

"Is this Mr. Grisham?"

He laughed. "You couldn't afford him so you had to settle for me, remember?"

"Oh, yeah, that's right. You're the cheap attorney."

"So go ahead. What happened? I've been waiting all afternoon for you to call me."

"Well, I don't know that anything was accomplished, but I laid it out there like you told me to."

"What was their reaction?"

"Mr. Cummings had none. He just stared a hole through me. Mrs. Cummings stopped her yard work long enough to turn around, but I didn't get more than a stare from her either. They are a stoic couple."

"All you could do was lay your evidence out there. Now you're going to have to play the waiting game. Even lawyers have to endure this type of thing."

"I'm not a lawyer, remember. I'm a journalist. No, I'm not even a journalist. I don't know what I am. But I know what I'm about to be: a tour guide wearing fifty layers of crinoline, melting makeup, and a bonnet that no self-respecting woman should be forced to don. How is it possible that I have already descended from published author to Scarlett O'Hara reject? I ask you, how is such a thing humanly possible?"

"At least you're positive."

"Oh, I am? You call that scenario positive?"

"Yes, you have a career to fall back on. Most put all of their hopes into one thing. But not you. You are a multifaceted individual with many gifts. If you can't write about Savannah, you can just tell people about Savannah." He laughed himself into a tizzy.

"I'm glad you find my life so amusing."

Gregory collected himself. "I believe you will probably have a phone call by Monday."

"You really think so?"

"I absolutely think so. I know you did extremely well. Were you nervous?"

"I was until she called me 'Savannah from Savannah.' Then all nerves vanished and I was ready for the kill."

"They'll call. I don't know what they'll tell you, but they will call."

"I hope you're right."

"Let's get us some dinner and those key-lime, I-need-to-marry-that-man squares."

"You are sad."

"Yes, I know. Then we'll watch *Law & Order*," Paige said from the other end.

"Ooh, yeah. I need to sharpen my skills, plus it will keep me from going home. I'll be there around six."

I retrieved dinner, made a fool of myself trying to catch a glimpse of the chef's left hand, and was headed back to the car when I heard the familiar siren. "Savannah! Yoo-hoo, Savannah!"

There she was, Miss Amber Topaz, waving as if from a runway on the opposite side of the street. She had to be stalking me. If I hadn't looked up so quickly, I would have tried to pretend I hadn't heard her holler my name. But dumb me had looked.

I waved as nonchalantly as possible, hoping my open car door would give her the signal I was headed somewhere. It didn't faze her a bit. Direct insults probably wouldn't faze her either, unless they were related to her clothing, hair, or makeup. She came to an abrupt halt right in front of my trunk. "Hey, Savannah. I just keep running into you all over the place. I think this has to be another sign that you and I are just destined to be lifelong friends. Don't you?"

I sat down in the driver's seat and placed dinner on the passenger's side, then put my keys in the ignition, trying to look hurried. "Well, we have seen each other a lot lately."

"Are we still on for Tuesday? I love The Lady & Sons and thought that would be a great place for us to go and tell each other more stories about our lives. And drink sweet tea until we burst," she said, patting me on the leg.

Turning the car on, I said, "I might have to reschedule our

lunch. I've run into a few deadlines and I'm trying to make sure I have my first article ready to go to press by Tuesday. So we might have to play lunch by ear, if that's OK."

"Oh, sure. We have the rest of our lives to have lunches. But I'll keep in touch with you just to make sure you're not working too hard," she said in that mock voice of concern, giving me another irritating pat. "So, did you enjoy looking at my program books? Weren't some of those girls just ghastly?"

"I thought all the girls were rather attractive. But I can't stay and chat, I've got a dinner appointment that I have to get to."

"Well, I just think some of those girls look like they've been rode hard and put up wet. You know that's an old saying in the South."

"Yes, I think I've heard of that one."

"I mean, in that book I gave you there were girls who couldn't even win the Miss Fried Okra Pageant, but somehow they made it to Miss Georgia United States of America. I figure they were the only ones who even competed in their local pageants. Some people's parents should just tell them, 'Honey, you're not really right for pageants; why don't we put you in mud-wrestling. With those thighs you could beat anybody.' You know what I'm saying?"

"Actually, I don't. And, not to be rude, but I have an appointment, and if I don't leave, I'm going to be extremely late," I said.

"Oh, OK. Well, I've got to go too. I have a mock interview rehearsal," she said, standing to her feet.

Before I could catch myself, I said, "What's a mock interview rehearsal?" I was now officially the biggest idiot in Georgia. It is one thing to be an unwilling participant in lunacy, but it is another thing altogether to become a willing one

She began like a whirlwind, arms flailing, hands patting, eyes sparkling, voice dancing. "Oh, Savannah, mock interview rehearsal is the most awesome thing. I get all three of my aunts and my mother and my stepmother, and for about two hours they bombard me with every type of question, from who the president is to how many pairs of shoes Imelda Marcos has."

"Imelda, huh?"

"Yeah, she's my favorite world leader. Then, they ask me what my thoughts are on everything from world peace and universal health care to what my favorite song is and why I named my dog Aqua Marine Lewis."

I did prevent myself from asking why she named her dog Aqua Marine Lewis. Instead, I put the car in park and leaned back in my seat. My watch read five forty-five. Paige's was only two minutes away. Surely she would be through in ten minutes. Wouldn't she?

I stared at her moving lips, realizing I might be forced to run her over. But I would at least be willing to write her obituary. "Miss Cubic Zirconia Childers was killed graciously by Miss Savannah Phillips after Ms. Phillips was tortured mercilessly for thirty minutes by the beauty-pageant junkie. In lieu of flowers, please send cash donations to the Miss Georgia United States of America Pageant for new opening-number outfits. Every dress will be emblazoned with precious stones symbolizing the precious jewel that Miss Childers was to all of us."

As I rested my eyes, she continued her lesson in interviewing techniques. "See, at the pageant—you know those five judges you saw at the pageant the other night?"

I nodded.

"Well, during interview, they sit in front of you at a big long table and for ten minutes they shoot you with questions and you answer them as rehearsed, yet as natural as possible, of course. They have a bio on each of the girls that they get before the pageant begins. Sometimes they ask you questions off your bio, and other times they ask you whatever comes off the tops of their heads. I've seen girls leave interviews crying. The judges asked such tough questions they couldn't hardly answer any of them. Then the next girl will go in and come out all smiles, saying it was the easiest thing she has ever done."

"Hmm," I said, keeping my eyes closed.

"One girl got asked a question one time about what she

would do to reform the EPA. Poor girl didn't even know what it was. She thought EPA stood for the Equal Protection for Animals, and she went on for two minutes talking about how she felt that every cow, duck, frog, and cat should be treated with the same respect as people. Then she gave four solutions, declaring that her plan would make the system better. She said the only thing the judge said was, 'I'm sure it would honey, I'm sure it would.'" When her roommate informed her that EPA stood for the Environmental Protection Agency, the poor girl walked straight into the bathroom and tossed her cookies. Her mother took her home that night. I'm telling you, you have to be prepared for anything."

"For anything," I agreed, nodding my head. And that was when I made my move. I reached out my hand, grabbed the door-knob, looked her squarely in the eye, and said, "I have to leave now. I'm sorry. But we'll talk this week."

"OK. Always great to talk to you. I love hearing all about you. You're just the neatest person," she said with a Vaseline-slathered-on-your-teeth kind of grin. "I'll talk to you soon. Toodeloo," and she skipped into the dusk. It was a wretched sight, but she nevertheless caught the attention of an elderly gentleman in the car across the street. He almost took out a fire hydrant. His wife slapped him with her purse.

CHAPTER TWENTY-THREE

O h, that was so good," Paige said, all but licking her plate for any leftover key-lime residue.

"Yes, it was."

"I want to marry him."

"Get a new line."

"It's true. I want a guy who can cook."

"I want a guy who can figure out the minds of sociopathic killers."

"I'm going to start making you watch comedies."

"Speaking of sociopaths, let's rehearse again what I'm going to say to my mother. There is the possibility I will never be seen alive again." I really had no idea how my mother would react to my discoveries, assumptions, and speculations. This was the woman who had been caught walking around with a tiara on her head, singing show tunes in the middle of the afternoon, when a group of tourists passed by her house and spotted her through the window. This is the same woman who invites former queens over to her house every year to watch the Miss United States of America Pageant in their old pageant dresses. This is a woman slightly off balance when it comes to beauty pageants. She was liable to horse-whip me with her sash. Her next ad in the *Savannah Chronicle* would probably read "New daughter wanted for extremely gra-cious, fun-loving, pageant-watching mother-daughter experience."

"Well, if you think I'm going to tell you how to handle your mama . . . Girl, you are the master with her. You just treat her gentle, compliment her shoes, and offer to go out to lunch with her this week. She'll forget everything else you have to say. You know that."

"That won't work this time. This will cut to her core. She lives and breathes pageants. If she thinks I think her beloved pageant is rigged or remotely less than authentic, well, she might think death would be sweeter."

"Well, at least you have a job, a place to live, a father who will provide you with Coke to cure your ills, and a best friend who can support you for a while if need be. And who will never, and I do mean never, force you to watch another pageant as long as you live."

"Say it's true!"

"It's so true! Now go. You can do it. Remember, gentle. Be very gentle. And compliment, don't forget to compliment. And call me. No matter what time. Don't forget to call me," she said, open-ing the door to let me out.

"I won't. But be fasting and praying."

"I'm starting now. But hurry, I'd like to get a bowl of cereal around eleven."

"You're sick."

"But I love you."

"I'll call you later."

"I'll be waiting, rest assured."

I entered through the front door. This simply needed to be faced head-on. A ball came bouncing in from the kitchen, and Duke came barreling out behind it. The ball hit the wall, bounced against the iron console, ricocheted to the other wall, hit my leg, and then landed at my feet. Duke took roughly the same path. His front paws slid across the hardwood as his back paws tried to slow his speed. Eventually his full body weight hit the foyer rug, causing his front paws to curve under his body, creating an odd somersault effect. The carpet ended up in a heap. He tried to recover himself, but his feet scrambled when he hit the hardwood, resulting in a bad Scooby-Doo impersonation. Finally, he landed at my feet, panting. I patted his head.

"No way, champ, will I touch that ball."

Dad called him a second later, and Duke gave up on me, retrieved his ball, and took it back to his faithful companion. I turned the corner to the kitchen and saw Dad sitting on the floor for the dog and ball show.

"Hey, sweetheart," he said, standing up to hug me.

"Do not touch me with those hands. You've been playing ball with a spit wad."

"Oh, but it's lovely spit," he said, still reaching out to me.

I ran to the other side of the kitchen island. "Where's Mother?"

Dad walked over to the sink to wash his hands. "You're a brave soul. She is wondering what in the world you are up to. I'm wondering the same, but her curiosity is exceptionally piqued since she got word you went to see Emma. Are you ready to talk to her?"

"Do I have a choice?"

"There's always a choice."

"Yes, to deal with or to delay. I'm too busy to delay."

"Do you want to practice on me?"

I gave him a hug. "You would not be practice for what I'm about to face. You wouldn't even be a warmup. Just wish me luck."

"Good luck," he said, hugging me back and pointing upstairs.

I slowly climbed the stairs, wishing I was in one of those magical children's novels, like *The Lion, the Witch and the Wardrobe,* and that my stairs would lead me to an enchanted forest where I would be crowned the queen of something. The queen of anything. I would settle for queen of the Dukes at this point, spitball and all.

Her door was shut. I turned to glance into my room before knocking and noticed that there was stuff all over my bed. It was like a Kate Spade store. There were four Kate Spade handbags, ten pairs of shoes, even some that looked like flip-flops. There was an entire travel ensemble, with a wheeled carry-on and makeup cases. There was an executive ensemble, with what looked like a new satchel and a Day-Timer, with a coordinating wallet and key ring. I couldn't help but smile. I also couldn't help but wonder how long it must have been since I had told my mother I appreciated something about her. This overkill was evidence that it had been a very long time. I was glad I'd seen all this before I entered her room.

Her door opened just as I was about to knock. She looked beautiful, as always. She was wearing a pale blue silk Christian Dior robe, with a nightgown of the same color peeking out at the top. She had on her one-and-a-half-inch heeled bedroom shoes and stood exquisitely finished in full makeup and surprisingly subtle accessories.

"Hello, darling! When did you get home?" She opened the door wider.

"Just a few minutes ago," I told her, coming into this room that held so many memories. During our at-home years, Thomas and I would always come up to Mother and Dad's room at night, sit in their sitting room in front of the fireplace, and talk about our days. Mother would read to us while Dad read his own book. Then we would watch a television show, pray, and they would tuck us in.

"Mother, I love all the stuff in there on my bed. That was very thoughtful. I even saw a couple pairs of flip-flops," I said, smiling at her and truly meaning it, not that I'd fight anything that worked.

She just beamed. "I'm glad you do. I thought it might help you with your new job. And if you have a lot of traveling to do, well, then you'll have some things for that as well."

I put my arm around her and led her to the chairs that we hadn't sat in together for so long. "I was going to take you for a walk outside. But since you already have your gown on, why don't we just sit here," I said, motioning for her to sit down in her chair. I sat across from her in Dad's well-worn chair.

She gestured to the closet. "Well, I could get dressed and we could walk down past the cemetery again."

"No, I really think this will be more comfortable, and I'm not really in the mood for being that close to dead people. And we haven't sat in here together for a long time. This will be a nice change of pace for us."

"Savannah, I declare, you sound like you've grown into a woman," she said as she perched her feet daintily atop her ottoman and wrapped her robe around her legs. "I remember how you and I used to cuddle in this chair every night. You would tell me the greatest made-up stories. One of my favorites was how you had written the president of McDonald's asking him to boycott the entire city of Savannah until he put a McDonald's downtown next to your father's store," she said, laughing.

"Mother, that wasn't a story. I did write him."

"Savannah, you did not!" she said, laughing even louder. "How many times have you written them?"

"Well, in total, about twenty-five. Some were to report poorly maintained Coke machines, others were to report poor carbonation, and my last was a letter of special thanks," I told her, not revealing it was for the machine they let my dad put in his store.

"What did you write to thank them for?"

"Just to tell them I appreciated their willingness to meet the needs of young children." She would think I was talking about the Ronald McDonald house.

"Savannah, you are like no child I've ever met. You're beautiful, yet not snooty. A trait you got from me, I might add," she said in absolute seriousness.

"Mother, I really need to talk to you about something important."

"Yes, I know you do. You have for a while. I figure it has something to do with beauty pageants. At first I thought you might be telling the stories of past queens. However, I figured out that wasn't it or you would have wanted to interview me and not Emma. Then, I figured you must have found something intriguing, or someone intriguing, who spiked your interest."

"Yes, I have."

"And since I thought I had revealed about everything possible to be known regarding the world of pageants, I knew I would just have to wait for you to tell me yourself. So, Savannah, what has prompted your sudden interest in pageants?" At that moment she looked so vulnerable, so delicate, so . . . my mother, so the last person in the world that I would ever want to hurt. And she was Jake's wife, and Jake's rare wrath caused me far greater concern than this woman facing me. So I proceeded gently.

"Mother, the last thing I would ever want to do is hurt you. And please know that I don't even know all the facts yet. There might not be a story here at all," I said.

"Well, tell me, and we'll see."

"Well, you need to know first that the story came to me. I didn't seek it out. And for that reason alone, it seemed necessary to pursue it. I hope you'll understand when I tell you what I know. But I hope you'll understand even more what I think."

"I trust you, Savannah."

I began with the day I had first walked into Katherine's store and finished with the events of the weekend, leaving out a few of my questionable activities. For almost two hours, Vicky did nothing but listen intently and nod her head when it was appropriate. She never asked a question, and for the majority of the time her head just rested on her hands as she watched every word come out of my mouth. When I was finished, she leaned back in her chair, rested her head, and closed her eyes.

"Are you going to say anything?"

"Well, first I'm going to say that that was a very long story, and you need to learn to go easy on the details."

"I'll work on that."

"Second, I'm going to tell you that truth is more important than anything. Your father and I have taught you that from the beginning. If there is truth here and you find it, then you should rightly reveal it. My only request is that you make sure you know the truth, that you don't reveal speculations. People have been ruined by speculation."

"I wouldn't want to ruin anyone."

"Savannah, if all the speculation that was said about me was believed, I would probably be locked up in a cell with former beauty pageant queens forced to watch reruns of *Miss Congeniality* all day. But I know what is true about me, and so do the people I love. So, make sure you never contribute to faleshoods about others. Those are the values we raised you by, Savannah. I don't expect you to act any other way."

"Nor would I want to."

She leaned in to make her point clear. "I know on Wednesday, whatever is in the paper will be the truth that you found. And I know that if it leads to speculation about me and how I won, or if I should have won, I will still know what is true and so will my family. All I ask for is excellence, and that's all you've ever given. I trust you, young woman. I trust you because I know you."

"Thank you, Mother."

"You're welcome. And I know that inside of you is a continual struggle to do what is right, especially if there is the possibility you might hurt someone. What is right is always right. The cost doesn't change that. And I will be just as proud of you no matter what you decide, because I know you'll do the right thing. You always have. Now, it's late, my mind's taxed, and I need some rest. If you need any help, let me know." With that she got up, walked over to me and kissed me on my head, and made her way to the bathroom to remove her face.

I rose in a stupor. I had expected flash and fireworks. I had expected screaming fits and tears. I had expected drama. But I got a lady. A gentle, understanding lady. A woman who at that moment cared more about my doing what was right than the conflict, speculation, or questions about her that it would cause. That was the depth of this woman's love for me.

Since tomorrow was my first day working a "real job," as they call it, I needed to make sure I had myself fully prepared to enter the world of the employed. I'd held down plenty of jobs before, but this was different. This wasn't one of those college standbys where I could call in at the last minute if I had a stomachache, boyfriend matter, or just felt more like taking in a movie. This one had designated sick time, vacation leave, working hours, and an actual desk I would have to sit behind. The thought of all of it began to make me extremely nervous.

I had really thought that I would spend my years strolling through parks, sitting in diners, carrying my laptop around with me, and documenting the life that passed by. My life would be devoted to developing characters and enlightening imaginations, with little structure and unlimited lunches with friends, being my own boss and creating my own schedule. In short, my life would be like Paige's.

Until now, these newly defined rules for living had been lost on me. Everything had been such a whirlwind since I had pulled the car up in front of my "Welcome Home" banner, that I hadn't thoroughly explored the concept of having a real job. Had I, I might not have shown up at all. Needing to redirect my energies, I focused on what I was going to wear. Vicky had provided me with substantial options.

I located a light-gray pair of silk pants with a nice line. I decided to pair them with a pale-pink cotton sweater and gray open-toed shoes.

The outfit wasn't truly me, but I wasn't going to be truly me until I could relocate my office to a front table in Jake's Coffeehouse. Looking out over Bay Street would be nice, but I would much prefer the view at the shop. As good as I was at the art of persuasion, I imagined I could negotiate that by the end of the first month. The possibility gave me added energy.

There I stood, staring at all those shoes and handbags, when this overwhelming feeling urged me to try it all on. For me this was strangely odd. I'm not the kind of person who cares about fashion. As long as an item remotely fits, remotely matches, remotely works, I'm remotely happy. I'm not obsessive about outerwear. I like to look nice, neat, clean, all of those things. But let's just say I've never left a store wearing my new shoes. I'm the kind of person that could bring home a pair of new shoes, throw them in the back of the closet, and forget they were there until I stumbled upon them searching for an old pair of flip-flops. So, this feeling, this need, this momentary weirdness, almost frightened me.

Still, I reached into the first box and pulled out a pair of shoes that certainly were from another time. They were espadrilles. There were a couple pairs of different-colored tennis shoes, and two beautiful pair of slip-on open-toed sandals with a slight heel. One was in camel and the other in black. These would go with anything. Though I wasn't a big heel wearer, these were so attractive I decided to slip my foot in one, then the other. Staring at my feet in the mirror, they looked slimmer, older, more refined. They didn't look like mine.

At that moment I was posing. I, Savannah Phillips, was striking a pose. My right foot went in front of my left, in kind of perpendicular form. It was a beauty pageant stance. I was metamorphosing! Then, I grabbed a handbag and slung it over my shoulder. Before I knew it, I was prancing toward the mirror, striking a pose and turning back, flinging myself around so my hair would whip around my face. It was the whipping action that did it. I whipped a tad too fast and about broke my neck. The fall was slow and methodical, but the results extremely fascinating.

Then I caught a really good look at myself in the mirror. There I was—rear in the air, one shoe off, the strap of a purse hanging around my neck, and my hair so whipped my face was invisible. The sight of myself and pathetic genes caused me to laugh so hard I fell over in the floor. "So much for my attempts at striking a pose," I said out loud.

Collecting myself, I turned my attention to Vicky's executive ensemble purchases, I picked up the Day-Timer. It was a little black number, fastened with a silver clasp. I transferred all my numbers into it and decided to record my upcoming activities. Monday, May 5, 2002, first day of work 8:00 a.m., lunch with Paige at Clary's 12:00 p.m., Tuesday, May 6, first article due! Now, I was ready: an outfit, matching shoes, a Day-Timer . . . absolutely no story.

I laid my outfit across the chair by the window to iron in the morning, picked up a gray purse and matching wallet and laid it by my outfit, then placed my newly organized organizer inside my purse. Then I crawled into bed; but feeling the need to say my prayers kneeling tonight, crawled back out. "Lord, I'm not sure what I'm about to embark on tomorrow. I'm not even sure if I've been chasing the right story, but help me know. Somehow, please help me know." I thanked Him for the day and even the new shoes with the heels. I got back into bed, and somewhere between thoughts of Amber's cockamamie stories, Emma's nappy hair, and Vicky's continual surprises, I fell asleep.

CHAPTER TWENTY-FOUR

A t five a.m., only Duke had perked. The sun wasn't ready, and I was too nervous.

I jogged and tilled and rummaged through my thoughts. My CD of the week was by CeCe Winans. My first lap was consumed with Mrs. Harvard, my first meeting with Katherine, Emma's first appearance at her door, and the mean old lady who wanted to make jokes with my name. I considered Gregory's question of whether this was a human-interest story at all.

As my thoughts grew more frustrating, I decided I needed one more lap around the park. This lap was for tilling and not thinking. Duke looked at me as if he would just as soon go back home, but I encouraged him to give it one more shot. After the pain in my right side began and the half-dead dog next to me stopped cold, we headed toward home.

Knowing I had to face work eventually, I showered, ironed, dressed, and made my way to the kitchen for something to nourish me until lunch. Mother was already downstairs. She had made a tremendous breakfast: bacon, eggs, homemade biscuits, cheese grits, and homemade hash-brown potatoes. At that moment, Victoria needed to be kissed. I was most willing to oblige.

"Thank you. Thank you! Thank you!" I said, planting a big one on her cheek.

"You're welcome," she said, laughing. "I knew you would be excited and would need some extra energy."

"You were so right!" I said, stuffing a piece of bacon in my mouth as I fixed my plate and sat down.

Mother leaned across the counter and watched me devour my food. "Savannah, you need to quit chomping like that. You have to make a good impression with these people, so if you are going to eat in front of them, you need to get ahold of yourself."

"I'm sorthwy," I said with my mouth full, then swallowed a mouthful of juice. "I'm just so nervous."

"You're going to do great. You just give them your best story and put your personality in it, and you'll do great," she said, standing back up and turning around to put the dirty dishes in the dishwasher.

"Do you have any more thoughts on your story?"

"No, ma'am. I'm just going to see what I find out today. I hope Mr. Cummings will call me, give me some more information, but who knows. I hope I haven't spent the last four days chasing a ridiculous story for no reason. If I have, then, we'll just have to pull out my handy-dandy 'Painting with Paige' article from sophomore year creative-writing class. I figure I'm creative enough to give even that a different twist."

She still had her back to me, but I could see she was laughing. "I'm sure you can."

I got up and headed for the door. "I love you, Mother. Have a great day."

"I love you too, darling. And I know you'll do a great job. I like your shoes."

"I do too."

"I wish you would have worn your hair down. You look so

much more ladylike with it down. Don't you want some jewelry? I have a great silver bauble necklace that would accentuate your gray pants perfectly. I even have a gray straw hat, if you would like that." I headed for a Coke.

When I entered the coffeehouse, everyone paused and then stared at me with their mouths hanging open.

"I know, I know, I look like a real person," I said in mock disgust, walking straight for the Coke machine. I picked up a glass that was far too small. "Please tell me you have something bigger than this. I am requiring extreme caffeine." Mervine smiled and headed into the stockroom behind Dad's office. She came out holding one of the biggest cups I'd ever seen.

She set it down beside me, patted me on the back, and simply said, "Enjoy, honey."

I was almost startled. In thirteen years, I had probably heard her speak no more than once per year.

"Savannah, what time do you have to be at your new job?" Louise asked.

"Well, I'm getting there a little early. I want to figure out where everything is and make a good impression," I said, filling up my thirty-two-ouncer.

"Well, you look wonderful, darling," Dad said, coming over to give me a kiss on the cheek.

Taking a long drink of my Coke, I took a breather to say, "Well, I'm not sure what newspaper people are supposed to look like, but this is my best shot at acting like I do."

Then as if a dam had burst, Mervine spoke. "Well, I think you look like a princess, Savannah. You're going to blow the roof off that paper, and I am so looking forward to reading your first article. You're going to set this city on its ear." By this time she had more motions than a tent-revival preacher on a Saturday night.

"And it's about time we had some fresh faces and new life around here. I think that editor up there needs some new perspectives, and I believe you're just the kind of person to give it to him. I also believe these young people with their pierced parts need to see a young and refined lady. Sure you have a little edge, but a little edge never hurt anybody. It's about time someone your age left a mark on their own culture. Who knows, us old people might even learn something ourselves." Then she stopped talking, returned to the counter, and simply smiled at us.

"I told you she talked," Louise said. "Doesn't even take a breath either. That's what she does from the time she wakes up. Talk, talk, talk. Talks to her kids' pictures, talks to the TV, my word, even talks to the Braves on TV." And she walked to the front of the store just shaking her head.

Mervine grinned from ear to ear. Didn't say another word, just grinned as she followed Louise. Dad and I just stared at each other, dumbfounded. "I have never . . ." was all I could say.

"I have never myself," Dad agreed, still looking through the door that led to the front of the store. "In all these years, that woman hasn't so much as asked what time it was. You might better watch out today, Savannah. I believe a new day has come."

"Well, it's calling my name. I've got to run. Wish me luck!" I did look back one more time, just to make sure that whole occurrence hadn't been a brief apparition. But when my eyes revealed Dad still leaning against the counter staring in the direction of Mervine and Louise, I knew it was true. Mervine had spoken.

There was little activity at seven at the *Savannah Chronicle*. People were beginning to mill about, but only a few. I drove to the back of the building and parked my car in what appeared to be the newspaper's parking lot.

Gathering myself and my new backpack, which I had settled on this morning instead of the purse, I decided to leave my Coke in the car and feel everyone out first. Who knew if they even allowed drinks inside? I wanted to fit in the best I could for the girl whose name had appeared in the paper more times than the mayor's.

I walked through the front door and at first glance saw no one at the front desk. Then a bright lady with a determined step headed in my direction.

"You look new," she said as she came around the corner with her hands full of papers. She smiled at my expression.

"So much for hiding my real feelings," I told her, smiling back at her.

"Well, my name is Doris, Doris Berry. I've worked here at this paper for over fifty-five years. Yes, ma'am, fifty-five years. I started when I was eighteen, right after high-school graduation." She looked good for seventy-three. Her hair was unashamedly silver and she wore little makeup. Only her hands told her age. I imagined this woman had lived well and enjoyed life. And the way she talked about this place caused me to believe she ran the ship tighter than Mr. Hicks.

I tried awkwardly to shake one of her hands, but they were encumbered with the files she was carrying. "Nice to meet you, Ms. Berry. I'm Savannah, Savannah Phillips."

"Well, it's Doris, and I know exactly who you are. Yes, ma'am, I know exactly who you are. You look like both your father and your mother. You have her nose and mouth and his everything else. Time will tell whose personality you have," she said with a wink. "Follow me and I'll show you to your desk." I followed her after first offering to help her carry her load. She refused. I didn't want to make her feel bad, so I never told her I had already seen my office.

We passed a small waiting area and the payment desk. "This is your corner," she said, leading me to a corner cubicle in the very back of the first floor—no windows, no fraction of a view of the outside world, nothing to see but gray, fabric-covered, Styrofoam-like walls all around me. Perched atop the desk was a computer and a desk calendar. Underneath the drab gray desk was a drab gray wastebasket. I guess the shock of my surroundings must have registered on my face. "Is something wrong?"

"Well, kind of," I said, hoping not to embarrass her. "I'm replacing Gloria. And I was here Saturday to do some work, and I've already seen my office upstairs, next to Mr. Hicks."

I could tell that she was trying to stifle a grin. "Oh, well, I see, and I hate to tell you this, but you have to work your way to that office, Savannah. Geraldine O'Malley, who has been here for twenty years and runs our classified section, is getting that office. This," she said, pointing to our dreary surroundings, "well, this, my dear, is your office."

"Oh," I said, mortified. "That was pretty presumptuous of me, wasn't it?" I was thankful no one else was around.

"It's totally understandable. And it will be our little secret," Doris whispered. I could tell by her kind smile she meant it, and my gratefulness increased. "So, Savannah, this is the world of newspapers. It's fast and furious with little glamour and long hours. Pretty soon you'll forget you can't see the world outside that you're writing about in here."

"Is it always this messy?" I asked, referring to the papers strewn about in every cubicle and corner.

"It's a newspaper, Savannah. Paper is a part of our name."

"After fifty-five years, haven't you gotten tired of staring at gray partitions?" I asked her as I stared aimlessly at the sea of blandness in front of me and the chaos that surrounded me.

"Oh, Savannah," she said, laughing. "After fifty-five years, you get an office on the third floor, surrounded with windows and looking out over Bay Street. Trust me, you'll adjust. You'll eventually adjust." Then she added, "Just an FYI: Most people have laptops today, if you know what I mean. Work is where you make it. Just get acclimated here, then you can work wherever you need to. The only requirement is that your work gets done."

I knew immediately I was going to like her. "Come on," she continued. "Let me drop these papers off and I'll give you the tour.

It doesn't get hopping around here until around eight thirty." She dropped the papers off on a desk settled even deeper in the monochrome dimness. It was a glassed-in office, however, with a window and a view of the alley. Doris informed me that this office belonged to the editor of the news division, Don Jefferson. Then she informed me that she was the head of advertising.

"No wonder you know me so well."

"Your mother has about kept this paper in business," she said laughing.

"My mother has about kept this city in business."

"That she has, my dear, that she has."

"Does everyone know that Victoria's daughter is coming to work here?"

"I'm afraid so. But they expect you to arrive in rhinestones, tiara, and four-inch heels, shouting orders and redecorating, so they're liable to be disappointed," she said, scanning my outfit.

"This will probably be the first time that I'm glad I've disappointed someone."

"I'm with you there, honey, I'm with you there. So let me show you where we eat around here," she said, going to the third floor. "This is our quaint break room." *Quaint* wasn't quite the word. It was old and tired, but it had a Coke machine, snack machine, and refrigerator. "Most people eat out," she said matter-of-factly. "These are the restrooms for this floor. I'll show you the others as we go," she said, pointing out the two doors next to the break room. "These are the major points. Printing has all of the fourth floor. Advertising and the main offices take up the third floor. Business, life and living, and classifieds take up the second floor. And the first floor is the news department, which handles everything from national to local. You are governed by Mr. Hicks, however. He edits all local articles himself. He was really fond of Gloria, Savannah. I'm honestly shocked that he hired anyone for that position at all. How did you do it anyway?" she asked, stopping to face me.

"The story hasn't gotten around?"

"No. No one is quite sure how you did it. Now, there has been a lot of speculation: new advertising from your mother, threats, bribery, and the like. But no one really believes any of that. And they sure won't when they meet you. So how did you do it?"

"That will be Mr. Hicks's story to tell," I said with a raised right eyebrow.

"You're good, Savannah. You're really good."

I stared at a computer I had never used, with the word IBM written across it. I had been a Mac girl since I learned how to use the computer in middle school. With each new one that came out, I would forgo anything—clothes, trips, food, anything but Coke—to get the next one available. My current models were the new iBook laptop and an iMac Cube, graduation gifts. That day I wished I had used an IBM at least once. If all else failed, though, the iBook was in my backpack.

After ten minutes of searching, I found the turn-on switch at the back of the computer. The screen popped up. Where was my AppleWorks, my Quark, my intimate friends? I decided to wait until someone came to show me how to use it, lest I begin my first day by melting down the mainframe. Hey, Mervine had spoken today; anything was possible.

Around eight o'clock, more people began to enter. I decided to unload my backpack and try to make this square, lusterless closet homey. I took out my pens, notebooks, pencils, Post-its, and my Day-Timer. Not that I had anything in the Day-Timer except my lunch plans, but no one else had to know that. By eight thirty the place was coming alive with chatter and people. I tried to look like I was working hard. Trying to write notes on my Emma conversation was virtually impossible, because it was so one-sided there wasn't much to tell.

People were busy even as they walked through the door, so

busy in fact that no one even noticed me. About eight forty-five, however, footsteps headed toward my desk. I heard them before I saw them—flip-flops. The flip-flops came around the corner; my eyes moved upward to the face of their owner. Curly Locks with the blue bike was standing in front of me. And to top it off, he held a cup of coffee in his hand. It was a white cup with that brown wrapper around the center. Coffee from that other place.

His eyes spotted me, registering shock at first before being over-taken by a wide, chafing little grin. "My, my, my. If it isn't the girl without a name. But now I know your name. Because we've all been wondering when Victoria's daughter was going to get here." As if my new cell wasn't enough, Curly Locks was going to be my cell mate.

Forget not having a story; being Victoria's daughter would be my greatest challenge in this new job. I would face it head-on. I would face it like Savannah. And I would begin today with the man in flip-flops.

"Actually, the name is Savannah," I said, rising to face him eye to eye. Well, eye to chest, but that's neither here nor there. I reached out my hand to shake his. He looked at me with a half-cocked smile and returned the gesture.

"Hi. Joshua, Joshua North. You're not quite what we expected," he said with that same annoying grin as he eyed my attire and footwear.

"Well, what did *we* expect, exactly?"

Not realizing he would be forced to begin his day describing his prejudices, he looked a smidgen embarrassed. "Oh, it's nothing. It's all in good fun. We're just glad you're here. I sit across from you. Let me know if you need anything. I know this is probably a dif-ferent world from the one you're used to. You know, where people do everything for you. You'll have to get your own coffee, I'm afraid," he said, turning around and heading to his desk.

I could have let it go, probably even should have. I could have let him sit his little wrinkled khakis down and sip his little brown-wrapped coffee and prop his feet up with that smirk across his face. I should have. But I didn't. I did, however, let him get good and situated, let him think for one brief moment he had left me speechless.

Then I rounded the corner of his cubicle.

"I did think about bringing my mother to work with me today. You know, to keep the *mean* people away," I said in mock fear. He spun in his chair to face me. "But then I remembered that I've never asked my mother for anything. In fact, I started my first job when I was fifteen and was elected president of my high-school student body—without using any of my mother's food or money to bribe the fellow students. I was the president of my college student body as well, and I didn't even need her to campaign for me. Then, lo and behold, I went off and won a publishing contract," I finished, leaving out the fact that she was totally responsible for that.

He leaned back in his chair as if to enjoy the show, which irritated me all the more. "Then I made a decision all by myself. Can you imagine that?" I said, slapping him on the shoulder and nearly knocking him out of his chair. "I made a decision and I decided to forgo book advances and fame and fortune to come here, to work beside you, to write stories that would influence the hearts of this city. I did it all without my mother's influence, letter of recommendation, or coercion. Instead, I decided those values she instilled in me would work fine on their own. And you know what? They did. Because here I am. Right beside you! Aren't you excited?"

"Extremely," he replied.

"And no pomp or circumstance, just me, all alone. Why? Because I'm totally capable on my own. Now for you, my new friend, the name is Savannah, not 'Victoria's daughter.' I get my own Cokes because, for your information, I don't even like coffee, and if I did, it would be from my father's coffee shop. If you have any more questions, remarks, or unsolicited comments, restrain yourself. I'll contact you when I have the time to discuss them." With that, I turned on my Kate Spade heels and headed back to my Styrofoam world.

CHAPTER TWENTY-FIVE

I stared at the ringing apparatus on my desk. Was I supposed to just say, "Hello"? Was I to introduce myself? Was I even supposed to answer it at all? After the fourth ring, the voice that belonged to the flip-flops came from the other cubicle. "You might want to answer that."

I picked the phone up as if it might be an explosive and said, "Savannah Phillips."

"Hey, Savannah. This is Marla at the front desk. I know we haven't met yet, but we'll get to know each other soon. But right now, I need to tell you that there's a man on the phone for you. I'll transfer him."

"A man, well, OK . . . how do you transfer him exactly?"

"Well, you just hang up the phone. Your phone will ring again, and when it does, you answer it just the way you did a minute ago and he'll be on the other end. OK?"

"OK," I said, hanging up the phone. I waited for about three seconds, and the phone rang again. I answered the same way, adding a hello.

"Yes, Savannah. This is Richard Cummings."

I froze. I had hoped he might call. But I had never considered what I'd say or how I'd say it, let alone what he might say in return. I didn't even know where to begin, so I just started with the first thing that came to mind. "Yes, Mr. Cummings. I didn't know if I would hear from you or not."

"Well, I am still appalled at your allegations and your intrusion. I wanted to catch you first thing this morning to let you know how out of line you were. You are extremely nosy, but you seem like you try real hard," he said with mock appreciation. "Now, past things are past things, none of which needs stirring up around here. You need to let things that have been laid to rest, simply rest. Nothing but trouble will come from your accusations." His anger had been giving way to weariness. "I'm asking you to simply let this be."

"I don't think it needs to just be, Mr. Cummings."

"Well, this thing was settled years ago. And if you try to stir up things now, we will have some trouble to deal with."

"Are you threatening me?"

He chuckled at that. "My dear girl, I'm too old to threaten people. I'm a successful, established businessman in a reputable community. My family and I are part of the fabric of this city, and to have a child from Savannah make such allegations against us is merely more than an annoyance. As for you, however, well, it would probably not be the wisest move."

"Well, I've learned that when people are duped by a person they put great faith in, they usually appreciate the knowledge of such things in the long run."

"I don't believe anything my family has done has 'duped' any-one. But I do believe your meddling will ultimately contribute to the well-being of no one," he said, his even voice full of hidden meaning.

"Are you saying that the things you have done have not had long-term ramifications on others' lives?"

"I didn't say I had done anything. But I do believe that any decision made by beauty pageant judges affects a young lady's life for one year. That's all. It's just one year out of her life. So don't waste your time on temporal things, my dear. Go write stories on things that really matter to people. That's all I have to say to you."

I jumped in before he could hang up. "Let me remind you of someone this story really matters to, Mr. Cummings. Her name is Emma. And your son's decision, your son's greedy choice, precipitated by years of your own greedy choices, have caused her to spend the last six years regarding herself as worthless. Did her own choices have something to do with that? Yes. Were your son's decisions the catalyst? I believe they were. Are you innocent? I don't think so. He followed in your footsteps, made the same choices you made for others countless times before. Besides the fact that you dictate destinies, you are a greedy man."

"Don't talk about what you don't know."

"Oh, I know. You chose a dollar over a life. You, Mr. Cummings, are the one who has let the temporal affect your future. You let one moment of decision, one pivotal moment of choice, determine that your life would be not one of character, but of compromise."

"You're treading on dangerous ground, little girl."

"Maybe so, Mr. Cummings. But you should be old and wise by now. Instead, you've missed what really matters. You've missed the opportunity to be a man of character producing children of character."

And with that, I heard a click from the other end of the line.

The bed-head from next door peeked around the corner and said with a quirky smile, "Do you talk to everyone in condescending composition form?"

I sat my elbows on the corner of my desk and laid my head in my hands. "No. No, I'm in rare form today. I'm sorry about earlier. Not a good way to get started," I said, looking up into his face.

His smirk softened. "Well, it was deserved, considering my smart-aleck comment. How 'bout we try again?" He stretched out his hand. "Hello, my name is Joshua, Joshua North."

I shook his hand as confidently as I could, trying not to act as defeated as I felt. "Hello, Joshua, I'm Savannah Phillips. Nice to meet you."

"Nice to meet you as well, Ms. Phillips. Do you need any help?" he asked, kneeling down beside my chair.

"Yes, I need a story. Because my first one just went bye-bye," I said, putting my head back into my hands.

"It can't be that bad. Maybe you just need to pursue it from another angle."

"The only angle I have not pursued would involve breaking into a bank or using my influence with Judge Hoddicks to retrieve information that really wouldn't produce a public-interest story. Except for maybe the *Star.*" I tried to laugh but proved totally unable.

"Well, if it's any consolation, my first story was a total disaster. I was writing about a meeting of the Savannah Chamber of Commerce and called your mother for some background. Then I referred to her in the article as "Vicky Phillips." It passed the editor, but I got a phone call at home at around six a.m. from one irate Vicky Phillips. It was pretty horrendous, and now I think your mother refers to me as 'the young man with deplorable research skills.'" He grinned.

"You know how to make a first impression," I said, looking at him and laughing as well. "If you only knew how much my mother detests being called Vicky. That's like calling Queen Elizabeth 'Beth.' Some things are just forbidden."

"Well, your father must not have minded, because he called me and told me he thought I did a good job for my first story."

"So you've already met my parents."

"Well, I wish I would have just been introduced to them as a normal person, but most around here would say I got what I deserved, and that I was anything but normal," he said, standing back up, as if he had revealed enough of himself.

I stood up too, feeling as if I needed a good stretch, and it wasn't much past nine o'clock. "Well, don't worry, by the time everyone here gets to know me, you and I will be in good company. Shoot, by the time my first article comes out, Vicky will probably be calling *me* a young lady with deplorable research skills. Trust me, she is no respecter of persons." Even as I said it, I wondered if that was true, considering her surprising response to news of my story the previous evening.

"Well, hang in there. It really will get better. You'll figure out your story. You'll write it, and everyone will love it. By what I hear, this town is crazy about you anyway. So, just do whatever it is that you've done for the last fifteen or twenty years, and I'm sure you'll be just fine. I have to get back to work, or whatever it is they have me doing around here. I think I'm covering the school board meeting this morning at ten."

"No more Chamber of Commerce meetings?"

"Oh, no! I got taken off of that beat immediately. Hey, maybe you can cover them," he said with that same sarcastic smirk.

"Or not!" I said with my right eyebrow raised.

"How did you do that?" he asked, trying to raise his own eyebrow and putting his face through hilarious contortions instead.

"Just one of those God-given talents. I have a few, you know. Despite my inability to communicate, there are a few things I can do."

"Well, that is too weird. I'm going to have to see that again sometime."

"I'm sure you will!"

"Well, I'll see you later. Don't work too hard."

"How can I? I still haven't figured out what I'm working on. Maybe I'll just sit here and decide which of my family members has secrets interesting enough to reveal to the world."

"That shouldn't be a hard decision," he said picking up his notepad, pen, and tape recorder. As he walked toward the door, he said, "See you later," and gave me a backward wave as the beautiful sound of flip-flops carried him away.

The latter part of the morning brought a sweet, timid girl named Margaret to my desk to give me an overview of my computer. She showed me all of its ins and outs and rehearsed me on the interoffice linkup and my deadlines for copy. We finished up around noon, and her parting words sent shivers up my spine. "You need to have your first article to Mr. Hicks for editing by two tomorrow. All stories will go to press by five. You're lucky, Savannah; two is his latest editing slot. He always gave it to Gloria. I didn't figure he would give it to you, but he hasn't said to change it." She smiled a sweet and gentle smile. "You'll do great here. Don't let them bother you about your mother, either. She's one of the nicest ladies I've ever met."

"When did you meet my mother?" I asked, afraid to know the answer.

Margaret's shyness evaporated. "Oh, one afternoon, right after I moved here, I decided to ride one of the trolleys and take a tour to learn the history of Savannah."

"A trolley tour, huh?"

"Yeah, little did I know, but I was sitting right by your mother. She was dressed in a pink linen dress, with a big straw hat and matching lipstick, fingernail polish, and pale pink shoes. She was the prettiest thing I ever did see, and I just couldn't quit staring at her. I didn't even hear the tour guide for staring at your mother. Finally, she told me who she was and what she was doing, but she made me promise to keep it a secret."

"I'm sure that wasn't hard."

"Actually, you're the first person I've told. Anyway, I shared a little bit about myself, and she took me to lunch and got me this job. So, any time anyone says anything about her, I just tell them to hush up. I say, 'You don't know anything about Miss Victoria, and you surely shouldn't be talking about things you don't know.' That hushes them for a while, and then, well, you know how people can be. But I just love your mother, and I'm sure I'll love you too."

"Well, thank you, Margaret. You've been a wonderful help, and I'm sure we'll get along great. Is there a set time that I can go to lunch?"

"Oh, people go whenever. Mr. Hicks just wants the work done right and on time. The rest is up to you. Well, have a great day. I hope I haven't talked your ear off," she said, lowering her head as if she was all of a sudden embarrassed at her candor.

"No, it was wonderful. Thank you for sharing the story about my mother."

"She really is a wonderful lady. Now, take care, you hear. And call me for anything," she said as she turned to leave.

"I'm sure I will." And I knew I would.

CHAPTER TWENTY-SIX

My breakfast Coke had settled itself in the most uncomfortable of ways. I headed down the hall to the restrooms and turned right at the first corridor, certain that this was where they were. Yet no friendly stick figures with skirts or slacks beckoned me. By the time I had rounded the fifth corridor, I was welcomed to the world of mayhem. It was the sports department. People were just loud in there. They talked loud and called each other by sport names: "Champ," "Sport," "Superstar." Televisions blared all around with golf, tennis, baseball, even reruns of last year's football games.

Now, far be it from me to be critical, but who in the world wants to watch a sporting event when you already know the outcome? Like me, these sportswriters had their own cubicle world, but theirs was red and white, the color of the Georgia Bulldogs. Seemed only fitting. There were a few black ones thrown in to add a flair of the Falcons. Yet, for all their excitement, they were none too observant of the fact that I was about to have to cross my legs and plop down on the floor right in the midst of them unless someone delivered me. Finally, a friendly soul took note. "You look lost."

"Desperately."

"Where were you headed?"

"The r-e-s-t-r-o-o-m."

"Ooh, that bad huh?"

"Uh-huh."

"Right down the hall, then take the first left."

I nodded in appreciation. As I made my way down the hall, it opened back to the place where I had begun, and there before me was a lovely left turn I should have taken instead of the right one I chose. I kept walking, hoping no one would notice that I had made a complete circle of the first floor.

My cell phone rang as soon as I put the key in the ignition. Mother's work number came up on the caller ID.

"Hello."

"Hello, darling. I hope you're not too busy."

"No. I'm actually just leaving to meet Paige at Clary's for lunch. What are you doing?"

"Oh, I'm just heading out to a meeting and wanted to see how your first day is going."

"Well, wonderful except for the fact that I'm not sure what to write," I said flatly.

"Why not? Have you not heard from Mr. Cummings?"

"Actually, I have. He called me this morning as soon as I sat down at my desk. He let me know in no uncertain terms that I really didn't want to pursue this story any further." I sighed. "I could call Gregory and we could dig a little more, but this whole thing is just out of my league. Part of me thinks I've missed the whole thing, wasted people's time, pursued the wrong story. I don't know. I should probably be writing books. I could ruin Gloria's legacy if I don't do a good job on this first piece. I just wanted it to be so perfect."

"Savannah Phillips, I have to say, I am ashamed of you at this very moment. You have said nothing but negative things since you started this job. You can do this. You will do it, and you will do it well. You will not let some old coot threaten you, and you surely won't embarrass me or Gloria by the article you write. But you will quit this pity party and write your story. Now, don't you say another negative thing, or your very words are going to trap you. Go, kick butt, and take some names."

"I know you did not just say, 'kick butt and take names,'" I said, laughing hysterically.

"Isn't that what they say?"

"I don't know who 'they' are, but you should not be saying 'butt.'"

"Well, whatever you need to be doing, start doing it. You are Savannah Phillips, and you are not a negative child. Now quit with all that doom and gloom and get in there with some heart and some life. Do you hear me?"

"Yes, ma'am, I hear you perfectly."

"Good. Now your mother's glad she called you. You must have needed to hear what I had to say. I love you. Will you be home for dinner?"

"I'm glad you called. I love you too. And yes, I plan to be home for dinner, but I might be late, working on this story."

"Well, I'll wait and have dinner around seven, so you can take your time. Now, chin up, young lady."

"Yes, ma'am, chin up," I repeated, laughing. "I'll see you tonight." And with good-byes, she hung up. Margaret was right. She really was a great lady.

By the time I reached Clary's, I had convinced myself I could write a story. Somehow, the pieces would come together, and my story would be what it needed to be and say what needed to be said. Paige was already inside at our usual spot, had ordered our food, and had a Coke waiting on me.

"Thank you, thank you, thank you," I said once I could breathe. My eyes watered from the powerful intake. "How is it possible you arrived before me?"

"I was bored. How are you, stranger? And where are your real clothes?" she asked.

"I found out that I can bring a Coke to my job, wear flip-flops, and work in the park if I want to, as long as my work gets done. You couldn't ask for anything better than that," I said, taking another drink.

"So how totally awesome is your office?"

"Well, it's not exactly an office."

"But you said it had big windows and overlooked Bay Street."

"Actually it has no windows and overlooks the path to the bathroom."

"You've got to be kidding me. You're taking Gloria's place. Do they think you can just work anywhere? Well, you can't, and you should tell them. So what's it like exactly?"

"It's exactly like a cubicle made of gray Styrofoam."

"Oh my stars. You poor pitiful creature. Are you totally depressed? If I had to look at gray all day, I would be totally depressed."

"I'm more worried about what I'm going to write inside those four pitiful, dreary walls."

She rested her elbows on the table and leaned in not to miss a word. "Right. Your first article. Tell me everything."

I tried to sound totally confident. "Well, I don't know exactly. But it's going to deal with beauty queens, a rigged pageant, and all of that."

"Savannah, I knew that a week ago. What is the story going to say?" she asked, looking disappointed.

"Well, I haven't worked it all out yet. But I will have it completed by tomorrow at two, and you can read it Wednesday morning with the rest of the city," I said with a smile.

"You have nothing, do you?"

"No! That is not true! I have a lot of somethings I've yet to combine into a perfect something. Just trust me. It will all come together. I promise."

"I hope you're right!"

"We must be positive, now. I'm sure I'm right."

Helen brought our BLTs and chocolate shakes, Paige caught me up on her weekend, and I told her all about mine. She had already heard about Emma from her mother, who had spent the majority of the weekend with my mother, shopping and working in their gardens. Paige said that Vicky had told Sheila that I was up to something that she had no idea about, but that she was going to find out as soon as I got home. I told Paige how Mother and I had talked, and then an hour was gone. I was not used to lunch on a time frame. But I felt like I needed to toe the line for at least the first month, then I could make everything more flexible.

Heading back to the paper, it dawned on me that Mr. Hicks had yet to visit my flavorless world. He had probably forgotten that I even started today. But I would let him seek me out. There was no need for me to go looking for trouble today.

I returned to my desk and decided to contact each involved party one more time. My first call was to Mrs. Harvard from Atlanta, hoping some twinge of compassion for me might cause her to reassess her reluctance to tell me everything she knew. I left her a brief but pathetic-sounding message on her answering machine, along with every number I knew, including my mother's cell phone. Who knew when she might break. The next call rang only twice before it was picked up by a determined two-year-old.

"Hewo . . ."

"Hello, is Emma there?"

"Hewo."

"Yes, this is Savannah. Is your mother home?"

"Mama go potty."

"Oh, that's nice. So is your mother in the restroom?"

"Potty, potty."

"OK, I got that part. Is your brother or sister there?"

"Hewo."

Finally, the line went dead. I decided I would try one last time to get Katherine to talk.

"Hello," said the voice on the other end of the phone.

"Hello, Katherine, it's Savannah."

"Well, hello, sweet girl. I haven't seen you in way too long. You must be working up a storm. You started your job today, didn't you?"

"Yes, I sure did."

"So, how are things going?"

"Well, to keep it positive, I believe I'll have something to talk about by tomorrow. No one has been willing to reveal anything much so far, and I'm trying to avoid becoming a sleazy undercover journalist."

"I'm glad you have chosen the path of least resistance."

"*Chose* is a harsh word." I paused, hoping she would ask about the pageant the other night.

"So, how was the pageant the other night?" Perhaps my tide was turning.

"Interesting, to say the least. But my mother is a former Miss Georgia United States of America, so I've had to endure them quite often in the past."

"Yes, I knew she was."

"You did?" I asked, feeling as if a door had been opened.

"Yes, that is pretty common knowledge here. Well, I'm sure you'd better get back to work. Was there anything else?"

"No, I was just calling to say hello," I lied. "I'll see you soon." As soon as I laid the receiver down, the phone rang, almost projecting me out of my seat. I looked at the clock in front of me. Three o'clock. I picked up the phone and this time actually said, "Hello."

"Savannah, hey, it's Marla again. Mr. Hicks just called down and would like to see you in his office."

Oh yeah, just the breather I needed. Carbon-monoxide poisoning. "OK, I'll be right there." I hung up the receiver and headed for the back staircase by the elevator. I needed stairs for this. I needed blood-circulating movement, brain-cell-birthing activity to deal with whatever was about to ensue.

After catching my breath, I passed the empty secretary desk and knocked on the half-open door.

"Come in," came the same gruff voice.

I opened the door, trying not to swing too hard. "Hello, Mr. Hicks," I said, reaching out my hand.

"Well, hello, Savannah," he said, shaking my hand in a professional manner. "Savannah, sit down. Uh, please, have a seat," he said, motioning awkwardly to the seat behind me.

"Oh, thank you," I said, taking a seat and trying to act in total control.

He took his own seat and began slowly. "Savannah, how's your first day?"

"Oh, it's been fine, sir. Everyone has been helpful and friendly. I'm really excited to be here," I said, thankful he'd asked a question I could answer.

His hands began shuffling papers around his desk.

"And how's your first story coming?"

"Wonderfully. My article will be on your desk by two tomorrow." Maybe this would be easy after all.

"So what's your piece about?" he asked as he created stacks of what I assumed were other writers' stories.

I hoped my face didn't reflect panic. "Well, I'm still working out the details. I feel that to discuss it now, knowing that things could change, might just confuse things." I examined my need for a manicure.

Mr. Hicks aligned a stack of papers with a brisk tap against the desktop and cleared his throat. "Savannah."

I looked up at him once more. "Yes, sir?"

"I took a great chance in putting you in this position." He looked me square in the eye and delivered this last statement with perfect clarity. "Now, I need you to deliver."

"I know you did, Mr. Hicks, and I promise you that I will." I stood, breathed deeply, and headed for the door. Feeling his eyes still staring at the back of my head, I turned to add, "And I appreciate the opportunity you have given me."

I got back downstairs and had no more than sat down when Curly Locks spoke. "Well, well, she has returned from the third floor alive."

"Did you doubt that I would?"

"I doubted a lot of things, Ms. Phillips. I doubted a lot of things."

"Then I'm glad I'm here to put your troubled mind at ease. I've got to get to work, if you'll excuse me." And I returned to my inanimate, passionless cubicle. Thankfully, he retreated as well.

Three thirty. I decided I should at least start working on something, anything that could be described as a story. I ignored the IBM and fished my Mac out of my backpack. Mr. Hicks would want a hard copy anyway, so it didn't matter what computer it came from. For the next hour and a half I stared at a blank screen. I tried to write something, but there was nothing to write. About five o'clock, Curly Locks made his way to my desk.

"Are you going to just stare at it or actually write something on it?" he asked, leaning against the partition.

"I'm actually going to cut it off and pray that between tonight and tomorrow a miracle occurs," I said, closing it up to pack and take home. I stood up, grabbed my satchel and purse, and waited to walk out the door with Joshua.

"You really can do it, Ms. Phillips. I'm sure that if you can talk like you do you can surely write well enough for somebody to want to read it. You just got to pull it out from your gut."

"You mean more like pull it out of my . . ."

"Savannah! don't you even," he interrupted.

"*But,* I just got to find something worth pulling out."

"It's in there. You've just got to find it."

"Is your name Victoria?" I asked, stopping to stare at him.

"Excuse me?"

"Never mind. Thanks for everything today. I'll see you tomorrow." He started to round the corner. "Joshua?"

"Yes?"

"Why do you call me Ms. Phillips? It is totally annoying."

"I just think it sounds like you. And as long as it's not Victoria's daughter, I think you should be happy."

I threw my hand up at him in a passing motion and headed to my car. I knew Vicky was holding dinner for me, but all I wanted to do was go home, close myself up in my room, and sit on the floor counting my new shoes.

I pulled up to the side of the house and turned off the car. Through my rearview mirror I saw her—Miss Amber Ruby Sapphire headed out of Clary's, flanked by two rather attractive gentlemen, headed toward my house. They were walking down the sidewalk that would cause them to pass right by my car. Doing the only thing I could think of to avoid detection, I hid. I tried my best to cram my five-foot-six frame all the way under my steering column. The last thing in the world I felt like facing was Miss Tape and Spray. I just didn't think I would survive that, not tonight.

Just when I was about to get my head fully under the dash, there was a knocking on the passenger-side door. Knowing who was there, I didn't rush to get up, but I still couldn't avoid banging my head on my steering column. My disheveled head turned to face the opposite window and there she stood, grinning from ear to ear in a key-lime-pie linen pantsuit that would have made Paige hungry. As soon as her eyes met mine, she waved as if she were ten blocks away trying to get my attention. I just rested my head on my steering column, thinking surely she couldn't be for real.

She opened the passenger door and positioned herself firmly in the seat next to me, having lost her suitors somewhere along the way. I didn't have the strength to raise my head, so I just kept it there, firmly planted on the steering wheel. I knew I looked frightful. I didn't care.

"Savannah, you look ghastly. Did you have a bad first day at work?"

I nodded.

"Did you finish your story?"

I shook my head.

"Are you going to be finished in time to do lunch tomorrow?" she asked with a pathetic mousy-sounding voice. I didn't hesitate.

I shook my head again.

"Well, don't you worry. We'll just shoot for Wednesday."

I nodded only to avoid actual conversation.

"You just get your story done and then we'll catch up on everything we need to. I've had such a busy day. I had to handle some things down at the tourism office. Your mother wasn't happy with some of the guides' descriptions of our fair city, so we had to do some rearranging today. Your mother, she runs a tight ship," she said as serious as she could be. "And tonight I have to go help this little girl down on Tybee Island with her talent for the Miss Georgia United States of America Pageant. I'm sure you're wondering why I'm helping another contestant."

I shook my head, but she didn't care.

"She's just pitiful; someone has got to help her. She used to sing. Poor child was tone-deaf. One time she even tried to do sign language with her song. People said she would have scored higher if she would have just signed and nixed the singing altogether. So, I told her she was going to have to change her talent. I tried her on the trumpet, but the sad soul about blew her brains out. I didn't think I would ever find anything she'd actually be good at, but finally I found something."

I allowed my right eyebrow to feign interest.

"I taught her how to play the cymbals. I just put one big cymbal in one hand and one big cymbal in the other. I gave her a tape of the "Star-Spangled Banner," and on about every fifth beat she clangs those cymbals with more enthusiasm than me getting a new dress. I still haven't told her it really isn't a talent, but poor child couldn't do anything else. I know she won't win, but I had to help her find something. But I've seen worse talent win."

I gave her another brief eyebrow raise.

"Yes, I have, I tell ya. It was my second time in Miss Georgia United States of America. The girl that won played the drums. Now, no lady should play the drums. You have to sit there with your legs spread-eagle and bang around and shake your head until your bun falls down. I don't even know the song she was playing. She clanged so loud on those cymbals and beat that big ol' front drum so hard you couldn't even hear her music. She was horrible. And she won. I sang an aria, fluttered around that stage like a gazelle, and didn't miss a note, including the climax of a C above high C. I have a tape of my song in my bag. Would you like to hear it?" she asked, eyes brighter than an exploding Fourth of July.

I should have stopped her there. But no, ridiculous me gave a nod. I just thought a head shake would be entirely too rude. I have no idea why I even cared. But I did. This was an unfortunate creature in front of me. She had no life. Well, no real life. She lived in a world of sequins, teased hair, and fake everything. And me, stupid me, gave her pity at the wrong time, because my nod took me to a place few should ever have to travel.

Now when someone tells me she has a tape of her song, my first thought is that she is actually singing on tape. Simply having to listen to a taped copy of her talent presentation would be persecution enough, but what actually happened teetered on the horrendous. This was no tape of her singing; this was her *accompaniment*. The actual singing was going to be done live and in person by Miss Savannah United States of America herself.

She hit an opening note that was so loud, my head flew back and embedded itself in the headrest of the driver's seat, where it stayed for the rest of the performance. For the next three and a half minutes, she performed an operatic aria, right there in the front seat of my car. She had motions; she had expressions; she had earth-shattering, only-dogs-could-hear piercing notes. Passersby stared at us. What was I to do? I did the only thing I knew: I waved.

At one point Amber became so animated that I actually believe she forgot she was sitting in an automobile, on the side of the road, *in front of someone's home.* I thought those few minutes would last an eternity. I thought I would never hear the final note. And when it finally came, I thought for sure every window in my car was going to shatter. I had just been presented an entire talent presentation. When she finished, I simply remained in my impacted, strained-neck, totally frazzled position and prayed for rescue.

"Now, can you imagine that being beaten by a drummer? She won and I left with some money and soon-to-be-dead flowers. The whole thing's rigged, I tell you. Because honey, the day I lose to a bong-bong player, you can bet your sweet rose-smelling britches that pageant is rigged."

With those words I should have jumped. I should have tackled that moment like Ellis Johnson tackles Steve McNair, but suddenly it just didn't seem to matter. The entire thing rested on the ridiculous. Grown women prancing around a stage, vying for the attention of five people, each trying to get the judges to view her as better than the one before. Grown women singing their talent numbers in the cars of virtual strangers. What did it matter? Why had I bothered with something so preposterous? Even I, for one fleeting moment, wondered if Mr. Cummings's words weren't true. Maybe it really didn't matter. Miss Amber Topaz didn't get it. So, maybe none of it really mattered. Maybe this whole thing had been a waste of time.

"Well, toodleoo, Miss Savannah. I'll see you tomorrow, and we'll figure out what we're going to do for lunch on Wednesday. You take care. You might need to get some major rest. You look a little stressed." And with that she closed the door and skipped her happy little self on down the street and out of sight.

I waited until she was completely gone to extricate my head from the headrest. It was now close to six, and I went promptly into the house and up to my bedroom. I laid myself across the bed.

When I woke up, the clock beside me read one a.m.

I decided to go downstairs and get a bowl of cereal. There was a note on the kitchen counter from my mother.

Savannah, I was going to wake you for dinner, but you looked exhausted. I hope your day went OK, and just remember that you were created for this job. I love you, Mother.

I still wasn't sure why she was so happy for me and this job, but at this moment I was too hungry to care. I poured a bowl of Cocoa Pebbles, walked over to the sofa, and turned on the TV. Tan Beautiful was being advertised. It is amazing how quickly those infomercials can snare you in their tangled web. Before I knew it, I had ordered two bottles with rush delivery.

When I finally returned to bed, I lay there staring at the ceiling and began to think of the stars of my beauty pageant story, and of how different each woman was: Victoria, so together; Emma, so traumatized; Katherine, so over that stage of her life. Very different women all uniquely touched by the same bizarre experience.

I bolted up in bed. That was it. My story wasn't so much about the pageants as much as it was about the people *in* the pageants. The thoughts began to come so fast and furious that by the time I fell asleep, the whole story was neatly written in my head.

CHAPTER TWENTY-SEVEN

I headed downstairs around seven forty-five. Mother had prepared my favorite breakfast: chocolate gravy and biscuits. Trust me on this one. It is absolutely the best stuff I have ever put in my mouth. She makes homemade biscuits, then prepares a chocolate gravy, similar to what you would use as icing for a cake, but not quite as thick.

It is because of Vicky's culinary skill that we even supported her decision to write a cookbook. She wanted to compete with her good friend Paula Deen, who owns The Lady & Sons, one of the best restaurants in town. Paula has her own cookbooks and her own show on the Food Network, which is perfectly charming and perfectly Savannah. One night after dinner, we were going on about what a fabulous cook my mother is, and she decided that since we loved her cooking so much, maybe she should write a cookbook. We all agreed, thinking it would keep her out of our business for a while. Well, it did, and the result is *Dining with Victoria*. We tried to get her to call it *Victoria's Vittles*, but she didn't think that sounded Martha Stewart enough. I know in the back of her mind she is trying to build her own

Martha Stewart conglomerate of the South. Well, maybe not so much anymore.

The cover picture has her standing in our kitchen holding up one of her silver platters with pork tenderloin, southern mashed potatoes, and green beans. It was pre-hair-fallout, when the color was still red. She was wearing a beautiful yellow suit, accessorized to perfection. She did look stunning. But now that she's chestnut, she wants to take a new cover picture. For that reason alone, it will probably never be published. If she took a new picture she'd have another hairstyle by the time the book came out anyway. It would be a cruel and vicious cycle for some local photographer, pity the soul.

And trust me, we will never mention the word *television*.

"Thank you for not waking me up last night; I was exhausted," I said, taking a plate from the counter.

Mother turned around at the sound of my voice. "Oh, I could tell that you were exhausted. I'm sorry things haven't turned out like you planned," she said, opening the refrigerator and pouring me a glass of milk. She walked over and pulled out the chair beside me. "When is your story due?"

I took a drink of milk before responding. "I must deliver my copy into Mr. Hicks's hands by two. So I have from now until then to create a story."

"Well, you need to remember that these are people, Savannah, not characters. You're writing truth, not fiction."

Now, where did that come from? I didn't have time to investigate. "Speaking of characters, I saw the lovely character creation of your own yesterday."

"Savannah Phillips, bite your tongue. I did not create that child. She is a creation of . . . I'm not sure what yet. She cracks me up, though, and I think she stands a great shot at becoming Miss Georgia United States of America this year."

"Don't you think she would have won by now if she could have?"

"I think there's a timing for everything in life, Savannah. Sometimes we think things should happen at a certain time, in a certain way, but there is a master plan. So we brush ourselves off and learn from our mistakes, and try not to make the same ones again, all the while doing what we feel it is we've been called to do."

"So at what point is it fair to ask yourself if maybe, just maybe, you aren't following the master plan? I mean, if I had tried to write three different books and none of them ever got published, I would start to wonder if that was what I was supposed to do."

Victoria smiled at me in the way she does when she is about to say something truly profound. "Yes, and you should. But only you can figure that out for yourself. What if all of those books that failed gave you the idea for a fourth book, the one that gets published? Then you could reasonably say each rejection paved the way to success. See, Savannah, you have to be careful not to put destiny into a mold. Each life has its own."

Then back to the world of Mary Kay we went. "Anyway, Amber really does do a wonderful job. She has the perfect personality for tourism director and she's delicate with the adjustments that have to be made over there quite often."

"Yeah, she told me about your adjustments. You need to leave those poor people alone, Mother. You have them so nervous! One day you're going to be on the back of a trolley and they're going to spot you and send that trolley right into the statue of General Oglethorpe. It's not right what you put those people through."

"Well, you don't need to worry about what I do in this city. I have it perfectly under control," Vicky said, standing up and pretending to put away dishes.

"Under control? Wait a minute. Aren't you the one who climbed into the horse-drawn carriage and screamed so loud when a wasp flew up her dress that the poor horse had to be sedated before they could hook him up to a carriage again? That's just wrong, Mother."

"Is that all you remember about me? Can you not recall sometimes the multitude of good I do around here?" She pretended to act all pouty, but I could tell she got a kick out of the memory too.

I wiped my mouth and took my plate over to the sink where she was. "Trust me, I know all of the wonderful things you do, and taking care of us is the most wonderful of all. Especially this," I said pointing to the empty plate in front of me. "I've got to go. I'll remember what you said." I kissed her on the cheek and headed out the door. "I love you," I called out on the way.

"I love you too, darling," I heard from a distance.

"Well, I guess you're ready to write that story?"

"Ready as I'll ever be."

Dad paused for a moment, then closed the top of the Coke machine and stepped aside to let me have my fill. He leaned against the counter, and by the look in his eyes, I knew he had something to say.

"You can say whatever it is you're wanting to say, Dad. Mother had her turn; feel free to take yours."

"You know you can tell me anything, Savannah. In fact, until now, you have always told me everything. When you were little, you actually told me more than I really wanted to know, from every stubbed toe to broken heart to bad prom dress. So why have you had trouble letting me in on this one?"

"What do you mean?"

"Telling me what this story is about. Your mother won't even tell me anything, and that woman is incapable of keeping a secret. But apparently she feels strongly that it should come from you," he said with an expression I'm not quite sure I had ever seen on his face before.

It wasn't a look of hurt so much as it was of perplexity. I could see in his eyes; he was wondering if the time to let me go had come yet again. I had slipped from his arms to the hairy halls of preschool; I had kissed him good-bye and climbed into the car with Grant for my first real date; I had closed my college dorm-room door behind him when he left me there to enter the world of adulthood. But I had never closed the door to our conversations.

I had always told him everything. But today, Vicky knew something he didn't. The poor man had to be suffering.

I hadn't realized until that moment that I was changing. Not everything would be known to my parents anymore. Not every detail of my life would be disclosed, because there's no need, really, to expose parents to unnecessary knowledge. Who wants her parents to carry her hurt when she knows she will recover, while they might not? Today was our shifting. It had happened without fanfare or even true awareness. I had become the protective parent; he had become the curious child.

I smiled at the concern in his eyes. "You know, when I was little you wouldn't let me watch something on TV because you didn't want it to scare me."

"That's because you were scared of your shadow."

"Still am. Then there were also the times when someone would be in here early in the morning talking about something, and you would quiet them because you didn't want me to hear."

"You were very nosy."

"Still am. But even though I didn't understand, I knew it was for my own good. I guess this is one of those times. But this time I've been protecting you. Not from anything horrible or sordid," I said quickly when his look of concern grew exponentially.

"See, I've been trying to protect you from the need to protect her. So, before you ask, just know, I will do nothing to hurt her, harm her, or cause her pain. As for us, maybe the tide has turned. But nothing will ever change the way I feel about you," I said, encasing him in a bear hug. Then I whispered in his ear, "I'm growing up, Dad. I won't be able to tell you everything anymore. But I'm sure I'll still tell you far more than you'll ever want to know." He held on a little tighter than he had in years. When he let go, his face registered that he understood.

"Are you ready for another day at work?"

"No."

"Are you ready for your story?"

"No."

He paused for a moment, not sure if he should ask any more questions, so he settled for the one he already knew the answer to. "Would you like another Coke?"

"Yes!" I said. He took the glass from my hand and filled it up. He looked at the clock, which read 8:15.

"Take this Coke. Grab a banana off of the counter if you're hungry. Get in your car, gather your thoughts, and go to work. And when you are there, take yourself, your very talented self, go to your office, and write an article like this city has never read," he said, his eyes just hinting at tears. "Do that, Savannah, and this transition will have been worth it."

I had spent my life knowing that my father was the finest of men. But there are encounters in life that take things we've known forever in our heads and channel them into the chambers of our hearts. I call it the "second look" moment. Most people stop at first looks, never taking a second glance to really see what has transpired in an experience.

Today, my father became a person, a person to discover, a person to cherish. In that moment my father became Jake, not just Dad. In my car, I gathered myself and wiped away the tears that had begun to flow down my face. I didn't know what awaited me today, but the unfolding of a story could never match what had just developed in the last few moments of my life.

"Hey, you must be Marla. I'm Savannah Phillips," I said, holding out my hand to the sweet face smiling behind the receptionist's desk.

"Well, Savannah Phillips," she said, refusing my hand and proceeding to get up and walk around her desk to face me. "I feel like I know you," she said, grabbing me in a bear hug. "You are just the cutest thing I've ever seen. We're so glad you're here. Mr. Hicks is a tad concerned, but we're thrilled to have Victoria Phillips's very own daughter working right here among us," she said. "Now, I'll just be right here, behind my little desk. I'm only a phone call away. So you just ring-a-ding me if you need anything," she said, returning to her place.

"Thank you. I think I'm good for now. But if I need you, I'll be sure to call. Oh, but would you mind holding my calls today, Marla? This is my first story, and I want to make sure I make it good."

"Not at all, dear. You just go write this paper one amazing story."

"Thank you. I'll do my best." When I arrived at my new home away from home, I pulled a stack of books from my bedroom library out of my backpack. A girl needed to have something inside this monotone mausoleum to add a little color, and nothing added color like books. I stood them up neatly and made a mental note to acquire some bookends. Curly Locks flip-flopped in during my designing moment. I could tell he wanted to have a conversation, but I stopped him before he started. "Don't. I've got too much work to do. I've got a story due by two, and it's got to be perfect," I said, holding out my hand and never looking in his direction.

"Your computer isn't even on."

I reached down and pushed a button. "It is now." He disappeared for the rest of the morning.

And for the rest of the morning, I shut myself off from the world. I typed, retyped, wiped out, started over, and all but turned the thing inside out and upside down until my first story was fully complete.

When two o'clock came, it was finished—a human-interest story that would set Savannah on its ears. When the last page had printed, I grabbed my "copy," as they call it in the newspaper world, put it in a folder marked "Savannah Phillips," and headed to the third floor.

After only one wrong turn, which put me in a broom closet, I arrived in the proper place, but Mr. Hicks was nowhere to be found. His secretary wasn't there either. For a fleeting moment I wondered if Mr. Hicks actually had a secretary. After much reflection, I set my folder on his desk and walked out. I had done my job. Mr. Hicks would now have to do his.

"Where have you been? Taking attendance in traffic court?" I asked, refusing to look up as Curly Locks appeared.

He pulled his uninvited chair up to my desk. "You are a regular comedian. No, Ms. Phillips, I am capable of more than paint by numbers. So. How do you feel now that your first work of art is in Mr. Hicks's hands?"

"I feel good, I think." I was surprised that I felt nervous. "We'll know tomorrow, won't we?"

"Yes, my dear, we sure will. Your critics will be silenced, I'm sure."

"Critics, I have critics?" I asked, thinking he was just trying to get me to react and hating myself that I was.

"Well, maybe skeptics is a better word."

"Well, they've been mighty silent."

"To you, yes."

"But not to you?"

He got up from his chair to return to his desk. "Let's just say, tomorrow they'll be silenced."

Poor Marla had been holding my calls since morning, so I went to her desk to thank her and see if I had any messages. She greeted me with a handful of pink While You Were Out notices. There were seven in all, each one from Miss Amber Topaz Cubic Zirconia Rhinestone Childers. She just wanted to make sure that we connected today to make plans for lunch tomorrow.

"She's a persistent little thing, Savannah," Marla said with a furrowed brow. "Just a persistent little thing."

"Yes, she is, dear Marla. I sure appreciate your intervention."

"Savannah, this switchboard is my domain. What I say gets through, gets through. And what I desire to hold, I will hold. What I say gets lost, well, it gets lost. And may I say, it has been my pleasure to get Miss Amber lost. Actually, I've lost her on a couple of occasions in the *last fifteen minutes!*" she said, trying to control herself.

"I'm really sorry."

"Don't you be sorry, Savannah. I'll protect you." With those words the phone rang and she returned to her seat. As I walked away, I heard, "Listen here, young lady. Miss Savannah is taking a lunch break. She needs her nutrition and cannot be bothered. And you have tied up my switchboard long enough. Now, I don't want to hear from you one more time today. Do you understand me?" I couldn't help but laugh all the way back to my Styrofoam paradise.

Mr. Hicks had not called me to his office by the time five o'clock arrived. That meant that either he was using my story or he was in desperate search of a replacement. I could only hope for the former.

The pink card underneath my windshield wiper was embossed with the words *Amber Topaz Childers, Miss Savannah United States of America.* I was being stalked by a crazed former beauty queen. Surely there were laws against women with big hair stalking women who were just trying to do an honest day's work. The note read, "Sorry I haven't been able to reach you today, but the lady at the switchboard is an absolute irritant. I'll just swing by tonight and we can make our lunch plans. Love ya, Amber." I made mental note to search out a good therapist. I might need one sooner than later. Just two weeks ago I was a healthy young woman. Now it seemed as though my mind was slowly becoming debilitated by mind-warping tales of marimba players and magicians—or was it ventriloquists? See, it was already happening.

I drove home, desperate to find something to do other than go home. I called Paige and asked if she wanted to go to a movie and grab some dinner. She was a go, so I risked a quick stop at home.

When I walked through the door, I could smell dinner. I knew Vicky would be disappointed that I wasn't staying, but she would eventually get used to this new rhythm of my life. When I walked into the kitchen, she was standing in front of the sink rinsing a dish, and Dad was behind her with his arms wrapped around her waist, saying something in her ear that had her giggling.

Dad noticed me first. "Hey, sweet girl," he said, coming over to give me a hug. My mother turned around too.

"Well, hey, darling," she said, walking to the stove to remove what smelled like green beans.

"Hey!" I said and hugged Dad back.

Dad went over to the table, pulled out a chair, then sat down in the one across from it. "Savannah, sit down and tell us what happened today. We want to know all about your story."

I sat down and went over the same thing that I had determined to tell everyone. "Well, you'll be glad to know I actually wrote one."

"Well, we thank the Lord for that," Dad said, laughing and taking a drink of his iced tea.

I stood up and walked over to survey what good food I might be missing. "But I really want you to wait and read it in the morning. That way everyone can have an objective reaction."

"Well, Savannah," Dad said, "we look forward to reading it in the morning then."

"And, Mother, I hope it's no big deal, but I really need a mental breather tonight, so Paige and I are going to go see a movie and grab a bite to eat."

She hid her disappointment, gave me a kiss on the cheek, and told me to have a good time.

Then I remembered I had one item of undone business. "Mother, by the way, your happy little director of tourism will be stopping by. Please let her know that I have been busy and will meet her for lunch tomorrow at The Lady & Sons at noon."

That night as I was leaving Paige's apartment, I noticed a small painting lying next to the door.

"When did you do that?"

"The other day. I was just trying something different."

"I love it. The color is so vibrant and bold."

"What would you expect?"

"Nothing less from you."

"Do you want it?"

"I can't take it."

"Yes, you can. Consider it a congratulations gift for your new job."

I scooped it up in my arms before she had any second thoughts. "OK. That sounds good. You hadn't gotten me anything yet anyway."

Home was wonderfully quiet. In less than ten minutes my head was on my pillow. My mind tried to run wild with all of the what-ifs that the morning could bring. But I put a halt to that and simply said a prayer of thankfulness that I had been able to write anything at all. Sleep came quickly, and it was the sweetest sleep I had known in quite a while.

CHAPTER TWENTY-EIGHT

For an instant, I forgot that today was the day that my first article would appear in the paper. But then I was fully awake. Today was the day that Savannah would realize that I was or wasn't a human-interest writer, was or wasn't a suitable replacement for Gloria, was or wasn't any kind of writer at all.

I jumped up, put on some jogging clothes, brushed my teeth, and ran downstairs. I grabbed the leash and attached Duke to it, grabbed the newspaper from the iron console, and didn't stop running until I reached a bench on the perimeter of the park's east side. I sat down and slipped Duke's leash over the arm of the bench so he wouldn't drag both of us after some fair lab. Opening the paper directly to the local section, there on the front page was my picture with my name under it: Savannah Phillips.

I was shaking so badly, I almost didn't think I was going to be able to read it. I tried to breathe in about six or seven times and refocus my eyes, but they were getting blurred from sudden light-headedness. I leaned back against the bench and enjoyed the fact that at least Mr. Hicks liked some of it. I mean after all, my picture was there, so he had to have kept at least part of it. Sure, maybe he had edited it to smithereens, but if he used my picture, he at least had to have used my premise.

"Just read the story already, Savannah!" I said out loud. I looked down and began to read the product of my so-called investigation.

I have lived most of my life never quite understanding beauty pageants. Not that there is anything wrong with them; there just doesn't seem to be anything necessary in them. They don't solve world hunger; they don't change the political climate; they don't even do much to affect a city. But I have recently come to realize that no institution truly changes any of these things either. Hunger organizations don't feed world hunger; people giving of their time, money, and energy do. The government doesn't change the landscape of this nation; people who care about issues, who serve in blood banks and listen to the needs of the elderly in small corner cafés and play with children and repair dilapidated playgrounds, they do. And cities don't change themselves, but people who love them, who give of their time and care about every detail from the trolley tour to the airport lobby, who build corner bookstores and open up coffee shops, and who raise the next generation to love their neighbor, they do.

So, as unnecessary as beauty pageants may seem, by this standard everything is unnecessary. What makes anything of value are the people who are a part of it. And yes, believe it or not, countless women who enter beauty pageants every year are some of the most productive, viable, and life-giving forces behind the very causes that matter most to each of us.

The time I have spent considering the relative value of beauty pageants has proven enlightening. I will spare you the many horror stories I have been forced to endure over recent days: tales of manufactured cleavage, dresses worn backward, and cymbal concertos. No, today I want to suggest that even though beauty pageants hardly fortify the fiber of a nation, they can shatter the life of an individual. And when a life is so shattered because of pride or greed, when it is thrown off its destined course, the fiber of a nation will ultimately be weakened.

Consider the story of one of the most beautiful women Savannah has ever seen. Today, her beauty is gone. Her glory is such a distant memory that I have wondered if even she recalls it.

Savannah's jewel once won every pageant, every homecoming, and every heart. Her inner spirit was as beautiful as her physical self. I know, because on one of my more desperate days at the tender age of thirteen, I was the unexpected recipient of her compassion and kindness. But as I stood at her door just days ago and stared at her dirty T-shirt and uncombed hair, as I witnessed her grim outlook on life, I didn't see how this could be the same person I once knew.

She had a dream too. A dream to be Miss Georgia United States of America. But when that dream was taken from her, the loss was too much to bear.

She came home, married a man who abused her, had four children, and has spent her life since forging a dreamless existence. I went to her home the other day, and as I wiped old Cheerios from the sofa, I tried to force her to see herself as she was, remind her of who she had once been. I wasn't eloquent. Frankly, I wasn't really even nice. But I was honest.

After I left her home, my anger at the people who had done this to her began to grow, so I went searching.

And what I uncovered was an age-old story of greed, deceit, and lies, all in the name of money.

Some of you may blame her for allowing such a "petty" loss to destroy her own life. But I would challenge all of us to consider our power to affect others' destinies. When we are entrusted with the life of another—to direct or guide or lead or aid—and we deem anything greater than that life, then we have devalued the greatest treasure any of us could ever have the privilege to bear.

If I could give Savannah's one-time reigning beauty anything, I would restore her ability to dream. I would wrap up a crown, place it on her head, and assure her she is a princess. I would wash her face and comb her hair and try to help her remember her true beauty. But what's done is done. We can't go back. The choices we make to affect people's lives are done. We can alter the future, but the path is forever littered with reminders of past losses.

I have much more to say, but today, I will urge you to nurture the personal destinies that fall within your realm of influence. Speak life into them, and help them find their wings. Because the life of a city is determined by the destiny and character of its individuals.

Until Friday,
Savannah Phillips

I sat back and realized I'd been holding my breath. I couldn't believe it. Mr. Hicks had edited me more lightly than I could have hoped. Not only was my story intact, but most of the words were mine too. I grabbed Duke, kissed him square on his nose, grabbed his leash, and took off toward home.

I took the first eight steps of the staircase by twos. "Vanni, if that's you, Mom wanted me to tell you that Amber is going to meet you at The Lady & Sons at noon," Thomas said sleepily. I stopped dead in my tracks, took a breath, and continued my climb by twos. Not even Amber would be able to ruin this day.

I showered and dressed in a giddy mood. And I don't do giddy. I sang every Barry Manilow song I knew. I danced around my bedroom like a woman unleashed. I swung on bedposts, tap-danced on the tile floor in my bathroom, even struck up a chorus of "I Write the Songs." I've never written a song in my life, but by George, I wrote an article. And it was a good article.

I flitted to the closet and picked out something extremely "out of control." I picked out a dress. Then I actually put it on. A black linen dress, but it was a dress nonetheless. I don't know what came over me, but something did. And then I picked out a pair of Kate Spade shoes in black, which I had come to adore, that still flipped when I walked, but weren't technically flip-flops.

"Somebody stop me!" I screamed at the mirrors that covered my sliding closet doors. Then I swirled around and about whipped myself too hard again, but this time I recovered with nothing more than disheveled hair freed from a ponytail holder. Hold on, Hannah. Savannah has let loose and traded her pulled-back do for a straightened mane of dark hair. I had forgotten how long my hair had become. I ran my hands through it, wondering if I could handle an entire day with this flopping around my head.

Well, today anything was possible. With one last gander at myself in the mirror, I took off down the stairs.

The seventh step from the top, my flip-flop-clad feet slid out from under me. The rest of the trip down was endured by my backside, though I tried to stop myself with one hand on the railing and the other descending the stairs beside me. I made such a commotion coming down that I thought surely the neighborhood would come in to check on me. Sitting on the floor in sheer agony, hoping for someone to kiss my boo-boo, it occurred to me that no one in the world would be hailing my latest achievement if they had witnessed my ungraceful fall.

The silence of an absent audience encouraged me to gather my dignity and my bruised behind. I headed out the door and shouted for all the world to hear, "Miss Grace has left the building."

CHAPTER TWENTY-NINE

In the mouth of the foolish lies one's arrogance, but the lips of the sensible will preserve them." No sooner had I read the words on Dad's board than Judge Hoddicks walked over, grabbed me by both arms, and pulled me to him in a bear hug. I couldn't breathe well, but at moments like this, you simply endure.

"Betty, I can't tell you how wonderful I thought your article was. I laughed. I . . . well, I didn't cry, but I thought about it. I just thought it was wonderful. I'll be honest: I loved Gloria. I wasn't sure you could pull it off, but you did. In fact, you more than pulled it off; you nailed it, baby. Caused me to think about how I treat those ol' ornery criminals. I can't wait until Friday. I cannot wait until Friday."

I waited for more congratulations, but none came. Everyone seemed rather preoccupied with customers and all. Even Duke didn't offer a lick, a wag of the tail, or a would-you-take-me-to-do-my-business look. I headed into the back to get a Coke and pulled Dad by the arm along with me. "OK. So tell me, what did you think?"

"I got up early to read the paper without interruption, but it was gone and so were you and Duke." I slapped my forehead and groaned. "I heard your mother get up earlier, around five, and I wanted her to have time to digest whatever you had written by herself."

"She read it already?" I asked wide-eyed, anticipating some dramatic retelling of every word and sigh and tear.

"Yes, she read it."

"Well, what did she say?"

"Nothing."

I considered this. "Well, did you know I was doing something about the pageant?" I finally asked, nudging his arm.

"That didn't take an Einstein, Savannah. An investigative jour-nalist you may be; a subtle one you are not." That made us both laugh. "So, I got ready, told Thomas to bring Duke on his way to the courthouse, and sat here with a cup of coffee and the morning paper. I wasn't sure what you would say, Savannah," he said, his eyes more intense than I had seen them in years. "I knew you wouldn't hurt your mother, but I also knew that you wanted a story that would declare your legitimacy. I wasn't quite sure how you could protect one and accomplish the other." He paused for a moment. "And to be honest, I'm not so sure you did."

Every ounce of my energy left. I put my drink down and tried to speak. "What . . . what do you mean? I didn't say anything bad about Mother. I didn't even talk about her."

"This isn't about your mother, Savannah. This is about Emma."

"I didn't say anything untrue about her. I didn't even use her name."

"No, maybe not technically, but you described her according to your opinion. Do you think anyone doesn't know who you were talking about? And did she ever tell you she wanted to be talked about? Or that she wanted her life told in the paper? Or that she even cared if she had lost the pageant at all?"

I stood there trying to get my taxed brain to register his bar-rage of questions. I had been through so much. It had been a long week. I had just fallen down the stairs, for goodness' sake.

"I thought I would be helping her. Trying to find out who did this to her and why. Putting a face to her pain."

"Savannah, you needed to know that she wanted a face to her pain. Now the only face she might see when remembering her pain is you."

That was so far from my intent that I hardly knew what to say. "Do you really think this will hurt her? I tried not to even make it about her."

"But it was, Savannah. The message behind the whole thing was Emma, or a bunch of Emmas. Or not becoming an Emma. Can you imagine someone writing about you, about how horrible your life would be if you became a Savannah?" He stopped, realizing that his words were cutting me to the core.

"But I didn't mean to hurt anyone. I would never have intentionally hurt her," I said, feeling the sting of tears forming in my eyes. "I wouldn't knowingly hurt anyone," I said, letting the tears fall freely now.

"I know you wouldn't," he said, wrapping me in his arms. "But I believe you probably did today. And you're going to have to make it right."

Dad released me and headed toward the front of the store, but stopped to add, "I love you, Savannah. I wouldn't hurt you for the world either. But you still have things to learn. You still have wisdom left to gain. And the best place to begin is in learning to guard your words. They are now more powerful than I believe you know."

I made my way to my desk undetected. Who knew how many other people would feel like my father? About the time I got to my seat, two girls I had seen before but never met walked by my desk giggling and whispering until they spotted me. I smiled, but they didn't. In fact, their faces went pretty much stone cold, expressionless. Not angry or malicious, just indifferent. Those two would probably take effort. I had no energy for effort today.

I wanted to hang my new picture. I had picked the perfect place, just to the left of my books on the top shelf. That way, anytime I needed a pick-me-up, I could just look up and catch a glimpse of its vibrant tones. But why hang it up when I would surely be fired before the day's end? I left Paige's artwork leaning against the bookcase and spent the morning trying to look busy, while Friday loomed like a stalker with pink stationery. If anyone felt half as much concern as my father, the only thing left to write was a formal apology to the city, Emma, Ichabod over the door, and resign myself to becoming a tour guide.

To my great relief, Joshua never appeared. Marla called me around nine thirty to tell me she had just "loved every little word" I had written on those pages. "It was like a painter had created a masterpiece." Then, she added, "But the lady who's headed back to you now, well, she might not feel quite the same way."

Emma, in fine form for a Spray and Wash commercial, rounded the corner while I still held the receiver in my hand.

"I can't believe you," she hissed, waving her newspaper in my face. I stood up to at least be able to block any blows she might be contemplating. "How could you?"

"Emma, I know. It was kind of insensitive . . ."

"*Kind of* insensitive? Who do you think you are?"

"Ooh, whoa doggies. Let's go outside and talk. We don't need to bring the whole office into this."

"Are you kidding me? You brought the *entire city* into this! I just want to know, Miss Priss, who died and made you judge and jury? When did you decide that I needed you to take me up as your cause?"

"Well, I was trying to—"

"*I'm not a cause,* Savannah; I'm a person. A person you single-handedly turned into a complete and utter laughingstock," she said. Every blood vessel in her face pulsed beneath her pale skin.

I caught her eyes. At once I saw both anger and hurt. Dad's revelation became my own. "Emma, you're right. I'm so sorry. I'll retract everything on Friday."

"Your retraction won't help, Savannah. It's done. It's all done. You can't undo it. You said it yourself, with your own words, in your own little paper. 'The choices you make to affect people's lives are done,'" she mimicked. "'You can alter the future, but the path is forever marked with reminders of past losses,'" she said, throwing the newspaper at my feet.

The sound startled me. "I said all that?"

"Yes, you said all that. Well, take a close look at what you've accomplished. Not only have you embarrassed me, but my children, Savannah. My children now get to go to school and listen to what other children say about their mother. You think about that, Savannah. Even if you had no thought about how this might affect me, I would have hoped you cared more about my children." And with those words, she turned her greased locks around and left me to wallow in my own misery.

"Long day?" Curly Locks appeared from nowhere, picking up the scattered paper and throwing it away.

"You don't know. And I don't want to hear your comments about my article," I said, flopping to my chair and laying my head on my desk.

I could feel him kneel down beside me. "Well, it wasn't all bad. I mean it was bad, but not all bad."

"Any bad negates any good," I said, starting to cry.

"Not all the good."

"Yes, any good."

"At least she didn't hit you."

I tried to stifle my laugh, but I couldn't. I sat up.

"Ooh, Ms. Phillips needs a tissue."

"Sorry," I said, reaching across my desk for a tissue. I blew hard and wiped off my face. "I didn't realize I would hurt her. What was I thinking? I am a complete idiot."

"A complete idiot. That's harsh. Partial idiot, certainly. But I'm not sure what you were thinking either. I mean, what were you thinking?"

"I don't want to have this conversation with you. I've had a long morning, and I'm tired, and I really can't stay here anymore," I said matter-of-factly.

"What? Are you going to quit after your first article?"

"I have no choice. You heard what I did to her. Have mercy! I have affected her children! I should have stuck to fiction." I stood up, feeling the anger rise. "I was supposed to write books, to make people laugh and smile. To tell stories of crazy people that weren't real. That way, at the end of the day, no one would be hurt or angry or remove their children from my path when I walk by. This is all my mother's fault."

"Obviously, you have deeply rooted, unresolved issues with your mother."

"Oh, that's good, Sherlock. Do you charge for your therapeutic services?"

"You couldn't afford me."

"Well then it's a good thing I don't need you." I turned on my heels and headed to the elevator. "I don't need counseling. I know what I have to do."

"You may know what you have to do, but you definitely need counseling. And if you want my opinion, you're making a mistake. And this isn't about your mother." I threw my hands over my ears and continued in forward motion, singing "la, la, la."

Of course, there was no secretary at Mr. Hicks's office. I knocked on his half-open door and waited for him to allow me to enter.

"Come in, Ms. Phillips."

"Mr. Hicks, I just wanted to let you know that I'll be taking my things and leaving today. I know I've done nothing but desecrate Gloria's good name, and I won't put you through any further embarrassment or shame by having my name associated with your paper. I'll write a brief apology for Friday and you don't have to worry about paying me."

"Oh, really."

"Yes, really, and truth be known, I should probably give you money for rent space. So, anyway, thank you for the opportunity. I'm sorry I wasn't capable of more, but I appreciate your taking a risk on me at all. Good luck, Mr. Hicks. I hope you find someone worthy to take Gloria's place." I began my exit.

"I did find someone worthy to take Gloria's place," he said, stopping me in my tracks. "And if she would learn to give other people a chance to speak before she makes such hasty exits, she might learn a thing or two along the way." He stood and pointed to a chair. "Sit."

He sat on the edge of his desk, arms folded neatly across his belly. I took the seat across from him. "You're a good writer, Savannah. You tell a story. You teach us lessons. You even taught me a lesson. You challenged me to see the potential in the people who work for me. It is precisely because of what you wrote in that article, Savannah, that I'm not letting you walk out that door and go home."

"Because of what I wrote?"

"Yes, when I first read your piece, I was furious at your carelessness. The things you said about Emma were downright indefensible."

"Yes, they were."

"They may have been true, but not your truth to put into print. But the other things you said made me realize you are one of those people within my realm of influence. You are one that needs to be guided and grown and matured. I'm here to help you do that. And today, you've learned the lesson you needed to learn."

"Remind me again of what that is."

"You've learned you have much to learn. That will make you from this day forward a better writer than you ever dreamed of being. You won't leave. Instead, you'll go down there and write an article for Friday—better, wiser, and more powerful than the one you wrote today. Now go. And I don't want to see you again until you deliver me your article tomorrow afternoon."

"Thank you," I said, swallowing my tears. "Thank you. You're a good man, Mr. Hicks. I'll see you tomorrow."

The clock on my desk said noon. The Lady & Sons was waiting. I would go. But only after I hung up my picture.

CHAPTER THIRTY

I t wasn't hard to locate my lunch companion. She was the one in the back, standing on her tiptoes, wearing a bright purple pantsuit with lipstick that matched her suit perfectly. "Yoo-hoo! Savannah! I'm over here." I sighed and made a point of avoiding eye contact with anyone. Today of all days, I didn't want the Purple People Eater yelling my name across a crowded restaurant.

I tried to sit Amber down with the wave of my hand, but she continued making a spectacle until I took my seat across from her.

"Savannah Phillips," she started, "I had no idea in this world that you were going to write an article on beauty pageants. I mean, you should have interviewed me. I could have told you a thousand stories," she began in her animated way, not stopping to breathe. "I mean, Savannah, I have competed in more pageants than most women this side of Decatur." And then she laughed a ludicrous laugh; a laugh that totally appreciated the fact that she probably *had* competed in more pageants than the sum total of all the women I know.

To my inexpressible relief, the waitress came quickly. I ordered Coke and asked her to keep them coming. I also ordered the baked spaghetti, voted the best in the South by *Fodor* magazine, even though I hardly had the appetite for it. Amber ordered a salad with no dressing but, true to her word, caved in and had sweet tea. "This is the only place I break down to have sweet tea. But I just can't help it," she said, as if this life necessity needed justification.

I stared at her in pity. This poor child was probably going to live her entire life eating less than a toy poodle. Chatty Cathy started up again, reminding me that the only pleasure in lunch with her was knowing I could eat without ever having to say a word.

"Savannah, I didn't realize everything Emma has been through. That child just sounds plumb pitiful."

I wanted to tell her she looked plumb pitiful, but it didn't seem appropriate.

"I think one afternoon I'm going to stop at her house and offer to take her out or something. I might even go to that Katherine's Corner Bookstore and buy her a book."

"You read?" I asked. I felt bad as soon as it came out; she was unfazed.

"Well, sure. I mean, just yesterday I was reading *People* magazine. Do you ever read that, Savannah? I just love hearing about the lives of the stars. I mean, did you know that Jennifer Aniston—"

I held up one hand. "Amber, there's one thing you need to know about me. I don't live in the land of need-to-know, unless someone deems I need to know. So let's not spend lunch talking about people. Why don't you tell me about you? Tell me about your job."

"Whatever you say, but you told the whole city about Emma."

I tried to catch my breath. Amber had just shown me myself. But she didn't stop to ponder the revelation with me. "Oh, I just love my job. You know, your mother helped me get it. Miss Victoria is just the sweetest thing I've ever met. She saw me at the pageant my last year and we got to talking. I had already been out of school for a year and was working at the bank. I knew I could do so much more, but nothing had opened up yet. When your mother mentioned the job as director of tourism, I saw doors swinging wide open. So I jumped at the chance, and between the two of us we have made this place come alive." I barely heard her, still mulling over my need-to-know revelation.

"But you know my greatest goal, that is if I don't ever win Miss United States of America, is to win *Mrs.* United States of America," she said, actually stopping long enough to take a sip of her tea.

"Do what?!" I asked, fully present again.

"Oh, yeah. When I get married—and I've got my eye on a fellow now—but when I get married, I want to be Mrs. United States of America. I mean, surely I can win that. I've already got the wardrobe. That's why I try to keep my figure, you know." She pointed to the uneaten salad before her. "Yeah, the pageant's in California, so once I get married, all I have to do is just keep rehearsing my talent and staying up on current events. You never know when you might snatch Mr. Right, and you need to be ready.

"I practice all the time anyway," she continued. "I practice walking in my evening gown and answering questions on stage. I just stand in front of the mirror in my bathroom and use my brush for a microphone, then I ask myself questions, like I'm the emcee. Then I step to the other side of the bathroom and answer the question I just asked. I did really good last night. I got all the answers right." Spaghetti about flew out of my mouth on that one, but I recovered. "So when I get married, it will just be a natural recession." I do believe a noodle lodged in my throat at that exact moment.

"You know, Savannah, you could have interviewed me," she said, getting all pitiful.

"Amber, my story wasn't about the quest to win a pageant," I said, trying to sound as diplomatic as possible.

"Oh, I know. It was about losing pageants."

"No, it wasn't just about losing pageants. Did you read it?"

"Yes, I read it. I do read, Savannah," she said, acting slightly irritated. "But I've lost pageants. I know what that's like. I could have shared my story."

"I told you, Amber, the article wasn't just about losing. The article was about different things. It was about the treasure of a destiny, the loss of a destiny, and the lessons we learn along the way. And a multitude have been learned by me today, trust me."

"What are you talking about? What have you learned?"

"Multitudes. But back to you. After your losses, did you make any life-changing decisions, other than just to compete again? I mean, if you don't win Miss United States of America, or Mrs. United States of America, are you going to start a Mrs. Senior United States of America?"

"You should bite your tongue. But actually there already is a—"

"Oh, please, tell me it's not true," I said, throwing my head back in utter disbelief.

"Well, I can't help it, but there is," she said, patting me on the arm and forcing me to look up at her purple mouth. "But I made a decision too, Savannah," she said, laying her fork down. "I made a decision after each loss, the decision to keep going, to keep trying. I'm not sure why. To someone like you, it probably sounds silly.

"But I determined a long time ago that of all the things I really wanted, I really want this. I really enjoy it all. Every aspect. Every moment of success erases every time I didn't hear my name called. So I keep trying. I keep waiting for the moment that some magical host will sing a song just for me. And everyone will stand around the stage and for that one moment, I will be the most special person in the room. Fortunately, I'll have the opportunity until I'm dead." She laughed in amusement at her ceaseless opportunity.

It struck me that inside Amber lay a desperate need to be approved. "But you've heard your name called, Amber. Every local pageant you've won has given you that moment, several actually. When will it be enough? When is it enough applause or enough adulation or enough praise? At some point, the need to be approved by others has to bow to the need to simply appreciate yourself, don't you think? You're beautiful. You're a tad extreme, but you're a nice young woman. You're talented. You have a great job. You get to take people into an unfamiliar place and make them feel at home."

"You think I do all of that?"

"Yes, you do. But I get the sense that's not enough for you."

"Not enough?"

"Well, is it? Let me tell you: I believe that inside each of us is a hole only one thing will ever fill. You can try to measure out its space and search the world over, but you won't find it there. It's an eternal purpose, and only eternity can fill what it created. No tiara or applause or walk down the runway with Lawrence Welk's bubbles will fill what heaven created in you. Every pageant judge this side of Dallas might declare you a perfect ten, but until you realize that's not true victory, you will never be happy. It's time to look up, Amber. It's the only place eternal things are found."

The tears that sat on the brim of her counterfeit eyelashes were proof that she had, for the first time, really heard me. And for the first time since I had met Miss Amber Topaz Childers, she was speechless. I was pretty wasted myself. Because as much as I was speaking to her, I was certain I was also speaking to myself.

Her brief inability to communicate gave me the opportunity to look at my watch, which read 1:10.

"I'm so sorry to have to leave, Amber, but I've got to get back to work." She still never spoke. And I wasn't quite sure what to do with her there. So I stood up, grabbed my purse, and put my hand on hers. I knew I might hate myself in the morning, but at that moment, there was only one appropriate response. "I'll be your friend, Amber. A real friend. I won't always tell you what you want to hear, but I will always tell you the truth. I'll get lunch. And we'll talk soon."

She looked up at me with dark brown eyes covered by green contact lenses, making them a lovely shade of ocean. She smiled slightly. A genuine Amber smile, not a smile of competition, not an interview moment. I returned it, understanding in that moment we really weren't so different after all.

CHAPTER THIRTY-ONE

W e need to talk. I have the information you want. I believe it is time you knew the truth. I'll meet you at the fountain at Forsythe Park at 2 p.m."

I would have completely missed the typewritten note had it not fallen to the floor when I laid my purse on my desk. I didn't know what to do. Should I run around screaming, "I've got the story. I've got the story!"? Should I call the police and request an escort? Should I even go at all? And was this even the story that should be told? After the fiasco of that morning, who knew what really needed to be told? But I knew I had to go.

My mind began to race. Maybe Mrs. Harvard had a change of heart. Maybe it was Mr. Cummings . . . or Katherine, finally ready to talk after what she had read in the paper today. Maybe she hated me now and wanted to slap me around. It was only 1:20. I would go stir-crazy before two. There was no way I could stay here. I had to get a Coke, get something.

I grabbed my purse and headed out the door, calling to Marla as I passed, "If anyone needs me, they can call me on my cell. I'm closing in on my story, and I'll be back later."

"You got it, girlfriend."

Curly Locks emerged from his car with a cup of coffee that looked mighty familiar. It was from Jake's. I knew he would want to talk, but there was no time. So I just answered his questions before he asked them. "I'm going to get a Coke. I have a lead on my story. I'll be back before quitting time, and I'm glad to see you finally got you some real coffee." With that, I got in my car and sped in the direction of Jake's. I grabbed my cell phone out of my purse as I navigated myself through Reynolds Square.

"Jackson County Courthouse," someone crooned.

"Gregory Taylor, please."

"One moment."

"Gregory Taylor."

"Grisham, it's Savannah," I said. "I believe something is about to break. My first story was a bomb, according to some, but maybe not everyone, but definitely my father and definitely Emma, and I'm not sure what my break is, I'm not even sure it is a break. I'm not sure even if it's anything at all; it could be nothing; it's probably nothing. No, it can't be nothing; I have to have something by tomorrow!"

"Would you stop and breathe? You're wearing me out, and I don't get paid enough for such nonsense. Now, take a breath and start at the beginning," he said.

I pulled the car in front of Dad's store and cut the engine. "I'm not even sure what the beginning is."

"Well, just start somewhere—you're driving me crazy," he said.

I started with the phone call from number III and went all the way up to the note on my desk a moment ago. "So anyway, now I'm going to get a Coke, because I couldn't sit in my office until two doing nothing except draft my 'Apology of a Loser.' So who do you think the note's from?"

"I have no idea."

"What do you mean you have no idea? I called you because I figured you'd know. Lawyers always know. And even if they don't, they act like they do. So start acting like you do!"

"Well then, I have a couple of ideas. Did Cummings act like he was in town?"

"No. Well, he never mentioned that he was. Not that he would have. You don't think it is him, do you? I mean if it is, I might need to take someone with me, just in case."

"Savannah, that man is not going to hurt you. He is old, well-known, and not in the business of killing local reporters who have never actually reported a thing a day in their lives."

"Oh, thanks! I'm just a fanny load of encouragement now!"

"You are so dramatic. Has anyone ever told you that you should really have been an actress?"

"Has anyone told you you should really not try to be a psychiatrist and dissect people's personalities?"

"Honestly, Savannah, I really don't know who it is. It could be anyone or no one. Do many people who aren't actually related to this story know what you are up to?" he asked.

"No, no one actually. I mean, I just told my dad the whole story. My mother knew, but she must be solving world hunger because I haven't even heard from her today." I gasped. "Oh my Lord, have mercy!"

"What? What?"

"I haven't heard from my mother today! Do you have any idea what that means?"

"I have absolutely no idea what that means."

"That means at this moment, my mother is somewhere in this city planning a party bigger than Texas. And she will have circus men and airplanes flying banners, and she's liable to have a billboard bigger than life with my face and name splattered across it. As soon as this is over, I have got to find her and stop her. She's the reason I'm in this mess in the first place."

"Savannah, it's time to let your mother go. You just go to the park, face whatever it is head-on, and see what it holds. You can handle it. Of that I'm sure."

"Do you really think I can?"

"You've proven it already. Look back, Savannah. Look back at all you've done this last week, and you'll know that nothing you can meet today will be more than what you've already had to face. Chin up, young girl. Counsel says, pursue," he said with a laugh. "But call me immediately."

"If you don't hear from me . . ."

"Trust me, I'll hear from you."

"Did this cost me? Because you were really weak today."

"Yes! For unappreciation I charge triple."

"OK, the check's in the mail."

Duke came over and put his head under my hand as soon as I sat down at a front table by the window. That was his way of letting anyone know he needed petting. Obliging, I took his head between my two hands and got up close, where his big black nose was almost touching mine. He thought that meant I needed to be kissed. Only my quick reflexes saved my face from being lovingly slathered with dog drool.

"Duke, do you have any idea how lucky you are?" I asked. His expression assured me he knew I was trying to give him a valuable life lesson. "People feed you, bathe you, kiss you, walk you, and pet you. You have no job, no bills, no responsibilities. Granted, you have issues with Vicky and that darling lab up the street, but don't we all? On the whole, you really have it made.

"And you are loved. Deeply loved. Maybe not by the people who have to buy a new pair of tennis shoes every other month, but by most. The women adore you." I could have sworn he smiled at that one. "And Dad, well, Dad would be hard pressed if ever forced to choose between you and Vicky. Don't take this for granted. Savor it, relish it, chase cats up trees, roll around in the mud, retrieve whatever your little heart desires, take baths in Vicky's pool. My stars, lick yourself if you want to. After all, that's what dogs do. You have only one life, Duke; live it well."

"You might want to see a counselor for that," Dad said as he sat down in the chair across from me.

"I've been hearing way too much about counselors lately."

"They make movies about people who talk to animals."

"You're thinking of movies about people who can hear animals talk. I only wish I knew what this old fella was thinking."

"No, it's probably best we don't," he said, laughing. "Especially for your mother's sake." I couldn't help but laugh at that. "What in the world are you doing back here in the middle of the afternoon? Please don't tell me you've lost your job already."

"No. I tried, but he refused. I'm here for the caffeine," I said, rising to go into the back. Duke followed me, hoping I might need more time to talk through things while rubbing his head. Dad followed too.

"I hear they have a Coke machine down at the *Chronicle*."

I reached the back room, pulled a glass out of the cabinet, and proceeded to the ice dispenser. "Actually, I have a two o'clock appointment at the park and had a few minutes to kill."

Dad came around to the side of the Coke machine where he knew he would be in my view. "What's going on?"

"I don't know," I told him, grabbing a straw from the straw box. I unwrapped it, placed it in my glass, and took a long drink. Then I backed up so I could lean against the counter. "I thought I had written a good story. But obviously it lacked wisdom. I got scolded by you and reamed out by Emma. My resignation was refused, I do believe my mother's planning a party bigger than one she would throw for 'Bushie,' and I'm headed to the park to meet a stranger who might want to kill me. And the day isn't even half over."

"So you have no idea who you're meeting at the park?"

"Absolutely no idea," I said, taking another long swig of my Coke. By then he was reaching for a Coke himself.

"Emma wasn't very happy, huh?"

"Madder than the wasp that flew up Victoria's dress."

"Let you have it, huh?"

"Both barrels."

"Still going to write a story about a rigged beauty pageant?"

"That or Dead Woman Walking."

CHAPTER THIRTY-TWO

The fountain stared at me from the south side of Forsythe Park. One fifty. It was time to do the work of a journalist. It was time to discover my story.

Unfortunately, it couldn't be done here in the car, even though my sore behind had finally found a comfortable position on Old Betsy's pillow. I wasn't sure I wanted this story anymore, or this job or this chaos or this changing relationship with my father. I wasn't sure I wanted anything to change. *Maybe I should go back and get my doctorate in how to become a professional student. Maybe I shouldn't move out. Maybe I'm pressuring myself to grow up before I'm ready. My word, I'm only twenty-four. I'm just a babe. Babes shouldn't be putting their lives in danger for a dumb beauty pageant. Babes should be curled up on chairs with their mothers. Sharing stories with their fathers. But I am not a babe. I, Savannah Phillips, am a grown woman.* Extricating myself from the car, I began a slow but determined walk to the fountain.

At five 'til two, I saw her at the top of the main path leading to the fountain. She was wearing a beautiful peach linen pantsuit. I stopped before she saw me. This was no time for a Vicky encounter. I was too frustrated to see her anyway, and whoever was meeting me didn't want to have to deal with two Phillips women at once. So I withdrew to the other side of the sidewalk. I watched her for a minute from behind some shrubbery. At least she wasn't tucked away in her office coordinating hula dancers and knife throwers. *You need to go to a meeting or a walking tour or a trolley ride or something.* But she wasn't with anyone. She was standing in front of the fountain as if she were waiting.

As if struck by a flying tiara, the realization hit me: She was waiting for me. Vicky was my appointment.

My thoughts ran out of control. *What did she know? Had she been a part of something? Did I know my mother at all?*

Must a woman have all her life-changing moments in the course of one day?

I looked at her again. Even from here I could see the concern on her face, the intensity of her brow. Now granted, Vicky was always intense, but this was a different expression. I saw a mother about to play a different role in her daughter's life than either had ever known.

I could run, but no number of miles would ever create enough distance to leave behind what I had seen at the fountain. I knew that going forward was the only option. Vicky knew too. I reset my step.

She turned around and saw me coming, then smiled at me in a bashful way never before directed toward me. Dad had received this smile a thousand times. It was half "I'm sorry," half "You'll appreciate me after you hear what I actually have to say" kind of smile.

"Hello, darling, I can only imagine what you're thinking," she said, trying to offer a faint laugh.

"I'm not sure that you can. I don't even know what I'm thinking." I stared at her blankly.

"Would you like to walk?" she asked, motioning to the side of the fountain.

"Sure." I followed her lead.

"I haven't really been able to sleep since our conversation the other night. And after your conversation with Mr. Cummings and after reading your article in the paper, I knew you needed to know the whole story. I wish I had told you earlier. It could have spared all of us pain, especially Emma."

"You know something that could have stopped me from writing that article?"

"I just need you to listen to me."

My agitation grew. "I'm not sure that I want to listen to you."

"Savannah, watch your tone. I'm sure you've had an eventful day, but I'm still your mother."

"Eventful? Eventful? I would say so. I've been reprimanded by my father, screamed at by Emma, and embarrassed in front of my entire office. And now you're here with information that could have stopped it all. Why now?"

"Why now am I telling you, or just why now?"

"Why, after all these years of sticking your nose into *everything* from the very beginning, would you wait until now, after a tombstone's being carved with my initials?"

"Savannah, what in the world are you talking about?"

"Don't act like you don't know what I'm talking about. You know good and well what I'm talking about!"

"I know good and well that my hand is about to meet your face if you speak to me that way again."

I tried to pull back my tone, but I was so angry that trying to contain twenty-four years of whys was virtually impossible. "You're why I'm here. I wouldn't be going through any of this if you would have just stayed out of my fiction contest at school. But no, you had to get involved. You couldn't just let me win on my own."

"You think I helped you win that contest?"

"Mother, please, let's lose the drama. I know you had everything to do with me winning that contest."

Vicky hooked her arm in mine and tugged my rigid frame along beside her. "You think you're all grown up, don't you, Savannah? You think you know everything, I can tell. Well, you walk and listen; I'll talk. Understand?"

I harrumphed. "Talk away." Her heels made an irritating click-ing sound on the sidewalk.

"During my reign as Miss Georgia United States of America, I found out that the pageant was rigged. One night during my preparation for the Miss United States of America Pageant I was over at Mr. and Mrs. Todd's house going over my schedule of appearances. Mr. and Mrs. Cummings were there as well. I had found out the families were good friends, but I had never thought much about it. That night, I left them at the table after dinner and went to the bathroom. As I was returning, I heard Mr. Cummings mention to Mr. Todd that the sale of the program pages had been extremely high. Something inside me told me to just stop and lis-ten. So I stayed tucked away in the hallway where they couldn't see me.

"Mr. Cummings asked Mr. Todd what he had done to encour-age such high sales. Mr. Todd started laughing and said that *some-how* the girls had gotten the idea that the more pages they sold the more likely they were to win. He said the girls had set themselves into competition with each other before the pageant had ever started. 'It's so funny, isn't it?' he said. 'Watching those girls try so hard, knowing I decide the winner on the final night myself. The god of the pageant, that's me. I know who I want, and I have to live with her for a year, so you bet I'm going to choose her.'"

"He said that?"

"Hard to believe, isn't it?" After all this time, judging the pag-eant had been about nothing but power. The craziness of it all was just settling in when she continued. "Well, then Mrs. Todd asked Mrs. Cummings if she had received her thank-you note and gift. Mr. Cummings answered for her, saying she had and that was what made him realize they had sold a substantial amount of pages."

"So it was true."

"Yes, it was. Mr. Todd thanked Mrs. Cummings for her com-pany's fine printing job and laughed again and called it the most expensive comped service anyone had ever been given. At that point, I didn't know how I was ever going to return to that room without my face giving away what I knew."

"How did you do it?"

"I just summoned all my acting experience and gave the best performance I'd ever given," she said, putting her hand on her chest.

I almost said, "Up to that moment," but I didn't want to stop her momentum.

She continued. "When they saw me come around the corner, they immediately changed the subject to the Georgia weather. Everyone finished dinner, and Mr. and Mrs. Cummings left. I told them I needed to leave as well. I climbed in my car and cried the whole way home. At that moment, I knew I hadn't won legitimately. I had been picked by two sickening individuals, not by five legitimate judges, and certainly not because of my all-around talent and personality."

"And you do have that."

"Well, I think so. Anyway, I didn't know what I was going to do. I didn't want to tell anyone, because I was so mortified. How could I tell people that I wasn't really Miss Georgia United States of America, but I was Miss Money Market Miss?"

"I know you did not just call yourself Miss Money Market Miss.'"

"Yes, I did. I felt cheapened, violated. I felt like someone had stolen my greatest dream from me."

I couldn't let her go with that. I slipped out of her arm and made her look at me square in the eye. "I can't believe that was your greatest dream. And I don't mean any offense, but I don't know how you can compare losing a beauty pageant to what I've lost. I mean, it is nothing more than a group of women strutting around in bathing suits, vying for five people's approval, and sauntering across a stage in expensive and hideous gowns."

"Not all of them are hideous."

"Mother, honestly, how can that be your greatest dream? Those women are a bunch of overcooked, overemotional, over-the-top phonies."

"That's enough, Savannah Phillips!" Mother said with a tone I had heard only in moments about to involve extreme contact. "Sit down and let me explain before you make me out to be some mindless twit."

She sat down and turned to stare me straight in the eye. Now she was scaring me.

"I've always known you have never understood pageants. I've always known that you thought I was whacked, or whatever word you girls use these days, simply because I enjoyed competing in beauty pageants. But let me explain it to you as clearly as possible, Savannah." I sat quietly. "It was never about fame or fortune to me. It was never about people's applause or even their approval. It was about being part of an organization that offered me opportunities to take the things that I believed in, that I enjoyed, and bring them to a more visible stage. I knew if I ever became Miss United States of America, that it would open doors for me like nothing else could ever do. And it was fun, Savannah. Believe it or not, it was just a lot of fun."

"Fun?"

"Yes, Miss Priss, fun. I got to meet wonderful women. They're not all as you say, Savannah. And after all of that—after the sequined dresses, big hair, and tacky talent costumes—I was able to travel the state and meet people and talk to them about my dreams and my ideals. And do you know what, Savannah? People listened."

"I have no doubt you captured their full attention."

"Well, they didn't listen to me because my name was Victoria Musick. They listened to me because I was Miss Georgia United States of America. Granted, times have changed. Granted, the women's movement has tried to make us look like a bunch of hollow, high-heeled, out-of-touch simpletons. But some of those women today are just like I was over twenty-five years ago. They have goals and dreams. They have things to say that people need to hear. And they see beauty pageants as the avenue to open those doors."

"I'm sure not all of them feel that way."

"Sure, some of them have other goals. Some of them just want to say they're the best at something, at anything. But there really are some who, just like you, want to author books or write articles to reveal to the world that they have something of value to say. Is it old-fashioned? Maybe to some. Is it still enjoyable to others? Absolutely. Does it hurt anyone? Obviously it does. Do we all have to know how to win gracefully as well as lose gracefully? Eventually. Because each of us will do both at one point or another. And I think you've learned that yourself today."

"Yes, ma'am. I think I have."

We are good women, with good hearts, though some push the limits with their obsession. But some . . . no, *many,* Savannah, are women just like you, except their book is a pageant. Their story is a song or a ballet or a moment in front of a willing audience. They may never get a record deal, or tour with the New York Metropolitan Ballet, but to their parents, every moment was exceptional."

"As it should be to any parent."

"And it is with yours, rest assured. So for that one magical moment they are living a dream. Now, you can dilute that to mind-lessness if you'd like, but you'd have to include me in your sweeping generalizations. And I may enjoy things that are different from you, Savannah, but that doesn't make me any less capable than you. It just makes me different. I have always encouraged your dreams. It is time that you at least try to understand mine." She paused. She breathed. But she did not cry. "For many girls, Savannah, losing can cause them to feel their lives are over."

"Mother, how can losing a pageant cause someone to think that life is over?"

"It's the death of a dream, Savannah. It's me watching them crown someone else Miss United States of America, when all my life that is what I thought I would be. It's you watching Grant marry someone else, or writing your first article for the paper and it not being received the way you had hoped. It's not that you don't think better things will come your way. It's that this one thing is lost forever. And like anything, it is a loss that you grieve. And for one moment, I thought I had lost my dream."

My anger flared up again, "I hope you can remember that feeling, because that's how you made me feel. You stole my greatest dream."

She looked at me exasperated, wondering, I'm sure, if I had heard one word she just said. "I didn't rig your contest, Savannah. A friend of mine from college noticed your name and where you were from and called to see if you were my daughter. He just happened to be the head of the publishing company. We hadn't spoken in years. I told him you were and that you were an excellent writer. I let him know, however, very clearly, that I didn't want you to know we had even spoken. If you didn't deserve to win that contest, then you shouldn't be the winner, regardless of our friendship."

"But your name was on my notification. I called them. They thought I was you . . ." Even as I said it and replayed the conversation, I realized that Mr. Peterson had said nothing to indicate that Mother had asked for their special favor in any way. It was only my assumption. My assumptions made me give away my publishing deal. My stupid assumptions made me write an article that should never have been written. My assumptions had me sitting on a park bench with my mother, realizing I had just totally and successfully screwed up my life. "I threw it all away!" I buried my head in my hands. "I threw it all away to prove a point to you!"

She sat down and wrapped her arms around me. "Well now, you're experiencing the loss of a dream. It hurts. And it blinds. But there was a greater plan for you, darling. And you found it, wrapped in a newspaper. You're a great writer. Today's experience will make you a more compassionate writer. Don't lose what you feel today, because it will forever change who you are and what you write."

I looked up at her and saw my mother in a different light. She was not trying to manipulate this moment. She was trying to help me encounter her feelings. She had stated her case, and I could accept or ignore it. But it wouldn't change it. This was who she was. She was a woman who'd experienced dreams and losses. A woman like me.

We would never dress alike, walk alike, talk alike, or ever think alike, rest assured. But we were still the same in this regard. Her dreams led her down runways; mine led me down hallways. Hers required lipstick and hairspray; mine required laptops and Post-it notes.

"Forgive me, Mom," I said, looking at her very similarly to the way I had looked at my father earlier that morning, knowing our relationship would never be the same.

She stared back at me. "'Mom.' I like that."

"All these years I couldn't understand what this fascination was, this craving for this type of life. Then I met Emma and Katherine. Each of you walked the same road and yet are so different. You are not mindless, and please don't ever think I have thought that about you. But today I've seen something in you I've never seen before. I see me."

"Well, now, that took a while, didn't it?" she said with a smile.

I laughed. "I always thought I got my drive from Dad, and this idea that I have a destiny, a place, an actual calling. But I got it from you."

"That knowledge is in the core of each of us, Savannah. And at the end of the day, there really is only one dream: to touch some part of the world with something of eternal value. The only thing that differentiates the call is the method."

"I love you. If I become half the woman you are, I will have achieved great things. Will you tell me the rest of your story?"

"Sure." We stood and continued our walk. "I called your father after I gathered myself. We hadn't been dating long, but I knew I was going to marry Jake the first time I saw him." She still spoke his name with tenderness, even after twenty-five years. "I've never met a stronger, yet gentler, man. He holds us together. He's that quiet strength. I'm that flamboyant moment!" Her face revealed a delicate smile. "He just did it for me. You know what I mean?"

"Would you stop trying to talk like a teenager? I do not want to know all of your intimate feelings. I know you love him. Now, focus. On with the story."

"OK, OK. But you're a lucky girl to have two parents who love each other like we do."

"Yes, I am," not adding how lucky we all were to have Jake to balance the chaos.

"Anyway, he told me that I needed to get to the bottom of it. Even if it meant finding out I was an illegitimate winner. He let me know that I couldn't be a part of something that was a lie. And if it meant giving up my dream, then I would have to give up a dream and wait for another to replace it. So the next day I went straight back to the Todds' house and told Mr. Todd what I had overheard the night before. He assured me I had misunderstood, that none of it was anything more than two old friends cracking jokes and acting crazy, that I had been the unanimous choice. I didn't know what else to do but believe what he told me. Your father and I agreed that I would continue with my preparation, and we would just try to find out anything to the contrary that we could."

"So Dad's known about this all along as well?"

"Yes, he has."

"You two are good."

"We know," she said matter-of-factly. "Anyway, for the next six months I prepared for the Miss United States of America Pageant and your father tried to find out anything he could to disprove what Mr. Todd had said. But we were young. We didn't have any connections with anyone and very little spare time. He was in graduate school full-time, and I was an eighteen-year-old dreamer. We were more concerned really with seeing each other when we could. And honestly, Savannah, once I met your father, all I was really excited about was getting married. Then, when I didn't win the Miss United States of America Pageant, I just wished the next six months away."

"When it was time to give up my crown, there was a beautiful young lady competing that year. She was so petite and talented, and people had been talking about her all over the state. She had emceed numerous local pageants and the word was that she was magical. She could captivate an audience. Well, everyone compared her to me," she said with a big smile, apparently proud that she was captivating and magical.

"But for some reason, every time her name was mentioned by anyone, Mr. Todd got irate. He accused her of taking another girl's song for her talent competition. I know it's totally ludicrous, but no one even gave her the opportunity to defend herself. Looking back, I believe it was her character in general he had a problem with. Word got back to me about another girl who was competing for her third time in the pageant. Mr. Todd had nothing but wonderful things to say about her. So I decided I would just watch. Not being in the middle of it gave me the ability to be far more objective.

"During the competition, the petite one just captured everyone's heart. She was a lady. She was extremely talented and even won the swimsuit competition. The other girl was beautiful, don't get me wrong. But the petite one stole the audience. But when the evening ended, the one Mr. Todd loved walked away with the crown. The whole audience gasped at the announcement. And I left knowing I was going to get to the bottom of that mess," Her southern indignation rose even now.

"Two days after giving up my title I went back to their house. I told him I didn't believe what he had said, and that I was going to be keeping my eye on them. If they were up to anything, I was going to make sure that they didn't ruin another girl's life in any way, shape, or form.

"I guess my naiveté thought mere talk would work. But it wasn't until Emma lost that I realized what they were actually doing. That year, I went into undercover mode. I used all the influences of Judge Hoddicks, got all of the bank records with the listing of every deposit made into Patricia Cummings's account from Mrs. Todd's account, knew every deposit and every note and everything imaginable. It was documented and categorized. I mean, they were so silly. They didn't even try to really hide anything. I finally got all of the past score sheets, and they revealed that in each illegitimate win, Mr. Cummings III or IV had scored a woman fairly in the preliminaries so he wouldn't rouse suspicion among the other judges, then gave her ones in every phase of competition on the final night."

"And you had actual proof of this?"

"I had every piece of evidence needed not only to prove but to prosecute."

"What did you do with it?"

"I gave it all to Judge Hoddicks. I asked him not to prosecute unless forced, because I really didn't feel Emma needed her name slathered in scandal with everything else that she was going through."

"Unfortunately, I took care of that for you."

"Yes, you did. But years ago I even went to her house and tried to help her, but she refused. She broke my heart, Savannah. Judge Hoddicks went down to Jackson. He met privately with Judge Tucker, and then they met privately with Mr. Todd and Mr. Cummings III and IV. Judge Hoddicks said it wasn't pretty, but it was gratifying. They reached a private settlement and all of them were forced to leave their positions. None of them have any part in the pageant anymore, and only by Judge Hoddicks's mercy are they not serving jail time.

"So that's what happened. That is all of it," she said, sitting down on another park bench and dabbing her forehead with a tissue.

I sat down beside her and turned to ask, "How did you feel when you saw your scores and realized that you had only won because they made you win, over someone else?"

"Well, that didn't happen in every situation. In the year I won and about nine other pageants through the years, the person that actually won had indeed been chosen to be the best by all of the judges. I had actually been the winner. Now, could I have handled it if I wasn't? I don't know. It's a question I never had to ask."

"You could have. I'm certain of it."

"I hope I could have. I hope that by now it would be enough for me to be the wife of an incredible man, the mother of fascinatingly passionate children, and a woman who is making a difference in the city she loves. But I'll never really know the answer to that question, Savannah. I'll never really know." We had come full circle, and she stared at the fountain in front of our bench.

"Why did you wait to tell me all of this?" I asked. I wasn't angry anymore, just puzzled.

"Because I was hoping you would see the bigger picture here, Savannah. There really is one."

"You're not the first to say such a thing."

"Then you might want to listen. The intrigue is great. The stories of mayhem would be entertaining. But are those the things you want people to leave with? Did you leave fiction writing to just uncover real fiction, or did you leave fiction writing to make a difference, to change a city?" She stood up. "What did you give up your dream for, Savannah? Beyond proving something to me?" She bent down, kissed me on my forehead, and simply walked away.

I called after her. "So all those contests I thought you influenced, I really won on my own merit?"

She just raised her hand and shrugged her shoulders. I knew her well enough to know. And I watched as her Coach embroidered sling-back pumps clicked all the way home.

I laughed out loud. I got myself so tickled I couldn't get up off of the bench. I laughed until my side hurt. I laughed at taping and dresses worn backward, at strange women singing in my car, and at the last week of pent-up anxiety. I laughed at the people who looked at me as if I were crazy. I laughed at the insanity of my life. I laughed at the thought of having to write another story by tomorrow afternoon.

Finally, I headed back to my office to pick up my computer. I had a story to write. Could I do it? Well, I am Savannah from Savannah. Victoria is my mother and Jake is my father. Oh yeah, I could do it. Wasn't sure I really wanted to, but at least I knew I could.

CHAPTER THIRTY-THREE

G irl, well, what can I say? You just did an amazing job. I'm not even sure that *I* would have been more interesting. There is a possibility, but I'm truly not certain," Paige said on the other end of the line.

"Well, not everyone appreciated it."

"Oh, the Emma thing. That was a little risky, but it was true. And you have always been a declarer of truth."

"Yes, well, I about declared my truth all the way to the unemployment line."

"You almost got fired?"

"Not exactly, but really I don't want to talk about me today. What have you been doing all day?"

"Well, I've eaten breakfast, eaten lunch, and jabbered with every plaid Bermuda shorts, kneesock-wearing gentleman that has a hotel reservation in this city tonight. But I sold three pieces of art, and that, my friend, is enough to take the rest of the week off."

"Ooh, I think that's a great idea. You should treat yourself."

"We should both treat ourselves. How about we go grab some dessert after Bible study tonight? You want me to just pick you up?"

"That sounds great. Come about six-thirty."

"OK. I'll just honk."

"I'm sure you will."

"Bye."

"Bye."

I entered the side door on the first floor and came up the back stairs that lead into the kitchen. There was no reason to return to work because the day was already over. Mother was busy preparing dinner and talking on the phone at the same time.

Dad and Duke apparently weren't home yet, and Thomas, well, who knows where he was. As I went upstairs to wash my hands and freshen up, I heard Vicky say, "I know. She's just fabulous. I think I might take out another one of those ads to surprise her. You know, in all these years she's never guessed that it was me," she said, laughing. The poor woman had no clue. I wasn't going to give her one either, but I would have a long talk with my dad about making sure she never placed another ad again.

The Wednesday-night message was timely. With excerpts from Jim Collins's book *From Good to Great,* the sermon revealed, "The only ones who accomplish great things that last are those who live a life not swayed by trends, but who hold fast to what they know to be true."

In the car, Paige put her key into the ignition but didn't turn it. "Savannah?"

"Yeah?"

"Do you think what I do has any real eternal value?" she asked in a rare moment of introspection.

"I think you have done exactly what you were destined to do. You've been given an amazing gift, and you've put it to good use. And each time someone steps into your gallery and purchases one of your amazing gifts, you give them joy and pleasure every time they pass by it hanging in their foyer or hallway. There is eternity in that."

"You think so?"

"I should know. I have an original hanging in my office."

"Did you get permission for that?" I asked, laughing at the two entertaining creatures sprawled across the sofa. Their heads perked up simultaneously at the sound of my voice.

"We don't have to get permission for anything, do we, Duke?" Duke simply laid his head back down on his side of the sofa, knowing he didn't need permission from anything or anyone other than the man by his side. "I think you forget who's in charge here," Dad said, patting Duke on his hind end.

I walked over and took a seat in the chair next to the sofa. "I'm not sure if it's you or the hairy creature lying next to you."

"It's both of us. When I'm too tired to be in charge, Duke steps into his rightful place."

"What about Thomas?"

"Duke has more authority because of his actual time spent on the premises. Pretty good sermon, wasn't it?"

"Yeah, it was great. It seems like that place has grown so much since I've been gone."

"Yeah, it has. They really have the pulse of this city. They're reaching people who haven't had a place to belong. They've given them a type of family. Those of us who have good ones forget some people have never known what that's like." He continued petting Duke without looking at me.

I scooted to the front of my chair, getting as close to Dad's head as possible. "Speaking of our family, I overheard a conversation with Vicky, I mean Mother, and one of her friends. Seems she's planning to put another ad in the paper."

Jake snickered.

"Dad, please. She doesn't even think I know it's her, and I wish I could put a stop to this. But you and I both know you're the only one that can pull the plug on her madness. People who aren't too excited that I have this job will be even more unhappy when they realize it's still mine on Friday. And the last thing I need is Mother making a declaration that she thinks my employment at the paper needs to be celebrated in print."

Dad cocked his head. "Trust me, you will see no more ads in the paper."

"Thanks." I stood up, leaned over and kissed him on the head, and turned to leave the kitchen. "You do know you are not only helping me, but you are sparing innocent generations to come. My children will thank you." He raised his hand that was petting Duke, then put it right back where it had been.

It was around nine-thirty when I made it to bed, and I was exhausted. For some weird reason I was thankful for all that had transpired this day. Thankful that even though it had been difficult, it had still been good. I finally fell asleep.

Somewhere in the wee hours of the morning I dreamed that when I showed up at work, everyone was standing in front of the door holding up the front page, which boasted a full-page ad of congratulations and a half-page picture of me and Vicky when I was eight and she had us dressed alike for Easter. We wore matching floral dresses with dangerously large bows planted on the side of our waists, I in black patent-leather shoes and she in her black patent-leather pumps. I woke up about three in the morning in a cold sweat. I ran downstairs and scoured our picture albums for any photo that could be totally humiliating if it were to appear in a newspaper. I put them all in a folder, took the folder to my bedroom, and hid it in the bookcase behind a stack of books.

I enjoyed dreamless sleep the rest of the night.

CHAPTER THIRTY-FOUR

We have a mini YMCA on our first floor, which Vicky designed years ago. When the world decided it was fashionable to do aerobics, so did Vicky. She bought Savannah out of every leotard it had, and when she couldn't find any more in town, she had someone design them for her. No one understood as well as Vicky did the importance of looking good when working out in your own basement by yourself.

A trainer from one of the finest state-of-the-art gyms in Atlanta designed her a fabulous workout facility. He did one whole wall of mirrors and about every weight you could imagine, along with a treadmill and a rowing machine. But the only thing Vicky ever did was aerobics. That lasted, in total, forty-eight days.

Every morning at six a.m., she came out of her room in full makeup, totally coiffed hair, and manicured nails. In exactly sixty minutes, she returned upstairs. The amazing thing was, she never came out perspiring. I assumed she never actually moved enough to produce perspiration. But regardless of what she actually did while she was down there, after forty-eight days exactly, she never returned to do it again. Not to say that she doesn't go down there.

Oh, she goes down there, all right, and we hear her singing at the top of her lungs. Usually it's when she's had a really bad day, on which she usually sings show tunes. On the days that have been significantly challenging, however, we are treated to Vicky's version of "Nobody Knows the Trouble I've Seen." Reality is, the only ones with troubles are the afflicted creatures upstairs forced to endure such recreation. Duke retreats to the top floor and hides under Dad's bed.

This morning, it poured outside. I silently prayed the rain would wash away the horror of yesterday. I spent time lifting a few free weights, for which I was sure I would pay the next day, then spent thirty good minutes on the treadmill, perspiring profusely. When I returned upstairs, I found Duke sitting dejectedly at the door. The one thing that rain brought him was the inability to be walked at all. He knew today was going to be one of those days.

"I'll see you tonight," I called into the kitchen to Mother as I raced for the door.

"You'll have to start dinner without me. I've got a five o'clock meeting tonight. I had to call an emergency meeting because some developer wants to tear down one of our houses and put in a singles' bar. Can you imagine me letting that happen? These people and their crazy ideas. I don't know what city they think they've come to, but this isn't sin city. This is Savannah. And it doesn't happen here unless it comes through me."

"I'm sure they'll figure that out soon enough."

"Yes, they will. And no singles' bar will be replacing a historical home in the heart of our city. I guess the next thing they'll want is adult entertainment and bathhouses. These people need to go to church. If they want to meet someone worth meeting, that might be a fine place for them to start. Singles' bars! When I was young, people didn't need help meeting people." She turned back to the sink, and I was certain the conversation could go on without me. I sneaked out.

My phone was ringing as I made my way to my barely pigmented world. "Savannah," I heard Marla say from the other end, "I just sent a lady back to your desk."

I pulled out some framed pictures of Paige, college buddies, and my family and placed them on the far corner of my desk. "Is she as uptight as the one yesterday?"

"No, she seems a lot calmer than yesterday's adventure. A little cleaner too."

"Well, thanks for telling me. I hear her coming." I braced myself, not certain who would appear around the corner. Much to my surprise and anxiousness, it was Katherine, looking perfectly stunning.

"Good morning, Savannah. I'm sorry to bother you at work."

"Oh, it's not a bother at all. Please have a seat," I said, motioning to the chair just inside my modular wall.

"Actually, the rain has stopped. Would you have a moment to take a walk?" *Wish Emma would have wanted to take a walk,* I thought.

"Sure. That would be nice. Here, we can just go out the back door," I said, motioning to the door that wasn't far from my desk.

"Cute cubicle."

I opened the door, and a blast of Savannah heat caught us off guard. "Well, it's not much, but it's mine. I guess you're here to talk about my article."

"I've known about your article since the day you invited me to the pageant. You're not the most subtle person I've ever met," she said gently.

"Pretty pathetic, aren't I."

"No, pretty fearless, I would say. I'm wondering how long you've known about me?"

"I found Gloria's tape of your interview the day that I went through some of her files. So when I came into your store the second time, I realized the voice on the tape was yours."

Her flesh-toned mules clicked in rhythm as we walked. "Why didn't you just ask me about it?"

"I honestly just wanted to get to know you. But now that we're talking about it, may I ask why you didn't tell Gloria your story?"

"Because for me, the real story wasn't about a rigged beauty pageant. It was about the decisions I made for my life after the pageant. I read your article, Savannah. You had some good points in there, but you had the wrong premise."

"What do you mean?"

"My heart breaks for Emma, it really does. And I do think your point about people in positions of authority using them wisely is a story in and of itself. But Emma's decision really had nothing to do with the decisions the judges made. The ultimate decision was Emma's and Emma's alone. Let me tell you the difference between disappointment and defeat."

"I'm listening."

"We all have moments of disappointment, Savannah. But we don't experience defeat until we invite disappointment to stay with us. Emma allowed disappointment to define her life. She made a home there; she got married there and had children there. She held hands with disappointment and it led her to abuse, lies, torment, and more unhappiness than she ever intended. Disappointment gave way to her defeat."

"I think I understand."

"It only takes one moment of real confrontation with the truth to force defeat out."

"I guess that's what you did?"

Katherine nodded slowly. "Yes, I met up with disappointment. But when I realized it was a thief, I made it leave." She paused to see if I was listening.

"So how did your moment of disappointment come?"

"Well, about thirty years ago, I competed in the Miss Georgia US of A Pageant."

"Did you just call it US of A?"

"Yes."

"That's not sacrilegious to you?"

"No," she looked at me as if I needed to be examined.

"Just checking. Go ahead."

"Anyway, I was twenty years old and had two more years of school left. A couple of friends who had competed in the pageant before talked me into being in it myself. Well, I had never been in a pageant in my life," she said, raising her hand in amusement. "But they told me they were going to do it again and we could all do it together. That made it exciting enough for me."

"You and I have different interpretations of exciting."

"Well, when I came away with the title of Miss Savannah US of A I was astonished. Are you sure you want to hear this?"

"Absolutely. Go ahead." I had been around beauty queens all my life, and I mean all my life, and Katherine was like none of these. I may have been mistaken about her story being the one I needed to tell, but it was still a story I personally wanted to hear.

"Well, the director of the Miss Savannah US of A Pageant took the Miss Georgia US of A Pageant extremely seriously. The day after they had topped my head with a tiara and announced me the winner, the director and I met to begin my preparation for the next competition. As far as she was concerned, I needed a total overhaul, and she had less than nine months to get me to competition level."

"Competition level?"

"My question exactly. All I knew was that I had sung in a borrowed dress, walked around in a two-year-old swimsuit, and interviewed in one of my mother's suits. I figured if that worked for Miss Savannah US of A, it should work for Miss Georgia US of A. But she was sure it wouldn't.

"So for the next nine months, every weekend I met with the former Miss Savannah US of A to go over every aspect of competition. She assured me that I had what it took to win. And by the end of nine months, with a new hairdo, fabulous clothes, a knowledge of every current event and any other event of most of history, I was ready to sing my heart out with my version of 'Where the Boys Are,' designed to make grown men cry. It even had choreography."

"Go, Katherine."

"I did. I won both the interview and evening gown competitions. But then I didn't even place in the top five. I was shocked. I had grown from a young lady who had won Miss Savannah US of A on a dare into a woman who was taking this event seriously. After they announced the winner, the night shifted into slow motion."

"How so?"

"I don't remember them crowning her, her walk down the runway, or the emcee saying good night. I just stood there in shock, wondering how in the world I had not only lost, but hadn't even placed. Somehow I got back to my hotel room, and I found a copy of the auditor's sheet underneath my door. Those sheets revealed something that to this day I've never told anyone."

"What?"

"I had the high scores in every category of the pageant. Beyond the interview and evening gown, I had also won talent and tied for first in swimsuit. Can you believe that?" she asked more of herself than of me. "But on the final night, for some reason, one of the judges gave me a one in every single category. Somewhere between Friday night and Saturday night, this judge was convinced by something or someone that I wasn't the one who needed to leave that evening as Miss Georgia US of A."

"But how do you know it was an actual copy of the auditor's sheet?"

"Well, each judge has to sign the bottom of their scorecard for authenticity and sign the final auditor's ballot as well. Earlier that week I had participated in my personal interview with the judges' panel. As a contestant, one of the greatest things you can do is to leave your personal interview with a memorable thought. So at the end of my session, I told the judges I was starting a time capsule that I would open in thirty years on my fiftieth birthday, and I wanted this experience to be a part of that. I had brought my pageant program book and placed it underneath my chair. I pulled it out and told them that each contestant had already signed it for me, and that it would be an even greater memory if they would be willing to sign it for me as well. You could tell they were all flattered, and I had obviously come up with a rather ingenious idea."

"All these years, I thought my mother had come up with that concept herself. I should have known better." We both laughed.

"So when I got a copy of the auditor's sheet, I was able to compare it to the signatures in my book. Each one was exactly the same."

A drop of rain hit my cheek, and I suggested we turn back. "Who would want you to have that information?"

"I've asked myself that same question a million times. It had to be either a judge or an auditor. Someone who realized what had happened in retrospect, or someone who had a conscience check a little too late."

"I know who gave it to you."

"You do? Who?"

"Mr. Harvard. He and Mr. Wilcox never audited for that pageant again," I said. Every piece of the puzzle was beginning to form a perfectly fitted whole.

"Why do you think it was Mr. Harvard?"

"Well, I actually met with Mr. Harvard's wife, and I'm sure that is why my questions upset her so. I do wonder, though, why he would give it to you. What could you do with it?"

"Well, I've had thirty years to ask myself those questions. I honestly believe that they hoped I would make this public so they wouldn't have to. They believed what had happened was wrong but didn't want to be the ones to reveal it. They probably thought I would be mad enough to go tell anyone who would listen."

"Why didn't you? Why didn't you go to a paper then or question the pageant directors or contact the judges or auditors?"

"I thought I would give it a couple of months to settle in, get over the shock, and then evaluate what I wanted to do. By then, I had started my last year of school and that is when I met Jim."

At the very mention of his name, it seemed Katherine left for a place reserved for only the greatest of lovers. As I watched the shift in her gaze, I knew that until my heart held that respect, that divine regard, for another man, I would remain alone. Having witnessed that kind of love truly exists, I would be foolish to settle for less.

She caught me taking in her transformed countenance, and she blushed. "Honestly, once I met him I didn't think about much else until years later. Meeting him was the best thing that ever happened to me. He transferred in from Mississippi State for his senior year, then he graduated. He went to the University of Alabama for only that one year. If I had been Miss Georgia US of A, I wouldn't have returned to school. The one year I would have missed would have prevented me from meeting the man I fell in love with."

"And you wouldn't be here today. Walking with me in Savannah."

"No, I wouldn't be a lot of things. But when I finally opened the time capsule, it seemed maybe it was time to tell my story. And Gloria seemed perfect. But sitting there, it was clear the better life had been lived."

"So would you say your loss was part of a better destiny?"

"Oh yes. Even though I could have spent the last thirty years being called a former Miss Georgia United States of America, I much prefer being called Mrs. Owens. And you can say that in your article if you want to. That love was my greatest achievement, gained only because of what seemed at the time to be my greatest defeat. I truly believe, Savannah, that a divine presence guided my life for an eternal purpose." Katherine finished her story just as we arrived at the back door to the paper.

"I've taken enough of your time; I'm sure you need to get back to work and I need to get back to the bookstore."

"You're an amazing lady, Katherine Owens," I said. "And I'm sorry for your loss—not the pageant, but Mr. Owens."

"To have a love like we had, Savannah, I don't deserve anyone's sorrow. I just hope you find someone to love that way in your lifetime."

"After today, there isn't any other option." I reached out and wrapped her in a hug.

"Don't settle for the Ishmael," she said in my ear, "when you can have the Isaac. In anything, Savannah."

I held on for a moment longer. She let me go. I tried to blink away my tears. "I'll come see you soon."

"I'd be disappointed if you didn't." I watched her go. The real story had found me.

CHAPTER THIRTY-FIVE

Before I walked into the paper, I took a moment to take in my city. It was different to me somehow. It took a moment, but I began to appreciate the fact that it wasn't really the city that had changed; it was me. I wasn't Betty anymore; I was Savannah. Savannah from Savannah.

I had somehow grown into myself, grown into the things about me that I liked and the things I had refused to see. The things that I had respected about myself and those denied would both have to be accepted. They were all me—the good, the bad, and the Vicky. They all made up Savannah.

As I made my way back to my prosaic world, even it didn't seem quite as flat as it had when I left. I tried to envision amazing things happening within my makeshift cosmos. But first, a stop by the ladies' room.

The voices coming into the bathroom after me were obnoxious and giddy. "She about got her prissy little behind fired, is what I heard," one of the voices said. "Every time I see her headed to Mr. Hicks's office, I just leave. I can't believe he hired her in the first place." This must be the always-invisible secretary of Mr. Hicks.

And the prissy little behind was undoubtedly the one now trapped in this stall.

"Well, don't be too hard on her," said the other, a very sweet, lovely young maiden.

"Oh, she needs somebody to set her in her place. Her mother thinks she rules everything around here. She's even trying to make my parents get rid of their satellite."

OK, girls, hurry it up. I looked through the small crack and noticed they were painting their faces.

Miss Two-Faced Tilda packed up her beauty makeover kit as my legs began to shake from the extended squatting period, then added, "Well, she's met her match with me."

Finally, they left, only to be replaced by a new visitor who headed to my stall. The hand pushed hard on my unlockable stall door, forcing me to fall firmly onto the very toilet seat that up until then had successfully been avoided.

"Oh, I'm so sorry," I heard a somewhat familiar voice say.

By then, my tumble signaled the automatic flusher, which plunged with such force I was sure I would end up somewhere the far side of New Jersey or it had just sucked a hickey on my hiney the size of Texas. Reaching for nonexistent toilet paper to wipe off every rudiment of germs, I moaned in agony.

"No paper?" came the voice next door.

"No."

"I'll send you some."

"That would be nice, because if you don't, I'll be forced to use this toilet tissue attached to my shoe."

I saw her hand come from underneath, bearing enough toilet paper for a small country. "It ain't quite that big," I said, and we both just died laughing.

I had less than two hours to complete my story. People came and went by my prefab world, but everyone could tell I was too busy to talk. Even Curly Locks left me alone. I saw him peek his head around the corner once around lunchtime, but I didn't look up. After the last couple of days, I needed a day off from conversation in general.

At one forty-five, the final page printed off. What needed to be redeemed was hopefully complete. I headed up to Mr. Hicks's office to turn in my story. His secretary was missing in action again. Mr. Hicks, however, was working diligently at his desk, so I knocked on the open door. He looked up and invited me inside but never looked up.

"Got another story ready, Savannah?"

"Yes, sir. I hope it will repair what I screwed up."

"I'm sure it will," he said still engrossed in what he was working on. "So what's your next article going to be about?"

I'm almost certain that my heart stopped beating and my blood stopped flowing through my veins. It was really true: I was going to have to work this hard to come up with a story every week. What in the world had I been thinking? This workaholic, crazed individual would never allow a moment's peace. I gathered myself enough to say, "You'll have to wait and see."

"Meet me in front of your dad's store as soon as you can," Claire said from the other end of the line.

"Why?"

"Because the apartment above his store has just been purchased and the new owner wants to rent it out."

"The Culpeppers' place? Dad never even said they were thinking about moving."

"Well, they moved out about two weeks ago. Mrs. Culpepper needed a little extra care and couldn't handle the stairs any longer. They sold it for not much more than they paid for it. I heard they really like the buyer and didn't want a long drawn-out process. But the new owner asked to remain anonymous, because they feared people might think they had taken advantage of the Culpeppers, when really the Culpeppers felt like they were keeping it in the family."

"Well, it doesn't matter. You know I can't afford something on a square. Those are the most expensive properties in the city. Your front yard's a square, for crying out loud. Look some more; this won't work …"

"Savannah Phillips, don't you hang up on me. Get down here now and at least look at this place."

"Well, meet me around back then. I don't want Dad to know anything yet."

I met Claire around the corner in front of the Lucas Theater. The Lucas Theater is Savannah's gift to the fine arts. Mr. Lucas built a number of theaters through the years in the South. But the one in Savannah is the only one that bears his name. After a ten-year restoration project, it reopened in 1998. I would tell you that Mother had something to do with it, but unfortunately, someone else thought of it first. However, the rumor floating around town says they stole the idea from her. One can only imagine how such rumors get started. As for me, my imagination is vivid and often accurate.

Across the street from the Lucas Theater is the Olde Pink House. The eighteenth-century mansion-turned-restaurant is a designated National Landmark and is, of course, pink. Its claim to fame is that the Declaration of Independence was read there for the very first time, and it's pink because the scored stucco was never removed and the color of the red brick is bleeding through.

Grant and I used to eat regularly at the Olde Pink House. He always ordered for me. He would hold my hand across the table and share his thoughts about life, his childhood memories, his dreams for the future. We had a regular table, from which I could see the Lucas Theater marquee, clearly in the winter and more partially in the summer, when all the leaves have taken their places on the trees. The last time we ate there it read, "Savannah Chamber Orchestra, June 28."

Claire touched my arm, returning my thoughts to the present, and we headed to the back of Dad's store, where stairs went up to the apartment. "So how can I make my rent payments if the owner is anonymous?" I asked her, not caring who owned it as much as whether I could afford it.

"They have an escrow account set up down the street at the SunTrust Bank. You'll just go there and pay to an account number each month."

We climbed the stairs. Despite thirteen years of memorizing every line of this entrance, I had never climbed the stairs to the Culpeppers' home. Claire opened the door. It was perfectly laid out and pristinely kept. It had old refurbished hardwood floors, high doors, and beautiful moldings. There was a living room and dining area, and in the back was the kitchen with what seemed to be brand-new appliances and a built-in breakfast area. One more flight of stairs took us to the two bedrooms, separated by a small hallway. The master was a little larger than the second bedroom, with an incredible master bath and a claw-foot tub haloed by a curtain rod that allowed one to draw the shower curtain all the way around. The other bath was ideal as a guest bath. The place was perfect, and perfectly out of my price range, I was sure.

"Claire, how in the world do you think I'll be able to afford this on my salary?" I asked, still perturbed that she would even show me this place.

"Well, that's what you're not going to believe. The owner got such a good deal, he's only asking $850 a month. Do you think you can swing that? This is the deal of a lifetime. If you don't take it, I'm going to!"

"There's no way this place is $850. You just didn't hear him right. This place has to be at least $1,850. You'd better go back and tell him he gave you the wrong price."

"I checked and double-checked, and he assured me that the rent was only $850. All he wanted me to do was find someone who would take care of it and not ransack the place with wild parties, like those that go on everywhere else around here."

"Well, I won't even get a paycheck for another two weeks." I ran my hand up the trim of a doorframe.

"Well, it gets better. And stop looking at me as if I'm some lying girl from lower Savannah. He said that he was so concerned about the kind of person that lived here, he would rather hold it for the right one than rent it for the sake of renting."

"Is there a candid camera about to pop out on my head?"

"No, silly. I told him I had a wonderful friend who had moved back to town and is one of the best southern girls I know," she said, smiling a ridiculous smile, "and she is looking for a place, and this would be perfect for her. He told me to just let him know what you thought. So, what do you think?" she asked me, grinning that "I already know what you're thinking but I'm going to ask you anyway just to be totally obnoxious" kind of grin. "You love it. I know you love it."

"Yes, I love it," I said, laughing. If there had been furniture, I would have flung my body on it in total disbelief. But since there wasn't, I just twirled around in absolute amazement at my good fortune. As I did, my eyes landed on something familiar. A tennis ball. A drool-encased tennis ball. The common bond between man and dog. A man and dog I knew very well.

The box on the top step declared my Tan Beautiful had arrived. I planned to try it that night, but when evening fell and I remembered the fright of tomorrow, a small spot of mildew in the far corner of my shower ruined me for two good hours.

When I finally got ready for bed, I remembered my Tan Beautiful. It recommended using gloves for application, but I didn't have any. So I just slathered myself from head to toe and went to bed expecting to wake up looking like I had spent the last week on the beach.

Sleep came easily after my two-hour workout. But somewhere in the wee hours of the morning, I began to smell smoke. It seemed faint at first, then it got stronger and stronger. I jumped out of bed and ran though the hall toward the door, screaming, "Fire! Everyone get up! Get up, THE HOUSE IS ON FIRE!"

Dad was in the hall in no time. Mother came out trying to tie a robe around herself all while carrying her mother's pearls and her own wedding album. She started screaming for Dad to wake up Thomas. We all started running down the stairs trying to find out where the smell was coming from, but none of us could see any smoke. We searched and searched, but the smell just wouldn't leave me. Mother scurried around the house trying to retrieve all of her priceless possessions. She threw things out windows and the front door and ran around snatching up baby booties and crowns boxed in acrylic.

Dad and Thomas were walking around with a fire extinguisher when, somewhere in the hubbub, I caught a sniff of myself.

I was the fire.

Tan Beautiful was the fire. I was the one that smelled like fire.

I put out a call far and wide for everyone to come into the foyer. Each one ran in frantically from different directions, Mother in her high heels with an eye mask perched atop her head, Dad and Thomas skidding to a halt in the foyer, Duke on their heels, convinced this whole escapade was a party. I simply stated, "There's no fire." With that I turned around and headed up the stairs.

Dad panted as he leaned over double, "Savannah, how do you know there is no fire?"

"Just trust me on this one, Dad, there is no fire." With that the stairs carried me back to my asylum. I'm sure it took my mother three hours to retrieve everything she had thrown onto the sidewalk, and I'm certain Dad kept looking for the fire anyway. I myself went to bed with the declaration that no other living, breathing soul would ever know the truth about that moment.

CHAPTER THIRTY-SIX

I woke up early and headed downstairs to begin what I was sure would be my Wednesday and Friday routine—at least until I moved and could read the paper alone at my own breakfast table. Duke was waiting at the door. Since I had returned home, Dad had an excuse not to walk him. "Why should Duke be walked twice?" he asked. Duke merrily led the way out the front door, and I saw the paper resting safely between the iron railing and the box-woods, perfectly placed by a hurried paperboy.

About the time we hit the sidewalk, I spied Grant's image two blocks down, coming my way. I did a one-eighty, ducked, and tugged at Duke's leash to follow. I climbed the stairs in a crouched position and headed safely back inside. As I closed the door quietly, I tried to catch my breath.

"Good boy, Duke," I said, reaching down to pat his head and feeling nothing. "Duke!" I screamed at the end of a leash that disappeared to the other side of the door. I opened the door just a crack. Duke was staring at me in disgust. I opened the door and snatched him in as quickly as possible. Then I waited. Duke sat by me, stoic and calm, while his master was fidgety and anxious.

"It's really nothing," I assured him. "We'll leave in just a moment. It simply didn't feel like the right time."

After a good ten minutes, Duke and I headed to the park where we nestled ourselves on the closest park bench. It still gave me chills to see my picture on the front page of section B with my name underneath, knowing my mother had nothing to do with it. Duke was thankful for the breather, and I strapped his leash around my ankle and began to read the second and final part to my first human-interest story.

I tried to savor it, knowing I'd experience this first only once. For all the pain of the week, I had come to realize how little I had appreciated first things. My first kiss, my first love . . . even my first public failure. These moments pass too quickly, moving from magic to familiarity. So I read slowly and appreciated every dotted *i,* comma, and period.

I owe this city an apology. But first, I must apologize to the woman who was the subject of my Wednesday column. To act as if it was my right to tell someone else's story was presumptuous and arrogant. It is a privilege to know a person; it is an honor to know her story. And it is a treasure to be given a person's time, which is what you offer me on Wednesdays and Fridays. Wasting it with thoughtlessness was inexcusable. I assure you, if you would entrust your time to me once more, I will handle it with grace and caution.

I have learned a great deal over the past twenty-four hours. I have learned the real human-interest story I sought had nothing to do with the story that I spent days investigating. There is much even for me to learn about my treatment of those entrusted to me. In a way, Savannah's beauty queen was entrusted to me, and I failed her. In desiring to help her fly again, I clipped her wings instead. I hope she will forgive me.

I've also spent the last twenty-four hours asking

myself many questions about loss and disappointment and defeat. No one wants anyone to see his or her failures. And by exposing another's, I lived my own. The lesson was hard. But the outcome will hopefully make me more aware—aware that failure and loss, when accompanied by a true desire to learn, is often the necessary road to achieving a dream.

We experience loss every day. I lost a book deal because of a misguided attitude. I lost a good human-interest story because of arrogance, and I almost lost this opportunity to commune with you, right here on these pages, because my failure tempted me to throw it all away.

My greatest failure, however, was the misconception that another's loss paled in comparison to my own. A fine lady taught me that one. She caused me to realize that even if the dream isn't yours, the death of it is no less significant.

This beautiful city boasts at least two women who know the secret of weathering loss. One stands on the corner of one of our squares, selling books and dispensing smiles. Katherine Owens has faced the loss of a dream and the loss of her love. The loss of a dream introduced her to the man of her dreams. And the loss of that man propelled her into yet another new dream. She could have wallowed in her world of disrepair. But she knew, even on dark nights, that opportunity awaited her. And morning always showed up. Mrs. Owens will tell you that to lose is only to begin something new, to discover something you would have missed had success taken you down a different path.

The other woman has taken on challenges I would never have the courage to face myself. My mother has loved her husband and children, breathed life into this city, and found jobs for people in whom she's seen hidden potential, and all this after losing her own greatest dream. Yet Victoria Phillips refused to allow that loss to define her future, and as a result, her life has touched the lives of all of us who live here, and none more than mine.

We experience loss in families, in football games, in the stock market. But what if in the midst of those losses we could remember the successes? What if in the moment the marriage seemed to be crumbling we grabbed hold of each other and remembered the wedding day, the birth of our children, the sharing of dreams, the telling of secrets, the love that we've made, and the heartbreaks we've shared? Could focusing on the fulfillment of the past allow us to realize that today's conflict will pass as well?

Today I challenge you to reject loss and disappointment as your companions. Let's resolve to face our crippling moments with the courage of Katherine Owens and Victoria Phillips. We will face lies and deceit, unfairness and cruelty, bad economies and sickness. What we do in the face of such circumstances is what will set our course. It is what will lead us to a corner bookstore or to the Chamber of Commerce. What will you do in the face of your life losses? Whatever you do, rest assured you will never be the same for having met them and faced them well. Nor will the life of our city.

Until Wednesday,
Savannah from Savannah

Someone sat down beside me and started petting Duke. When Grant's face registered, paper, park bench, and me all about went flying. So much for avoidance.

306

"Have mercy! you about scared me to death," I said, crumpling the paper to my chest so I could grab my heart.

"Well, you were so focused I didn't want to bother you. So what did you think?"

"What did I think about what?"

"About your article."

"Oh," I said, embarrassed that I had been caught reading my own work. "Well, I just wanted to see if it had to be edited much."

"Savannah Phillips, I know you. You would read me everything you wrote. You would call me at three in the morning just to read me something, whether I was cognizant or not," he said, laughing.

I couldn't believe he would bring all of that up. They weren't things I wanted to remember just then. "Well, that was a long time ago," I said. I stood as if to go.

"I'm sorry. Just wanted you to know you made the right decision. Well, I'm sure I'll see you soon. And I would really love for you to meet Elisabeth."

"Well, I'm sure we'll meet eventually. I really need to hurry. I hope you have a good day. It was nice to see you," I said as I walked past him.

"It was nice to see you too. Nice tan," he said as he headed in the opposite direction. I turned to watch him jog away and knew I must choose how this loss would define me. There was the convent option, which might afford me a teaching position at Saint Vincent's Academy. That wasn't appealing. There was the "I'll never love again" recluse option. Paige would never allow it. Or there was the option to live my life, write well, and perhaps one day meet a man who would rock my world like Jake did Victoria's, or Jim did Katherine's, and experience that cataclysmic risk of marriage. Or maybe not.

I stared into my closet. Each color represented something to me. Khakis reflected my nature of somewhat predictability. All the black represented my desire to fit in while standing out.

And my flip-flops represented my need to feel free. Today, I wanted to reflect something different. Something less safe. Something, dare I say, more Savannah. Today required a dress, a blue denim sleeveless wrap dress. So I put it on and slid my feet into my cute leather-between-the-toes Kate Spade sandals with matching bag.

Vicky was pulling out of the garage as I came out the side door. She backed up to position herself beside my car, stopped, and rolled down her window. "Savannah Phillips, you look absolutely breathtaking. Have you met a man?" she asked, staring at me.

"No, it's Friday and I feel like wearing a dress. I do that sometimes, you know," I said, opening my own car door and sitting down where I could see her eye to eye. "I was hoping I'd see you before I left. Would you have time to go to lunch today? I have somebody I'd like you to meet."

"You must be ill! Do you have a fever? We need to get you checked. Maybe you have Lyme disease. You know, Duke is probably loaded with ticks and you might have gotten one on you. Get out of the car, go upstairs, and let me take your temperature. That thing could be sucking the blood out of your brain as we speak," she said, turning off her car.

"Mother, please. I am fine," I said, starting my own. "And Duke doesn't get out enough for a tick to even find him. Seriously, I want you to have lunch with me. Today is a special day."

Well, that stopped her ranting. "Then yes, Savannah, I would love to have lunch with you, and it is a special day. Your article was one of the nicest things I've ever read. I am supremely proud of you, supremely proud. But promise me, if you ask to go shopping with me too, we will head straight to the emergency room."

"Would that really be so shocking?"

"As shocking as if you said you had always had a secret desire to enter a beauty pageant yourself."

"If I ever say that, I'll need more than an emergency room, I'll need to be admitted for psychiatric evaluation. I'll see you at noon. Let's meet at The Lady & Sons."

"I'll see you at noon. Get checked, honey. Really, get checked," and she drove off in her Mercedes coupe convertible that she bought purposefully so Duke could never ride in it. Dad bought the SUV so Duke could ride in it whenever he wants.

I placed another call on the way to Dad's shop. Another invitation to lunch. It was accepted. Then I called Claire. I told her that I should have enough money to move into the new place in about a week or so. I asked her to see if that would be OK with the landlord. She assured me it would. But I told her to check anyway.

CHAPTER THIRTY-SEVEN

As I pulled into a parking place a couple of stores up from Jake's, I saw the back of a man leaning over and petting Duke. Duke's tail was wagging feverishly. As I approached the gentleman from behind, he stood up. It was Joshua.

"Oh, hey, Ms. Phillips," he said, startled.

I tried not to act as surprised as he. "I see you've met the master around here." Duke got up to greet me and I patted him on the head.

"Yeah. Thanks to you I've become more addicted to your father's java than I was St—at that other place. I think that's what you call it." He started swirling his cup around as if he didn't know what to say next. "Do you smell something burning?"

Apparently Tan Beautiful's promise of a lasting tan wasn't the only thing that lasted.

"That would be Duke. He lost his ball in the fireplace and was bound and determined not to let it escape."

I turned to look inside the store, and when I did, every head whipped around. Surely they had far more interesting things to do today at work than glue themselves to the window.

"You must have been pretty busy yesterday. I didn't see hide nor hair of you," I said, walking to the door as two of the ladies who work at the courthouse came out with their coffee in hand. They said hi to us both, and after they passed Joshua, they turned around to check him out.

"Yeah. I had to contend with two board meetings and a local petition about satellites brought up by the Chamber of Commerce."

"I heard about the petition. That must have made for an interesting afternoon."

"Actually it made for an interesting evening as well." He reached down to pet Duke again, who was persistently nuzzling Joshua's hand.

I decided to take the opportunity to ask what I felt was a rather pressing question, since he had brought up the satellite issue. "Joshua, do you know Mr. Hicks's secretary very well?"

"Why, have you met her?" he asked with a slight smirk.

"I wouldn't say we have actually met," I said, thankful that she hadn't witnessed my encounter with ceramic in the ladies' room, "I hear she doesn't care for me much."

"Ms. Phillips, I told you earlier, not everyone is thrilled that you're here. I know it's hard for you to believe, but not all the world is going to celebrate you."

"I don't need celebrating. It was just a question."

"Well, you worry too much. She's just a silly girl with a stressful job. She probably wanted yours. But don't worry. You'll win her over in time. Might be a long time, if I know her, but eventually you'll become friends, I'm sure. And if you don't, you'll still have the likes of me to run around with." He gave me an obnoxious wink. "Well, the tourism department calls." He said as he gave Duke one last pat on the head and began to walk past me.

"You cover the tourism department?" I gave him a slight smirk of my own.

"Yes, I have had it for the last year. Can't say I enjoy it though. The new director has a crush on me." He wrapped his satchel crossways around his rather defined chest.

"Well, that's flattering," I said, trying to stifle my growing smile.

Joshua and Miss Amber Topaz? The mere thought of the two of them together made me laugh out loud.

"Laugh if you want, Ms. Phillips. But I have job to do, a professional job. And I can't have a giddy director of tourism winking at me when she needs to be directing meetings. Not to mention it makes all the other journalists there slightly jealous." He turned back around to continue his walk to his bike that was parked up the street.

"Well, flatter her. I bet she's a fine young lady."

"Aren't they all, Ms. Phillips, aren't they all?" His voice trailed off down the street. I didn't know what it was about these newspaper people always repeating themselves. "Good article, by the way," he called out, turning around with an incredible smile. I refused to act like I even heard him.

I wanted to stop there for a moment and take in what had happened to me with his smile. But had I stopped for any length of time I would have invited a set of twins, an aged African American, and an anonymous landlord to hit me with a thousand questions, none of which I had either time or desire to answer. So instead of stopping to think about anything, I walked straight in and straight to the back and only acknowledged the stares with a casual hello.

I poured myself a Coke and was putting the lid on it when the only one brave enough to come back and ask questions entered the room. "He seems like a nice guy. Do you see much of each other at work?" Dad asked.

"Inquisitive, aren't we? But that's not why I'm here. I found an apartment."

"Yeah? Well, tell me you can afford it!" he said, coming around the counter to sit down.

"Don't you want to know where it is?" I asked.

"Of course."

I grabbed his hand and said, "Well, come out here and I'll show you." I dragged him out the front door, and even Duke jumped from his slumber when he saw us headed to his location on the sidewalk. I turned Dad around to face the front of his store and said, "Look up!"

He turned his gaze upward and said, "What am I looking at?"

"The Culpeppers' place. It's going to be mine," I told him, punching his arm and jumping up and down like a teenager.

"Savannah, are you sure you can afford that?" he asked, still looking up.

"I know! I didn't think I could either. But apparently the man who bought it just wanted to have a responsible kind of person living there. That would be me." I pointed to myself as if I were a two-year-old. "Do you know who bought it?"

"No, uh . . . I heard he likes to keep to himself though." He returned to the shop.

"Well, don't you love it?" I asked, following him back inside.

"Yes, I think it's perfect. If you can afford it, I think it's perfect. But I really think you just wanted to be a hop, skip, and a jump from your father."

"Don't kid yourself; I wanted to be a hop, skip, and a jump from free Coca-Colas and Duke."

"So how soon are you moving?"

"Well, my, my, don't we seem quite anxious?"

"Well, it's not like I'm getting rid of you," he said, looking up.

"I should have my money together after I get my first paycheck. Hopefully I'll get paid by next week, so I should be moving out in a couple of weeks, maybe sooner. Won't you be a happy man?"

"Oh yes, now I will have one Phillips woman to dictate my days and another my nights. Won't I be the lucky one?"

"Yes, because now you really can sleep at the store if you need to. I'll have an extra bedroom anytime you need a break."

"So back to this Joshua kid."

"There's nothing to him. He's annoying and arrogant and we have to sit right next to each other." I would not allow this conversation to become interesting.

"Well, anyway, I didn't get to see you before I left the house. Your article was wonderful, Savannah. I can't tell you how proud I am of you. You did exactly what you needed to do," he said, leaning back against the counter on the other side of the Coke machine.

"All I did was write down my own questions," I said, turning to look at him. "I figure if I'm asking them, surely someone else is asking them or has asked them. I just hope that with all the questions there are some answers in there as well. Life hasn't given me many experiences. I mean you and . . . Mother have sheltered Thomas and me from a lot of things."

"I think it came across loud and clear. I've got to get back up front. I'll see you for dinner. You're welcome to invite your friend sometime," he said with a wink as he headed out the door.

"Paige would love to come by. She was just talking about you the other day," I yelled loud enough that he could hear me even though he tried to act as if he couldn't.

As I passed Dad's "Thought for the Journey" on my way to the car, the words resounded with my new discoveries: "In his heart a man plans his course, but God determines his steps." Nothing clearer needed to be said. Nothing truer either.

Marla was already busy answering phones. She gave me a thumbs-up sign as I walked through the door. I headed back to my desk and sat down to open up my laptop and rack my brain for a new story. I might as well resign myself to a life of sleepless nights.

Paige's, Jake's, college-student-turns-human-interest-writer were the best story possibilities that occurred to me in the hours I sat typing out asinine concepts. I looked at my watch to discover it was almost lunch time, but I wanted to speak to Mr. Hicks before going. As my feet exited the elevator, I saw his secretary's petite frame actually sitting where I imagined it was supposed to. I stopped at her desk and introduced myself, extending my hand.

"Hello, I'm Savannah Phillips. I don't believe we've met."

She looked up at me said, "I know who you are," and turned around to put a file in the cabinet behind her. This one would definitely take some effort. I proceeded to ask if I could see Mr. Hicks. "Mr. Hicks is busy at the moment. You should have called before you climbed all those stairs with your delicate legs."

I was looking forward to a good day, and getting into it with this little girl wasn't on my agenda. So I simply said, "Actually, I took the elevator."

The back of her head replied, "Whatever."

"I'll just come back later."

All would have gone off without a hitch if she just hadn't added under her breath, "Oh yea! She's coming back later."

I was halfway down the hall when I heard it. I promptly stalked back to the desk of that bleached-blond, overdone Prissalina. "Do you have a problem with me?"

She turned around, and gave me a rather menacing glare for such a little one. "Yes, I do have a problem with you," she said. "You prance yourself in here, demanding a job you don't deserve. You walk around here like you are the queen of the world and think everyone is supposed to jump when you say jump. Well, I won't be jumping. You'll respect the rules around here like everyone else. There are no exceptions, and no one gets to that man in there unless they come through me. I only wish I would have been here on your first visit, because I would have made sure that meeting never happened. So you can act like you're some cherished prize around here, like your mama does, but you ain't all that, sister, and neither is she."

Why can't some people just leave well enough alone? Attack me, talk about my clothes, make cracks about my flip-flops, I don't care; but for heaven's sake, when they talk about my mother, they leave me no options.

"Number one, I don't prance. Number two, the only thing I've ever been queen of was the okra seed–spitting contest. Number three, my dog doesn't even jump when I tell him to, let alone any human I know. Number four, I've always respected every rule, every law—well, except an occasional breaking and entering—but that's none of your business. And lastly, sister, my mother *is* all that."

She shook her head and tsked at me! "Don't suck your teeth at me. Victoria Phillips is everything she thinks she is and more. And I want you to know something. I got this job because Mr. Hicks gave me an opportunity, just as I'm sure you have yours for the same reason. I don't want your job. I don't want your attention. But I do expect your respect."

"Dream on . . . dream on."

"If I need to speak with Mr. Hicks, you'd better make sure he gets the message. And if I turn in an article to you, you'd better make sure he gets it exactly the way I left it. And if you ever, and I do mean ever, talk about my mother to me or anyone else, well, let's just say there is not a set of stairs high enough that I won't find you and deal with you. So let's make a truce here. You don't have to like me. You don't even have to talk to me if you don't want to. But you will respect me. And I will respect you. I'll call for appointments, and I'll turn my stories in on time. We can get along. But that choice is yours."

She looked puzzled, but I knew she was just trying to sidetrack me. "You are a weird child."

"Well, you're whacked."

"What did you say?"

"I said, you are in lack. In people skills, that is. So, if you can, would you tell Mr. Hicks I need to see him. I'll be downstairs." While I was still standing over her desk, I heard the click of Mr. Hicks's door.

"What's going on out here?"

Miss Thing put on the most phony smile I had seen since the Hinesville Pageant. "Oh, nothing, sir. Ms. Phillips just came up without an appointment, and I was trying to explain to her," she said, rolling her eyes at me, "that she needs to have an appointment."

Mr. Hicks chuckled and said, "Thank you for guarding me, but I don't mind if someone needs to talk to me." He reached over and patted her hand, which had a death grip on the edge of her desk. Then he turned to me. "Savannah, I have a few minutes now, would you like to come in?"

"Yes, sir, it won't take a second."

He motioned for me to go in front of him. I offered one last smile to the warden, hoping it might soften her. It didn't.

"Savannah, have a seat." He shut the door behind us. "Jessica is a little rigid about how she wants things to run around here. I imagine she'll lighten up in time." I sat down in one of the two worn blue leather chairs in front of his desk. "Did you need to talk about your next story?" he asked with a delighted smile on his face. I wasn't sure why he was so anxious to hear about my next story. He acted more anxious than me, if that was possible.

"No, sir. I'm here to make sure today's article was OK."

"Actually, I thought it was an improvement," he said, leaning his larger frame down into his own blue leather desk chair, as every spring let out a sound of extreme tension. "You still have a lot to learn, but at least you won't bring on needless litigation."

"Well, I'm learning."

"Well, we'll learn together," he said with a smile I'm sure he had given to a multitude of young dreamers who had stood in this same office many times before. "Time will teach you the difference one person can make."

"One person can't make that big a difference."

"Oh yes, they can. Look what Gloria did for years. One person can light a fire under a multitude of people. You need to remember that every time you write an article."

Well, that was just a glorious ounce of pressure added to an already draining morning. "Thank you for that pep talk. Well, I've got to head to lunch. I'll see you later."

"Have a good one. By the way, I noticed the book on your desk when I walked by the other day. You'll enjoy it."

He was referring to the new book I picked up after Wednesday's debacle, Peggy Noonan's *When Character Was King: A Story of Ronald Reagan*. "Didn't think it could hurt, with my track record and all."

"Never hurts any of us. Have a good lunch. Oh, when you pick up your next Coke, tell Duke I said hello," he said with a sly grin.

"Point taken, sir."

Jessica was standing by her desk sifting through some papers as I walked by. And suddenly I was overcome by exactly what I needed to do. So I walked right over to her, grabbed her by her shoulders, planted a big ol' kiss on her cheek, looked her straight in her eye, and said, "I'm going to make you like me." And I walked back to the stairwell and down the stairs, laughing all the way.

Victoria eats at The Lady & Sons about once a week, just to trade recipes with the owner, her good friend Paula Deen. She says Lady & Sons knows how food should be cooked; no boxed stuff found here. When I pulled in, she pulled in beside me. I got out of my car first and walked over to open her door.

"Hello, darling," she said, removing her blue floral Kate Spade mules from the car first, then lifting the matching bag from the other side, and finally bringing her blue-suited self out of the car.

I closed her door and wrapped my arm around her to walk into the restaurant. "This suit looks almost identical to the white one you had on yesterday."

"That's because it is. I loved the style so much, I bought three; a white one, a blue one, and a pink one. So how was your morning?"

"It was more interesting than you can imagine." I opened the door so we could go inside.

"Well, what in the world happened?" she asked. She was quickly sidetracked, however, when Miss Paula greeted her at the door. They caught up for a few moments, talking about Paula's boys, Miss Paula's new television show, and Thomas and me as if I wasn't there. When they were through catching up, I asked if we could have a table in the back. When we sat down, and I positioned myself where I could see the front door. Mother ordered a sweet tea and I ordered a Coke. "Now tell me, young lady, what in the world happened today?"

Her ringing cell phone spared me from answering. The only

thing that was mentioned was TV crews and that she would be there when she was finished.

Katherine walked to our table as my mother ended the call, looking as good as I hoped to in another twenty-five years. She was wearing pressed khakis with a black sleeveless sweater, a black belt with a simple silver buckle, and another sweater draped over her shoulders. Her silver hair fell fresh and naturally around her face, framing her beautiful smile. I wrapped my arms around her and gave her a warm hug, which she returned as warmly, and then I was able to introduce two of the finest women I knew to each other. "Katherine Owens, this is my mother, Victoria Phillips."

"What an absolute pleasure to meet you," Katherine said as she took my mother's extended hand and placed it inside both of hers. "Can I give you a hug? I feel like I know you."

Victoria smiled as the two women shared a greeting. "Absolutely. I feel like I know you as well."

"I thought you two needed to meet," I explained. "After all, I wouldn't be here without either one of you." The emotion of the moment as I looked into the faces of these women I had grown to love and admire was almost overwhelming.

"Now, that's not true," Katherine said. "You know, Savannah, your determination to make your own way is what brought you here."

"Isn't that the truth?" Mother replied.

"But that's not why I've stayed," I assured them. "I stayed because somewhere between proving points and losing dreams— not to mention torturous pageant stories—I realized this is where I was really meant to be."

We all got a chuckle at our pageant horrors.

"Amazing, isn't it?" Mother added. "Look at us. Three very different women, all having lost something. And yet we've each discovered, because of our willingness to believe in an eternal purpose, that every loss eventually reveals something better that we've gained."

This table and my life revealed plenty.

CHAPTER THIRTY-EIGHT

The blaring date on my cell phone seemed to be important, but I couldn't quite remember why. Then the memory lured me back to a party in New York I would have attended this evening. Today, however, I was confident I had made no mistake. I was home.

To many, my home exists in a time gone by. But Savannah has its own rhythm. Life still happens here. People still die. Babies are still born. Dreams are still shattered. Successes achieved. You can find it all here. And I'm not sure that changing the world was ever really my goal anyway. I just wanted to touch a soul, so that he or she could touch another, and the ongoing cycle—the cycle of life, the reason for living—would produce change. And I was glad at this moment, with the almost-summer sun beating through my window, that Savannah had welcomed me home.

At the office, I saw the pantyhose-covered legs and cranberry sling-back pumps before I turned the corner of my tiny cubicle. When the full body came into view, I found myself face-to-face with Amber, decked out in a cranberry suit with tiny fabric-covered buttons running up the front of her jacket. Her hair had not moved

320

since I saw her the other day at lunch, and her jewelry reflected her, shall we say, illuminating personality. As soon as she saw me, she stood to her feet. "I'm sorry to bother you, Savannah. I know I shouldn't just stop here without even calling first. I just wanted to see you for one minute since we haven't talked since lunch the other day."

"It's OK," I said, setting my satchel on the far side of my desk. I motioned for her to sit back down and pulled my chair up to sit across from her. "What's up? You look beautiful."

She looked down at herself with a surprisingly shy smile. "Oh, this is an old suit. I've had it since I competed in Miss Georgia United States of America the third time," she said, lowering her head. "Pretty sad, isn't it? That's how I remember the time frame of major events in my life, what pageant I was in."

"We all need points of references. Mine are ads in the paper. So how have you been?"

"I've been good. Really good," she said and I believed her. "I've done a lot of thinking since we talked. You said some hurtful things, Savannah," she said with a pouty look. "But they were true. Every one of them. I've spent my entire life allowing other people's opinions to define me. And I made a decision that I'm not going to do that anymore. I mean, the last time I lost Miss Georgia United States of America, I went home and sat in front of the TV eating an entire chocolate cake and replaying the pageant video in my VCR over and over. In the middle of the forty-ninth viewing, I called my mother and said, 'I've watched this thing forty-nine times and I still haven't won.'" She broke into a light laugh. "It was really pitiful. I realize now that only one thing will give me that kind of self-worth. You called it an 'eternal perspective,' I think. And thanks to you, I believe I've been able to find that."

"So are you hanging up your pageant dresses?"

"Well, no. I'm just getting a new perspective. I'm going to do pageants for the enjoyment alone. Because I do enjoy them. Just like you enjoy writing. But I'm just not going to do it for approval. I'm going to tell myself, 'Self, you are beautiful. You don't need these people's approval. You don't even need to win. Now, it's OK if you do, but you don't have to win. So, self, you just go out there and sing your little heart out, answer your questions, and let the whole world see those great legs. And if you win, you need to tell those other girls how wonderful they were and not to let the judges' decision make them feel worthless.' What do you think about that?"

I just smiled at her sincerity, patted her skinny knee, and said, "That's a wonderful place to begin."

"I thought you would agree," she said. "So I've got to get back to work. And I've got a busy weekend because I think I might get asked out soon, and I also need to practice changing from my swimsuit to my talent competition outfit. I've got my time down to a minute and thirty seconds, but I really think I can cut ten seconds off of that. If it wasn't so hard getting my swimsuit unstuck, I could probably do it in a minute flat. 'Always be prepared.' I learned that motto in Girl Scouts. And I hear the Mrs. United States of America Pageant has a lot less time to get ready than you do in the Miss Pageants. Who knows, I could be there by this time next year."

I knew the next thing we might need to work on was her motivation for marriage. I also wasn't about to be the one to inform her of Joshua's feelings for her. So I simply raised an eyebrow and stood up. She continued to talk incessantly until I had to use more abrupt measures by saying, "Amber, it was great to see you, but I've got to get back to work."

"Oh, I'm sorry," she said, standing up with a slight, very slight, hint of embarrassment. She straightened her cranberry attire and headed around to the other side of the cubicle. As she turned the corner, Joshua's nameplate that hung on the side of his cubicle caught her eye. "Savannah! that's him. That's the man I think I'm going to marry. Oh, my side. If I knew that was his cubicle right next to yours, I'd have gone weak in the knees. And if he would've heard us! Oh, heaven help me, I would've had to have a face transplant and move to Katmandu." Her face morphed into that of a lovesick pup. "He's the most beautiful thing my eyes have ever beheld. The way his hair kind of flops on his head. And those curls. Oh, they are just like a bowl of noodles. And his hands, have you ever looked at his hands, Savannah? They are the strongest, most breathtaking hands I've ever seen. I bet they could hold your hand in theirs, and you wouldn't even be able to see your fingers. I need to go. I'm getting annihilated."

"I'll see you later," I said, laughing, knowing even I had never seen "exhilarated" in quite that way. I watched as she half swayed, half strutted back up the aisle. I hoped she wouldn't introduce herself to Marla, because she'd probably never make it through the door again. *Well, Rome wasn't built in a day,* I thought as she disappeared into a sea of gray.

I peered around the corner of Joshua's cubicle. It was totally sparse except for a University of Florida banner hanging on one of the Styrofoam beams and a picture of him and a group of guys about his age. There was little to reveal the full character of the man that rested in this chair. I figured what I didn't know, Miss Amber Topaz would reveal. The ringing of my phone called me back to my desk.

"Hello, Savannah Phillips."

"Vanni, you were worried about your next story?" came a unique tone of excitement, so rare, in fact, the last twenty-one years had never revealed such enthusiasm. "Well, I've found it. Get up here to the courthouse as soon as you can."

"What is it, Thomas?"

"Just get up here, now."

"OK, I'll be right there," I said, reaching for my satchel.

"And Vanni."

"Yeah?"

"Don't be shocked when you get here, but Mom has chained herself to it."

"I'll be there in three minutes," I assured Thomas and hung up.

I grabbed all coordinating paraphernalia and my cell phone. "I've got to get my attorney on speed dial," I muttered. I left, not sure if this was the story I would want or not. But a reporter must go. A reporter must go.

ACKNOWLEDGMENTS

Most of you can skip these pages. After all, the only people who will read it are those who are dying to see if I mention their names. So, for those who read it and you weren't mentioned, I can only blame such reprehensible actions on my weary being. For the rest of you that I did mention, my words are sincere and words that I hope I have said to you personally at one time or another and not just on the written page. If I haven't, I'm glad the opportunity arose that I could.

Many authors would tell you that they had some profound idea when they began writing a book. I did once. However, that book received a substantial amount of rejection letters, thirteen to be exact. (But who keeps a count of such things?) So, I simply wrote this one instead. It didn't start with a prolific idea. I simply knew beauty pageants and thought a story of one being rigged would be an enjoyable adventure. Since I began this idea almost three years ago, many other books with tiaras gracing the cover have been published. But like any good writer will assure you, I had mine first!

This book was written because of a dream I thought I had lost. My multiple rejected manuscript was how I wanted to be introduced to the publishing world. It seemed that it would offer true hope on this chaotic adventure. But no one wanted to publish it. A wiser person might have given up on writing books altogether after the thirteenth rejection letter declaring her book "Not what we are looking for." A statement which cuts as deeply as "She's got a great personality." But call me crazy, or stubborn, neither would be foreign to me, but I believe it was those closed doors that allowed me to get quiet enough to hear the direction the Lord had for this time in my life. That direction is Savannah.

I can honestly say I've fallen in love with these characters. Partly because they were created and developed in one of the darkest times in my life. They gave me laughter and an outlet to be creative and produce a work that I can honestly say I am proud of. I feel like I know them. Even gotten sick of them a time or two. But I must clarify here and now that they are not me, nor my mother, or any beauty queen I have even known, and any resemblance thereof is totally due to way too much Coke consumed during the writing of these pages.

Speaking of my mother, few things of life are possible without one. Life itself being the main thing. But for me she has been a wonderful example of grace and beauty in a world where those words are used to describe very few things. And my father, whose love made it easy to believe Jesus loves me too. For the cars you bought me, for the college you sent me to, for the trust you had in me (because if you had known better, you would have locked me in my room until I was forty, as you threatened), and for letting me climb in an old dilapidated Saab of my own and spread my wings to the hills of Tennessee. I love you and I thank you. But for allowing me a safe place in a dark time and being true believers in miracles, and for giving me a heritage in Jesus, I love you and thank you even more.

To the two grown men who are my brothers, one of which I will forever boss around and the other who, even though he is almost a foot taller than me, will forever be know as "the baby," know this book is not about you and you, and no, you cannot receive any royalties. But you can forever know that it is a privilege to call you on the phone, laugh at your stupid jokes, and pray with you for our needs and dreams.

To my priceless friend Deneen—I know you hate to read, but at this point, until there is a book on tape, you have no choice. You helped finishing this become possible. Through your prayers, through your love, and through your belief that God could somehow use the likes of me. Few people will live this side of heaven and know such a treasure as our friendship has given me. I'm glad I didn't have to wait until there to find it.

To the two women who have been friends and sisters—Beth and Joan. Distance has prevented our getting together as often as we would like. But it will never prevent us from our wonderful memories and invaluable friendships. You two are a part of my best moments.

To Esther Fedorkevich—this would still be lying on a shelf in my office if it hadn't been for your belief, dedication, and hard work. And often persistent attitude. (Aren't we a pair!) This was part of God's plan for both of us. I will always believe that. And I will be forever thankful that He let us have this new path in our lives together.

To Ami McConnell, my editor—I knew you were my kind of girl when you asked if it was "McDonald's calibration system." That was just plain freaky. You have made me mad. You have made me laugh. You have made me better. And you have believed in Savannah like I did. I didn't think people did that unless they were married to you, gave birth to you, or owed you money. But you just got it. From the first day you got it. Here's to believing you'll get the next one as well. Shoot! Here's to believing I'll get the next one as well.

To Bridgett O'Lannerty—thank you for your energy and effort. You were a joy to work with.

To Erin Healy—thank you for making Savannah dance. You

were gentle and "surgical." You took the heart of something and made it beat more powerfully. You are a master at what you do. And such a kind lady. Even though you edited out my husband, you redeemed yourself in fabulous ways. I look forward to seeing what you do with the next one.

To Allen Arnold at WestBow Press—what a risk taker you are. How grateful I am. I'm proud to be part of your team.

To the rest of the WestBow team—Jenny, Amanda, Andrea, and Rebeca—you are here because of your talent. Thank you for sharing those talents with me.

And to my sister-in-laws Janey and Deborah, my cousins Patty and Carol, and my wonderful friends, Heather, Jackie, Valencia, and Cyndi—first thank you for being women of prayer. Your prayers held me up and kept me alive. But also thank you for selflessly reading my book and critiquing my book. Even though I told you a thousand times this is not autobiographical, I know you still don't believe me. I thank you and love you.

To my precious mother-in-law—your strength astounded me. Your faith challenged me. And your life taught me invaluable lessons. I love you for who you are and the treasure you gave me in your son.

To Hannah, Lauren, Abigail, Daxtyn, and the newest addition Jake, Aunt Niecy or Aunt Nina—whichever it is you call me— wants you to know that your destiny is going to be powerful and you are going to be a part of changing this world. I can't wait to see what you will become.

And to the rest of my family, extended and immediate—our treasure is our heritage. Our joy is having the privilege of shared experience and love. All that I know is a part of who I have walked this journey with. I'm thankful God allowed me to be a part of you. And I'm thankful I come from such fine people.

And to my Pastors Rice and Jody Broocks—you loved me, prayed with me, and believed with me. I count it a privilege to walk with you in ministry and to call you pastors. To Pastors Tim and Lechelle Johnson—you challenged me and loved me at the same time. Then, assured me, "No one's getting out of the boat." I know that is true. You have proved it. To Pastor Jim and Kathy Laffoon—your prayers have been felt, and the word of the Lord you have spoken over my life has been foundational in allowing me to continue to believe. To David and Sandy Houston—thank you for giving us such a beautiful love to emulate and the defining words of "original intent." To John and Maretta Rohrer—you have loved me with an undeserving love. You gave when I had nothing to give in return but my gratitude. You grieved and rejoiced with me. I smile when I think of you, and am glad this journey will be traveled with you. To my Bethel family—I am never more proud than when I'm riding down the road and catch a glimpse of those two distinctive hands touching each other, declaring that we are "Reaching a City to Touch the World." I am honored to be a part of such a beautiful body of believers.

And to those who dwell under my roof. My Maggie and Chloe, who have let me cry in their fur and laugh at their inability to ever tire of chasing a ball from one end of the room to the other. Thank you for being just as excited to see me if I've been gone for two weeks overseas or ten minutes to the grocery store.

And to the man I fell in love with in what seems a lifetime ago. Marriage is a journey. It will make us smile, bump and bruise us, challenge us, grow us, and hopefully, at the end of the day, lead us somewhere. My prayer is that it leads us to our original intent. Thank you for your sacrifice to let me pursue the gifts I felt God had given me, even when they seemed to cost more than they brought in. And thank you for being a man with as much character as talent. Your abilities amaze me. But your heart amazes me more. And at the end of the day, when our children sit on the steps as we swing on the front porch, we're going to tell them the stories about how Mommy and Daddy kept loving when everything in the world screamed at them to stop. And then we're going to tell them how they fell off their bikes and we patched them up, how they had dreams and we nurtured them, and how their hearts got broken and we helped mend them. And then "when there are lines upon our face, from a lifetime of smiles, and when it comes time to embrace, for one long last while, we will laugh about it, how time really flies. We won't say good-bye 'cause true love never dies. You'll always be beautiful in my eyes."

And to the Man who lives in my heart: Jesus Christ. You've taught me much these past years. You've broken me to pieces, then graciously rebuilt me. You've disciplined me, then held me. You've listened to my secret dreams, then given me new ones yet to share. And You've loved me. When I wasn't sure anyone could see my failures and really love me, You showed me that not only could You, but You did. At the end of the day, the only thing that matters is that You are pleased with me: with my life, with the way I love, and with the way I use my gifts. My greatest desire has always been for You to use me, someway, anyway. Thank You for allowing me to be used in a way that I sincerely love. You are the Christ of my soul, the Healer of my heart, and the Deliverer of my dreams, and the One I can't wait to see.

MARION COUNTY PUBLIC LIBRARY
321 MONROE STREET
FAIRMONT, WV 26554